Twins in Time

A Fantasy Adventure

Ray Wenck
Glory Days Press
Columbus, Ohio

Ray Wenck

Copyright © 2020 by Ray Wenck

All rights reserved. No part of this publication may be reproduced, distributed, or transmitted in any form or by any means, without prior written permission.

Glory Days Press
Columbus, Ohio

Publisher's Note: This is a work of fiction. Names, characters, places, and incidents are a product of the author's imagination. Locales and public names are sometimes used for atmospheric purposes. Any resemblance to actual people, living or dead, or to businesses, companies, events, institutions, or locales is completely coincidental.

Book Layout © 2016 BookDesignTemplates.com

Twins in Time/ Ray Wenck. -- 1st ed.
ISBN 978-1-7360350-2-3

Twins in Time

Dedication

This story is dedicated to my sisters Carol, Val, and Laura. It may not have been a fantasy life, but that doesn't mean we can't get lost in one. Enjoy.

Acknowledgement

This was such a fun story to write. It was easy to get lost in the fantasy world. I would have liked to do more with it—to flesh it out into an epic world, but the story was already long and I didn't want it to be tedious or get lost in the creation.

Though I have no plans for a sequel, it doesn't mean one might not happen somewhere down the road. Though I spend most of my time writing post-apocalyptic tales and most recently, mysteries, I have always loved the fantasy genre. In my youth, I devoured J.R.R Tolkien and went on to David Eddings and Robert Asprin's *Thieves' World* anthologies. More recently, J.K. Rowling brought me back into fantasy, and G.R.R. Martin brought new interest and excitement. There were many others in between.

I got my first taste of writing fantasy in my young adult story, *Warriors of the Court*. That was fun but was told more from a modern point of view. More recently I co-wrote a trilogy with Jason Nugent that also involved time travel.

Next up is an urban fantasy titled *Jeremy Kline and the Invisible Village*, which I plan to make into a trilogy.

So if you like Twins in Time, check out my previous works, and rest assured that there is more to come.

I'd like to thank Jodi McDermitt for her usual masterful editing work. And credit to MiblArt for the cover design.

Thank you for your support, and as always, read all you want—I'll write more.

Ray Wenck

CHAPTER ONE

The memory of the assault was still fresh in Esmarelda's mind. His crazed look bordered on demonic. His disgusting odor and foul breath. His surprising strength. The sheer brutality of the act. Anger and hatred raged within her. Unsure what had made her more furious—the rape itself or that she couldn't fend him off—she forced her attention back to the ancient book. Just because he was the so-called ruler of these lands did not give him the right to take her like she was property to be used or a field that needed sowing.

Barely able to think, she tried to concentrate on her work. She stood naked, not taking the time to dress after he finished with her. The promise that he'd be back for her again spurred her to complete her task long before the idea of a second assault entered his mind.

Chanting the proper words, she took a pinch of the dark red powder derived from a root her mother had her dig up and grind into its current form. She tossed it into the fire. It flared, rising high enough to heat her sex. Her first reaction was to step back, but she let the fire singe the hair between her legs, hoping it would burn out the evil seed he'd planted.

She glanced at the book of spells. It was her mother's and she was forbidden to use it, but this was an emergency and called for something more intense and more punishing than the weak spells she knew. Her mother's warnings filled her head. Her mother repeatedly told her she was not ready to cast such complex spells and not strong enough to control them. The potential for a mistake if the spell was not followed exactly was great, and she was in a rush, both to take out her revenge and finish before her mother discovered the book missing.

Wait! How much of the powdered root did she need? Had she put in too much? She reread the ingredients and couldn't remember. She'd allowed her hatred to distract her. The words faltered. They had to be firm and spoken with confidence and authority.

"Esmarelda!"

The young woman froze. Her mother was calling her. Had she discovered the book missing? Perhaps she felt the growing magic.

But Esmarelda had to finish. Her assailant had to be punished and sent to a far-off land. She didn't care where. The people of this land would be better off without him.

She continued to chant as she added the last ingredient, the head of some ugly little swamp creature ground to a fine powder. With quick, vigorous movements, she stirred the combined ingredients and dumped the batch over the fire. With a jolt of fear, she realized in her haste she'd poured out the entire potion when the recipe clearly stated only half was needed.

The fire doused and sputtered, then flamed back to life. A strange vibrating current ran through her slight body. She lost all thought of the spell, fearing for her life. Then, like something summoned from the depths of the Earth, two fiery balls emerged from the middle of the flame and ascended toward the heavens. As they rose, the color changed from glowing red to a cool translucent blue. They rose side by side, passing in front of the sun. Sunlight filtered through them, casting a grayish shadow over her. But the hazy light was cold, chilling her to her soul. *What had she done?* The two spheres drifted away, picking up speed, then separated and moved in opposite directions until she could no longer see them.

What had she done?

"Esmarelda, if you're using my spell book, I'll turn you into a tree frog."

The threat might have been funny to another child, but in this case, she knew her mother was more than capable of doing just such a thing.

She slammed the book shut and ran for the cabin she shared with her mother and sisters. She was caught. No need to lie; it would only make her mother angrier. Telling the truth was the only way to lessen the punishment she knew was coming. An image of her rapist appeared in front of her, rekindling the anger within. His fate was sealed and she would make her mother understand why. But as fast as her anger flared, it dampened from doubt. What else had she unleashed? The second blue orb bothered her. There should've been only one.

She reached the clearing where several wooden structures stood. Her mother was on the porch of the largest one glaring at her. Esmarelda had to talk fast. She wouldn't get much of a chance to plead her case.

She thought about life as a tree frog and swallowed the lump in her throat. Had it sounded like a croak?

Ray Wenck

CHAPTER TWO

"Ha! Ha!" He thrust again. "Take that! Oh, you want some too, eh?" The sweat-drenched shirtless man pivoted and performed a series of parries and attacks on imaginary opponents. He'd dispatched many such foes in the last thirty minutes, his graceful movements like a choreographed dance.

With two long athletic strides, he leaped for the bed, landed, blocked an invisible lunge, and swung a vicious backhand slice. "Off with your head, Sheriff of Nottingham." Bouncing twice, he propelled off the bed, landing on the polished wood plank floor. His socks slipped out from under him and he landed hard on his butt. "Oof!" He rolled. "Son of a…that's gonna leave a bruise."

He brought the blade level with the floor. "Strike a man when he's down, eh, Blackbeard? I'll teach you." He rolled backwards and came to his feet, swinging. His cuts were a blur of motion. Then, in an upward diagonal slice courtesy of his Kendo classes, he said, "Take that, pirate."

He paused for a moment, breathing hard; long, wet hair plastered to his face and neck. Then, in slow motion, he pivoted. He widened his eyes in mock surprise. "So, Mr. Vader, you wish to test your force against mine? So be it." He rushed to press the attack as his phone came to life playing the theme song from last summer's big fantasy adventure movie, a blockbuster based on the novel he'd written.

"Time out, Lord Vader."

He picked up the cell phone, looked at the screen, and winced. It was Jackie, his ex-wife and literary agent.

"Shit!" He sucked in two quick, deep breaths to calm his exertion and answered cheerily. "Hey lovely, how are you this bright, wonderful morning?"

"Cut the crap. Where're my pages?"

"Pages?"

"The pages you promised me last week. God, you're so full of shit. Why do I bother with you?"

"Because you still love me and you know it."

"Fuck that! Have you written anything?"

"Well, yeah—I, uh..."

"Wait a minute. Are you breathing hard? You've been sword fighting again, haven't you?"

"I was just getting some exercise."

"Oh, bullshit! You forget I know you probably better than you know yourself. You sword fight when you're blocked. It clears your mind. Motivates you. Gets your creative juices flowing. How long have you been fighting?"

"Jackie, I—"

"How long, Derek?"

"Ah, I don't know. Thirty minutes, maybe."

"Thirty minutes? Wow! That's a bad one. How many days?"

His voice a defeated whisper, he said, "Six."

"Six!" Her voice exploded through the phone. "Six...dear God. Why can't you be like most men and sword fight with that little dagger between your legs? That might get your juices flowing."

"I think something's coming."

"If you use the other sword, you'd *know* something was coming. Wait—you think?" Her sigh was loud and long in his ear. "Damn it, Derek. You're under contract. You have a deadline and it's coming up fast. They advanced you based on your last book's success, and an amount almost unheard of in today's publishing world. They will not hesitate to come after you for that money if I can't convince them you've got something good enough to wait for."

"Jackie, I'm trying. I really am. It's just—"

"Just what? The idea of fighting imaginary villains is more alluring than being able to pay your rent? That studio apartment is costing you dearly. If you want to continue living there, you need to earn big. And not just a once-a-year thing."

"I know. I know. I'm busting my brain here trying to come up with something fresh, but..."

Her voice softened. "What, Derek? Talk to me."

"With the success of *Swordsman's Gambit*, I'm having trouble coming up with something that's even equal to it, let alone tops it. The fame and fortune are great, but anything I write now pales in comparison. I think I was happier being a mid-level fantasy writer. My fans loved me no matter what I wrote. Now that millions of people have read the book or seen the movie, there's a lot of pressure not to disappoint."

"Then don't disappoint—especially not me, and definitely not the publisher. You screw them over, and you'll never get published again."

Now he sighed, the effort draining him of all energy. "I know."

"Oh, Derek. How can I help?"

"I'm not sure even your considerable charms can help me right now."

"If you mean what I think you do, you're right. They won't help because it's not happening."

"No, I didn't mean that, but while we're on the subject, what would be so wrong?"

"You want a list? How about 'cause we're divorced. I'm living with a guy. I have no interest in you that way. It would cross a professional line. You had your chance and tossed it away. You want more?"

"No, that'll do."

"Derek, if you're stalling in hopes of me coming back, it's a huge mistake."

"No. I would never do that. I know better. I blew it. It's over. I still love you, but it's finished. I'm trying to move on like you have. I'm just having a bad case of writer's block, and to answer your question, there's nothing you can do. I have to work through it myself. Don't worry; I'll come up with something."

"Well, not to add extra pressure, but don't just toss some words on a page and call it a story. You owe them your best effort."

"What if that is my best effort?"

"Derek, we both know it isn't. You're a very good writer. I've always enjoyed your stories. I believe in you one hundred percent. You can do this. Put down the sword and pick up the pen."

"Nice sword and pen wordplay. Well played."

"Writers write. Sit that nice ass down and give me a few pages to work with. I'll even take a synopsis or a few great ideas if you have them."

"So you still like my ass."

"And that's what you took from that? I should have known better. Yes, I've always liked your ass. It's the asshole part I couldn't live with."

The words stung. She was deadlier with her tongue than he ever was with his sword. He stared at the phone, long after Jackie disconnected, his heart mortally wounded.

CHAPTER THREE

Derek slid the expensive longsword into the scabbard mounted to the side of his writing desk. He kept it close for inspiration and to help work out fight sequences. It had cost him a lot of money, but after the royalties began pouring in, he splurged. He took sword fighting lessons from a European-style trainer and a Japanese sword master. He also took fencing lessons and competed at a local gym.

The European master had also taught him knife fighting skills and hand-to-hand combat, and the Japanese master taught him judo and karate. He used the weekly lessons for exercise as well as research. The knowledge and training had paid off, which was evident by the success of his first three books.

Swordsman's Gambit was the third. The book had sold reasonably well, and after Jackie negotiated a contract for a movie deal, sales soared. She was currently pitching the next book to movie producers, but since it wasn't a sequel, she was finding it difficult to land a deal.

The publisher bought the first two but balked at the third due to sluggish sales. The first book earned out, but the second hadn't; at least until the movie based on the third book came out. Then the backlist took off and the publisher offered a new three-book deal, which he jumped on. It seemed too good to pass up, but in retrospect, the success and acclaim was too much for him to handle. He went to Hollywood as a consultant on the movie, which really meant he was only slightly more important than the caterer. He had no say or control, but that was all right with him. He just liked being on the set and watching the production unfold before him. He partied and hung out with the fast crowd. Several paparazzi captured his antics with wannabe starlets, and that had chased Jackie away. Derek regretted it every day since. He didn't doubt for a minute that guilt was the underlying reason for his block.

He didn't have even the merest hint of an idea for the first story. He stared at his chair, dreading sitting there. Inhaling, he caught a whiff of his body odor and a practical excuse presented itself. He went to take a shower.

Under the hot water, he tried to relax and allow thoughts and ideas to naturally present themselves. Soon, however, he was forcing them. Each one was nothing more than a rehash of previous work, an alternate version of a book he'd read, or a movie he'd seen. By the time he stepped from the shower, his anxiety had grown.

He dressed and went into the large apartment. It had more than enough space for him; in fact, it had more square footage than most apartments in the area. Its open floorplan didn't have many interior walls. The kitchen was along the northern wall. The bedroom area was on the east side. The southern exposure where he placed his writing table and workout area was half brick and half glass and allowed for plenty of sunlight and a decent view. The living area with the massive smart TV mounted to the wall was on the west side next to the outer door.

The only two enclosed spaces were the bathroom and another room split into two sections. One half housed the furnace, water heater, and washer and dryer. The other side was meant for storage, but he used it as his closet. The ceiling was twenty feet high and had six paddle fans.

Without looking in the direction of his desk, Derek beelined for the kitchen. He made a ham and cheese sandwich, put a handful of chips on his plate, and grabbed a bottle of water. He started to sit at the kitchen table but looked up as if the desk had called his name. He frowned, picked up his plate, and went to the desk.

Over the next two hours, Derek wrote, deleted, wrote, deleted, and wrote again. He was rereading his latest effort and only seconds from erasing the monstrosity when the phone chirped at him. It was a text from Jackie.

I do believe in you.

He stared at the message for a long moment. A twinge of sadness hung like a weight on his heart. He placed the phone down and looked at the six pages he had just written. He drummed his fingers on the table, gnawing at his lower lip. Derek attached the pages to an email and sent it to Jackie. They weren't good, but it would keep her occupied and off his back for a while.

He stood and reached for the sword and paused with his hand on the ornate hilt. Jackie's words came back to him.

You sword fight when you're blocked.

He released the sword. *Yeah, so what?* He walked toward the workout area, tying his long dark hair back in a ponytail.

Stepping onto the mat, Derek moved through a series of stretches and warm-ups before going through his karate forms. He'd show her. He could avoid writing just as well by doing other things. He didn't have to use a sword. He realized the absurdity of his thought but didn't care. He was still angry about her final words to him.

It's the asshole part I couldn't live with.

In truth, it wasn't her or her words he was angry with; it was himself. He *was* an asshole. He had no one else to blame for the failed marriage but himself.

Derek was in good shape. He had no ultimate goal for his workout regimen; he just liked the way he felt afterward. He had once tried his hand at professional tennis but wasn't quite good enough to remain on the tour. In truth, he didn't have the drive or competitive nature that those who beat him regularly displayed.

He finished, toweled off, and forced himself back into his writing chair. He called up the story but refused to reread the whole thing, knowing he'd only delete the drivel he'd written. Instead, he read the last line, and having no clear idea of where the story was going, picked up from there. He had always been a "pantser" in his writing style, preferring the story to unfold as he wrote rather than outline it beforehand. But this storyline was weak, even for him. The plot was thin, but he wanted to get something—anything—down. He'd worry about rewrites later.

He worked through character development, forcing one scene after another. It was a waste of time, knowing that once he finished for the day and read through it, he'd erase it, but he had to keep going. Something would click soon. A tiny thread of a good idea would come from this. He had to believe it, yet after nearly four straight hours of pounding the keys, he pushed back, shoulders aching from the tension of knowing the story was crap.

He stretched in his seat and looked out the wall of windows. The sun was already deep into its decline. He should call it a day, fix dinner, and try to relax by watching TV. Derek stood and bent at the waist, stretching to touch first his toes then the floor with his fingers, then palms. He was agile with good flexibility. He reached farther, pushing his muscles as far as they'd go without strain.

Derek straightened and looked at the kitchen clock. Seven forty-three. He debated going out to a club for a while. Lord knew he needed the diversion. No; he wasn't in the mood. He'd only sit at the bar and drink himself into a stupor, and tomorrow he'd be nursing a hangover rather than getting any work done. Of course, that was the point, wasn't it?

He ate a simple dinner of grilled chicken breast over a salad and went to bed.

CHAPTER FOUR

Derek didn't usually dream; at least he never remembered, and was not prone to nightmares. Whether spurred by his inability to write a decent story or by Jackie's hurtful words, this night was different.

He was inside a dim spotlight surrounded by total darkness. Something or someone moved around him just beyond the light's reach. He turned in fast circles, trying to catch a glimpse of whatever it was. Then, in a sudden disorienting flash, he was falling through the darkness like someone had turned him on his side and dumped him into a void.

The light still surrounded him, blackness still engulfing the light, but now he was falling. His arms and legs flailed as he fell endlessly. Somewhere in the distance, a light hurtled toward him. His already intense panic escalated to near hysteria. Derek tried to air paddle out of the path but could not alter his course. His eyes strained wide with fright. The light bore down on him as his speed accelerated.

The light grew larger until in a burst, it passed within inches of him. To his shock, he thought he saw a man haloed within the light just as he was, but the vision had gone by too fast for him to be sure. A few seconds later, his speed dwindled. He slowed at a steady pace, like braking on a roller coaster after all the drops and high-speed twists had ended.

He felt his breath return to a normal rhythm. His heart, though still pounding, lessened its assault on his chest. Then the light vanished, leaving him in only the surrounding darkness. He landed in a whiplash-like collision with something soft. He slammed into it butt first, whipping head and legs down a fraction later. He moaned against the cushioned thing. His head hurt and his vision swirled.

Feeling more secure now that he'd settled on something firm, he kept his eyes closed to fight off the wave of nausea. He gripped rough cloth on both sides as if holding onto a lifeline. As the sensation of falling subsided, Derek tried to recall how much he'd drank last night, although he didn't remember going out. This was the worst hangover in recent memory. It was so severe that it brought vows of giving up drinking for eternity, but having seen how short eternity was from previous recitation of such vows, he gave up and just tried to stop the room from spinning.

He had no idea how long he lay there, but the longer he was still, the better he felt. After a while, he forced one eye open. A thin, blurry crease of light filtered through the windows. To his surprise, it caused no pain.

Derek opened the other eye and tried to focus. Something didn't look right about his room. It was darker and more bricky. His walls were drywall on three sides. These walls were stone. He took a chance and pushed up to balance himself on his elbows. Yeah, something was wrong with this picture. Encouraged by the lack of pain, Derek swung his legs over the side of the bed. Still no headache. If he'd been drinking as heavily as he thought, the lack of a headache was a first.

He caught a whiff of something musty. Was that him? Didn't he shower after his workout? He sniffed his armpits. Nope. The smell wasn't emanating from him. At least not all of it. A damp, musty odor hung in the air.

His feet found the cold stone floor.

Wait! What? He looked down at the large gray rocks. As if he'd stepped on hot coals, he recoiled. Where was his beautiful oak flooring? He bent his knees and placed his feet on the bed. The bed was too hard. And lumpy. This wasn't his bed. Where the hell was he?

Then he noticed he was naked. *What the...?* He seldom slept naked unless he...

There was movement next to him in the bed. He glanced back and saw a woman under heavy covers, her left arm and breast exposed.

Derek gasped and jumped off the bed. What had he done? He tried to remember but grasped nothing but blankness. He stepped away from the bed, trying not to wake the woman, whoever she was, and searched for his clothes. They were nowhere to be found. Perhaps they'd started their adventure in another room. At least he hoped they had; otherwise, he'd arrived sans clothes. Awkward, but unfortunately not a first.

He spied two large wooden doors, unlike those in his apartment. These were heavy wooden planks held together by wide bands of black steel, like those in a castle. *A castle?* He did a slow three-sixty scan of the room. That's exactly what this was. A castle. How the hell did he get here?

The woman moved again. Derek reeled backward. He searched in vain for something to cover himself with but came up empty. He kept a cautious eye on the bed's occupant to see if she woke. The bed was massive and made from full logs. Ten foot tall posts reached upward from each corner toward the thirty-foot-high ceiling. A circular stone stairway spiraled up one long curved wall.

Curiosity making him forget his strange situation, he moved to the series of translucent glass windows and peered out. The ground was fifty yards below. A large stone wall surrounded the building like that of a proper castle. People bustled around all in period garb.

He must be in some historical replication of a medieval castle; one of those places where people pay to relive a time long gone. He'd been to Renaissance festivals before, but this one with the huge castle was by far the best. He touched the wall. It was cold and real stone. This must have cost some company an enormous amount of money. Enthralled by the realism and relaxed by the rational explanation, he'd forgotten about the woman until she spoke.

"What a nice view, m'lord."

Shocked, he jumped, striking his head on the stone at the top of one of the windows. He cried out, holding his head.

Instead of concern, the woman burst into a hearty laugh. He turned to speak and found her sitting up, exposed to the waist. Her large breasts hung low. Her pale skin appeared never to have been touched by the sun. She beamed.

"Care for an early morning bit before I go?"

Reminded of his nakedness, he released his head and bent a bit, covering his manhood.

"I'm glad you weren't that shy last night, m'lord. It mightn't have been nearly as much fun." She tossed the covers aside, exposing her ample dark muff. "Well, what's your decision? Another go?" She opened her legs.

"Oh. My. God."

"Maybe not a deity, but I'll let you worship at my altar if you wish."

"Ah, no thank you, uh, M'lady. I'm fine."

"Oh. M'lady, is it? Do you mock me now?"

"No. No. No mocking intended. But perhaps you can tell me where we are. Maybe more importantly, tell me who you are and how we got—uh, here. I don't have any memory of last night."

The woman slid off the bed, hands on hips, and pouted. "I'm not memorable to you?" She scooped up a dress. "I can understand, I suppose, considering how much you had to drink."

There it was. He had been drinking. But if so, and he drank enough for his mind to go blank, why didn't he have a headache or cotton mouth or—anything?

She disappeared behind the bed and Derek figured she was being modest as she dressed. Then he heard the sound of dribbling water. Did they have plumbing here? He supposed they would have to, if only for health regulations. He plucked a small pillow off the floor and held it in front of himself. He wanted to use the bathroom next, and as he walked past the bed he found the naked woman squatting over a pot and peeing.

She looked up at him and smiled. "Almost done."

He backed away in a hurry. He decided to wait until she was out of the room before using the facilities. If there were facilities. If the creators of this adventure were seeking realism, a chamber pot was going a little too far.

Someone pounded on the door. "I suppose that's housekeeping wanting us to vacate the room." More pounding, vigorous this time. He wasn't about to answer the door naked, and he didn't have to. The door exploded open, slamming against the wall and almost bouncing closed again.

A hostile woman with flaming red hair burst into the room, smoke trailing from her ears.

Now what?

The woman stopped in front of him and pointed at the nearly dressed woman. "What does that trollop have that is any better or different than your wife has?"

Huh?

CHAPTER FIVE

"You! Get your round rump out of this room. If I catch you up here again, I will flog you myself."

The woman paled even more, if that was possible, as she hurried from the room still not quite dressed. The red haired woman slammed the door before she was completely out.

"My lord, Husband."

He looked behind him in hopes there was another *my lord, Husband* in the room she was speaking to. This was too bizarre. Was this all part of the act? Was this like the TV series *West World*, but as a medieval fantasy world for his enjoyment? Or perhaps he had paid for a dinner theater version that came complete with a storyline. Even their accents were Old English. Well done. But did the complete package also come with his nightly entertainment, or had that been negotiated separately?

Then a new thought entered his confused mind. He felt the color drain from his face. Was he being pranked? Did some of his friends drug and kidnap him? He looked around the massive room for cameras. If they existed, they were well hidden.

"I understand you are angry with your father for arranging this marriage, but the sooner you get used to it, the better for us both. I know you do not like me, but I do not care. All I ask is that you do your husbandly duty and make me with child. Once that happens, I will fade away and you never have to touch or see me again. But you are not to bed any of your stable of whores until you give us an heir. Is that understood?"

Derek nodded, mouth agape at the proposal and the thought of giving her a child. If this was all a stage act, it was extremely good. He'd have to fill out a comment card to say so.

"Are you too exhausted from your late night adventures to perform now? Or perhaps still too drunk?"

"Huh?"

"Don't be daft. Did you wear yourself out with your trollop?"

Not knowing what to say, he shook his head.

"Fine. Then since I have you here, do your duty."

She pushed him aside, hiked up her dress and all its layers of skirts, and lay down on the bed. When he didn't move, she said, "Well, what are you waiting for?"

Despite his confusion, he was getting aroused. He pressed the pillow tighter against himself to keep the erection covered.

"My lord, I'm begging you. Please." Her voice softened as she pleaded.

"Ah, sure. Okay. As long as this is allowed."

"I'm telling you it is. And why would it not be? I am your wife, after all. If anything is not allowed, it is your constant need for women you are not married to."

Sensing some sort of honey trap, he looked around the room again for hidden cameras.

"Do you need me to do something to get you ready?"

"What? Ah, no. I don't need any assistance."

"Well, obviously you do because I'm still waiting."

Tentative, he edged closer to the bed. A tuft of silky red hair awaited his approach. He crawled up on the bed and positioned himself between her legs, still feeling as though someone was about to burst into the room and say either, "You've been pranked," or "You're under arrest for sleeping with a minor." *Minor?* Where had that come from?

He looked at her face. Now that she wasn't red-faced with rage, she did look young. No, there was no way he was doing this. Statutory rape would put him away for a long time. He backed off the bed, but she sat up and grabbed his arms.

"Am I truly so repulsive that you cannot bring yourself to be with me? You didn't seem to have any problem on our wedding night or that last time."

"No, you are not repulsive. You are very beautiful."

"Then what prevents you? Do you despise me so?"

"No. I don't know you. How can I despise you?"

"Then I am begging you, my lord. Please. Both families call for an heir. We have been wed four months now, and you have touched me only twice. Sire an heir and I will not bother you again. You will never have to force yourself to my bed."

"God, this feels so wrong."

She lay back, pulling him forward to her. "It is a simple act, and by previous efforts, shouldn't take more than a few seconds to complete."

Did she just slam me?

She yanked the pillow from his hands and gripped his erection. "See, my lord? Part of you is willing." She pulled him toward her. He went more from fear of pain than a willingness to perform. She inched him closer until he felt the ticklish wisps of hair.

"How old are you?"

"I'm old enough to be the lady of these lands and your wife."

"Okay, but that doesn't answer the question."

"I'm old enough to bear your children."

"Again, no help."

The tip of his erection touched something moist. He started to recoil, but she squeezed harder, making it clear he wasn't going anywhere.

This had to be a dream. My God, that was it. His subconscious was giving him a story in his dreams; something to write about when he woke. But would he remember it? If it was truly just a dream, he wanted to make it as vivid as possible to etch it into his memory and better recall the details.

He allowed her to place him at the precipice.

"Please, my lord. There is no need to be hurtful or strike at me this time. You do not need to beat me into submission or punish me for what angers you."

"Seriously? Someone beat you during sex?"

"Don't be crude, my lord. Ease yourself inside."

He looked into her green eyes and saw the pain and sadness there. He also saw fear. Whoever she'd been with before had hurt her and she anticipated more of the same.

She gripped his hips as he slid deeper. God help him, she felt good. He reached the extent of his length and held there. He touched the sides of her face and held her lightly, but the mere touch caused her to flinch and gasp.

"Relax. I will not hurt you."

He lowered his face to hers and placed a tender kiss on her quivering lips. He wanted to believe it was from her building excitement but couldn't help but feel it was more from fear. She did not return the kiss.

He lifted his hips and began a slow, rhythmic rise and fall. Her eyes widened with surprise, and a small gasp escaped her. He watched her, unable to pull his gaze from her mesmerizing eyes.

His pace increased as his climax built. Her breathing came in short, quick bursts. A low growl filled her throat, but she swallowed it. Her hips rose to meet him, then stopped, as if realizing it was wrong. Caught up in her rising pleasure, she was unable to stay still or silent. Her hips moved in rhythm with his.

His explosion grew near. God, if this was a dream, it was the best one he'd ever had.

She released a low groan, her eyes rolling up before she closed them. In the midst of her orgasm and just before his, she said, "Sixteen."

He drove hard now, lost in the throes of his satisfaction.

"Huh?"

He was close.

"You asked my age."

About to explode.

"I'm sixteen."

"What?"

It was a trap. He tried to pull out, knowing it was already too late, but she wrapped her legs around him, squeezing tight, and dug her nails into his buttocks to hold him in place until the last drop of seed was wrung from him.

CHAPTER SIX

He lay on top of her, spent, in shock, and incapable of movement or thought.

"Ah, my lord?"

"Huh?"

"Are you finished?"

"What? Oh. Yeah." Derek slid off, rolling to his back. "Sorry." He placed an arm across his forehead. This had better only be a dream because otherwise, he was in deep shit. He stared at the ceiling. Everything looked so real.

The woman—correction, teenager—straightened her skirts and sat up. She looked down at him, questions forming beneath the expression on her face. "Thank you, my lord." She stood. "I'll take my leave now." She took two steps, stopped, and grabbed a bedpost for support. She stood for a moment, then looked back at him. Her face was flushed. She blew out a breath. A quick tremble rippled through her. She exhaled again and straightened, more erect as if now composed enough to move. "Are you all right, my lord?"

"Oh, great. I just slept with an underage girl, but other than that, I'm fine."

"I-I don't understand. What does my age have to do with it? I am your wife."

He turned to see her. She was very attractive and did look older than she was. For a moment, he contemplated using that as his defense, but it was ridiculous to even consider. No, he was going to jail.

Why had he given in to his urges? Had he needed sex that badly? He must have. One woman left and a second took her place. At least the first one was mature enough not to send him to prison. He didn't understand anything that was happening. Not himself, not the bizarre scene surrounding him, and not the need for two women. What had he become? Why?

He remembered thinking it was okay since it was obviously a dream. How would that sound in court? *I thought it was a dream, your honor.* That would certainly be good for some chuckles around the courthouse.

"My lord?"

"Yeah, I'm fine." She gave a tentative nod, then turned to leave again. "Wait."

She stopped.

"Can you tell me where my clothes are?"

She pivoted, and for a second, her face clouded. He thought she was going to launch into another tirade, but then it faded and she pointed at the floor. "I would say last night's activities got wild. Your clothes are strewn all about the floor." With that, she turned and stormed out, slamming the door.

"I don't know why she's so angry. I'm the one going to jail," he said aloud. Then, a more nauseating thought struck him. What if she gets pregnant?

Derek looked down at his penis, lounging happily on its brown thatch. Absurdly, he thought about the movie *Splendor in the Grass.* He released a derisive snort. "Since you have so much more control over me than my other head, maybe you should write the stories," he muttered to himself.

He rose to search for his clothes and felt faint. Nauseous, he lay back down and curled into the fetal position. He lay still for a while, feeling drowsy. Then, with a sudden lurch that drove the air from his lungs, he was falling again. Once more, the ball of light engulfed him. He sped through the darkness like the *Enterprise* rushing through space on its way to places man hadn't yet been. He knew one place this man shouldn't have gone.

Again, the other ball of light approached at warp speed and blew past. This trip was equally as frightening as the first but didn't seem to take as long. He landed, curled in a ball, and stayed there.

Derek waited for the dizzying sensation to pass and opened his eyes. The familiar surroundings were heartening. He leaped from the bed, but the sudden rush brought pain and a wave of vertigo. Lightheaded, he reached for the bed. He missed but was able to slow his fall to the floor. He sat still for several long moments until he felt better. Only then did he risk looking around again.

To his great relief, he was back inside his apartment. It *had* been a dream. He broke into hysterical laughter. He laughed loud and hard until his stomach hurt. Then he began to sob. As the cries lessened, exhaustion took hold and he fell asleep on the oak plank floor.

Derek was awakened by the sound of his phone. Stiff and achy from sleeping on the floor, he made his way with slow progress toward his desk. He snagged the phone and answered without looking at the caller ID.

"It's about time," Jackie said. "I know you've been ducking my calls. I was about to come over there and beat you to death. At least that would be a more fitting ending than the slow death you'll have if I ever submit a piece of rubbish like this. They'd bury both of us in the same grave without the benefit of embalming or a casket."

"Gee, Jackie. Tell me how you really feel."

Silence.

"Tell me the truth, Derek. Are you done? Have all the creative juices dried up?"

He sighed. "I don't know, Jackie. Maybe. I'm sorry."

"Well, it was a good ride while it lasted. They'll want their advance back."

"Yeah. I should be able to handle that."

"What will you do now?"

"I honestly don't know."

"Look, you've still got a little time before the first draft is due. Think about it and let me know."

"Okay. Oh, Jackie?"

"Yes, love?"

"Thanks for everything you've done for me."

"Sure."

He disconnected and stared at his computer. Then he shifted his gaze to his body. To his surprise, he was still wearing the same clothes he was wearing yesterday. He couldn't remember getting dressed, but then it came to him that his nakedness had all been part of the dream; the very vivid dream that had survived his waking.

The memories flowed back in perfect sequence, the reality expressing itself in the tiny details. He sat in the desk chair as he recalled the flawless beauty of the young woman. "Well, at least you have great taste in dream women."

Derek stopped and stared at the computer in confusion. It was not in its usual place. He racked his brain trying to recollect when and why he had moved it. Looking left, he found his desk lamp wasn't on the desk. He rolled the chair and saw it on the floor.

"What the..."

He bent to retrieve it and set it back in place and discovered the bulb was shattered. Had he thrown it to the floor in a fit of frustration? Or had someone else been there? But when? While he slept?

Concerned, he rotated in his seat to take in the rest of the apartment. Everything looked to be in order. At least nothing appeared to be missing. He turned back to his desk, spun the laptop to its proper position, and lifted the screen. Derek tried to shake the feeling that someone had been there. Something was still off. He sensed it stronger now.

Then he saw it; rather, he didn't see it. The sword was gone from the scabbard. In a panic, he leaped to his feet and scanned the room.

It was standing in the corner just beyond the mats, but it wasn't leaning against anything. He walked to it, alarmed at the sight. Someone—him?—had embedded the point into the wooden floor.

Derek stared at it for a long moment before pulling it free. What had happened last night? Had it all been part of the dream? Had he been sleepwalking?

"What the hell?"

Derek looked at the door. Curious, he went and opened it. Not sure what he was looking for, he checked for scratches on the lock, like he'd seen in numerous TV crime shows. His neighbor across the hall, Mr. Jenkins, stepped out of his loft, pulling the door closed behind him. The elderly man frowned. "Carving a big turkey, Derek?" He pointed.

"Huh?" He realized he still held the sword. "Oh," he chuckled humorlessly. "Funny. I was just working out a fight sequence."

"Must have been a pretty violent one, considering all the crashing and shouting coming from your apartment last night."

Derek was stunned. "The what?" He recovered. "Oh, yeah, sorry about that. Got a little carried away and accidentally hit a lamp."

"Uh-huh. Do try to keep it down, will you? We old people need our sleep." He smiled and walked toward the elevator.

Derek shut the door, slid the sword back inside its berth, and sat down. No doubt about it; he had been sleepwalking. The dream must have had a strange effect on him. The dream. The images came flooding back.

He saw himself in the computer screen. He stared at it for a while, mesmerized by the wide smile on his face.

Then he noticed something else. The tension that had knotted his stomach and strained the muscles in the back of his neck and across his shoulders for weeks now was gone.

He turned on the laptop and the screen came to life. He called up the document file and opened the trash he'd written the day before. He didn't bother reading it. He knew it was rubbish as he was writing. He deleted everything, paused a moment, and began to write.

His fingers flew across the keyboard. In a trance-like state, the story came to life on the screen. It was well after midnight when he stopped.

CHAPTER SEVEN

He woke the next morning with a start to the sound of someone pounding on the door. For a moment, he was gripped by fear, remembering the scene from his dream. He expected the beautiful woman to barge in yelling at him again.

Derek scanned the room to make sure he was still in his apartment. To his relief, he was. Then he patted the bed next to him. Vacant. Again, relief. He got out of bed and found he was naked. He stopped in his tracks. How odd. He never slept in the nude. He glanced around the room. Finding his clothes folded neatly on a chair, he yanked on his pants and grabbed the shirt. He was pulling it on as the door opened.

Jackie bustled in and approached him with obvious intent. Fearing harm, he recoiled as she wrapped him in a strong embrace and kissed his cheek.

"Done, my fine ass." She stepped back and held up a handful of printed pages. "Derek, this is brilliant. Of course, I know it's just a sampling and needs editing, but if the rest is like this, it might be your best work yet. I have to say, I was worried about you. I honestly thought you were done. How did you manage to overcome your block? Oh, no matter; just so you did. Do you have any more?"

"Jackie, slow down. I just got up."

"Well, get to work. I'll make coffee." She gave him a gentle but firm push toward his desk, then hustled into the kitchen. "God, I'm so excited. Do you have more?"

"Give a guy a chance, Jackie. I worked until midnight last night. I sent you what I had."

"Okay. Sorry. Stop talking and get to work."

Derek yawned and stretched, then sat at the laptop. He fired it up and opened the untitled document. The aroma of brewing coffee reached his nostrils and he inhaled deeply. He watched his ex-wife working in the kitchen and smiled at the old familiar scene. He missed those days; missed her. His smile faded at the memory of how he'd thrown that and so much more away.

Jackie walked across the floor, heels clacking loudly. She held two steaming cups and wore an excited smile. It was exactly like the old days. "Hey. Get to work. You've got better things to do than watch me."

He accepted the cup and breathed in the smell. "Important things maybe, but never better."

Their eyes met. Tenderness shone in hers, or was it sadness? Maybe she was recalling the past as well. She put on a smile that didn't reach her eyes. Yes, she was remembering, but he could tell it wasn't the good things. He turned away before the mood became too dark to recover his muse.

"So how did you come up with the idea?"

Derek set the cup down. "It came to me in a dream."

"A dream! Really?" She lifted her cup in a toast. "Well, here's to more pleasant dreams."

Derek reread his last paragraph. He'd stopped at a new chapter. A sudden sick feeling hit him. He'd finished the story as far as it went. He had nothing else in mind to progress the narrative. As he sat there unable to add another word, he felt Jackie's presence like a weight on his neck. The longer he sat, the more apprehensive he felt. The old tension returned. Tightness encircled his shoulders and neck, causing a headache to form behind his eyes.

After nearly fifteen minutes, Jackie walked back to the kitchen and washed her cup. She returned and forced a smile. "I'm sorry. I should go. I'm putting too much pressure on you. Guess I'm not the muse I used to be."

"Nothing's as it used to be." He didn't know why he'd said it. The words came out before he could lock them inside. They seemed to sting her.

She stiffened. "No; nothing is, but we move on, adjust, and do the best we can. Good writing."

She walked toward the door. Her leaving brought deep sadness. "Jackie." She paused without looking back. "You'll always be my muse."

"Not always. But if it works for the moment, that's fine."

She left him hurting as he had once hurt her. One sentence was all it took to ruin the moment. One stupid sentence. Why hadn't he typed it instead of saying it out loud? He was a fool, but then he'd known that for a long time, back to when he'd allowed himself to be swayed by the glitz and glamour of a Hollywood scene where he did not belong. Just like if his tryst with a teenager was real, one night could ruin his life.

It was too late to earn that trust back. All he could do now was be thankful she'd kept him as a client. At least he still had her in his life, if only on the fringes.

Derek began writing thoughtlessly, trying to take his mind off his foul mood. By mid-afternoon, he'd advanced the story a mere four pages. Three and a half of them were trash. He got up and paced. He walked to the mats but wasn't motivated to work out. Walking back to his desk, he slid the sword free of its scabbard. He stared at its shining length. Looking at the intricate etchings and the fine-honed edge, he wondered how would it feel to be penetrated by the blade. To have it run through his body and exit out his back, or have it slice across his abdomen, spilling his intestines at his feet.

Over the past few months, he'd often thought the sword would be the mechanism of his own destruction. He stared at the blade and a long, slow, bone-chilling shiver crept through him. The realization that indeed his death *would* come from a blade, either by his own hand or that of another struck him like a premonition, but it wouldn't be today. He would not let Jackie down. When he bowed out, it would be after he had made her proud of him one last time.

Derek slid the sword back in place, looked at the screen, then went to fix lunch. He might not be ready to die yet, but he wasn't ready to write yet, either.

He fixed a sandwich, poured a glass of milk, and went to his bed. Derek plumped up the pillows and sat back against the headboard. He took a bite of the turkey and cheese sandwich, chewing but not tasting and trying to recall any forgotten details of the dream.

He was halfway through the sandwich when he felt the strange sensation begin. Fear surrounded him once more, but he was awake.

Wasn't he?

He sat up, intending to get off the bed. Then, he was falling. A scream fought its way up from his core and was choked out beneath the half-chewed bread, cheese, and meat.

Darkness came. The second light flashed past. He thought he heard a scream, but had it come from him?

He landed fast, whiplashing on the somewhat soft mattress. His eyes fluttered and blackness took him under.

CHAPTER EIGHT

Derek had no idea how long he'd been unconscious, but when he opened his eyes, he found himself back in the castle room. This time, however, the bed was empty of the remains of any late-night diversions. He was alone. He was at once excited and afraid.

He climbed from the bed and saw he was naked. Again. *What was it about this dream world that he didn't wear clothes?* He looked around the floor, and not seeing any of his own, picked up the clothes scattered on the floor. He dressed, surprised that everything including the boots fit, then went to the window. The day was still bright; perhaps an hour before dusk. This time, he took in as much as he could. Armed men walked the ramparts on the castle walls. The grounds below bustled with activity. Beyond the walls, men, women, and children worked the fields; the crops they tended unrecognizable from this distance.

He decided to explore his surroundings in hopes that when he woke, he'd have more to add to the story. Feeling an electric jolt of excitement race through him, Derek opened the heavy door to an empty stone corridor running left and right. Across the hall to the right was another large wooden door. The hall continued and ended at a window. To the left, it curved out of sight. He followed the curve.

The hall led down a stairway with wide stone steps curving along the wall. Derek followed, trying to keep the sound of the hard heels of his boots from reverberating off the stone walls. He studied everything from the size and shape of the stone to the black wall sconces and the feel and smell of the chilly air.

He reached the next floor. A long hall ran the width of the castle. The curve of the wall at the opposite end suggested another stairway. Four doors, smaller than the ones above, dotted each wall. He continued down the stairs to the ground floor. Four more doors stood to the right. To the left were two large arches leading into a huge open room. At the near end on a raised platform sat a large ornate wooden throne atop a white stone base. Two smaller seats, hand carved with decorative swirls, sat on either side of the throne.

Pillars on both sides supported a narrow balcony. Large wooden double doors almost twice his height stood at the far end. He walked toward them. Even trying to tiptoe could not prevent the echoes of his footsteps. He glanced behind nervously, hoping not to be discovered.

He stopped and pressed his ear to the place where the two wooden constructs met. A chilly breeze came through and he heard muted sounds beyond the doors. Derek was sure they led outside.

He gripped the heavy metal handle and pulled. Though it took an initial hard tug, once it was in motion, the door opened as if on glides. The air hit him in the face, causing a shiver. Two men in castle arms and dress snapped to attention as he stepped out. In unison, they said, "M'lord."

Not knowing the customary response, Derek said, "At ease, men." That brought a confused look to the one on his right, but neither man relaxed.

He strode out and found himself on the top stone step of a flight of twelve leading to the castle grounds. The inhabitants moved about, performing their tasks and chores. Some noticed him, but none greeted him or even nodded. Most ignored him; some hastened their pace to get away from him. One old woman curled up a lip in a sneer.

"Wonder what that was about," Derek muttered.

He could hear the sound of swordplay from somewhere on the grounds. Intrigued, he walked down the steps in search of the metallic clangs, taking in the details of his surroundings. The castle itself was not large, but the grounds were vast. The gate was open and the fields beyond were in view.

Along the castle wall and underneath the parapet were small shacks. They looked too small to be lodgings. At the edge of the castle, he turned left and stopped. To his astonishment, he discovered the outer walls abutted against a massive sheer-faced mountain. It seemed the mountain was actually the rear wall of the grounds. He pivoted and took in the surrounding area. No other mountain was near. The others were far off to the west. He continued his exploration.

Along this side was an assortment of structures that looked more like hovels. Here, the population was more dense. Women cooked on open fires and did laundry. Children ran and played.

The sword clangs came from somewhere beyond the hovels. A strange mix of aromas assaulted his sense of smell. Some were easily recognizable, like the smell of roasting meat or charred burning wood. A few he could discern by process of elimination, like sweat or musk. But others were just repugnant and crinkled his nose.

Derek noticed that most of the castle folk averted their eyes as he approached. He didn't know why they seemed to despise. Behind him, a woman mumbled something he couldn't make out, but he got the distinct feeling it was some sort of curse.

He passed the structures, moving to the rear of the grounds. In front of him, the open land stretched fifty yards to the mountain. Along the mountain wall were stables and a large wooden structure that likely housed the men-at-arms. A group was training with swords in the courtyard and the sight excited him.

He watched for a moment, then turned to take in the castle. Attached to its rear was a large porch-like area that spanned the width of the castle and extended ten yards out. A big stone fireplace sat at one end. Women worked at various tasks. His eyes wandered upward, taking in the full scale of the castle. There appeared to be a walk at the very top of a circular tower. He thought of the stairs in the bedroom. Was that where they went? He would find out. Another smaller tower was to the right and toward the front.

His eyes were drawn to movement at a top window. A woman stood looking out. Derek shielded his eyes against the sun and focused on her. To his delight, he saw it was his teenaged lover. He smiled and waved at her. To his surprise, she glowered at him and disappeared with a fast spin. Her reaction confused him, but he shrugged it off as being too far away and too much sun to be sure of what he had seen.

Derek turned his attention to the practice session. To the left, facing the far wall, a dozen men practiced with bow and arrow. He advanced on the fighters, watching their form. He'd done enough training to recognize different attacks and parries. He stopped short and clasped his hands together behind his back like a general observing his troops.

He noted most of the men were merely going through the motions. Their attacks were slow and cumbersome; their feet barely moving. It looked like a poorly choreographed routine. They were probably bored and tired of doing the same thing repeatedly, day after day.

A tall older man stood to his left, sword at his side, watching the practice. Derek walked toward him, and the man glanced his way with a look of scorn. He was taller than Derek and at least ten years his senior. A wicked scar ran diagonally across his right eye almost to his ear. He was bald and had a full beard.

In a disrespectful tone, he greeted Derek. "M'lord."

Derek said, "Sir."

The man's eyebrow went up in question.

"Tell me, are you responsible for their training?"

That seemed to be an affront to him. He faced Derek, his hand resting on the hilt of his sword as if daring him to repeat his words.

"Aye, m'lord, you know I am."

"Do they always practice with so much lackluster?"

"Lackluster, m'lord? Meaning what?"

"They are just going through the motions. There's no energy; no intensity. How can they ever hope to improve if they don't put out some effort?"

"Do you question my techniques, m'lord?" Clearly, he was hoping to show Derek his skill, but Derek did not quake from the man's intense glare. Derek had served in the Rangers and had seen combat. The training he'd received instilled self-confidence in his abilities that did not allow him to back down from bullies. He'd fought side by side with true warriors and knew one when he saw him. This man might have had the fighting spirit within him at one time but gone was the pride in his training that was needed to teach and lead men.

"Not so much your technique as your leadership."

The man's face went beet red. "And what would I be leading them for, m'lord? When was the last time anyone from this keep went into battle? There is no need for proper training when we cower behind these walls and allow others to fight our battles."

Derek was confused. He didn't understand the political scene of the era, nor what battles the man was referring to. It was also clear the master-at-arms blamed him for this situation.

"And how do you think they'd fare if forced to defend this castle?"

His head snapped upward. "Castle, is it? Ha! Those men are more than ready if someone had the nerve to give the word."

"Someone?"

"Aye." He cocked his head to the side while continuing to stare at Derek. "Perhaps m'lord would care to test one of them?"

Derek fought back a smile at the challenge. This man thought Derek too much of a coward to fight.

"The thought amuses you, I see," said the big man. "But I haven't heard your acceptance yet." They locked eyes. "No. I did not think so." Then with a sarcastic tone and mocking bow, he added, "M'lord."

Derek felt the blood rush to his face. He narrowed his eyes and hardened his stare. "Pick one." Equally sarcastic and more caustically, he added, "Sir."

The man's face reddened again, recognizing the challenge for what it was: a slap in the face of his abilities as leader, soldier, and man.

"With pleasure."

CHAPTER NINE

The master-at-arms spun and strode toward the men, many of whom had been watching the exchange. He said a few words and the men ceased their session and gathered around. As Derek approached, he heard grumbling. Whatever the master-at-arms had said was not popular with them. He heard the big man say, "Will no one volunteer to uphold your honor?" No one spoke. "Very well. Bran, it is you."

Bran was none too happy about the so-called honor. Others gave him a pat on the back or offered encouragement. The men stepped back to give him room. Derek faced Bran, an unwilling participant in the duel.

"I shall need the use of a sword," Derek said. No one moved to offer theirs.

"A soldier always wears his own," the big man said.

A few of the men chuffed a laugh. Derek was sure he heard one man mutter, "Fluff."

"Be that as it may, I still need a sword."

The big man motioned to one of his men, and with a grunt and a frown, he stepped forward and passed his blade to Derek. He hefted it and took a few practice cuts. It was not well balanced and better suited for chopping wood than swordsmanship. It was blade-heavy. That would cause a soldier's arm to weary sooner in a battle, making it difficult to keep the tip pointed upward. His offense, and more importantly, his defense would suffer, leaving him open for an easy strike.

Derek thought about asking for a different blade but decided it would make him look weak or like he was stalling.

"Shall we?" he asked.

"Indeed," the trainer said.

His opponent took a reluctant stance. Derek stood erect as if unprepared, but his years of training kept him calm. He was ready and looking forward to the contest. The man stood frozen in place. Derek swiped at the blade, knocking it from the man's hand. The fighter glanced at the trainer, hoping it was the end of the exhibition.

"Go on, man. Pick it up and give a better accounting."

Grudgingly, Bran picked up the sword and resumed his stance. Derek advanced on him again, swatting the sword aside several times before lunging for a kill. The blade touched the man in the chest and Derek stopped. He pushed the sword tip forward, forcing the man back.

"So you refuse to give me your best effort, or are you just that bad?" He shoved the man back another step. Derek could hear the comments and feel the hatred emanating from the group around him.

"Go on, Bran, stick him," one said.

Derek shoved again. This time, anger flared in the man's eyes. Derek shoved, then pressed close to his opponent, locking eyes with him, and said, "Yeah Bran, stick me if you're able." He pushed the man backward, then turned his back on him. He knew what would happen and readied for the attack. Bran did not disappoint. With a wild scream, he charged.

Derek pivoted to meet him. Sword raised high and eyes wide with rage, Bran whipped the blade downward. If Derek had not anticipated the stroke, it would have cleaved him in half. Instead, he stepped to the side, avoiding the blow, and brought the flat of his sword down across the other man's wrist. He knocked the blade from his hand, then drove his elbow into his face.

The strike cracked into the man's teeth, sending pain flashing up Derek's arm. Blood spurted, and the man staggered and went down. Derek drove his sword into the ground and whirled on the master-at-arms. "Make them work harder, sir, or I will find someone who will."

He strode away, both angry and pleased. He had created something to write about. He wanted to make sure that whatever caused this dream world to spring to life would continue. He hustled up the steps. The two guards snapped to attention again. This time, he said nothing. Derek clomped through the hall, no longer concerned about the noise.

He went through the arches, ran up the steps and into the bedroom. There he headed straight for the winding stairway. It ended at a landing with a ladder attached to the wall that led to a wooden hatch in the ceiling. Derek climbed the ladder and pushed up on the hatch. He put his shoulder into the task and the heavy door flopped over with a thud. He climbed to the top. The space was a twelve-by-twelve square. The surrounding stone wall stood about four feet high. Since the tower was round, he expected the top to also be round. It was the highest point in the castle. He looked down on the shorter tower on the front side of the castle. The two guard towers at the front corners of the wall stood much shorter.

Derek walked the length and looked out over the land. One side was the mountain, its sheer gray face stretching high above the castle. To the east about a hundred yards from the castle wall was a forest that reached beyond his vision. In front of him and to the west as far as the eye could see was a blanket of gold and green. Beyond the gate, a dirt road parted the fields and rose in the distance before disappearing over a rise.

He figured the total population to be roughly two hundred. Not many, but perhaps just the right amount. He'd have to get to know some of them to write about them. To do that, however, would mean he'd need to change the perception many seemed to have of him.

Derek thought about the woman in the window. Was it the lady of the castle, his wife? He definitely had to win her over. He remembered how she looked. Her fiery hair was outshined only by the flames in her eyes. He closed his eyes, remembering how she felt and smelled and her moans of pleasure. He wanted her on his side. Despite her age, he wanted her. She was sixteen years old, but that was acceptable here in this world.

Then, a new thought came to him. If this dream was a creation of his subconscious, did that mean deep inside he had a thing for sixteen-year-olds? He shuddered. No. That wasn't him. He'd have to change her age in the book.

Even so, he was determined to see her again before he woke. Derek climbed down the ladder, closing the hatch. He descended the stairs and went into the hall. There was only one other door on this level. It made sense that it was her room. Her. The first thing he would do was ask her name.

He marched to the opposite door, paused to listen, then rapped. No one came, so he knocked louder. He was about to bang a third time when the door cracked open. A woman slightly older and only a little less attractive than the lady poked her head out. She wore an angry scowl and didn't speak.

"Is the, ah…is the lady in?" He felt foolish trying to figure out how he should speak.

Whether he'd made some blunder, he wasn't sure, but this woman was clearly mad. She glowered at him and said, "I'm sorry, my lord." She almost choked on her words. "My lady cannot see you at the moment."

"Oh? And when will she be able to see me?"

A voice inside the chambers shouted, "Tell the ass *never*!"

The tone and choice of words surprised him. "Who was that?"

The woman at the door paled and seemed to shrink in on herself. She was yanked backward, and the door opened wider, revealing a short, plump older woman. "You have your nerve, showing yourself here after what you've done. I don't care who you are, lord or not; no one should treat a lady the way you have. I've half a mind to throttle you myself. Wait 'til her father sees how you've abused her."

Perplexed and becoming annoyed at the woman's boldness, Derek said, "What are you talking about?"

Her voice went glass shattering shrill. "What do you mean, what am I talking about? You fool. The damage you did to her. I don't see how anyone can consider a lout like you a nobleman."

"Damage? What damage?" Concerned and confused, Derek pushed past the woman, despite her best efforts to prevent his intrusion. He stormed through the ante room and into the lady's bedchamber.

He found her in a large canopy bed, lying propped up on a mountain of pillows.

"You cannot barge in here," the old woman said. "I don't care who you are. You get out of here now before I send a rider for her father."

Upon seeing him enter, his bride pulled the covers up high, leaving only her face exposed; her long red hair covering most of it. The lady who answered the door fled, cowering in a corner when he entered. The older woman tried to stall his advance by grabbing at his arm. She wasn't strong enough to stop him but was determined to try.

He pulled up short of the bed and stared at his wife. "My lady, what has happened?"

The older woman said, "How can you pretend you don't know? You're the one who beat her."

Angry, confused, and frustrated at the constant chatter, Derek turned on her. "Woman, close your mouth now. I'm talking to my...my lady, not you."

Despite her bravado, she quieted, though did not retreat. She stood, ready to pounce.

He stepped closer to the bed and the woman defender did the same.

"My lady, are you all right? What damage is this silly woman speaking of?"

The red-haired girl looked frail and frightened. A single tear ran down her cheek, soaking into the hair that lay across her face.

"Please show me, or at least explain it to me."

"Go ahead, my dear. Show the bastard his handiwork," the older woman said.

The girl turned her head away from him and pulled back her hair on the left side. A large red welt covered her face; half of it a long abrasion. Her eye was blackened.

Derek gasped. "I don't understand. How did this happen."

"You have nerve, playing the innocent."

Derek glanced back at the old woman.

"What are you talking about? I didn't do that. I wouldn't do that." This didn't make sense. If this world was of his creation, why would he ever abuse a woman? Was this another deep-seated perversion? First, he'd made love to a sixteen-year-old, and then he beat her? No. Never. Not even in a dream. Something was wrong here.

Perhaps his vivid imagination was creating a conflict for the hero to resolve. Yes. That must be it. But then, why was he the villain? That didn't make sense either. She would know her husband, unless there was something else at work here and he had to puzzle it out. Yeah, that was good.

The lady found the fire in her spirit and it came out in her voice. "It was you. You burst in here last night, mad and ranting about some spell I'd cast on you that sent you to hell. You threatened me, beat me, and then had your way with me." Her energy dissipated. Her voice softened. She was on the verge of tears. "And after," she sobbed, "you were so kind. I should've known it was just an act. You can't change your nature. You're a brute and I pray I never bear your children. Then we can end this farce of a marriage."

"My lady," he said, moving closer. She shied away and cowered beneath the cover. "It wasn't me. I would never treat a woman like that. Maybe there is some truth about a spell, but I didn't do this to you. I've only just come back, and—and..." Derek didn't know how to explain.

"Leave, you bastard," the older woman snapped. "Leave now, or so help me, I'll cut you myself."

She grabbed him. He was so dismayed and in such shock over the revelation, he allowed her to pull him away.

"My lady, don't you see? This is all just a dream. I didn't hurt you."

"Dream, my ass. More a nightmare, if you ask me. Now get out and don't show your face here again."

She shoved him into the hall. He pushed against the door as she closed it. He caught it short and began inching it back open. The woman poked her head around the door and said in a low but intense voice, "None of your people like you, but they all love the lady. If they saw what you did to the poor girl, how long do you think it'd be before they rose against you? And you'd deserve whatever you got."

Derek was so taken aback by her words that he neither offered further comment in his defense nor any force against the closing door.

CHAPTER TEN

Back in his bedchamber, he sat on the bed and tried to understand what had happened. He'd been feeling so good about this entire scenario, but now he just wanted to wake up and write.

They were all so positive that he was the one who had beat her that he began to doubt his memory. Had he blacked out and attacked her? But why? For sex? She was more than willing the first time. She'd been very insistent, actually. And if he had to say so himself, it was rather good. It certainly sounded as if she had enjoyed it.

What the hell? Couldn't he do anything right? This was his story, his creation. Where had it gone wrong?

It was impossible. This was his dream world. He was the only one allowed to play his part, and he knew himself. He would not strike a woman, especially not over sex. Somehow his creative mind had fashioned a plot twist. He didn't have to go with it, though. It was his story. He'd write it the way he wanted to, and he'd be damned if he would portray himself—er, his hero—in that manner.

Derek paced the floor until he grew tired. No answers were forthcoming, so he flopped on the bed and stared at the ceiling.

Several minutes later, he felt the strange sensation coming on. He recognized the signs. The blackness, the glowing ball of light, nausea. Then he was falling, but this time, he welcomed the change. He wanted to get home and write. The globe of light rushed through space. He saw the other ball of light approaching, and as it passed, his jaw dropped.

He saw a man. He'd only gotten a glimpse, but he was sure it *had* been a man. Was someone else trapped in this same type of time traveling bubble? Maybe it wasn't a dream after all, but some strange form of time travel. But that was a different story than the one he was writing. Wasn't it?

By the time he landed, his mind was blank. His eyes rolled up and he slept.

This time, however, his dreams were true nightmares. He chased young women around a hazy, undetailed city like Jack the Ripper, but instead of cutting them, he beat them, laughing as he did. A community of a mixed assortment of modern and medieval men and women chased him through time. When they finally cornered him on the roof of the castle, they beat him to a pulp, lifted him over the wall, and tossed him down.

He fell endlessly until he crashed down on the hard floor, waking with a cry of pain.

He wrapped his arms around his head and writhed until the pain subsided. When he could open his eyes, he realized he'd fallen out of bed.

"What the hell!" he shouted, rubbing the point of contact. He'd probably given himself a concussion.

He stood on shaky legs and staggered to the kitchen. He filled a plastic sandwich bag with ice and pressed it to the small knot forming above his left temple.

The cold felt good. He closed his eyes and leaned back against the sink. His arm struck a glass and it fell, shattering on the floor.

"Shit!" *Why the hell was a glass there?* He bent to pick up the pieces. He never left dirty dishes in the sink or on the counter. Had Jackie left it when she was there? No. She had made coffee and he'd washed and dried the two mugs and put them away.

He stood to throw out the larger pieces of glass and saw the food cartons, silverware, dishes, and unopened packages all over the counter. *What the hell is going on?*

Derek tried to relax so he could think. Maybe Jackie had come in, but even if she did, she'd never leave such a mess for him to clean up. But it was the only logical explanation. He hadn't left the apartment in several days.

He looked for his phone and found it next to the TV, which was odd. He pushed the thought aside and called his ex-wife.

"Got anything new for me?" she said as she accepted the call.

"What? No," he snapped. He drew in a deep breath to control his rising concern and budding panic. "Hey, uh, I was wondering if you have been in my apartment within the last twelve hours."

"No. The last time I was there was when I was excited about your new story. You going to send me more?"

"Ah…yeah, sure. So you weren't here?"

"No. Why? What's going on? You sound a little spooked."

"I think someone's been in my apartment. The place is a mess. There's food and dishes all over the place and things have been moved."

She didn't respond.

"Jackie?"

"Yeah?"

"Did you hear me?"

"Yeah, I heard. Look, Derek, I don't want you to take this the wrong way, but were you on something last night?"

"What? No, I haven't done any of that since—well, for a long time. I don't do any of that stuff anymore. I swear. Thanks for your support here."

"Okay. I'm sorry. Have you called the police?"

"No. You think I should?"

"You're the only one who can answer that. Did they take anything?" In a more concerned tone, she said, "Oh, please don't tell me they stole your laptop. I know when you get excited about a story you forget to back it up."

"No, the laptop's still here. I don't think anything's missing."

"Whew! That's a relief."

"I have to go. Sorry for bothering you."

"That's . . ."

Derek hung up on her. He was annoyed by her suggestion that he was high. It had been part of his Hollywood life and he hadn't touched anything but alcohol since she left him...although he had to admit if he didn't know any better, he might have suspected the same.

Derek took a slow tour of his apartment to note things out of place and to make sure nothing was missing. When done and satisfied, he decided to go down to the lobby and talk to Marvin the daytime doorman.

He walked into the hallway and headed toward the elevator. His apartment was on the sixth floor of an eight-story building. Most of the time he took the stairs down, but as he drew even with the elevator, the doors slid open. Mr. Jenkins stepped off and stopped when he saw Derek.

"Nice to see you remembered to get dressed before you left your apartment."

"What?"

"Ah, youth. Such a waste."

Confused by the statement, Derek watched his neighbor's unsteady path to his apartment door. *Was the old man going senile?* The elevator door slid shut. Derek slipped an arm through, forcing it open and stepped inside. By the time he reached the main floor, he'd forgotten the old man's comment.

His steps echoed off the tiled floor, bringing back the memory of walking through the castle's hall. He pushed through the inner door and went to the large front desk. A small black man sat with his feet up on the desk. He wore the stereotypical uniform of a New York City doorman.

His small frame made him look like a boy who'd dressed in his father's clothes.

Derek had always gotten along well with Marvin, but not so with Marvin's counterparts on the second and third shifts. Both of those men maintained a more professional and distant relationship with the residents. Not that they didn't do their jobs; they just weren't as personable as Marvin.

"Well, looky who it is," Marvin said, lowering his feet to the floor and sitting up. "Got your key today?"

Derek patted his pants pocket, relieved to feel the key there. "Yeah. Why wouldn't I?"

"Ah, okay. You want to play it that way, huh? It's okay by me. We'll pretend it never happened."

"What never happened?"

"Exactly."

"No. I'm being serious, Marvin. What are you talking about?"

The man eyed him, trying to discern whether he was being put on. "Are you telling me you don't remember?"

"Ah, I guess that's what I'm saying, 'cause I don't know what you're talking about."

"Wow! I used to have that problem back in the day too. Not no more, though." He brought two fingers up to his mouth like he was holding an invisible joint. "Were you...you know?"

"What? No. You're as bad as my ex-wife. I don't do that."

"Uh-huh." Marvin smirked.

"Please tell me if you know something, 'cause I'm starting to think I'm losing my mind. Someone's been in my apartment. You let anyone go upstairs looking for me?"

Marvin cocked his head and narrowed his eyes. "What are you talking about? I never let anyone upstairs without permission from the tenant. And ain't nobody asked to see you since Jackie came calling. You don't mean her, do ya?"

"No. It was after she was here."

"No one's come in on my shift. Let me check the log."

Marvin rolled his chair a few feet and turned pages in a large three-ring binder. "Nope. I don't see anything here going back a few weeks. You want me to ask the other two anyway?"

"Yeah, would you please?"

"You want me to call the cops?"

"No. I don't think that's necessary. Nothing's missing."

Marvin nodded in a contemplating way. "And you don't remember 'bout locking yourself out of your room, bare-ass naked?"

"What? When was this?"

"Last night."

Derek stood, mouth open, shaking his head. He was asleep all night. The only explanation was that he had started sleepwalking. He sighed.

"Hey Derek, you all right, man?"

"I don't know, Marvin. I have no idea."

Derek walked to the elevator, stunned by the revelation.

CHAPTER ELEVEN

Derek entered his apartment, closed the door, and leaned against it. This was so unreal. What was happening to him? He glanced at the mess in the kitchen, then at the laptop. He wanted to sit down and write but knew he would not be able to concentrate with the clutter staring back at him. He forced his feet to walk to the kitchen and went about tidying things up.

Thirty minutes later, having scrubbed down the countertops, Derek went to the laptop and fired it up. He reread the last few paragraphs, formed some thoughts, and began typing. In a few short minutes, Derek was in the groove, having relegated everything else to unimportant.

The words seemed to materialize on the screen. His fingers flew across the keys, recreating every little detail from his last dream. The story came to life in front of him, and again the feeling of elation returned.

He worked non-stop until late afternoon. Derek took a break for dinner, mulling over his recent pages in his mind. He thought about making a few small changes to the manuscript and after cleaning up the kitchen, he went to work again.

Near midnight with his eyes blurring and burning, he pushed back from the desk, exhausted yet thrilled. The story was good. He twirled circles in the chair, pushing faster and faster, his feet pounding on the floor like he was running. He gave one final push and lifted his feet, allowing the chair to whirl on its own. Derek jumped to his feet and paced, then he ran to the mat and did several touchdown dances. The feeling of accomplishment was exhilarating.

He spied the sword and ran to it. Whipping it free of the scabbard, he moved through a series of practice routines before sparring with a mental image of the master-at-arms. After slaying the man several times, he set the sword back in its housing. Then he took a long shower and debated whether to eat. He'd only had one meal yet did not feel hungry. He was too excited to eat or sleep.

Derek decided to watch TV for a while, hoping it would make him drowsy. He sprawled on the couch with only a towel wrapped around his waist. His eyes grew heavy. An assortment of images flashed through his mind as he began to drift off. A vision of Jackie bloomed. He smiled. Then a memory connected, and his eyes flew open.

He jumped up, turned the laptop back on, and sent the new pages to her. Before he shut it down, he remembered what she'd said about backing up his work. He dug in the desk drawer for a flash drive and copied the file. Feeling more secure, he threw himself back on the bed.

As he lay there allowing the story to unfold in his mind, he was jolted to his feet. He strode back to the laptop, turned it on, and sat. He searched for causes of sleepwalking. The list included heredity, lack of sleep, fatigue, inefficient or interrupted sleep, illness or fever, medications, noisy or different sleep environment, going to bed with a full bladder, and stress or anxiety. None of them fit until he read the last one. That made sense. His writer's block and the fast-approaching deadline had taken a psychological and emotional toll on him. But that was over now, wasn't it? This story was flowing, and extremely well at that. He didn't feel stressed at all. He shut the laptop down and returned to bed confident his sleepwalking nights were over. He lay back, feeling relaxed. He closed his eyes and drifted, hoping the next installment of his story was on its way.

Derek's sleep was uneasy for a while. In his dreams, he chased a constantly moving bubble of light. At last, the bubble stopped and engulfed him, and soon he was falling through space and time once more.

He landed on the bed. When his body recovered from the journey, he stood, naked. He dressed, thinking about how his mind used the bed as a time machine of sorts to take him to his dream world. There had to be something Freudian about the imagery.

At the window, Derek discovered it was night. A few torches were lit below, and a line of them flared along the castle walls. Shadows passed as the guards walked by. Derek wondered if the watch was purely routine or if there was a reason to be vigilant.

He thought about what the master-at-arms had said, wondering if there was more to his words. *There is no need for proper training when we cower behind these walls and let others fight our battles.* Was there a war waging somewhere that they were ducking?

Then Derek understood. The man was accusing Derek of being a coward and hiding from the fighting. Well, Derek would show him. He couldn't wait for daylight. But since he was already awake, he decided to go exploring.

He spotted what looked to be the same clothes he'd worn the last time. Derek pulled on the pants, sniffed the shirt, and recoiled. It was ripe. He searched for another one that was at least less odoriferous, if not cleaner. He found one tossed over a chair. It smelled, though not quite as bad.

Starting for the door, Derek noticed a sword hanging from the bedpost. He took it down, remembering how the master-at-arms had commented about his lack of a weapon. The scabbard was ornately tooled with assorted gems inlaid down each side. The gold hilt was designed as a dragon's head with two ruby eyes.

He drew the blade back but not out. The shiny steel was intricately etched with swirls down its length. He turned the sword to look at it. It barely had an edge, and the lack of nicks told him the sword had never been used for anything more than decoration. That wouldn't do. He placed the sword back and left, unarmed.

He tiptoed down the hallway and stairs, stopping outside the large hall. He'd gone that way already; now he wanted to try the four doors. The first one opened on a dark, narrow stairway leading down. Without a torch, exploring it would be too dangerous. He closed the door and moved to the next. This was a small room of perhaps ten-by-twelve feet. A table with two chairs sat in the center. At the back was another chair with a hole in the middle and a pan beneath the hole. Derek stared at it for a minute then laughed, realizing it was a toilet.

The third room was much larger and held a table, six chairs, and a large box full of rolled parchment. A partially unrolled parchment lay on the table. It was a map of an unfamiliar area. A thick layer of dust covered everything, including the map. It was obvious this room hadn't been used in quite a while.

The last door led to a storeroom full of tables. The tops and legs had been separated for storage purposes. Stacks of chairs and shelves of folded linen lined the back, and shelves of torches, rags, oil, and other supplies were to the right. *This might prove useful*, he thought.

An archway at the end of the hall led to the kitchen. It was a space half as large as the hall. At this hour, the kitchen was empty. Bowls of rising dough sat on a table. It came to him then that he hadn't eaten any meals in this world yet. He would have to remedy that, as so much happened during mealtime and it would be important to have an accurate description for his manuscript.

Derek walked around the table and studied the details of the room. There were two hearths on each side of the room. Stacks of metal plates and bowls were arranged on a flattop. To his surprise, the room looked very tidy and orderly. He made a mental note to praise the cook.

There were three other doors in the kitchen. Derek went to the first on the right. It led down a curved stairway that he assumed was the food storage area. The path was dark, so he moved to the next one. This door opened to the dry goods storage. It was filled with bins and barrels of vegetables, beans, and large amounts of assorted foods. He grabbed a handful of walnuts.

The third and fourth doors led to the outside porch he'd seen on his previous dream visit. Derek went out onto the porch. The night air was chilly but invigorating. He sat on the short wall that surrounded the porch and let his legs dangle over the side.

Palming a walnut, he slammed it down on the stone three times before it cracked. He peeled out the meat and popped the pieces in his mouth. As he chewed, Derek looked out over the courtyard. Lost in thought and amazed at the detail of his creation, he was startled when a voice behind him said, "M'lord, pardon. I didn't know it was you. Can I get you something?"

He turned to see a large woman wearing a dingy white apron and a white cloth covering her hair. He figured she was the cook.

"I was looking at the kitchen."

"Yes, m'lord."

"It is clean and well organized. You're doing a good job."

"Thank you, m'lord. Kind of you to say. We do work hard at it."

"I can see that. Keep up the fine work—and tell your staff I said well done."

"Yes, m'lord." Her tone was excited and she gave a slight curtsy.

Derek turned to look out at the sheer cliff in front of him. When he glanced back, the cook was gone. Behind him, kitchen sounds announced the morning meal preparation. As the sun began to rise, the castle residents stirred.

He thought about finding his wife, but after the last visit, he decided it was better to keep his distance.

How strange that sounded—his wife. Why was it important to him that in this dream world he be married? Was it a subconscious desire to return to a time when he was still married to Jackie? If so, why hadn't he created a happier relationship here? Why did it have to be as belligerent as theirs was at the end? Was this dream world his mind's way of wishing things were like they had been in the past? That made a strange sense.

He finished the rest of the nuts, then hopped down from the ledge and walked through the kitchen. The aroma of fresh bread hit him. Eight women and young girls bustled about. He nodded to several of them and stopped as he recognized the woman from his bed on that first visit. He gave her a smile and her face reddened.

"You're all doing a great job. Thank you."

For a fraction of a second, no one moved. Then, as if a director shouted, "Action!" movement began again.

CHAPTER TWELVE

Derek walked through the hall and out the front door. Two new guards leaned against the wall. They snapped erect upon seeing him. Again, Derek said, "At ease, men," and again they stood stiff and still, perhaps not understanding the command, but he didn't bother to explain.

Walking to the wall, Derek found stairs leading to the parapet and climbed. He stood next to a torch and stared out into the darkness. How could these men ever see anyone approach in the dark? An attacking army would be on top of them before they knew what hit them.

Maybe their vision was better than his, but even so, penetrating night as dark as this was not easy. He should be able to come up with a more effective and modern warning system, but did he want to change this setting?

As the sun rose, the landscape revealed itself in a slow striptease. Most of the crops in front of the wall were wheat and beans. That made sense, as both were staples. They reached the rise about a hundred yards out and disappeared. What lay beyond that was a blur at the horizon. Looking left, he followed the line of trees. They did the same. *How much of it belonged to this kingdom?* Looked like quite a lot. He wondered if the lands continued past those points. Maybe all he saw was what he needed to see to make the scene real.

He walked left, nodding at two guards as he passed, and did a ninety-degree turn at the corner. Curious, he paced the entire side, stopping where the wall abutted the mountain. It was the perfect defense against invaders, as it was too high to climb down, although he wondered if an enemy could find a way up from another direction and rain down arrows. That was something to consider as he explored and created other parts of this world.

Derek leaned against the mountain face and looked back at the castle and the courtyard. He'd done an impressive job of adding realistic detail. Now he just had to develop a storyline worthy of the setting.

He scanned up the castle wall until he found the window where he'd seen the lady looking out. He stared at it for a long while hoping to see her, but if she was awake, surely she had better things to do than look out the window.

Derek climbed down the ladder and walked toward the stables, curious to see what type of horse he'd dreamed up for himself. It might be fun to ride the countryside to get an idea of the scale of the world and discover if the landscape extended as he neared the border, or if what he saw was all there was. More people walked the grounds. He entered the stable and was met with the musky smell of animals. Derek was surprised at the size of the structure. He stopped, curious.

He left the stable, backing away from the wooden building, and looked at the roofline. Sure enough, the roof only went back about thirty feet. The stable was built into the mountain. Derek went inside and paced, looking at the wood ceiling. The room went at least another eighty feet.

There were forty stalls all filled with horses. He toured the stalls, examining each horse. Most were huge draft horses with long, well-groomed manes. Except for one, they were all black or brown. A few had white spots. The lone white horse looked taller and leaner than the others. Derek didn't know enough about horses to recognize the breed, but it looked like it was bred for speed instead of power. If he had to guess, the lord of the land rode this horse.

A young man entered carrying a bucket and a shovel. Derek smiled, knowing the lad's duty. The boy stopped upon seeing Derek. Unsure what to do, he set the bucket and shovel down, bowed, and said, "Morning, m'lord."

"Good morning to you." As the boy picked up the bucket and shovel, Derek said, "Can you tell me who to speak to about getting a horse saddled?"

"Saddled, m'lord?"

"Yes. You know, so I can go for a ride."

"A ride, m'lord?"

Derek wondered if the boy was a bit slow. "Yes, a ride. Is that so unusual?"

"Well...I mean, no, m'lord. I'll fetch the horse master for you." He ran out of the stables like he was escaping a fire. Several minutes later, a small, rail-thin man entered, tucking his shirt into his pants.

"Sorry, m'lord. I wasn't told you'd be needing a horse today. I'll get right on it."

"It's all right. The urge was spontaneous."

"Spon...er, yes, of course, m'lord. You'll be wanting Gwen, then. I'll have her saddled in a moment."

Gwen was the white horse. Derek was right. He watched the horse master work. In short order, he led the animal to Derek.

"Here she is, m'lord. You can trot her around the courtyard."

"That wouldn't be much of a ride now, would it?"

The man gave him a look of amazement. "You-you're leaving the grounds, m'lord?"

"Why is that so shocking?"

"Beg your pardon, m'lord. It's just—"

"Just what?"

"Nothing, m'lord. Enjoy your ride."

Derek had one more stop to make before riding out. All along the grounds, fires were being lit and food prepared. He led Gwen to the building attached to the stables and tied her to a post. Men were up and moving.

Idle talk and laughter met his ears. Like the stable, this structure was also built into the mountain.

He was aware of the sudden absence of noise and realized the men had stopped talking and were looking at him, but no one spoke to him. He was in the barracks. The space was as large as the stables. The only light came from the sun filtering through the two front doors and a fireplace in the wall to the left. An unpleasant smell wafted forward to greet him. Derek gave the room a general nod, then feeling uncomfortable for intruding, he left. As soon as he was out the door, the men found their voices again.

He untied Gwen and climbed on. The horse whinnied and backed a few steps. Derek patted her to put her at ease. Then he walked her toward the front gate. Along the way, he found what he'd been looking for. A blacksmith was kindling a fire, getting ready to start his day.

Derek stopped and called down to the man. The heavy bald man came out to meet him.

"Beg pardon, m'lord. I didn't hear you over the fire."

"I need a sword. Can you help me?"

"Yes, sir. But where is the one you commissioned me to make for you? Is something wrong with it?"

"No. As a showpiece it's fine, but in a fight it's worthless. I need a sword I can take into battle."

He nodded. "Do you want it like the other one?"

"No. I don't want anything fancy. I want a good, solid sword that won't break in a fight and holds a fine edge."

"Of course, m'lord. If you'll step down, you can try a few to find the one that best suits you."

Derek did so and the blacksmith handed him an old sword that had seen better days. "Yes," he said, hefting and swinging the weapon. "Only I like it with a little more weight on the handle side."

The man grunted and turned away. He rummaged through an assortment of old weapons sticking out of a barrel before pulling out one with a slight curve to it. It reminded him of an old cavalry sword his grandfather had given him, except this blade was much wider. He held it, performing a series of swipes and lunges. The weight and balance felt good. Nicks and scratches lined one side down to the point. This blade had seen its share of action.

"This is perfect."

"Very good, m'lord. I'll make you up a right pretty blade."

"No. I don't want another sword I can't use. Rework this one. Put an edge on it, find a scabbard, and I'm good. Can you do that?"

"Aye, I can. You just want a plain sword, then?"

"That's right. When can I come back?"

"I can have it ready for you later today."

"In the meantime, I'm going to need to borrow something until that one is finished."

The large man scratched the top of his bald pate. "I can fix you up with something useful."

"And a knife too."

The blacksmith disappeared inside. He returned about ten minutes later with the requested weapons. He handed them up to Derek. They weren't in very good shape, but both still had an edge on them.

"Those are from my scrap pile, meant to be melted down. I suppose they'll do all right if you need to defend yourself."

"Yes, they will. Thank you. You'll have them back when I return."

"Return, m'lord? You mean you're leaving the grounds?"

"Why does everyone ask me that? Have I never left the castle?"

"Castle? Oh, of course, m'lord."

That was the second time someone questioned his use of the word castle. He was going to have to find someone to pump for information on proper terms, rules, and customs.

"You're not riding out alone, are you?"

"That was my plan. Is something wrong with that?"

"I was just wondering about safety, m'lord. There are brigands and other unsavory sorts on the road these days. Might not be good to venture too far."

"I'll keep that in mind. Thank you."

With that, he heeled Gwen into motion and aimed for the front gates.

CHAPTER THIRTEEN

Two guards were in the process of opening the gates and a group of workers stood by waiting. Derek halted his mount behind the group to allow them to pass. One of the guards noticed him and ushered the people to the side.

"Stand aside for the lord. Make way." He shoved a man back.

Derek moved forward, stopping by the guard. "That's not necessary. They have more important tasks to perform than I do. Let them get on with it. I can wait."

The guard looked at him, bewildered and mouth open. He recovered and said, "As you wish, m'lord. You heard him, get moving."

Some grumbling occurred as they moved through the gates, but Derek didn't blame them. He'd have complained too.

He waited until the workers were a short distance down the road, then urged Gwen into a trot. Although Derek had been on horseback before, he was far from an expert rider. Trying to find a comfortable position on the bouncing horse was a constant issue. As he got used to the rhythm, he was able to settle in.

In only a few minutes, he was over the rise and down in a valley. The castle disappeared beyond the horizon. It seemed his creative mind was working overtime developing the land as he rode. The forest curved toward the road on the left at the end of the fields. Open ground continued to the right for several miles before it narrowed with trees. After a while, Derek came to a forest.

He slowed Gwen to a walk and took in the nature around him. It was peaceful and relaxing. He wondered if the world he'd created had any actual boundaries or if it would just continue to scroll on as he traveled. His subconscious mind was amazing, from the detail of the trees and foliage right down to the sounds of the birds and insects. He looked for patterns in the trees to determine if the scene just repeated itself, but not finding any, he figured he was adjusting the scenery as he searched. He laughed out loud, happy his mind was so sharp and creative to adjust with such speed and variety.

The saddle chafed the insides of his thighs and he changed his position. If he was the creator of this world, why didn't he just eliminate pain from the equation? To that end, he concentrated on making his legs feel less raw, but nothing worked. If anything, his legs were getting sorer and his body stiffer.

Derek was about to dismount to give his body a break when a shout filtered through the trees. He lifted his head and listened but didn't hear it again. He nudged Gwen forward at a quicker pace, curious to see what interesting scenario his mind had created for him now.

After nearly a minute and still hearing nothing more, he halted Gwen. He rotated in the saddle to listen behind him. Nothing except the normal forest sounds. Thinking it might have been the cry of some animal, Derek turned the horse to start back toward the castle.

Gwen hadn't gone two strides when the shout occurred again, this time carrying a note of desperation. Derek had no doubt where it came from. He whirled Gwen around and urged her into a run. Within seconds, several loud voices reached him. It sounded like cheering at a sporting event.

Slowing Gwen, he located the commotion. He stopped the horse and scanned the foliage. A dark form darted between trees. Another shape followed.

"Keep her penned in. Don't let her get away!"

"I've got her. Ow! You witch. I'll hurt you for that."

Derek aimed Gwen into the woods. The closer he got, the louder the voices became.

"I got her."

"Get off me!" a female voice shouted.

"Hold her still."

"She's a wild one."

Derek saw them now. Four men huddled over a woman. He leaped from the horse, tossed the reins loosely around a branch, and ran. He closed on the group in a hurry. The men were having trouble controlling the woman who kicked, clawed, and tried to bite her attackers.

Derek burst unnoticed into the small clearing. One man straddled the woman, struggling to pin her hands down. One pressed her feet to the ground while the other two knelt on each side of her and tried to restrain her arms.

"Ow! She bit me!" the man closest to Derek yelled. He stood and delivered a kick to her head.

Derek ran up behind the man, grabbed him by his shirt, and yanked backward. He flew off his feet and Derek flung him to the ground. The straddling man looked up as Derek delivered a kick straight into his face. The contact lifted him off the woman, rolling him into the man holding her legs and knocking them both back.

The woman scrambled to her feet as the fourth man stood stunned at Derek's sudden appearance. Before he had a chance to react, Derek pivoted and snapped a side kick into the man's chest. The woman broke free and ran.

The four men regrouped, but this time their focus was on him. Two of the men drew long knives. The straddling man pulled a short-handled ax. The last man slid a sword free.

"Big mistake. Now you pay," the ax holder said. The men separated and surrounded him.

Derek almost forgot his sword. Heart pounding, he tried to pull the blade too fast. It was longer than he'd anticipated, and he got it hung up in the scabbard.

"A real swordsman, this one," the leader said. He laughed and moved toward Derek.

Derek used his left hand on the blade to lift it higher, putting a slice across his index finger. He winced but got the sword out.

The ax man laughed again. "You're gonna get more than that little nick by the time we're done with you." He swung the ax on a diagonal, his intent to end the fight in one swing by lopping off Derek's head.

Derek stepped back and the ax flew past, just inches from his face. His breath caught in his throat. He parried the next attack, a vicious backhand swing, but his effort was more panicked than controlled. Unable to handle the assault, Derek ran. He stopped as he got distance from the men. Their laughter followed him. One of them made clucking sounds.

Derek stopped, pressed against a large tree, and tried to gain control over his racing heart and leg-weakening fear. The laughter grew louder, and with it, his embarrassment. In his first real encounter in this make-believe world, he ran. He had never thought himself a coward, but when was the last time he'd faced a life-threatening situation? Yes, he'd been in battles during the war, but he had a weapon capable of killing at long range and was in the company of other well-trained men. The bouts he fought during his training or while fencing had little chance for serious injury. He'd fought multiple opponents in practice sessions to improve his vision and quickness. It had been fun and good training, but seldom did the one stand victorious over the multiple attackers. This felt more real; more deadly, but it was just a dream. He had no actual chance of dying unless he suffered a heart attack while asleep. No. He was not going to let this scenario end like this. It was his world. He controlled the outcome.

Anger fueling his actions, Derek stepped away from the tree and marched back toward the men still laughing and hurling insults at him. The men quieted as he approached.

"Well, well. The coward has decided he wants to play after all."

"That's right, butthead. The question is if you're man enough to face me alone, or if you can only fight when you have your opponent outnumbered."

Ax man's eyes flashed with anger. "I don't need anyone to help with the likes of you." He ran at Derek, ax up. He brought it down in a fierce arc aimed at the top of Derek's head, but Derek didn't block the strike. The blow had significant force to knock the sword from his hand, so instead, he stepped to the side and used the longer reach of the sword to lunge at the man's gut.

The tip of the blade pierced the man's skin. Though not deep, it was enough to slow and alter the path of the ax. The man cried out and doubled over, his free hand gripping the sword.

Derek pulled the blade back, and as the man tried to straighten up, he whipped the sword sideways and sliced through his foe's neck. Blood spurted, the ax fell to the ground, and the man to his knees, clutching at the wound.

The other three looked at their fallen comrade in shock. Then, as one, they raised their weapons and charged.

The swordsman was the greatest threat, having the longest reach. Derek swung the blade back and forth fast in front of the two knife holders, then spun to face the swordsman. With the knifemen backed off for the moment, Derek went to work.

Feeling more confident, Derek met the other man's sword and went into a patterned assault. In four fluid moves, he found an opening and stabbed the man in his side. He dropped his sword, ran several steps holding the wound, and collapsed to the ground.

Derek pivoted just in time to avoid taking a knife in the back. His opponent was too close to use the sword, so he fired an elbow into the man's face, then kicked him.

The final attacker froze, not wanting to end up like his friends. After a moment's thought and a menacing step toward him, the man fled, leaving his wounded comrades to their fate.

A sudden cry from behind made Derek's heart jump. He whirled in time to see the other knife man fall to the ground, a blade protruding from his back. Derek blinked in confusion, then glanced up to see the woman glaring at him.

"Thank you."

She didn't speak, but her eyes were so full of hate that he preferred the silence. She bent, put a foot on the dead man's back, and yanked the knife free. She wiped the blade on his shirt. She stood facing Derek, knife in hand, ready to do battle.

Derek held up his hand. "Easy. I'm not one of them. I mean you no harm."

The woman cocked her head as if trying to understand his words. She was younger than he'd first thought. Her hair was a wild, dark mess. Her clothes were torn and dirty. Dark eyes seemed to change colors as she glared at him. Since she hadn't yet attacked, he slid the sword back in the scabbard.

"Are you all right?" he asked.

Still she did not respond. She studied him with a curious look.

The ax man groaned and rolled to his knees. The woman walked to him, grabbed his head, and pulled it back. She sliced her blade across his neck and pushed him to the ground. Then she went to the wounded swordsman and plunged her knife into his chest. He screamed and cried, then begged for mercy, but his words only ignited a rage. She stabbed him in a frenzy until long after he stopped moving.

Derek watched in shock. As the woman's attacks ended, she stood, face splattered and clothes sodden with blood. She took two menacing steps toward Derek. He held up his hands.

"Wait. I came to help you. I had nothing to do with them."

She hesitated, and Derek could tell she was having an internal debate whether to let him live. Derek wanted to leave while he still could but was afraid to turn his back on her. He lowered his hands.

"If you're all right, I'll go."

He backed away. The added distance between them seemed to relax her. Her shoulders slumped and the tension and anger faded. She lowered the knife to her side.

Derek took that as her permission to leave without worrying about being attacked.

"Why are you here?" she asked, still breathing hard from her efforts.

"Because I heard you cry out for help"

"Why would you think I'd want *your* help?"

Her words confused him. "I don't understand. You mean anyone's help, or mine specifically?"

"Yours, of course."

He still didn't get what she was saying.

"Would you rather I left you in their hands? I'm sorry if my presence messed up your plans. From appearances, you were about to be raped and possibly killed. I'm sorry if you had them right where you wanted them. I was trying to help. If I didn't, I apologize." He turned to walk back to Gwen.

"You, of all people…why would you want to help me? Why care if I'd been raped, especially after..."

Something in his perplexed look made her stop talking.

"Have we met before? If so, I don't remember. I'm sorry."

She stepped closer and studied his face. "You're not him." She smiled. Her entire body relaxed, making her look smaller and less threatening. Her face beamed with delight, confusing Derek even more.

"I can't believe it. It worked! It actually worked! Come with me," she said.

"Where and why?"

Her eyes sparkled with amusement. "You'll see, and because I said so." She turned and walked, expecting he would follow. "Come. It's your reward for helping me." Her face lit with a wicked smile.

CHAPTER FOURTEEN

Derek couldn't help but think it was better to leave rather than follow her. She glanced over her shoulder. "Don't be afraid. Get your horse and come on."

Derek took Gwen's reins and led her through the woods. They walked for nearly thirty minutes before coming to a clearing where four log buildings sat. A cone of sunlight fell directly over the grouping. A river ran next to the small village. Three women worked a small plot of farmland. They stopped when they saw the girl approaching with Derek.

The three carried their tools with them as they converged with caution. They eyed him suspiciously, holding the tools like weapons.

The tallest one asked, "Are you all right?"

"Of course," the rescued woman said in a cheery voice.

"Ma!" the one with the lightest colored hair said. "Ma, come out and see this."

What was he, a carnival exhibition? The women were wary of him, but for some reason, he felt it was something other than because he was a stranger.

The woman holding a pitchfork held the tines toward him, ready to defend should he attack.

A tall gray-haired woman came out on the porch. She squinted against the sun. "Who do you have there?"

"Come see," the woman he rescued said. "Look who I brought home to dinner."

They must recognize him as the lord of the land. That had to be it.

The mother came closer, still squinting. She shielded her face with a hand to get a better look. Drawing closer, she stopped and gaped, recognizing him.

Derek offered a smile.

"I, uh, brought this young lady home. She was being attacked by some men in the woods."

None of them spoke, but they all looked at her.

"Since he was so brave to save me," her tone mocked, "I thought I should invite him home for dinner. Is that all right?"

The older woman looked from her daughter to Derek and back again.

"That will be fine. Felicity, see to our guest's horse."

"Sure, Ma."

The lighter haired woman took the reins from Derek.

"Thanks, but that won't be necessary. I'm heading back to the castle. I just wanted to make sure she got home all right."

"Don't be silly. I won't hear of it. You'll stay." She made a strange motion with her hand and whispered something, and just like that, his will faded as if it hadn't existed. Try as he might, Derek couldn't recall why he wanted to go. This was the perfect place for him right now.

Felicity led Gwen to a building and they disappeared inside.

"Come inside and sit," the mother said. "Tell me about this dangerous encounter."

Derek was apprehensive to go into the cabin. Something inside him warned he might never leave again. Still, he was compelled to follow, and the three women followed him in.

Derek at a wooden table and chairs. The mother sat across from him and the three girls stood behind him. The young woman he'd rescued stood behind her mother and stared at him with the curiosity of a spectator entering the tent of the two-headed man.

"So tell me this story."

It was if a stranger was inside him relaying the story. When he finished, the woman stared at him, trying to penetrate his eyes with hers. Derek shook his head as if shaking off the hangover of a nap.

"Who are you and why are you here?"

"My name's Derek. I'm the lord of the castle back up the road."

"Derek?" she asked. "You said Derek, right?"

"Yes. Derek."

The name caused her concern.

"See, Ma? He's gone. Like I told you. I sent him away."

"So it seems, my dear, but something tells me there's a problem with what you did."

"I don't understand. Who got sent away? And who are all of you?"

"Let me ask you something. Do you remember the last time you came for a visit here?"

Perplexed, Derek tried to recall something he was sure didn't exist. "No."

"So no memory at all? Of being here or being with my daughter?"

"Sorry. No. If I've been here before, I don't remember."

She sat back and looked from him to her daughter. "This could be a problem. I warned you about side effects."

"I took precautions. I had to do something. You know I did."

"Be that as it may, you should have heeded me and waited."

"You're talking about me like I'm not here. What is going on?" Derek demanded.

"Nothing, m'lord. Will you stay for supper?"

Derek eyed the woman with suspicion. Part of him wanted to stay and find out the mystery concerning him, but the stronger urge was to be away from there as fast as possible.

"Thanks for the offer, but I think it best if I return to the castle."

"Yes, perhaps you are right."

Derek mounted Gwen and was riding away three minutes later. Confusion filled his head, but even though he had so many questions, a nagging fear kept him from even looking back.

He found the road and turned north. Ten minutes later, the sound of heavy hoofbeats pounded on the ground toward him. He reined in as a host of riders appeared. The man in front was the master-at-arms. His expression was a cross between annoyance and concern.

"M'lord, you know it is not safe to be riding alone. You should have talked to me about an escort."

The intensity of his words startled Derek. He hadn't given any thought to his safety. After all, it was his world. Wouldn't he always leave himself an out?

His first thought was to lash out at the man for his tone, but he refrained. "I apologize if I caused undue concern. I wanted to explore, and since I wasn't going far, I thought I'd be safe enough."

The man brought his horse next to Gwen. "You are the lord of the land, and as such, you have a target on you at all times. Brigands may find you a tempting source for ransom. Enemies of the land are roaming the country and would think nothing of dispatching you. You must take care. This cannot happen again. I will not allow you to be slain under my watch."

With that, the scarred man pulled back on the reins and moved his mount behind Derek. The rest of the patrol fell in. Derek was now leading the small band. If it was so dangerous for him to travel because of who he was, why did they allow him to ride in front without protection? That'd be like the Secret Service allowing the President to walk unprotected through the streets. Maybe these men were hoping an attack would occur.

Not for the first time, he was aware of how much work he had to do to win the peoples' respect. He reflected on the women at the cottage. They'd exchanged strange knowing looks and had much unspoken communication between them. Something was going on there that had to do with him. They'd acted as if they knew him beyond just being the lord of the land. So he now had a strange plot twist and a storyline full of intrigue. He couldn't wait to go home and write. He needed to fill in the details.

CHAPTER FIFTEEN

They reached the castle and the master-at-arms said, "Dismount here, m'lord, and I'll have one of the men take Gwen to the stables."

Derek eyed the man with suspicion, searching for a slight or ulterior purpose, but the man met his gaze with an unwavering and empty expression. He slid from the horse, patted her a few times while his legs got the feeling flowing back to them, then backed away. One of the riders spurred his horse forward and grabbed Gwen's reins. The group disappeared around the castle and Derek headed for the front entrance.

The guards, seeing his approach, were already at attention. Derek nodded to each man, then pushed through the doors. Loud voices greeted him as he entered. The midday meal was in full swing. The voices silenced upon his entry; the quiet almost louder than their chatter.

Four long tables had been set up, two on each side of the hall. An even longer table was placed horizontally to the others at the far end of the room. Since the lady was seated there, he took that to be the head table. All eyes turned toward him. He nodded once to each side. "Eat. Eat," he said, smiling broadly.

He strode toward the front table, looking at the lady. She stopped eating and openly glared at him. The hair on the left side was loose and covering the bruise on her face. Anyone watching her could see her disdain for him. Derek was at a loss how to overcome her hostility. If he had any chance to win over the people, he needed her on his side. Slowly the noise returned, but didn't reach the level of volume or joviality it had before his arrival. He walked around the table to the chair next to the lady and sat down. She purposely averted her eyes and began a conversation with the woman seated next to her.

"Good day, my lady," he said, trying to keep the tension from his voice.

She looked at him, mouth agape, as if to ask, *You dare speak to me?*

"How are you today?"

He thought she would ignore him, but she said, "Why would you care how I am?"

"Because I do care."

"I'm sure you do." She spat with sarcasm.

"I do. After we eat, I would like a chance to explain myself."

"Only with a room full of witnesses will I meet with you. I shall never be alone with you again." Fire sparked behind her eyes.

"Very well. Whatever you decide." He reached for a loaf of bread and tore it in half. He plucked a slab of cheese from a heavy metal plate and reached for a plate of white meat that he assumed was turkey. He built a sandwich big enough for three people.

"I'll leave you to enjoy your meal, then. Until later." He stood and walked out the back archway. Once in his room, he set the food down and paced. There had to be some way to explain to her that he was not the one who had hurt her, although he was unable to offer any alternatives. It was impossible. If the world only existed when he was asleep, how could he have abused the lady when he wasn't there? He was missing something.

Derek stopped at the window and gazed out. His mind fogged and he yawned. The day's ride must have worn him out more than he thought. Pain in his inner thighs reminded him of the chafing. He should have started with a shorter ride to get his body used to being on horseback.

He unbuckled his sword and knife and set them on the table next to his food, then went to lie down. He sprawled on the bed and yawned again. After a short nap, he would speak with his wife. Wife. That still made him smile.

Then the world fell away.

Derek stayed alert during the trip. He wanted to see the other bubble. With only a few seconds of close viewing, he didn't want to miss it.

He saw the light approaching and pressed his face to the side of his bubble like it was a pane of glass. To his surprise, he felt no resistance. His face pushed outside of the light into the vast darkness.

The opposing light bubble closed fast and lined up with his face. He pulled back as the sphere reached him. As it blew past, Derek pushed forward again and caught sight of a frightened man. His features were blurred by the speed and the fuzziness of the light, though he did notice something familiar about the man.

His hair was long and about the same color as Derek's. His mouth was open in a continuous scream. Derek only caught a glimpse of the profile, but he could see the man was scared. It made Derek aware of his own lack of fear. He understood now that the bubble was a means of traveling between the dreamland and being awake. He was in no danger. He rather enjoyed the journey now that he was used to it. It was what he'd imagined space travel to be like, but these explorations only occurred in his mind.

Once again, he landed safely in his bed. He shook off the aftereffects of the trip, then went right to the computer. While the details were still fresh, he wanted to add to the story. He wrote at a feverish pace, almost afraid that the longer it took to record, the greater chance he'd forget something important.

Two hours later, he had to pee. He stood and stretched, then winced. His body ached and his muscles were sore. He stretched some more to work out the knots, then walked to the bathroom. To his surprise, his inner thighs burned. He stopped and rubbed them. "What the hell did you do, dude?"

He dropped the towel to the floor and stared open-mouthed at the red rash on his legs. *What the hell?* He touched the raw spots and winced. They hurt like he had actually ridden a horse.

In the bathroom, Derek ran cold water on a facecloth. As he wrung it out, a sharp pain shot across his hand. He looked and saw a small seepage of blood coming from a two-inch-long cut on his hand. *What the...? Where did that come from?* Mystified by the injury, he placed the cold compress against the chaffed area, then rubbed triple anti-bacterial cream all over. The rash cooled, though still made itself known. Then he washed the cut, placed the cream over it, and covered it with a band-aid.

Derek went into his closet and put on sweatpants. They would rub less than the jeans. On his way back to the desk, he noticed the kitchen was once again a mess. He froze. "Oh, come on!"

Just then, a loud knock resonated through the room. He was preoccupied as he opened the door, his mind on the disaster in the kitchen. Two large men in suit coats stood there. They did not look happy.

"Can I help you?"

"Derek Lawson?" The man on the left said.

"Yeah?"

They stepped forward together and grabbed him.

"Hey! What the hell are you doing? Let go of me." He struggled to no avail. Cold metal snapped over one wrist as his arms were leveraged behind him. The second man said, "You are under arrest for assault and attempted rape."

"What? Bullshit! I haven't left my apartment in days."

"Perfect, since it happened here." As the first detective began reciting his Miranda rights, Derek fought through the panic to make sense of this accusation.

"Who did I supposedly assault?"

"That'll all be explained at your interrogation. Do you understand your rights?"

"Fuck, no. I don't understand any of this."

They dragged him out of his apartment.

"Hey! At least close the door."

"Yeah, you're right. It's a crime scene. Thanks." He reached back and closed the door.

Mr. Jenkins opened his door and peered out. He nodded knowingly. "Yep. Figured it'd be just a matter of time."

CHAPTER SIXTEEN

Derek was carted to the police station housed in an aging three-story building less than a mile from his apartment. They put him in a typical interview room and cuffed him to a table that was bolted to the floor. The detectives left him to stew for the better part of an hour before entering and sitting across from him. The darker-haired detective tossed a folder on the table.

The lighter-haired one with olive skin spoke. "I'm Detective Smidi. This is Detective Reynolds. Derek Lawson, you have been arrested for assault, sexual assault, and attempted rape. Some very serious charges. You want to tell us about it?"

He stared at them, the shock causing pain in his brain. How was this possible? He hadn't seen anyone in days. Who would have mistaken him for a rapist?

"Who did I allegedly assault?"

"Well, first of all," Smidi said, "we're well past alleged. We have quite a bit of evidence. Enough that we consider this pretty much a slam dunk. Secondly, the accuser is very well respected."

"And that is?"

"Jackie Owens."

Derek started to bolt upward, but his hands were restrained. Just as quickly as he tried to stand, he was whiplashed back down. "Jackie? My ex-wife? Why would she say that?"

"Well, maybe because you did it."

"No. No way. I love Jackie. I would never do anything to hurt her."

"And yet, you did." He leaned closer and spoke in a low, conspiratorial voice. "Did you take something? Were you on any drugs that might explain this unusual and violent behavior?"

"No. Hell no. I don't do drugs."

He leaned back and smirked. "But you have in the past, haven't you?"

Derek could feel his anger rising. Only Jackie could have told him that.

Reynolds said, "All we need is your side of the story. If there were mitigating circumstances or some strange explanation for your actions, now is the time to get them on record. It can only help you in the end."

"Oh, so you want me to confess? Well, why didn't you just say so? Of course. Let me confess to something I didn't do. Seriously, does anyone ever fall for that bullshit?" He was too emotional. They were trying to trigger an outburst. He had to calm down before he said or did something to bury him further. "I want to speak to Jackie."

"Yeah, that's gonna happen," Smidi said.

"Then I want a lawyer."

"Sure. We can do that, but any deal we might have for you will be gone once that call is made," said Smidi.

"You mean you actually use that line? I thought it was just on TV. Does it ever work? Lawyer. I'm not going to let you guys railroad me. Lawyer."

The two detectives looked at each other, resigned that they would have to do things the hard way, and stood up.

"Last chance," Reynolds said.

"Bring me a phone. I'll call my lawyer."

"Give me the number and I'll call."

"I don't know the number."

"Could be a long wait, then." Reynolds opened the door and exited.

Smidi pulled out a notepad from an inner jacket pocket and slid it and a pencil across the table. "Write down his name."

Derek did and the detective left.

When he was alone, Derek was flooded with emotions. Why would Jackie do this to him? What did she hope to gain? They had been getting along, especially now that he had a good story going. He didn't understand any of it. Sure, he flirted with her. Yes, he wanted her back, but he would never force himself on her...or anyone, for that matter. He wanted her back. To do something like that would be to lose her forever; not just as a lover and friend, but as his agent too.

He thought about his dream. Was it a coincidence the same thing had happened there? Could he have been sleepwalking again and attacked Jackie? Perhaps the assault on the lady was his subconscious mind's attempt to tell him what he had done to Jackie in the real world.

No, this couldn't be happening, especially now when things were falling into place again. Maybe he had a split personality. What if the dreamland was how he saw the real world through the eyes of another persona? Oh dear God, what was he going to do?

More than an hour later, the door opened and in walked Mark Drury, his attorney. Mark handled his contracts and his normal business dealings. He was not a criminal attorney, but Derek had never needed one. He wondered how many people had criminal lawyers on their phones.

Mark extended his hand as he approached.

"Derek, I'd say good to see you, but..."

Derek tried to take his hand but was restricted by the handcuffs. Mark clasped his arm, gave a quick squeeze, and sat down opposite him.

"Tell me what happened. Wait. Before you do, I have to remind you this is not my forte."

"I trust you, Mark. I have to talk to Jackie and find out what's going on."

"So are you disputing the charges?"

"Oh, hell yes. I would never hurt Jackie. I've been trying to figure out how to get her back ever since I messed up our marriage. I certainly wouldn't do something to jeopardize any slim chance I have. Besides, that's not me. I don't care who it is; I'd never sexually assault anyone." He blanched at the statement, thinking about the lady's claims to the contrary.

Drury straightened in his seat. Derek realized he must have noticed and deduced he was lying.

"Mark, please believe me. I can get this all straightened out if I can just talk to Jackie."

"And what would you say to her that would change her mind about going through with these charges? You can't threaten her or try to bribe her."

"What? No. Mark, I did not do this. I don't care what those detectives say about having evidence. It's impossible they have anything against me."

He cleared his throat. "Having heard some of it, Derek, it's my professional opinion that you let me contact a criminal lawyer for you. I think you're going to need one."

"What? Mark, talk to me. What do they have?"

"Blood. Skin. Hair. Semen. They've got it all."

Derek's mouth dropped open. "No. It's impossible. It wasn't me." The desperation in his voice made him sound like a tormented soul.

"Also, let me give you some names of other legal counsel for any future work you have."

"Wait. What are you saying? You're dropping me? You don't believe me?"

"Out of courtesy for our past business relationship, I will contact a criminal lawyer for you, and then we're done."

Derek was speechless and watched, stunned, as his now former attorney walked out the door.

CHAPTER SEVENTEEN

Derek was led to a holding cell to await his new lawyer. He lay down on a bench and closed his eyes. Try as he might, he could not reach his dream world. Too much stress and nervous adrenaline prevented him from relaxing enough to drift into sleep, and without sleep, there was no light bubble to travel in. He tried to force a yawn but only succeeded in causing his jaw to ache.

Late in the afternoon, a policeman unlocked the cell and ushered him to a different interview room. This time, he was not cuffed. Several minutes later, the door opened and a tall, lean black man wearing an expensively tailored dark blue suit came in. His short black hair had white flecks. He was all business. He sat next to Derek.

"I am Arthur Lawrence. I was contacted by your former attorney, Mr. Drury. I am here as a courtesy for the moment. Whether or not I take your case depends on what you have to say. I have just spent a half hour with the arresting detectives, and the evidence they've compiled in such a short amount of time is quite substantial.

"You should know I only play to win. That being said, I will not take the case if it's a loser, and right now, that's a toss-up."

He studied Derek with hard, penetrating eyes like a scientist examining a specimen.

"I didn't . . ."

Lawrence held up a hand to stop him.

"Don't want to hear it. Don't care. My only interest is winning. Now, lay out the facts."

"Not sure how much I can tell you. I woke up alone. I started working on my new novel, then the cops were at the door. That was the first I heard about an assault."

"Were you drinking or doing drugs?"

"No. I don't do drugs and I haven't had a drink in several days."

"When was the last time you saw your ex-wife?"

He thought for a moment, wanting to be accurate. "Two days ago. The night before, I emailed her some pages I wrote. She came over, all excited about how good they were. We talked for a bit, then she insisted I sit down and write. She stayed for a few more minutes and left. I haven't seen or heard from her since."

"So you're saying you did not see her last night?"

"Last night?" Derek pulled out the memory. He wrote, he fell asleep, he traveled to another place in his dreams, he woke. Had she come over while he slept? She still had a key, so she could get in any time she wanted. The only thing that made sense was that he'd attacked her in his sleep, but he certainly had no memory of doing so. Maybe he'd blocked it out.

"No. I did not see her last night."

This was all so strange. The home invasions. The neighbor and the doorman seeing him naked in the hall. The kitchen left in disarray.

"Mr. Lawson, having seen the evidence against you and you not being able to offer any defense, I'm afraid I'll have to decline this case. Unless you can offer some acceptable explanation or have an evil twin out there somewhere, I'm done here. I'll have the detectives contact a public defender for you."

Derek barely heard him. Something flashed across his mind like a glowing ball of light. That was it. The traveling ball of light with the familiar figure inside; one that looked like him.

The pieces fell into place then. Lawrence stood to leave, but Derek's hand shot out and grabbed his arm. "Wait!" The man paused, wide-eyed, like he was afraid he was about to be assaulted. "It's coming together. Give me a minute."

What if there's two of me? When I travel back to the dream world, the me from that time travels forward. That would explain a lot of things. But who would ever believe him? Only one person.

Jackie.

And at that moment, he knew exactly what to do.

He looked up at Lawrence, who had pulled free from his grasp.

"That's it."

"That's what?"

"Mr. Lawrence, the evil twin scenario is a reality."

He gave an irritated look of disbelief. "Please, Mr. Lawson, don't waste my time."

"No. I'm serious. Look; you came all the way here. What's another few minutes? You wanted an explanation. I have one. Please sit."

"All right, but you do not touch me again."

Derek nodded. The attorney sat.

"All week long, strange things have been happening around my apartment. I've woken three different times now to a mess. I'm normally obsessively clean. I tidy everything up before I do anything else. It's the way I've always been. Once, things were moved; twice, there was a huge mess in the kitchen. Dirty dishes, food left out cupboards open. I couldn't explain it. At first I thought it was Jackie, since she has a key, but when I called her, she said she hadn't been there since I saw her last.

"One of those times, my sword was stuck in the floor, standing straight up. I keep it in the apartment to work out fight scenes for my novels. Mr. Lawrence, I spent a lot of money on that floor. I would never scar it like that. I had a cow when I dropped a steak knife in the kitchen once and it nicked the floor."

He stood and walked around the room.

"Then, I supposedly locked myself out of my apartment, naked. My neighbor, Mr. Jenkins, found me and gave me a blanket. Only it wasn't me. I went down and talked to the doorman and he confirmed what Mr. Jenkins said. Someone who looked like me was in my apartment. Both the doorman and my neighbor swear it was me, but it wasn't."

"So what are you saying here? That you have a twin somewhere?"

"I don't know if he's my twin, but I think I have a stalker, and he looks enough like me to fool others. What if he was inside my apartment when Jackie came over?"

"This is all very far-fetched. Do you expect a jury to believe you?"

"It is bizarre; granted. But some things Mr. Jenkins told me I said were weird. He thought I was on drugs. I'll take a blood test to prove I haven't done drugs in a very long time."

Derek dropped back into his chair and almost put his hand on Lawrence's arm, but stopped himself. "Sir, someone is impersonating me."

"And how do you propose we prove that? They have DNA samples from skin, saliva, and semen. The victim, your ex-wife, identified you. A stalker cannot be just a lookalike; he would have to be a blood relative."

Derek slid down in his seat and ran the entire scenario through his mind.

"I don't know, Mr. Lawson. I still see a losing case."

"The answer is with Jackie. We need to interview her."

"I can tell you right now, if I were her attorney, there would be no way I'd allow her to see you."

"Then we'll have to force the issue and you'll have to ask her some questions I pose to you."

Lawrence hesitated.

"Mr. Lawrence, I realize this all sounds strange. I admit it. I'm the only one who believes I'm innocent. Just do this for me, and if after you talk to her you still think it's a losing case, there's nothing lost but a little time. Time that will be worthwhile, and that I will pay you for."

Lawrence nodded slowly. "All right. What have you got?"

"Something a copycat will not have and couldn't possibly know."

Ray Wenck

CHAPTER EIGHTEEN

Derek told Lawrence what he wanted to do. To his credit, the attorney accepted Derek at his word. After all, he was getting paid and didn't have to decide whether to take the case until after the gambit had played out.

While Lawrence went to put things in motion, Derek was placed back in the holding cell. Left alone, he tried to puzzle out his situation more completely.

If there were indeed two of him from different times and different worlds, what was the likelihood of them being exactly alike? He knew there was a resemblance, but what if the bodies had the same markings and scars? He tried not to dwell on the fact that time travel was impossible. He'd deal with that part when he was released from jail. If he got released.

If the figure in the other bubble was a distant relation, that meant they were exchanging places. Traveling to the future had to be more overwhelming than the reverse. That also explained the mess in his apartment and why things were moved. Of course, he'd thought the whole thing a dream; just a clever manipulation of his mind to help him break free of his writer's block. In that regard, it had worked, but never in his wildest dreams did he ever think it was real.

He rubbed the inside of his legs. They still tingled with irritation. He looked at the cut on his hand. That was real enough. He wanted to puzzle this theory out before the detectives came knocking. Though he doubted his dreams were real, something was definitely wrong.

Derek's thoughts settled on his wife in that dream world. If the other him was as violent as he appeared, no wonder she hated Derek. She thought he was the one who'd beaten her. How could he convince her otherwise?

Then another thought hit him. What if he never returned? He might not get the chance to tell her the truth; not that she would believe him. He wasn't sure he believed it himself. Derek was surprised to find the idea of never seeing her again depressed him.

Before he could examine his feelings any further, a policeman came for him. He was escorted to a larger interview room this time. Lawrence and Smidi were already there, seated across from each other. Derek took the chair next to Lawrence and started to speak, but the man held up a hand.

"Everything has been arranged as we discussed."

The door opened and Reynolds entered, followed by another man in a suit. Reynolds leaned against the wall near the door and the suit sat next to Smidi.

Derek gave Lawrence an inquisitive look.

"Ms. Owens is in the booth behind the window," Lawrence informed him.

The other suit said, "My client will not meet you in person. Whatever you have to say will be addressed to me. If this is nothing more than a plea for her to drop the charges, I will end this interview. Do I make myself clear?"

The man's tone angered Derek. He didn't trust himself to speak, so he merely nodded.

"Also, this interview is being recorded."

Derek looked at Lawrence.

"It was the only way they would agree to meet," Lawrence said. "With what you want to do, it will be to your benefit anyway."

Derek nodded.

Smidi said, "We have been led to believe you will present evidence to prove your innocence. I would like to go over the facts and then have you tell your story from the beginning."

"No," Derek said.

"Excuse me?" said Smidi.

The other attorney glanced at the detective, then started to rise.

"I won't waste our time rehashing things that don't have any effect on my release. What I have to say and show you will end this in seconds."

He looked at the window and pictured Jackie there.

"Jackie, you know me. You know I love you. Though I've made a lot of mistakes and am solely to blame for the failure of our marriage, I will always love you."

"That's it. This interview is over." Jackie's attorney stood and moved toward the door.

"Hold on a minute, counselor," Lawrence said in a loud, authoritative voice. "Let him finish. It will be better for you to hear him out now rather than be embarrassed in court."

That stopped the man. "Get your client under control. I will not allow him to address my client."

"Jackie. The man who attacked you. Did he have his shirt off?" Derek asked.

"What?" her attorney said.

"Counselor!" Lawrence's voice boomed. "Sit your ass down and let the man finish."

He remained standing, fuming.

Derek stood. Reynolds pushed off the wall, ready to pounce.

Eyes locked on a spot on the window, Derek envisioned Jackie's face and began to unbutton his shirt.

"We were lovers for many years. You have seen me naked countless times."

The opposing attorney moved in front of Derek to block Jackie from seeing whatever Derek was trying to show her.

Smidi reached up and pulled the attorney to the side.

Derek talked over the protestations. "You know my body." He opened his shirt wide, revealing his torso. "Did he have these?"

The room went quiet as Derek revealed bullet wounds and knife scars. "The man who has been stalking me and impersonating me could not possibly know about these, because you're the only one who's ever seen them besides the medical teams that worked on me. I've never shown anyone else but you."

Her attorney sputtered sounds but couldn't form words. Lawrence stood and came around the table to see the wounds for himself. Smidi and Reynolds both eyed Derek.

"Jackie, if the man who assaulted you did not have these scars, then it wasn't me."

"Mr. Lawson," Lawrence said, "will you please explain to the officers what these are."

Derek looked at his attorney, who nodded toward the detectives.

"Yeah, sure. I was an Army Ranger. Our squad got ambushed in Iraq. I took three rounds; two to the chest and one in the left arm."

Lawrence nodded. "And the other scars?"

"One of our attackers saw me writhing on the ground. I was not able to defend myself. He stood over me with a smirk on his face, then bent to finish the kill with his long knife. Though I was weak, I attempted to stop him. I kicked his legs out and he fell. The blade penetrated and sliced me here." He pointed without looking. "We struggled and during the fight, he stabbed me here." Again, he pointed without looking. "I managed to call up every bit of strength I had and ripped the knife from my attacker and buried it in his throat. After that, I passed out and woke in a military hospital."

Smidi leaned forward in his seat and pointed. "And what of that one? It looks much newer than the others."

Derek looked down. Across his abdomen just below the rib cage was a fine scabbed line. The sight puzzled him for a moment before the memory came to him. "Oh yeah; forgot about that one. That was just two days ago. I was working out a sword fighting routine and accidentally sliced myself."

Lawrence said, "You will also note the lack of scratches. If Ms. Owens had skin under her nails where are the scratches?"

Derek stepped toward the window, still holding the shirt open.

"Jackie?"

Her lawyer said, "I will meet with my client and discuss this. We'll let you know our decision."

Just then, the door opened, and Jackie stood there, tears filling her eyes. "Oh Derek, I'm so sorry. The man who attacked me had pale skin and no scars. He was pretty strong, and he was thinner too. And now that I think about it, his hair was long and greasy." Her hand went to her mouth and her eyes went distant. "He called me a witch-whore and said I had cast a spell on him." Her eyes refocused. "He had an accent. I was so terrified that I only realized it now." She looked at Smidi. "I-I want to drop the charges. Derek, please forgive me."

He was elated to see her but unable to speak. The mix of relief and anger in his own emotions caused his throat to constrict. She had bruises around her eye and cheek and her lip was swollen. The sight angered him. He wanted to rush to her. To wrap her in his arms and hold her tight. To kiss away her pain and vow to always be there to protect her. But that was not to be. That thought morphed into anger at Jackie because she believed him capable of such a horrid attack. He looked away and buttoned up his shirt.

"Just a minute," Smidi said. "You told us you haven't left the apartment in days. How do you explain this so-called imposter being there and you not seeing him?"

Reynolds added, "The evidence samples all come back to you. There's no way it's not you."

"Please," Lawrence said. "I'll bring in a DNA expert that will tear that apart. If this attacker is a lookalike. maybe it's because they are blood relation. Now, I believe the lady said she was dropping the charges. I'd like my client released."

Smidi stared at Derek, lost in thought. He shifted his gaze to an emotional Jackie. "For what it's worth, you're making a big mistake here. It's just going to happen again."

"Careful now, detective," Lawrence said.

Smidi shook his head. "Hal," he said to Reynolds. "Would you get the paperwork ready, please?"

"Yeah. Sure." He left the room.

Jackie stepped into the room. "Derek? Say something. Yell at me or something."

"Nothing to say." He turned to Lawrence. "Get me out of here."

"I'm on it," he said.

Derek walked past Jackie, who put a hand on his arm. He hesitated, then exited without a word. She should have known him better than that. He just wanted to get back to his desk and write. Later he would think about his revelations and where he would go from there.

CHAPTER NINETEEN

Jackie called him several times, but he ignored her. He rationalized that when he was writing, it didn't matter who was calling; he wouldn't answer. He knew that wasn't true. He always wanted to talk to Jackie, but he had to sort out his feelings before speaking with her. He turned the phone off to prevent distractions and the temptation to answer.

Once Derek fell into the zone, he was too focused to be aware of anything else. His fingers flew across the keys as if driven by some mysterious force. The story unfolded rapidly, but Derek felt something was different. He wasn't as excited as he had been before. Instead, his pace and emotion were angrier. Even his touch on the keys was harder than normal.

Each time he felt the anger boiling over, he took a break to pace the room for a few moments, then returned to the story.

During one lap around, his anger exploded as he thought about Mark Drury, his former attorney. Derek called him and was surprised he answered. "Hey, asshole. Acquitted. All charges dropped. Case dismissed. You're fired."

It was at times like that he missed not having a home phone that he could slam the receiver down. It felt much more satisfying than the press of a button.

He wrote deep into the night without stopping for a break. Whether motivated by the story itself or the need to ignore everything else, chapter after chapter developed before his eyes. When his eyes burned too much to see what he was typing, he saved the work to two different storage devices, pushed back from the desk, and stared at the computer screen.

Derek wanted to read what he had written but was too tired. None of it would make sense. He wondered if he should send it to Jackie. He rubbed his face, maybe to wipe away the image of her in his mind.

He decided to wait. He shut down the computer and stood. As he turned toward his bed, he heard something. Derek froze and scanned the room.

"It's just me, Derek."

From the far side of the bed where she'd been hiding in the shadows, Jackie stepped out.

"I'm sorry. You weren't answering your phone and I couldn't stand it that you wouldn't talk to me. I knocked but you didn't answer, so I used my key. You were so lost in your work that you never heard me, so I sat here and waited."

She stepped closer. The last time he'd seen her this upset was when she told him she was leaving.

"It was strange yet comforting to see you so, ah…in the zone, you know, like you used to be. I'm happy for you. I used to love watching you work."

"Yeah, well, used to was a long time ago."

He walked past her and went to the bathroom. When he came back, she was sitting on the edge of the bed, crying. His heart sank. *Not tears. Anything but tears.*

"Why are you here, Jackie? I would think you'd be a little concerned about being alone with me. You know, not knowing if I was a rapist or not."

She lifted her head, displaying the free-flowing drops.

"Derek, please. I'm so sorry. I was so scared. I couldn't believe it was you. His voice didn't sound like yours and he kept saying weird things, like, 'What kind of spell did you cast on me, witch?' At first, I thought you were just talking in character like you used to, but when you—I mean, he—struck me, I was so shocked. I lost all focus.

"Then he tried to tear off my clothes. I should've known it wasn't you. He said, 'I am your lord. You will give me what I want.' There was so much hate and anger in his voice and eyes. I screamed and cried.

"He slapped me and got me half undressed before I managed to kick him. He fell back and I ran for the door. I got outside and I ran for the stairs, and when I reached the lobby, the night doorman saw me and called the cops. By then, it was out of my hands. I was too upset to think."

Derek listened to the story and his anger switched focus from her to his counterpart. "So, the night man knows, which means the entire building knows. Soon the story will get out and the media will be banging at my door."

"I explained the mistaken identity to the doorman. He was the one on duty then. I warned him that someone was stalking you and that he should be fired for allowing strangers into the building. I doubt he'll say anything.

"As for the media, just have them call me."

He nodded but did not speak.

"Do you know anything about him at all?"

"I'm learning."

"Derek, can you forgive me?"

"We'll be all right, Jackie."

She leaned her head against his chest and cried. Derek put his arm around her like he had done when she announced she was divorcing him. She cried then too and had asked for his forgiveness, even though it was his fault. He'd forgiven her, but he'd never forgiven himself.

Derek let her cry out. While he comforted her, he tried to think of a way to tell her what had been happening to him. How could he make her believe him? There was only one way.

She sat up and wiped her face.

"I should go. I never could have slept without talking to you."

"Don't go, Jackie."

She looked at him with tenderness, then placed her palm on the side of his face. "Derek, I have to. As emotional as I am, it would be very easy for me to give myself to you. But then what? We both know it would be a mistake."

He smiled. "No, that's not what I meant. I have something to tell you and maybe something to show you, but I can't do either if you're not willing to stay."

"Ah…okay. Now you have me curious, at least. What are you talking about?"

Derek climbed up on the bed and leaned against the headboard. He patted the mattress next to him. Jackie gave him a suspicious look.

"I don't think so, cowboy."

"Come on. This is the best place to hear this."

She scooted back hesitantly and sat next to him.

He tried to start twice, but the words fell from his mouth, incomprehensible.

"Out with it." Her tone was more confident now, like the old Jackie.

"I'm not sure where to start to make it believable."

"Is this a new story?"

"Well, actually it's the source of the story I've been writing."

"Okay, now you have to tell me."

"It's going to take some time. Are you going to be all right if you stay the night?"

"Why would I stay the night?"

"Not for what you're thinking. I promise. I just don't want you to get in trouble with your boyfriend. . ."

"Fiancé."

"Huh? Oh! It's like that now."

"Yes. I'm sorry. I should have told you."

"Anyway, I don't want your *fiancé* to be mad at you for staying here."

"You still haven't explained why I need to stay."

"Yeah. Well, that's just it; I'm not sure if you'll need to stay or not. Now that I think about it, it might not be the smartest thing to do. It may be too dangerous for you."

"What the hell are you talking about?"

He blew out a long breath. "All right, but first I have to get you ready."

"Get me ready? Derek, I swear, if you're about to tell me you're in contact with a ghost from the past or something ..."

"Relax." He jumped off the bed. "It's far worse than that."

Derek rummaged through a junk drawer and pulled out some rope. He cut it into two pieces and tossed them to Jackie.

"Excuse me. You are not tying me down."

Derek ignored her and went about collecting what he needed. Returning to the bed, he laughed at the shocked expression on Jackie's face. He flashed back to happier times. His heart ached at the loss.

"Derek?"

He shook off the memories and climbed onto the bed facing her.

"A knife? I don't think I'm going to like this at all."

"Like it? You're gonna hate it."

"Are you going to explain it to me?"

She was nervous. "Yep. Right now."

"Well?" she prodded.

"Okay. Here goes. First of all, if you agree to stay, you have to have these things. Deal's off otherwise." He laid out the rope, the knife, and a stun gun.

"Who are you expecting?"

"The truth? My counterpart."

"Your what?" Then it came to her, and her eyes widened. "Oh, hell no." She moved off the bed. "You've got to be crazy if you think I want to face that lunatic again."

"It's even worse than you imagine, because if you decide to go through with this, I won't be here to help you."

Jackie became serious. "Maybe you should tell me what's going on. I'm not saying I agree to do whatever it is, but I want to know."

"I think so too. Just don't stop me until I'm done and keep an open mind."

"Oh boy!"

Ray Wenck

CHAPTER TWENTY

"I can't tell you how or why it started. For a while, I thought it was a creation of my mind, since it occurred when I was sleeping. The story I'm writing is based on what I thought was a continuing dream. It was only today that I realized it was more than that. Not only is it real, but I travel back in time to get there." Derek paused for effect and to give her a chance to react.

"Time travel, Derek? That's your big revelation?"

"Look, I know it sounds crazy. I thought so at first too. Just…please. Hear me out. I fell asleep and I had a feeling like I was falling. I was wrapped in a ball of light and it fell through a dark void. I landed in a bed in some medieval kingdom. That's where I got the story from. The things I wrote about actually happened."

"Wait. So you're saying you really had sex with a sixteen-year-old?"

"Just listen. You promised. Now, as I was falling between worlds, I noticed a second ball of light moving the opposite direction. I didn't know what it was at first, but this last time, I saw a man inside. He looked familiar, but it wasn't until you had me arrested that I put it all together. The other man was the medieval time's version of me. Somehow we transported and switched lives and times with each other."

"You're saying that was you from the past? Like some evil ancestral twin?"

"Yes. And stop interrupting. I've traveled back three times now, and each time was different and I was there longer than the previous stay."

He watched her, anxious to hear and see her reaction.

"Are you done?"

"Yeah."

"So I can talk now?"

"Sure."

"So you had sex with a sixteen-year-old?"

"Seriously? That's what you want to know about?"

"Well, yeah."

"Look, I can prove it to you."

"No thanks. I'm not watching you have sex with anyone."

"Why? Jealous?"

"No. I, ah..."

"Never mind about that. I can prove about the time-traveling. But here's the thing. If I go, my evil twin comes. That's why you have this stuff."

"Wait. I'll have to subdue him?"

"Yes. I want you to be safe. That's why I brought you these things."

"If this is the guy who attacked me, why don't we just have the cops here waiting for him?"

"Well, first of all, you think cops will believe this story? You don't believe it. How you gonna convince them? And second and most importantly, if something happens to him, I don't know if I can get back. I'm not sure, and I don't want to find out."

"Derek, you know how crazy this sounds, right?"

"Yes, but I don't have a choice. Once I fall asleep, I'm gone. I'm not able to stop it, though in truth, I haven't tried. I've wanted to go because each time it advances my story. So what do you think?"

"I can't wrap my head around it. If nothing happens, you're crazy, and if something does happen, the whole thing's crazy. And that means—" She froze, not finishing her sentence, and cast a guilty look his way.

He finished for her. "That I might have tried to rape you." He sighed. "You should go."

Jackie sucked her lower lip into her mouth and worried at it. Derek saw her indecision. She thought he had gone off the deep end, but the only way to prove it was to put herself in jeopardy. He worried about the risk to her.

"It's okay, Jackie. You should go before I do."

"Let's say I believe you and this pervert shows up. If no one's here to stop him, he's free to wander and attack someone else?"

"That's my concern. But I also don't want anything to happen to you. But if you don't think you can handle it ..."

He let it hang in the air like a challenge.

"This had better not be some extreme plot to get me naked."

He knew he had her then. "Having seen you naked, such a plot would be well worthwhile, but it's not. Cross my heart and hope to return."

Her eyes moistened. "Oh Derek, if only..."

"I know, babe. It was all my fault. I blew it. I'll never forgive myself. I want you to know I haven't been with anyone since you left."

"Except for the sixteen-year-old, you mean." She gave him a half-hearted smile.

"Yeah, but that wasn't real. I hope."

She held his hands.

"So we doing this?"

"I guess."

"Good. Oh, wait." He hopped out of bed and went through the junk drawer again, returning with a roll of gray duct tape. "You're going to have to keep him quiet. Stun him, tie him, and tape him. Then keep away from him. Got it?"

She nodded.

Derek squeezed her hand and lay back and snuggled down. He closed his eyes and tried to relax his breathing, but with her there beside him like she used to be, it was too much of a distraction. He opened his eyes and sighed.

"Relax, honey. Everything will be all right," she said.

He smiled at her. When he closed his eyes again, he had a perfect image of her floating in front of him.

Moist and tender lips pressed his. He opened his eyes to see her hovering over him.

"For luck. Come back to me, time traveler."

"I will. I promise. Especially if I can have one more of those when I do."

She gave him a playful smack on the chest. "We'll see. I'm getting up so you have a better chance to sleep."

"Okay, but don't go too far away. You need to be close when he gets here. He'll only be disoriented for a few moments."

"How will I know if it's not you?"

"I'm not sure, but I think you'll know."

"What about when you return?"

He hadn't thought about that. "I'll give you a code phrase."

"That's good. What?"

He thought for a moment before saying, "I love you, Jackie."

She frowned. "Okay."

She got out of bed and Derek tried to get comfortable. He was tired. If only he could burn off the adrenaline. He knew a good way to do that, but he also knew Jackie wouldn't go for it.

"What are you smiling about?"

"Nothing."

"You're doing it again. You better not be thinking what I think you're thinking."

"Not me."

"Right."

It took longer than he thought, but finally the bottom fell out of his bed and he was flying in his bubble again.

As the other one passed, his alter ego was looking at him. Derek pointed a threatening finger at the surprised man.

"Oh, Jackie. Please be all right."

CHAPTER TWENTY-ONE

Once his equilibrium stabilized, Derek got dressed. He hunted for the sword and knife and found them tossed in a corner at the far side of the room. He strapped them on and was out the door. He had a lot to do and a lot to learn. Most importantly, he needed to figure out what had caused the time shift. He was sure that the catalyst was not happening in his time, but he had no idea where to begin looking for whatever it might be. His best recourse was to engage the locals in conversation and gather intel.

He was surprised to discover it was early morning. He hadn't thought about it, but he assumed he entered this world at the same time he left his own. It had been nearly three in the morning back home. Maybe it had to do with time changes. If this was medieval England, it was what—six hours earlier, or was it nine? He'd have to look it up when he got home.

Derek went through the kitchen and out the back. He greeted the kitchen staff as he exited and acknowledged everyone he met, still most of them made an effort to avoid him. *What was that all about?* Perhaps the real lord had come back in a foul mood, still clutching the family jewels from where Jackie had kicked him. Maybe he took it out on the locals.

He froze for a moment, wondering if that meant he'd also beat the lady. Damn! He wanted to talk to her, but the chances of her being receptive to him were unlikely if she was still sporting bruises.

The soldiers were not yet on the practice field, but ten archers were out stringing their longbows. Derek moved toward them. He watched them shoot for a bit. Most ignored him. He tried to engage two of them in conversation, but after their monosyllabic replies, he gave up.

An archer came out of the armory carrying a bow and a handful of arrows. Derek entered the ranch-style building and found a bear of a man, one arm severed below the elbow, sorting and stacking weapons.

He glanced up and spied Derek but went about his business. When he finished, he strode at Derek.

"And what can I do for ye this morning?"

Derek noted the lack of *m'lord* in the sentence. The man might be trying to provoke him, but Derek, not being a lord, didn't care about the title.

"I need a bow and some arrows."

The weapon master hadn't been expecting his reply. He blinked hard, then said, "A bow and arrows, you say? Are ye going hunting?"

"No. I'm going to practice with the archers."

"With the archers, are ye? And I wonder why that is?"

"Do you question everyone who comes in here in such a manner, or is it just me?"

He snorted. "Aye." He turned and went to the wall where the bows were stacked. He searched them, then reached through the pile to retrieve it. He grabbed a handful of arrows and shoved both at him.

Derek noticed several of the arrows were minus a row of feathers. He set those aside, then exited. Most of the targets were taken, but he found one, stuck the arrows in the ground as the other archers had done, then strung the bow. The string was still loose. The bow was something a small child might use.

Fuming, Derek strode back toward the armory. He stormed in, tossed the bow on the floor, and went through the stack of bows until he found one to his liking.

"Hey! Hey! No one goes through the weapons, save me. Don't care who it is."

Derek strung the bow. "If you can't recognize a proper bow from a child's, perhaps it's time to find someone else to do this job." He pulled back the string, feeling the resistance. Much better. He snatched a few more arrows and walked out, hearing the man mutter profanities behind him.

Derek took up his stance and nocked an arrow. He watched a few of the others loose theirs before he fired his first. The arrow soared high, striking the top right outer ring. He had to adjust.

The second hit the third ring and the third was a fraction from the bullseye. He had the range now. In rapid succession, Derek seated and fired six arrows. Four hit the center and the other two were a fraction out. It was a good grouping. Finishing, he looked up to see the other archers watching him.

He nodded to the nearest man.

"Got the range now, m'lord."

"Yes. Seem to have zeroed in."

He counted out his remaining arrows and counted the rings. *Let's see if I can pull this off.*

Taking careful aim, Derek loosed an arrow that flew off course. It struck the outer ring on the top left. Derisive snickering erupted. He fitted another arrow in place, aimed, and fired. This one landed in the top right-hand outer ring.

Derek lined up his next two shots and nailed the bottom two corners. Many of the swordsmen had wandered over to watch. The laughter had increased with each errant shot. Over the next five minutes, Derek hit shots in the next two rings, lined up with each of the first shots. The pattern developed enough for his audience to realize the shots were planned. The laughter stopped.

He finished off his design with a shot dead center. Other than one arrow slightly out of line, Derek had created a perfect X across the target. He unstrung the bow and walked to the target. One of the other archers ran past. "Allow me, m'lord."

Derek stopped, surprised at the gesture. "Thank you," he said loud enough to be heard by the others. He went inside the armory, handed the one-armed man the bow, and said, "Nice bow, that. Thank you."

He left.

On his way across the yard, the master-at-arms stopped him. "Will m'lord be joining us today?"

Derek eyed him with suspicion. The man was up to something; most likely a plan to embarrass him. He was more confident in swordsmanship then his archery. "I'd like that."

"I see you are wearing a sword. Are you ready?"

"Let's do it."

The master-at-arms called one of his men over and gave him instructions out of Derek's earshot. He noticed the man eyeing him. He smirked and said, "Aye, I can handle it."

Derek imagined his opponent was one of the better men, if not the best in his service. He drew his sword and took a few cuts with it.

The master-at-arms called, "Ready, m'lord?"

"Aye," he said.

No sooner had the word left his mouth than the man charged him. He screamed and cut downward with a heavy stroke, clearly not holding back. Derek managed to just block the swing before it cleaved him in two. He used his free hand and the man's momentum to thrust him forward. Derek pivoted and swung the blade fast, striking the man across the back. He turned the blade flat to avoid hurting the man but did not hold back. The man grunted and stumbled to his knees.

He jumped to his feet, growled, and attacked again. He was somewhat more controlled this time. They fenced for several seconds before Derek landed another strike. His opponent attacked again, his swings so wild and hard that Derek made deadly strikes at will.

Finally, the exhibition was halted. Derek's opponent doubled over, breathing hard.

"Seems your man not only needs additional training but maybe some exercise. He's winded."

"I'll see to it, m'lord," the sword master said through clenched teeth. "But perhaps you would be interested in a more competitive match?"

"You mean against you?"

"If m'lord feels up to it, of course."

"M'lord would enjoy the opportunity."

The master-at-arms took off his cloak and handed it to one of the men. He withdrew a monstrous blade but did nothing to warm up his arm or his body.

Derek sized him up. The man was too relaxed to be a braggart or brute. He exuded confidence.

He readied but his opponent stood still. He wanted Derek to attack. He obliged him. The larger man moved with speed that belied both his size and age, swatting Derek's initial advance aside with ease.

Derek made note and engaged with more caution. This time, they exchanged attacks, catching each other on their blades. He stayed light on his feet, dancing in and out of the action. He worked hard but noticed his smug opponent had barely worked up a sweat.

He realized his mistake as soon as he made it. In a flash, his sword was knocked aside and the point of the other sword sped toward him. Panic swept him, visions of his life raced past. He sucked in his stomach as the blade neared it, but knew if the man hated him enough, his life was over.

The tip bore in. He winced but refused to cry out in pain or scream in fear. The blade stopped its penetration and Derek looked up to meet his would-be killer's eyes. A spark of fire burned behind them, yet they remained calm, and his face expressionless. He held the blade where it was for a moment as if to let Derek know that his life was the master's to give, then the light flickered out and the sword was withdrawn.

Derek tried to control the sigh of relief. The two men stood silently facing each other. Then Derek stepped forward and whispered, "You wanted to. Why didn't you?"

The master-at-arms slid his sword back in its plain scabbard. "You'll find, my lord, that swordplay and fancy footwork may help you on the practice grounds, but when facing a man in battle, it's speed, power, and brutality that will keep you alive. End the fight as fast as possible and move on to the next. The longer the fight lasts, the more chances for an inferior opponent to land a lucky strike."

With that, he turned and walked away. Derek was confused. Should he be angry at the rebuke, or did the man just show him respect? He noticed the *m'lord* he was usually greeted with was changed to *my lord*. Was that a sign he'd gained some respect in the man's eyes?

Just then, a rider barreled toward him. The frantic look on the man's face gave Derek concern. He turned and raised his sword, ready to defend or dive aside. Others ran behind the rider.

He pulled up short of Derek, hopped from the saddle, and gave a quick bow. Derek relaxed.

"M'lord, we are under attack!"

CHAPTER TWENTY-TWO

Derek's eyes swept the castle walls. He looked back at the rider. He didn't recognize the man. His uniform's colors did not match their own. "How many and how far out?"

The rider looked confused.

The master-at-arms said, "He's from Castle Gratham, m'lord." He directed his next question to the rider. "I assume the attack is there."

"That's right, sir. A large army led by the brigand Bertrand. They have laid siege but had not yet attacked when I was dispatched."

"An estimate of their strength?"

"Lord Benton says more'n two thousand."

Derek stepped in. "What's the castle's numbers?"

"Under three hundred, m'lord."

Derek looked around his castle. If they had sixty men, he'd be surprised.

"M'lord," the master-at-arms said, his voice a blend of desperation and pleading. "We cannot sit back and let this go. We must act. The castle is strong and will hold for a while, but against those numbers, they will not last."

Derek listened to the impassioned man's plea. His mind worked fast on a plan of action. The master-at-arms must have read his indecision as a refusal to act.

"It is only a matter of time before they are at our gates, and there be no way we can stand against them." He paused, expecting Derek to respond, but before he could, the man continued. "It is our duty to go to their aid. To sit and wait is cowardice."

This time, his voice challenged. Derek bristled at the man's tone. Before he could respond, the lady ran down the stairs with her gown hiked up to mid-calf. She cried out to him.

"What is it? What has happened?" Fear lit her eyes. She breathed heavily at having run across the courtyard. "Tell me."

Derek opened his mouth to speak but was cut off by the sword master. He bowed. "My lady, Castle Gratham is under siege."

A hand flew to her mouth as an anguished cry escaped. She faced Derek. "Oh please, my lord, you must send aid. My sister's life depends on you."

Sister? Derek studied her face, desperation and fear making her look older.

"I beg you, my lord, I'll do anything." Her hands grasped his arm.

Derek cleared his throat. "Of course we'll help them, my lady. That was never a question. You need not vow anything more to me than to be my loving wife."

She flinched at his words, but Derek turned to the master-at-arms. "I assume you have maps of the area?"

"What need have we for maps? We know where the castle is." Disgusted, he spat the words.

"Maybe you do, but I want to see them. Now." He stepped closer to the larger man and spoke through clenched teeth. "Do not challenge me. If you have something of importance to divulge, you may offer it. If it's more of this belligerence, do it in private. Are we understood?"

The sword master gritted his teeth and said, "Yes—my lord."

"Show me the maps." He pointed at the rider. "You come with me."

"My lord ...?" the lady said.

"Of course. You may join us."

She looked relieved and followed the men.

The sword master led them to a lower level of the castle that Derek was unaware of. They descended several flights of stairs to the underground. The halls were dark and smelled damp. The door was pushed open and the sword master stepped aside to allow Derek to enter first. Lit torches exposed a large wooden table. To one side, a wooden cabinet with multiple cubby holes, each holding rolled parchment, was mounted to the wall. Unlike the room on the main floor, this one looked as if it was used. The sword master selected a parchment and took it to the table. He unrolled it, pinning the corners down with large stones.

Derek bent over the map, taking in the details. The master-at-arms was visibly annoyed.

"The keep is here, m'lord." He tapped the map. "And the castle is there." This time, he slapped the table.

Keep? No wonder all the strange looks when he referred to the castle. He traced the road from the keep. It wound a long way before turning toward the castle.

Exasperated, the large man said, "M'lord, we are wasting time. You bloody well know where the castle is."

Without looking up, Derek said, "I know you're a fighting man; a warrior, but even the best soldiers take a few minutes to form a plan of attack before riding into battle."

"At least a soldier rides into battle and doesn't cower behind his walls." The master-at-arms had reached his limit. All pretense of respect toward his lord was gone.

Derek whirled on him and stepped inches from him. "You call me coward once more and you will find out just how well I fight. If you don't have anything positive to add to the discussion, feel free to leave the room. Otherwise, sir, shut your mouth." He glared at the man for a few seconds before turning back to the map.

"How far a ride is it?"

The question wasn't asked of anyone in particular, so after a moment, the rider said, "Three days; two and a half if at a pace."

Derek examined the map again. "That's too long." He wasn't worried as much about the length of time as he was concerned about being zapped back to his own world before he accomplished the task. He pointed to a direct route through a large forest. "How long if we ride through there?"

"There, m'lord? I don't know. It hasn't been done."

"Why?"

"It's thick woods, m'lord. There's no path. Plus, there's the river."

"Is there no place to cross?"

"The river is deep, my lord," the master-at-arms said, his voice more leveled. "But we might be able to cross here." He pointed. "There hasn't been any rain for a while, so the level may be low enough to cross. It's a gamble, though. If we can't cross, we will have to cut along the river through dense forest to the bridge."

"How much time will that add?"

"Perhaps another half day."

Derek nodded. "What if we can cross?" He looked up at the sword master. He had a curious look in his eyes and his voice had an excited edge as he warmed to the idea.

"A little more than a day; maybe a little more, depending on the going."

He looked at the rider. "Show me where the opposing army is camped."

The rider leaned across the table and dragged a finger along an area in front of the castle. "From about here to here, m'lord."

"Tell me about their set up."

"Set up, m'lord?"

"Their staging. Their, ah..."

"Preparations?" the sword master offered.

"Yes. Exactly."

"Well, m'lord, they were setting camp when I slipped away. You know. Pitching tents, starting campfires. Spreading out to cover all sides of the castle."

"Did you see any siege machines?"

The rider looked at the master-at-arms, confused.

Derek was surprised. Surely they had siege machines in this time.

The large man said, "Battering rams. Towers."

"Yes. Catapults. Stuff like that."

"I-I don't know, m'lord. I didn't see any of those things as I left."

Derek nodded and stared at the map. An idea formed. He faced the master-at-arms. "Here's what we're doing. I need twenty archers mounted and riding light. Send someone to get them started. Tell them only bows and arrows, swords, food, and water. Oh, and torches and oil. And rope long enough to span the river."

The sword master nodded to one of the men standing near the door. He turned and sped away.

"What else?"

Derek shook his head. "Nothing else. We're going to attack quick, do as much damage as possible to disrupt Bertrand's plans, and even the odds. Then we're gone."

CHAPTER TWENTY-THREE

"What? You're fooling. This is an absurd tactic." The master-at-arms was all but frothing.

"No, sir. This is guerilla warfare."

"What? What are you blathering about?"

"Despite your insolence, I'm going to explain this to you. How many fighting men do we have?"

"Near seventy, if we arm them all."

"I saw forty horses, so our force will either be slowed or arrive at separate times, and we will either attack immediately or wait for the entire force to arrive.

"Seventy against two thousand. So we take everyone out to confront the enemy on the battlefield. How many men do you think Bertrand will use to kill us all? A hundred? Two hundred? And when he's done, who will be left to defend this keep?" He looked at the lady, whose beautiful face was contorted into a pained and anxious mask. "I am going to help your sister the best way I can without sacrificing the lives of every person here.

"By leading a small but fast group, I can inflict maximum damage, create chaos, and hopefully turn the attack aside, still keeping everyone alive. If need be, I will do it several times until Bertrand breaks off his attack."

"This is unheard of," the sword master stammered. "You send a fly to bite a bear."

"Which is exactly why it will work. They will not be expecting an attack from the rear. We will target their stores and their horses. Without food, the siege cannot go on for long. Without horses, they will be less mobile and slow to move."

He pointed at the rider. "If I can get him back into the castle to coordinate a frontal attack, we can leave them stunned and give Bertrand a chance to rethink his attack."

When Derek finished, the master-at-arms said, "Aye. I do see the merits. What would you have me do?"

"You, sir, are staying here."

The man almost exploded. "No! You will not leave me behind. That is not the way of it. I am the master-at-arms of this keep. I have been for many years. I fought battles long before you were an idea in your father's loins."

Derek cut him off. "That is why you're staying here. I need you to set the keep's defenses. If we are successful, we will incur Bertrand's wrath. It won't be long before he figures out who was responsible and sends an army here. We have to be prepared. If something goes wrong with my plan, we cannot risk both of us going down. One of us has to be here to protect the people and my lady."

"Then that someone should be you."

"No. The people can afford to lose me, not you."

The words stymied the man. His jaw worked silently.

Derek looked at the lady. She was equally as dumbfounded. By now, she had to be wondering who this strange man was that she'd married. If only he could explain it to her.

"Besides, sir, I can't have you out there challenging everything I say. My lady, I promise to do my best to keep your sister safe, or I'll die trying."

She took a step forward and for an instant, Derek thought she might hug him, but she stopped, her face now a roiling sea of emotion. She curtsied and said, "Thank you my lord—husband."

"Now, if there's nothing else, I must go."

Men gathered in the courtyard, making last-minute adjustments to their gear and saying goodbye to loved ones. Derek went to the armory to get a bow and quiver.

Before he asked the armorer, the one-armed man handed him a bow and full quiver.

Derek looked at the bow and saw it was a good one. He nodded his thanks to the old man.

"Good hunting, uh, m'lord."

"Thank you." He turned to exit and stopped. "I'm counting on you to help keep everyone here safe while I'm gone."

The man perked up, "Aye, m'lord. You can count on me."

Derek turned to leave and stopped. "If we are successful...well, even if we are not...the keep will need a lot of arrows. You might want to start on them now."

Derek found his horse already saddled. The sword master held Gwen's leads. "Can't say I'm happy 'bout being left behind, but I like the plan. Good luck, my lord."

Derek mounted. "And to you. If I'm not back, it will fall to you to keep my lady and the people safe. I know they will be in good hands." Derek offered his hand. The man flinched, a look of surprise crossing his face, but he engulfed Derek's with his own massive one.

Derek urged Gwen forward and his medieval minute men fell in behind him. As they made the gate, an old woman was entering. Upon seeing Derek, she hailed him. "M'lord. M'lord. I must speak with you."

"I'm sorry. It will have to wait." He continued past. She fell into step next to him. She looked familiar.

"But it's urgent, m'lord. It has to do with your, uh, travels."

Her words startled him. He glanced down, trying to recall where he'd seen her. "I'll talk with you when I return."

They exited the gate and he spurred Gwen into a run, leaving the woman and her words trailing behind him. It sounded as if she'd said, "It will be too..." but he missed the rest. What was it? The only word that made sense was *late*.

The raiding party left the road and raced toward the trees. The woman's face remained before his mind's eye until he knew. It was the mother of the woman he'd rescued in the woods. What could she possibly want with him? And what did she mean by his travels?

Derek remembered thinking something was off about that encounter. He recalled feeling like they had something to do with the creation of his dream world, only now he knew it wasn't a dream. Regardless, it had to wait until he returned from battle.

If he returned.

They were engulfed by the woods and raced toward…what? The end? He tried to picture what they might face at the castle, but no matter how hard he tried he couldn't keep his attention from wandering back to the lady.

Somehow, he had to make her understand that he was not the one abusing her. He wanted her to like him, although he couldn't understand why it was so important to him. What was he feeling? Perhaps a better question was what his intentions were. Did he want to remain there in this world, if it was even possible? He supposed none of it would matter if he was killed. What would happen to his body if he died here? How would Jackie handle his disappearance? It wasn't like she could explain it to anyone.

He rode on, unsure of everything except that he was about to enter into a fight against far superior numbers without a clue about what he was doing.

No better way to end a chapter in his story.

CHAPTER TWENTY-FOUR

They reached the river late in the day. A crossing did not look promising. Derek had the riders spread out and test different spots. The rider from Castle Gratham found the best one. He rode out into the water and nearly reached the halfway point before the water rose above the horse's legs. The horse balked at going farther, but the rider spurred him on.

The rest of the group watched as the tense crossing became more perilous. The horse, no longer able to step on the river bed, swam hard against the current for the opposite shore. The men cheered when the horse rose from the water and clambered up the rocky shore to level ground.

"Ropes," Derek said. "We'll need the ropes."

Four men untied long curls of heavy rope. Derek took one length and rode out into the river. He stopped where the ground fell away. Tying one end of the rope under the horse and around its front legs, Derek threw the other end as hard as he could. It fell just short of land.

The rider who'd crossed climbed down to the edge of the water as Derek wound the rope in. He tossed it again. This time, the end reached far enough by mere inches, but the rider missed. As he wound it in again, Derek knew what he had to do.

He urged Gwen forward into the water. As her back hooves left solid ground, Derek gave the rope another heave. With the added distance of the horse's body length, the rope made it, but the rider missed the catch again. As he scrambled after it, Derek felt the pull of the current taking Gwen downriver.

Gwen strained hard to make headway. He feared for his horse, and in turn, for himself. The rider snared the rope before it fell into the water and floated away. Putting it over one shoulder, he turned and struggled to climb up the slope. Unable to pull the combined weight of horse and rider, the man wrapped the rope around a tree and tied it off. Then he grabbed the rope in front of the tree and began to tow them in.

Gwen made steady progress. Once she made shore, Derek released a loud sigh.

He rested a few moments and had another rider cross. With two of them working to tow in the horse, the job was made easier. Once they figured out the process they crossed two, then four at a time until everyone was across. They were tired from the exertion but had no casualties. Derek allowed them to rest and take food, but too much daylight remained to set camp. Though they groaned, he ordered them back on their mounts.

They rode until it became too dark to go farther without risking injury. They made camp, set a watch, and settled in.

After eating, Derek took one of the first watch positions. He was afraid to sleep, fearing he'd go back to his own world. As he paced his post, he thought back to the times he'd traveled, noting the bed was involved in each. Did that mean he had to be in the bed to be transported, or just asleep? Since he'd only fallen asleep in his bed, even at the keep, he wasn't sure.

Maybe the spell or scientific power that created his time travel only worked like that, or maybe it only worked if both he and his counterpart were in bed at the same time. Still, he wasn't about to take the chance. From what he'd learned so far, he doubted his double had the interest to continue his plan of attack.

After being relieved, Derek walked around but was exhausted. He sat next to a tree and leaned back, determined to stay awake through the night. He was afraid of the impending battle, but an exhilaration also ran through him. He wanted to see this through, whether out of morbid curiosity to compare warfare from two different periods of time, or because he wanted to win over the lady. Of course, he had to survive first, a feat made more difficult by knowing this was no dream.

He thought about the lady. The way her thick, flowing red hair framed her pale soft face. He smiled, remembering the fire in her vivid green eyes the first time he saw her. When she was beneath him, faces inches apart, eyes locked for just that brief moment...

A horse whinnied. Derek snapped alert and scanned the camp. The men were all up and moving. His confusion was momentary until he realized he'd dozed off. He sprang to his feet and glanced around. Trees, horses, men. He slept but was still here. He sagged with relief.

He walked toward the center of camp and asked, "Everybody almost ready?"

Several men nodded. A few muttered, "Yes, m'lord."

Ten minutes later, they were mounted. They rode for several hours before resting the horses.

The castle's messenger was irritated by the stop. "M'lord, if we keep riding, we will be there by midday."

"That's good. I don't want to get there too soon."

The man stared open-mouthed.

"I want the horses fresh, not worn out. We must get out of there as fast as we can. You need a horse that can run when you've got a hundred men chasing you."

The messenger didn't respond. Derek hadn't shared his plan yet. He wanted to scope out the area before making his idea known. It worked well as he ran it through his mind, but reality could toss even the best plans into the fire.

He forced them to ride an easy pace for the next few hours to the dismay of the messenger and several of his men.

With the day nearing its end, the messenger, who had been scouting ahead, rode back to Derek. "M'lord, the castle is just ahead." He drew his sword. Some of the others did the same.

"Whoa! Slow down. Dismount and walk the horses closer. I want to look before we do anything."

Tension filled the woods as the men dismounted. Derek handed Gwen's reins to one of the men, and after instructing them to stay, he followed the messenger. They crept through the woods and crouched at the tree line. Ahead stood Castle Gratham. It was nearly four times the size of his keep. Its large towers and steeples rose high above the massive walls. Like the keep, it too was pressed against a mountain at the back, but with the castle standing taller and the apex of the mountain lower, attacking from above looked more possible. Large tents filled the open ground in front of the castle like a scene from Woodstock.

The battle was in progress. Men scaled ladders pushed against the walls. Others rammed the huge wooden gates with a twelve-foot-long tree trunk. Archers from both sides fired constant competing volleys. At this point, there were no breaches in the wall, and only a handful of men could scurry over the top.

Derek noted the absence of siege weapons. That surprised him. What year was this? He wasn't sure when they became the modern warfare of the day, but they made defending much easier.

He switched his gaze to the attackers' camp. The tents were about a hundred yards from the walls and too many to count, but he did take note of the larger tents. There were six, with one twice the size of the others. That would be Bertrand's.

Derek studied the scene in front of them. They had to cross a good sixty yards of open land to reach the camp. The ground where the camp was situated was elevated above where they now squatted. They were on an incline leading to a ridge ten yards from the edge of the camp.

He closed his eyes and visualized what he wanted to happen in this live action chess match, then opened his eyes to place his pieces on the board. Satisfied, he motioned the messenger back, but before they could rejoin the others, the sound of pounding reached his ear. He put an arm out to stop the messenger as he listened. He had a good idea of what the sound meant. "This way," he said. They crept along the bottom of the incline until they reached the opposite side of the camp. Behind a line of trees, men constructed their war machines. That made more sense. The initial assault was a softening up and feeling out effort. The real attack would occur as soon as the siege weapons were finished. He studied the different groups, noting two towers and three catapults in various stages of construction. Those had to go. Satisfied, he led the messenger back to the men. Derek called them to him.

"We stay here for now."

"But m'lord—"

Derek cut him off. "What would you have us do? Ride into the battle? Twenty men against a thousand? It is not my intention to sacrifice your lives. We will do the maximum amount of damage possible to disrupt the attack on the castle and still be able to ride to safety when we're done." He glanced up through the trees and into the fading light.

"Sit and relax. Make sure of your weapons. You will need at least two arrows fixed for fire; more if we can. We will attack after dark when surprise is on our side. Until then, no fire, keep your talking to a minimum, and keep the horses calm in the woods."

Derek took his quiver from Gwen's saddle and sat against a tree. He took out each arrow and examined it, making sure it would fly true. Done, he set the quiver down and closed his eyes. He wanted to appear relaxed and confident to his men. He heard them grumbling in low voices.

Derek fell asleep and dreamed about Jackie. She was in a constant battle with his counterpart. She fought, danced away, and he attacked again. Over and over the same scenario replayed with no end.

"M'lord."

He blinked but found only darkness.

"M'lord. It is deep into the night," the messenger said.

Derek stretched, wiped the sleep from his eyes, and stood. "Gather the men."

The twenty-one shapes converged and Derek spoke. "One man will stay with the horses. This is an important job because we will be running from pursuit and will need the horses here. Also, he must guide us through the trees to the horses. Who can whistle?"

Three men raised their hands. He selected the youngest, a boy of sixteen or seventeen. "Make sure they are all secure. We can't afford to lose any. You understand?"

"Yes, m'lord," the boy said, upset to be left out.

"Good lad. If we are in close pursuit it will be up to you to protect our retreat. Have your arrows where you can fire in a hurry. The rest of you, come with me."

Again, he stopped at the tree line. In the distant blackness loomed the darker shape of the castle. To the right and to his small band's advantage, many fires lit the camp. The white of the tents stood out against the black backdrop of the night. The fires made many of them appear to glow. Derek pointed to the rear of the camp.

"Two men will make their way around the back of the camp. The horses are tied up there. As soon as you see us launch our first volley, you scatter those horses as far as you can, then join in the attack. Here's what we're going to do. There's a ridge just below the camp. We'll stop there. We'll light a torch and light our first two arrows from its flame. Target the tents with the first two arrows, then fire randomly at the targets you see.

"You all have twenty arrows. Make them count. Set the largest tents ablaze first. The officers, stores of food and weapons will be there. After the last arrow leaves the string, run for the trees. We are too few to stand and fight. Our job here is to disrupt and even the odds as much as possible. Understood? You are not to stand and fight unless there is no choice. I want that entire camp on fire."

Derek faced the messenger.

"Do you have a way to get back inside the castle?"

"Yes, m'lord. We arranged a signal. I'm to go toward the back of the wall and a rope will be lowered."

"Good. Here's what I need you to do. Once inside, go directly to Lord Benton. Tell him to assemble as many archers as he can and have them ready at the front gate. Once he sees our attack, send the archers out until they're in range for their bows. Have them fire as many rounds as possible until the enemy either breaks and runs or attacks. They'll be firing mostly blind, but the burning tents should help them target shadows. They should have plenty of time to get back inside. Tell Lord Benton to keep some archers back on the walls to cover the retreat and fight off any attack. With luck, together the two forces should be able to cut the enemy's numbers by a considerable amount. Questions?"

"No, m'lord." Now that he understood the plan, he was anxious to go.

"On the far side of the camp, they are building siege weapons. Instead of firing at the camp, I want you two," he pointed, "to set those weapons on fire. It's important, so if you're not sure you can do it with arrows, get up close and torch them. You will be farthest from the horses, so don't worry about targeting the enemy. As soon as you're sure the wood is ablaze and can't be put out, start back. I don't want you cut off from us. Give ten of your arrows to the others."

To the group, he added, "Don't make any noise. Hold your equipment. Spread out so you don't run into each other. Go in pairs. Okay. Let's go."

CHAPTER TWENTY-FIVE

The small band raced into the darkness toward the glowing camp. They reached the ridge, dropping to the ground with collective heavy breathing. The ridge turned out to be higher than Derek had thought from his observation through the trees. Only his head and shoulders were visible when he stood. To his relief, no one ran toward them. He ducked down and called the messenger to him.

"Go now. We'll wait. Give us a signal once you get inside. If we don't see anything, I'm going to assume you were caught and will start the attack. It won't be as effective if the castle's archers don't get involved, so don't get caught."

The man nodded at him.

"Okay. Go."

He ran off, disappearing into the darkness with only a few strides.

Derek sent the two men responsible for torching the siege machines on their way, then called to the two men selected to disperse the horses. "You two go now. Take a wide berth around the camp. Once you reach the horses, get as close as you can without spooking them and wait for us to start shooting. The horses will be guarded. Take the guards out first as quick and quiet as possible, then scatter the horses. If you're still safe, shoot your arrows and get back here. Understood?"

The two men nodded.

"Off with you, then."

Derek stood to scan the camp again. Nothing had changed; no signs they'd been sighted. He squatted with his back to the ridge and motioned the men to him. He swept his gaze across their faces. In the dim starlight, he could see the signs of pre-battle anxiety and anticipation in their expressions. That didn't change from era to era. Few things in life were more stressful than facing a battle with violence being the last thing you might experience.

"Several of you will need to spark a fire to light the arrows. Once that is done, we'll rise together and loose them as one. Before that happens, though, you each need to decide on your targets. You four move around to the rear of the encampment and target tents on the far side. Communicate with each other to make sure you're all not aiming for the same one.

"Those of you who are better shots, go for the farther tents. We need as many as possible on fire. I'll take the big one at the back. When you've loosed the first, do not wait for me to give a signal. Just shoot. After the last fire arrow flies, target the men silhouetted by the fires. When all your arrows are gone, wait in the trees. We'll all depart together to avoid leaving anyone behind."

He locked eyes with each man to make sure they all understood him.

"Once we're back on the horses, we will ride to the river and cross, and ride straight through to the keep without making camp. Once Bertrand figures out who has attacked him, he will come for us, so we need to get the keep ready. Good luck, men."

He dismissed them and watched them spread out along the ridge. Derek squatted and closed his eyes. He thought about Jackie. He hoped she was all right. This was longer than he'd planned on being gone. He cringed at what he might find upon his return.

A strange, familiar sensation swirled around him. Panicked, he forced his eyes open and bolted to his feet. His breath came in short quick bursts; his heart pounded hard against his chest. He glanced to his left. Several of the men watched him, perhaps concerned their lord was getting cold feet.

He had to stay awake. The spell or whatever it was, was trying to send him back. Derek couldn't allow that.

"M'lord, the signal."

Derek looked at the man who pointed toward the castle. At the backside above the wall, someone waved a torch. He nodded more to himself than the man. It was time. He drew in a deep breath and exhaled in a long, steady blow.

"Light 'em up, men."

Four men bent and set about getting a spark with their flints. Several minutes later, two were flaming. The men pushed their rag-covered soaked arrowheads in the fire, igniting them in small balls of flame. Derek waited his turn, then looked down the line to make sure everyone was ready.

"Take your positions and keep the arrows down."

He gave them a few seconds to move into formation. The flame began to obscure his view of them.

"Lift arrows."

A line of fire stretched across the ridge. "Aim."

He sighted on the large tent. "Loose."

The fire swept upwards across the sky. Derek watched the flight of his arrow as it arced toward its target. It struck the top of the large tent near the center pole. He was so engrossed in watching to see if it ignited that he forgot to launch his next arrow until he saw the second line of staggered fiery spears in the air. He lit his second flame arrow, adjusted his aim a bit to the right, and sent it soaring. It stuck just above the tent's flap.

A cacophony of alarmed voices rose through the camp.

Derek nocked his next arrow, took aim at the front of the big tent, and released it as he saw a figure dart out. A man ran up to the figure just as the arrow arrived. Instead of striking Bertrand, it embedded in the other man's back, pitching him into the arms of the brigand leader. Bertrand released him and let him drop. He looked in Derek's direction for an moment, then ran for cover behind his burning tent.

Unfortunately, Derek had already sent another arrow at Bertrand, but it landed too late. He waited, watching the burning tent for another sighting, but the man was too smart to show himself. A few more fire arrows fell as some of his men shot extras. Multiple fires raged through the camp. Although the light they cast made it easier to see, most of what he saw was fast-moving dark shadows.

Though disappointed at losing Bertrand, Derek still had a job to do. One after another, he seated an arrow, aimed, and fired. It didn't take long for his quiver to empty. He looked down the line of archers and saw the majority looking at him.

"M'lord!" a man near the end called. "The castle gate is opening!"

Derek shifted his gaze in time to see two long lines of men running out of the castle. One broke left; the other, right. They formed two rows on each side of the gate. He was able to see the men raise their bows but could not see the arrows launch. Screams from the camp, however, announced many of the arrows had found a target.

He looked to the right for any sign of the two men he'd sent to fire the siege weapons. He heard the horses whine, but they were beyond the reach of the firelight. He tapped the shoulder of the man nearest him, "Go to the end of the ridge." He pointed to the right. "Let me know when you see our men coming back." The man ran off.

"Are all arrows gone?" he asked.

"Yes, m'lord." They answered in unison.

"Douse all those fires, save one."

The small fires vanished.

"Get ready to run," Derek said.

Something whizzed past Derek's face. One of the men screamed and fell.

Arrows.

The enemy was returning fire.

"Everyone! Press into the ridge." He ducked. "How is the wounded man?"

Something snapped, and the man cried out again. "Hit in the shoulder, m'lord."

"Can he run?"

"I can make it, m'lord," the injured man said through his pain.

"Two of you help him and start back to the woods."

He caught sight of shadows moving away. Another flight of arrows landed; two within a foot from him.

"M'lord!" a voice called. "They come!"

Derek lifted his head to look over the ridge. A shudder sprinted down his spine. Death could be in the air at that moment and he would never see it coming. To his shock, he caught sight of shadows heading toward them.

Shit!

"Let's go. Stay together. Run!"

He sprinted toward the trees, imagining being chased by another flight of arrows. The thought motivated his legs to longer, faster strides. The darker shadows of the forest loomed ahead. He entered the trees and immediately ran into a branch. Fortunately, it was not a thick one that could have knocked out teeth. Instead, it scraped his cheek as it bent away. He staggered to the side but kept his feet. However, to avoid further contact, he was forced to slow his pace.

He heard the men crashing through the trees but could not see them. He looked with desperation for the single torchlight to alert him the horses were close. A whistle. It felt like an eternity before he spotted the dancing light through the trees. He angled toward the light.

Once through to the small clearing, he discovered only four others had arrived, and two of those he'd sent earlier with the wounded man. They were helping him onto his horse.

"You four go. Stay together. We'll meet you at the river. Cross when you get there and wait on the other side. Be ready with the ropes."

The men didn't hesitate or object and vanished in seconds. Derek took the torch from the remaining man. "Mount," he commanded, then did so himself. The wait was eternal until one by one, the men emerged and ran to their horses. Once six of them were mounted, he sent them after the others with the same instructions.

Ten gone, ten more to come. Waiting was becoming more difficult, not knowing if the next man out of the trees would be friend or foe. The next five were friends. Two of them dragged a wounded man between them. Derek couldn't see the severity of the wound, but the way the man slumped on his horse looked dire.

He sent those five and waited, his nerves sparking with anxiety. To the right a short distance, he could hear the sound of steel clashing with steel. The enemy was close. He wanted to ride in to help his men but knew the folly. In the dark, he would be lucky to find them. Carrying the torch was not much aid. It would mark him more than give help. An enemy could be on him before he had a chance to defend. His only choice was to wait. He drew his sword.

Three more men burst from the trees, causing him to jump and Gwen to rear up. The men paused for an instant, then ran for their mounts.

"Have you seen the other two?"

"No, m'lord, but the enemy is upon us."

Derek nodded but said nothing.

"M'lord, we must be away before it is too late."

"Yes, of course." Yet still, he hesitated. He did not want to leave two of his men behind. It might be more acceptable in this time period, but he was trained in a time when the mantra was *No man left behind.*

A renewed clash of swords sounded close. Without thought, Derek handed the torch to one of the mounted men and kicked Gwen into motion. He rode toward the sound as six men entered the clearing. His remaining two men backed away as four attackers worked together to outmaneuver and outflank them. One of his men took a nasty cut across his left arm. He fought hard, but against two opponents, he had little hope to survive.

The second man faced one, but the second attacker circled and was about to cut Derek's man down from behind. Derek rode up fast and sliced his blade across the back of the man's neck, almost severing his head from his body.

His man lunged and drove his sword through his opponent's gut. He yanked the sword free as two of the mounted men Derek had sent away came to the rescue of the last fighter. They dispatched the other two attackers as the sound of running and shouts of directions filled the woods.

"Quick! Get to your mounts."

The two still on foot ran for their horses. Derek noted the men already on horseback stayed close to him. Two more enemy soldiers ran into the clearing. Derek tried to move toward them but was blocked by his men. They charged and engaged the foes, chasing them back into the woods.

Derek realized they were protecting him. He'd finally earned some respect. He glanced left and saw all his men were mounted. "Let's ride," he said, and the last members of the assault team rode off.

CHAPTER TWENTY-SIX

They slowed their pace an hour later, and by dawn had reached the river. To his relief, he found all his men there. They had been smart enough to cross the river, even though it had to be more dangerous in the dark. With dim shards of light piercing the veil of leaves overhead, the remaining men crossed to join their comrades.

They passed water around as the wounded men were tended to. Though he desperately needed more rest, Derek urged his men back in their horses.

He picked out two men who looked rested and appeared to be uninjured. "You two stay behind as a rearguard to allow us a more leisurely ride. If you see pursuit, do not engage. Ride to give us a heads up."

"A heads up, m'lord?" one asked. He glanced skyward.

That made Derek smile.

"To alert us."

They rode off.

The men ate in their saddles, most struggling to stay awake. Derek found himself drifting off several times; once, snapping awake before he fell off Gwen. He called a halt toward midday.

The men moaned, their stiff muscles stretching when their feet hit the ground. He gave them fifteen minutes. His rearguard caught up to them and informed Derek they had seen nothing. "Stay with us, then. I think we're safe for the moment."

Derek wondered what had happened after they fled. Were their efforts in vain, or had they made a difference? Even if all four hundred arrows they'd fired struck an enemy soldier...well, that was significant, though unlikely. However, even if only a quarter of them struck, coupled with what Lord Benton's men did, they may have slashed Bertrand's army by twenty-five percent or more. He may never know, but whatever the result, he felt good about what they'd accomplished. They disrupted the encampment, and although there were several wounded, they hadn't lost a man. That was a good day in his book.

"Okay. I hate to push, but we need to go. Water your horses and we'll walk for a while."

They made their way through the woods in two staggered lines. Periodically, he sent two riders back to ensure they were not being followed. During the rest of the day, they alternated between riding and walking to keep the horses as rested as possible. It also helped prevent the men from falling off the horses. As night fell, he kept them moving. If the men were upset with his decision, they never voiced it. Of course, Derek knew they might just be too exhausted to do so.

As the quarter moon began to slide down the night sky, Derek ordered a halt.

"We'll sleep for a few hours and start at first light. I'll take first watch."

One of the men said, "No m'lord. You rest. We'll handle the watch."

A lot had changed since the battle. He recognized his new status in their eyes, but he was also afraid that if he lay down, he'd be transported away. He couldn't risk it.

"Thank you, but I'll serve my time. We're all in this together. Besides, I'm too keyed up to sleep," he lied.

"As m'lord wishes."

Derek smiled to himself. The man might have been trying to show respect, but he didn't argue when told no.

He paced the camp in a continuous circle, not wanting to stop for fear of falling asleep standing up. After they'd slept for about two hours, he roused the camp. He gave them time to shake off the sleep still enshrouding them, then gave the command to mount.

They rode until daybreak. Two hours later, the keep came into view between branches. Derek halted the column. "I know you're exhausted. Once inside the castle, I will grant you all leave of your duties. Sleep as long as needed. But right now, let's look alert and victorious as we ride into view. Ride with the pride you deserve."

He watched as each man forced an upright posture and rode into the open.

They hadn't ridden far when someone on the wall sounded their return. Workers in the fields stopped to watch their approach. They reached the road and fell into two columns with him in the lead. As they drew near the keep, the number of people on the walls doubled. The gate crowded with onlookers.

Derek swelled with pride. Adrenaline pushed aside his exhaustion, though he knew he'd pay the price later as his body crashed.

Thirty yards from the gates, Derek spied the lady making her way to the front of the mob. The gathering parted as they entered. A buzz of excitement ran through the crowd. The lady fell in beside his horse and looked up with tear-filled eyes. He knew she wanted to ask if her sister was safe, but she held her tongue for the moment.

He stopped and dismounted. Someone took Gwen's reins. "See to it she's watered, fed, and groomed, please." He called out. "We have wounded. See to them." People swarmed around the riders. Two men, all but unconscious, were helped down from their mounts.

He turned to see the lady in his face expectantly. He didn't wait for the question.

"We did what we could, my lady. I do not know the outcome or if we had any effect, but we certainly disrupted the camp and lessened the odds. I will send a rider for word, and if need be, we'll go back."

The master-at-arms pressed through the crowd. "My Lord," he greeted.

"Sir." He looked back at the lady, who was wiping her eyes. He wanted nothing more than to scoop her into his arms and hold her tight. For a moment, he thought she felt the same. She took an involuntary step forward, her body leaning in, but then she caught herself and straightened.

He looked at the sword master. "Let us go inside." They moved toward the keep's front steps. As they walked, Derek spoke. "How are the defenses progressing?"

"Well. And how was your excursion?"

"I think it went well. Please send a rider to ascertain the damage. Make sure he takes the road, as I fear the woods will be guarded. He's just to survey the situation and return."

"I'll see to it immediately."

"My lord..." the lady said.

"My lady, I have nothing definitive to report. When we arrived, the castle was already under attack. The opposing force had made no headway on a breach. We made our attack that night. We torched their tents and ran their horses off. At the least, we delayed any further attacks. At best, we did enough damage to force them to retreat. We won't know until the rider returns."

To the sword master, he said, "Let's go to the war room."

"War room, m'lord?"

"Uh, the map room."

He nodded.

The lady followed, still wanting to hear more, but there was nothing else he could say. He just didn't know.

Derek went to the map still spread out on the table. He leaned over it, found the spot, and placed his index finger on it.

"We staged the attack from here. We waited until night, then set the camp on fire. The horses were back here. I sent men to run them off. I sent the messenger from the castle to get inside and inform Lord Benton of our plans. Once the chaos began, he sent his archers out to get in range. A steady barrage of arrows fell into the camp. Though dark I have to believe many found a target.

"We were forced to flee as the attackers found us."

"Flee, m'lord? Why didn't you stand and fight?"

"To what end? Our certain deaths? We took twenty men facing twentyfold, if not more. We would have been slaughtered. We did what I set out to do: disrupt the enemy and cut down their numbers. If need be, we will return and do it again and again until they flee these lands. We cannot stand against them in open battle. What benefit would have come from our deaths? We lived to fight again. There is no glory in a death thrown away."

The big man eyed him with a glint of disgust. Derek was too tired to argue further.

He pointed to the river. "In the future, we need to establish a path through the woods and build a bridge. It will save more than a day's journey to the castle."

No one spoke for a few moments. Derek said, "I have some suggestions for the defense of the castle—er, excuse me, the keep—but first, I want to rest. Is there anything that can't wait?"

"No, m'lord." The sword master gave a slight bow.

Derek looked at the lady, who was about to speak, then changed his mind. He needed to talk to her but didn't want to do so until they were alone. He walked from the room and went upstairs. Too tired to think, he entered his room, closed the doors, and stared at the bed. He was exhausted but was afraid to lie down. He still had much to do to protect the keep before he left again.

He glanced at the two cushioned chairs. Derek pulled them together, undressed, and grabbed a lumpy pillow from the bed. He wiggled into position, twisting and turning several times to find a comfortable spot. As his eyes grew heavy, a knock on the door opened them. He was too tired and unwilling to leave his position and ignored it.

Sleep enveloped him with its warm embrace. He became vaguely aware of moving, but he wasn't falling. Instead, he felt like he was floating. He recognized the feeling of being carried. He wanted to wake and was close to it when his body touched the softness of a cushion beneath him. His slumber deepened.

Then, to his shock, he was falling.

No!

He fought awake, but it was too late. The now-familiar glow surrounded him. He forced himself alert enough to look for the other ball. It flashed by too fast for him to see if anyone was inside.

This time, his landing was softer than before.

Someone shook him violently.

"Derek! Derek! Is that you? Derek, wake up."

His eyes opened a slit. Jackie's concerned face hovered above him. Her eyes pierced his, searching. The stun gun was poised like a coiled snake, ready to strike. From the depths of his memory, he conjured the words. In barely a whisper, he said, "I love you, Jackie." Then he slipped into darkness.

Ray Wenck

CHAPTER TWENTY-SEVEN

Derek woke with slow-developing awareness. He stared at the ceiling, not understanding what he was seeing or where he was. Consciousness returned with a start as Jackie leaned over him.

"That is you, right?"

He blinked a few times, then stretched. "Yeah, it's me. That doesn't mean you're any safer in my bed, though."

She smacked him on his bare chest. "Not funny. Don't even joke about that."

"I'm glad to see you're all right."

"I was scared shitless." She smacked him again, harder. "What took you so long? You weren't banging that sixteen-year-old again, were you?"

"No. It was a bit more exciting than that. I went to war."

Her mouth fell open as she studied him. "You're kidding, right?"

"Nope. I led a small band of men into battle."

"My God! What were you…how did you...why would you do that? Are you crazy? What happens if you get killed in the other world? Who's going to finish your book?"

"Seriously? That's why you want me to live?"

"No, dummy. But it's just as stupid as saying you led men into battle." Her voice softened and she leaned closer. She stroked the side of his face, igniting old memories and rekindling his desire for her. "What's going through your head, Derek? Please tell me you're not taking all these chances for the story."

He smiled. "You don't think it's interesting that instead of discussing the absurdity of time travel, we're talking about it like it's normal? Like we're living in some sort of sci-fi world where it's common?"

She stopped stroking his face and placed both hands on his chest, leaning on him. Her eye had turned several shades of blue-black. Her lip was still puffy. "If I didn't see it with my own eyes, I would have thought you a candidate for a rubber room."

He sat up and scooched back against the headboard, pulling her up on the bed and into the crook of his arm. His hand caressed her arm casually as he had done almost daily when they were together. "Tell me about it."

Jackie rested her head on his chest. He felt the air blow from her held breath. "Derek, it was frightening. One second, you were there, then you were gone, and a few seconds later, you were back. Only it wasn't you. It was—the other you. Like some cloned abomination from a horror movie.

"Even though I was sort of prepared, the transformation from you to him was so terrifying that I froze. He looked stunned at first, but once he recovered, he said, 'You,' with such hatred. I just reacted and stunned him as he leaped for me. One of us wet the bed. Don't worry. After taping him up, I rolled him to the floor and changed the bedding." She sniffed. "He revived as I was lifting him back into bed. He squirmed and tried to kick, so I stunned him again."

Something moist touched his skin. He tried to pull her up to see her face, but she clung to him tighter. "No. I don't want you to look at me. Okay?"

He hugged her close and released her. "I'm sorry, Jackie."

"It's okay now. I always thought I was this tough broad, able to dish with the best of them, but this scared me."

"What happened next?"

"Once I had him under control and you hadn't returned, I felt guilty about keeping him tied up and gagged. I figured I should at least give him some water. I didn't want him to die; at least not until you came back. But I also didn't want to change the bed again, and I damn well wasn't holding his winky for him to pee in a container." She wiped a hand across her face. "Anyway, I yanked the tape from his mouth and he screamed like a baby. It was then I noticed his eyes. His first words weren't threats. He said, 'What manner of witchcraft is this?' Once I understood that he was more afraid of me than I was of him, I relaxed. I gave him some water and fed him. Then we talked. His name is Erek. He is lord of Mountain Keep. His family arranged his marriage to the Lady Eldina. Her family owns the keep and the lands around there."

"Wow! You got more information in one visit than I have in all the time I've been there."

"It takes a woman's touch. Erek resents the marriage and the fact that everything belongs to his wife. Regardless, he's a little shit. I think he's a spoiled kid who's used to having his way. After he got comfortable with me, he started putting on the charm.

"Even with his hands taped together, he managed to snag my arm once. He may be a skinny weasel, but he has strong hands. I panicked for a moment and he drew me closer, but then I cleared my fear and grabbed the stun gun, and that was the end of that.

"I crushed up some sleeping pills and stirred them into his water." She sighed. "After seeing him again, I can't believe I thought he was you. He's a skinny, pale man of maybe twenty or twenty-two. He's got cold, hateful eyes until he tries to sweet-talk your clothes off. I imagine he's a real terror back in the keep."

"But he didn't hurt you, right?"

She lifted her head to gaze into his eyes. "Were you worried about me?"

"Yes. More than you can imagine."

"Oh, I think I can imagine. And no, he never hurt me. After those first few scary moments, he never really had the chance. I don't doubt he would've if he had gotten free, but that wasn't going to happen."

They lay there, absorbing the silence for several minutes. Then, Jackie rested her head on her hands so she could look at him. "So what happens now?"

"I'm not sure. I have to find a way to end this spell or curse or whatever it is. My stays are getting longer. If I don't figure it out soon, I may be there more than here."

She pressed on his chest and rose higher. "Wait! Does that mean I'll have to do this again?"

"I'm afraid so."

"Marvelous."

"At least one more time if I can come up with a solution. I have to talk to Eldina and somehow convince her so she understands what's going on."

"I'll bet you do. Just make sure you both have your clothes on."

He smiled. "Are you jealous?"

"Don't be absurd. I'm just afraid you'll be charged with statutory rape. If they don't catch you there and chop off your wee-wee, the charges will stay on record and someone will eventually find it in the extra cold cases and come and arrest you."

Derek laughed. "You are too funny."

He rubbed his hand up and down her back and gazed lovingly into her eyes. Her expression matched his. Slowly, he lowered his face toward hers. It startled her and she backed away. He stopped, the disappointment a fresh pain to his heart. "I'm sorry. Guess I got caught up in the moment."

She sighed and put a palm to the side of his face. "I'm sorry too. Guess being in bed with you isn't the best idea."

"It's an awesome idea. Just holding you is enough for me."

"Is it?"

"Yes. Besides, it has to be. I know that."

She leaned forward and gave him a quick peck on the lips. "I'm glad you're back and all right. I should go. I need to touch base at home and work if I'm going to have to babysit again." She stood. "Besides, you have work to do."

"There's the whip-cracking agent I know."

"Bet your ass. By the way, I'm already shopping this story to producers, so get your ass moving."

Derek watched Jackie gather her things and leave before climbing out of bed. He was hungry and had to use the bathroom. He ran his tongue over his teeth. *Nasty!* He wouldn't have kissed him, either.

He finished up in the bathroom, made a pot of coffee and two turkey and pepper jack cheese sandwiches, and sat at his desk. He fired up the laptop, took a moment to reread what he'd written, then started typing.

Derek typed for the better part of eight hours. The story leaped from his head to the keyboard. He never remembered being so consumed by a story. The more he wrote, the more excited he became. The more excited he became, the faster the story appeared before his eyes. As he wound down, he sat back and stretched. He noticed a sandwich on a plate and realized it was from the morning. He'd been so engrossed in the story, he'd forgotten about it.

He thought about Jackie and their almost kiss. If only he hadn't been such a fool. An image of Eldina formed in his mind. There could be worse things than getting stuck in that world. What if he was caught there, unable to return? How many people would miss him? Not many. His mother and sister. Jackie, of course. But other than his fans, no one would even notice his absence. The reality saddened him. He used to have friends; lots of them. But since Jackie left, most had fallen away. Sure, he could've reached out to them and kept in touch, but he had been so depressed at the breakup that he became reclusive.

He sent the new chapters to Jackie and got up from the desk. Withdrawing the sword, Derek went through a vigorous routine. The sword master's words came back. *Quick and brutal.* He forgot his routine and practiced forms and went wild until his arm could no longer hold the sword. How long had that taken? A minute? Two? He'd be dead soon after his arm gave out. He needed to build up his strength and stamina. As the sweat glistened, he finished the workout and went to take a shower. After wolfing down the dried out sandwich, he sat on the couch to watch TV.

Derek hadn't been sitting long when he felt a strange, almost magnetic pull to the bed. He had an uncontrollable urge to lay down. He didn't feel tired, but the need to be in bed persisted.

Was it the spell calling to him?

He glanced at the clock. He'd been back less than ten hours. He pushed the thought of bed from his mind and focused on the show, but he was unable to keep from thinking about his bed.

Angry, he stood and stomped back to the desk. He pulled the sword free, but a moment later slid it back. He looked at the mats and forced himself to go through a martial arts routine. Concentrating was difficult. His anger and frustration grew with each mistake he made.

Derek stopped and glared at the bed. He'd never hated and wanted anything more at the same time as he did that bed. He didn't mind going to sleep, but he didn't want to travel until Jackie returned. He didn't want her to walk into a surprise. He should call her.

With that solitary thought, he picked up his phone and found it was dead. He growled a curse at it and went to the nightstand where he kept the charger. Without thinking, he sat on the bed while he plugged it in. The pull was stronger. He sat back, flipped through his contacts until he found Jackie's and pressed send. It went to voicemail.

Derek lifted his feet and leaned against the headboard as he waited for the prerecorded message to finish. "Jackie," he yawned. "It's me. Hey, I wanted to give you a heads up. I think I'm gonna be traveling very soon. I don't seem to be able to fight it off. How soon before you get here? Please hurry. I don't want you to walk into a bad situation." Yawn. "Call me."

He set the phone down and yawned again. He couldn't control that, either.

"Come on, Jackie. Call me. Or better yet, come through the door."

With a start, he realized he had slid down onto his back. A succession of yawns drained him of all resistance.

His eyes closed, and in seconds he was traveling again.

CHAPTER TWENTY-EIGHT

Derek landed with a jolt. The soft crying was the first sound he heard. He glanced around the room and found a woman sitting on a chair with her legs drawn up to her chest. There was a blanket draped over her shoulders.

Son of a bitch!

Of all things to come back to. The bastard had done it again. How could he ever hope of winning over the people if this Erek asshole kept abusing the women?

He slid from the bed and blanched at the sight of blood on the sheet. *Oh no!* He was naked again. No surprise. He found pants on the floor and slid them on, then advanced cautiously toward the woman.

"Excuse me."

She jumped and cried out, then cowered, pulling herself smaller in the chair.

"Are you all right?"

She cried louder. "Oh please, m'lord, don't hurt me again. I'll do whatever you say. Just please don't hurt me." The crying turned to sobbing.

The girl was not much older than Eldina. Her face looked battered. Dried blood had crusted in several places. Somehow, Derek had to teach this asshole a lesson. He thought about Jackie. He prayed she'd gotten his message and didn't walk blindly into his apartment.

"I'm sorry. I won't hurt you. I promise. Are you hurt?"

She eyed him with suspicion. This Jekyll and Hyde routine must surely have her confused. He edged forward and extended his hand. She flinched away.

"Easy. Let me look at you. Nothing's going to happen."

Derek gripped her chin as tenderly as he could and turned her face toward him. She had a plump, round face.

One eye was swollen shut. A large bruise covered half her face.

"Don't move."

He walked to the water basin and dampened the cloth next to it. Taking the basin back to the chair, he set it on the floor and took her chin again. "I'll be as gentle as I can." He touched the cloth to her face and she winced and whimpered.

God, he wanted to hurt Erek. He cleaned away the blood, then told her to hold the cloth to her face. "I know you're not going to believe me, but I didn't do this."

"Whatever you say, m'lord. I promise I won't tell a soul. Just please, don't hit me again."

"Hush, child. Relax. I'm not going to hurt you. That was the other guy. I'm the nice one."

She furrowed her brow. He didn't blame her. How would he ever explain away what had happened to her?

"Please wait here for a minute. I'll be right back."

Derek pulled on a shirt and yanked on his boots. He left the room and went to Lady Eldina's quarters. He knocked, but no one answered. He tried again with the same results. Walking to the end of the corridor, he looked out the window. The sun had been up for about three hours. Eldina had gotten up long ago.

He jogged down the stairs and checked the hall. It was being cleared from the morning meal. Six women scrubbed the tables and the floor. Derek continued to the kitchen. The staff was in full prep mode, but everyone stopped when he entered. Most curtsied but avoided his eyes. Some glared openly.

Damn! All that work to be liked, and that asshole Erek ruined it.

Derek nodded a greeting. "Cook. Ladies. Has anyone seen the lady?"

No one responded. He sighed and bit his lower lip, searching for any words to win them over, but none presented. It was a small keep. They were probably all aware of the pain and whatever else his counterpart had inflicted on the young woman upstairs. There was nothing he could do. He went outside.

He walked the courtyard and found Eldina dressed in work clothes, bent over a small garden at the side of the keep. He stopped and waited for her to notice him. After a few moments, he realized she'd seen him but had chosen not to acknowledge him.

"My lady."

She ignored him.

"My lady," he said with more insistence.

She turned her head and looked through him. She made no effort to respond.

"A word, if you please."

"I do not please."

"My lady, it is important."

"Is it?" Her tone was hostile. He couldn't blame her. But somehow he had to explain; had to convince her of the truth. He had no idea how.

"Please, my lady."

She stood and brushed her hands vigorously together to clean the dirt. She stepped carefully from the garden and strode at him. She stopped and glared in an open challenge to him.

"Can we speak somewhere more private, my lady?"

"No, my lord." The title was spoken with venom. "We cannot. If you wish to speak with me, it will be in a very public place."

"I-I need to explain something to you, but I don't wish to discuss it in front of everyone."

"Then you will have to keep your explanation to yourself. I do not wish to hear it. There is nothing you can say to excuse your actions. You may be lord of this keep, but that can be changed. You will cease from abusing the women of these lands. Lord or not; powerful family or not; I will send word to my father and you shall be removed."

He rocked from the power of the words and their implications. Despite his best efforts, anger bloomed within him.

"Until you have a complete understanding of what is going on with your lord husband, any decision you make will be a mistake. We will speak, and it will be in private." He pivoted and walked toward the front of the keep. Every person he passed glared at him. Not one bowed, curtsied, or greeted him.

Derek stopped in the front courtyard and looked at the walls. He scanned the yard. Nothing had changed. Why hadn't the master-at-arms begun preparations for an attack? He spun hard and marched to the practice grounds, choosing a path on the opposite side of the keep from Eldina's.

He found the man watching as his fighters packed up for the day. Derek stomped up and stopped in front of him. "Sir, why haven't any preparations been made to defend the keep?"

The larger man eyed him with a mix of confusion and hatred. His jaw worked back and forth as if chewing his words before spitting them out. In a measured tone, he said, "Because, m'lord, you instructed me not to."

Erek. That bastard.

Derek couldn't blame the man, but still his anger flared. "And now I'm instructing otherwise."

"Beggin' your pardon, m'lord, but perhaps if you made up your mind and kept to it, I'd know what you wanted."

Derek swallowed his initial words. "I can't argue with that. You have my apologies. But is it your thinking that no reprisals will be forthcoming?"

"No, m'lord. I think it will come and will be swift and overwhelming."

"Do you think that as we are, we can withstand an all-out assault?"

"I doubt we can hold out for more than a day, regardless of what measures we take."

"So should we go down without a fight?"

That stymied him. "It was my understanding that you not only didn't believe an attack was imminent, but that you had no interest in putting up any resistance."

Derek was confounded. He had no response. "No matter what contradicting words you hear from me, I have no intention to give up this keep without a fight. Are you with me, sir?"

The man cocked his head, clearly confused, but his words and tone left no doubt of his commitment. "Aye, my lord."

Derek nodded. "Then we have much work to do. Come."

The two men walked to the front of the keep and out the front gate. Derek turned and examined the outer wall. "Everyone in the keep will be given a job to prepare for a siege. I will give you a list of what needs to be done. If you have suggestions when I'm finished, I welcome them."

"Very well."

Derek almost said, "Very well, what?" forcing the man to say, 'my lord,' but for the moment, he let it go. Besides, from what Erek had done to destroy any good will he'd earned, he didn't deserve the title.

Yet.

"First, I want rows of large spikes in front of the wall. From what I've observed of their attack on the castle, they used ropes and ladders to scale the wall. We won't be able to keep them away, but we can slow them down and make it more difficult." He looked at the sword master. The man nodded but did not reply.

He looked at the fields. "Any ripe food should be harvested. Send out hunting parties to build up our stores. We will need as much water as possible. Have any who are unable to perform heavier tasks start on that."

Derek walked inside. He stopped at the gate and studied the stone walls. The wooden gate was thick and heavy, but under the constant pounding of a battering ram, it would not hold up. The arch was ten feet high. The gate was recessed six feet on each side. He touched the wall, then turned to the sword master. "Do we have a mason?"

"Of course, m'lord."

Derek flashed a quick smile. Whenever he did something that met with the man's approval, he got a *m'lord*. Whenever he reached respect level, it was *my lord*.

"When I'm finished explaining what I want, send him to me." Derek moved inside the gate and looked at the inner wall. Another idea formed, but he was going to have to show someone rather than explain it.

He climbed the ladder to the parapet. He stood at the wall and was shocked to discover how low they were. He called to one of the guards. "Stand right there." He positioned him next to the wall. To the sword master, he said, "Look how much of him you can see above the wall. He is too easy a target for opposing archers. We must build this up to protect them, or the battle will be over in short time."

"We could lower the parapets, m'lord, but it will take some time to rebuild."

"I've got something else in mind. I'll explain it to the carpenters. I assume we have some?"

"Yes, m'lord."

Still getting *m'lords*. While he was on a roll, he pressed on. "Let's go to the smith."

CHAPTER TWENTY-NINE

The blacksmith saw them approaching and met them at the front of his shop. "What can I do for you," he paused, glanced at the sword master, then added, "m'lord?"

"I have a big project for you that will take precedence over all other jobs."

"Is that so?" He looked at the sword master again, anger ringing in his voice like the strike of an anvil.

"It is. How much scrap metal do you have on hand?"

"Quite a bit if I melt down the old pieces I've got in back."

"Enough to make five metal sheets as thick as my finger," he showed his index finger, "as wide as the gate, and as high as my knee?"

The smith looked at Derek as if he were daft. Then he switched his gaze to the sword master and asked, "What is he on about?"

Derek was annoyed. He snapped, "I'm right here if you have a question. And I'm talking about the defense of this keep. Now, can you do it or not?"

"Aye, I suppose, though I'm not sure about five. It may be sparse at the end."

"That's okay. The bottom ones will be the most important. I'd rather have four good ones than five weak ones."

"Beggin' your pardon, ah, m'lord, but do you understand how heavy they will be?"

"Yes. I'm counting on that. How long?"

"To melt down and work the shape…if you just want it rough and not polished, I'd say two days each."

"I need at least three of them in two days. Recruit some help if need be." He turned to the master-at-arms. "See to his needs. This has to be done as soon as possible." To the smith, he said, "Get started."

Derek walked toward the armory alone. He walked in to find the armorer eating. "Sorry to interrupt your meal, sir, but when you are finished, I have a large task for you."

"And what would that be, m'lord?"

"In a very short time, I anticipate we are going to need a great many arrows. You should start on them now. Recruit however many people you need to make it happen. If you need wood cut, send them out now. We might not have time later. Can you do that?"

"Aye, I can, but can you tell me why?"

"I expect we'll be invaded in a few days. It's best to be prepared. That's why I told you start when I was here last."

"Beggin' your pardon, lord, but last time you were here you told me to forget it."

Derek fought not to snap at the man. It wasn't his fault. "We need those arrows. Please. Get started."

"Can you give me an estimate of how many you will need and how long I have to make them?"

"As to the first question, thousands. To the second, I don't know. But as long as we have what you need inside the keep, you can continue to make them even after the attack begins. I do not want our men standing there without anything to shoot. Understood?"

"Yes, m'lord."

"Good man." He turned to leave, but the one-armed man said, "M'lord, will everyone be given a chance to fight?"

Derek eyed him, then said, "Sir, I'm counting on your expertise as a leader."

The man puffed out his chest. "Aye. Thank you, m'lord. I'll get started."

A few minutes later, the sword master caught up as he gave directions for the archers to report to the armorer to lend assistance.

"I need to speak with the masons and carpenters. Can you have them meet me in the war room?"

"Yes, m'lord."

"Please do that at once. Time may be shorter than we know."

"Of course."

"And see to the water and food collections too. Thank you." He left the man standing there and headed for the back entrance.

Derek snagged an apple from a bowl in the kitchen and went downstairs to what he called the war room. As he munched on the apple, he pulled out all the maps from the cubby holes and looked at each. He put back the ones that had no relevance and spread two out on the table side by side.

The first was the countryside in front of the keep. It looked to span several miles. The second was the keep itself. He studied that one first. By the time he moved on to the area map, a group of men entered the room followed by the master-at-arms. He walked around the table to Derek's left and looked at the maps.

"And these are?"

"The carpenters, m'lord," he said, a note of surprise in his voice.

"Good. Good. Here's what I need from you. Two projects to start." He looked around the room, his gaze stopping on a crude pencil. He picked it up and scanned for paper. Seeing none, he flipped over the castle map and began drawing a diagram, which made the sword master gasp.

Derek ignored him. "This is the first project." He pointed to the parchment. "The length doesn't matter as long as it's sturdy and can't be easily broken. This X on each side supports this cross beam. It should be thick. These pointed spears can be any size, but they must be smaller than the cross beam and thick enough that a man's weight cannot snap them. They need to be as sharp as possible." He looked up to make sure they were following.

"I want these around the entire outer wall. Questions?"

The men looked at each other with surprise and confusion.

"No questions? Good. Some of the spears should point outward at an upward angle and some straight up. They need to be in place in two days."

The room exploded with protests.

"M'lord," one man said, "That's a lot of cutting. It'll take time. We can't get it done in two days."

"Then when the castle falls and your loved ones are slaughtered or raped, you remember you said it couldn't be done. I'm not asking this for myself. I'm doing this for the safety of every man, woman, and child here." Derek looked from face to face. "And that's only job one. The second task is to make enough two-foot by two-foot shields to go around the entire wall. After they are constructed, I'll give you more details. That's it for now. Gentlemen, you have your jobs. I suggest you spend no time to complain or protest and get to it. Recruit whoever you can to chop the wood. I'm sure the sword master will lend you some of his men. Thank you. You may go."

The men left, shocked.

A few minutes later, a new group entered.

"The masons, I presume?"

The sword master nodded once. He appeared as overwhelmed by it all as everyone else was.

"Gentlemen, I have two tasks that need your immediate attention." He drew a diagram again. "On the inner wall of the arch in front of the gates, I need a channel built on each side that can withstand the pounding of a battering ram. The channel will have to hold five heavy sheets of steel, each about an inch thick." Not sure if they understood inch, he pointed to his index finger.

"The channel must have an open slot at the top to place and lift the sheets. The sheets will withstand the beating. The weak point of this will be the stone channel. If constructed well, it will prevent an invading army from penetrating through the gate. They will be forced to climb the walls, which will be to our advantage. Understood?"

The men nodded. They were easier to talk to than the previous group. Or maybe the word of the lord's insanity had spread.

"Your second task is to carve out a small niche on each side of the gate large enough for two men to pass through. I'll show you where to tunnel through the inner wall. I want two slots on each side big enough to poke a spear or shoot an arrow through, but not so big as to get the men inside killed."

Derek glanced around the crowded room. All eyes were on him. "What? No complaints about how impossible the tasks are?"

"No, m'lord," one man said. "We can get it done."

"Good men. So far, you're my favorites. Oh. Did I tell you it has to be done in two days?'

Now the men looked at each other.

Derek smiled. "Come on. I'll show you what I want."

As the men filed out, Derek looked at his second in command. "Getting the picture yet?"

He nodded.

"Still think I'm crazy?"

"Aye, but not about your plans. They are sound."

"I'm glad you approve. Speak up if you see anything I'm missing. Oh, and send out a scout. We'll need a heads up when Bertrand is coming." A thought hit him. "Has the first rider returned with word?"

"No, but it is still too soon. His ride was long."

Derek headed for the door but stopped abruptly. He faced the big man. "You do think they're coming, don't you?"

"Oh, aye. You may be wrong about many things, but not about that. They are surely coming for us. And sooner than later."

"Aye."

CHAPTER THIRTY

The courtyard was abuzz with nervous energy. Everyone was in motion, from the youngest to the oldest able to walk and carry. Word spread fast of the lord's belief of an impending attack. By their gazes and mutterings as he walked past, it was obvious to Derek that some thought him a fool. Others, having extra chores added to their daily burden, became angrier. Already festering over his abuse of the woman in his room, their hostility was open and near revolt.

Oh, damn! The woman in his room.

He'd forgotten about her. One more problem to deal with.

Derek led the masons toward the front wall. Ahead, near the gate, stood a familiar older woman. She was the only one not moving or performing some vital task. He paid her little attention until she moved to intercept him.

The sword master saw her too. Before she got within five strides, the large man was in front of him, blade in hand. Derek stopped as abruptly as she did. Her eyes went wide, then clouded with a malevolence that made Derek take an involuntary step back. She hissed. An electric current danced around her.

"Begone from here, witch," the sword master said.

She directed her reply to Derek. "My lord, it is urgent I speak with you."

"If you do not move, I will drive my sword through you," the sword master said.

The woman backed a step and crossed her arms in front of her, palms inward. Her lips moved, but no sound emerged. Nothing happened, but the sword master tensed, ready to strike.

Derek placed a hand on the man's shoulder. "Put your blade up." To the woman, "I don't doubt the urgency of your purpose here, but I am in the midst of preparing this keep for battle. Whatever it is will have to wait until I am finished, although I warn it may be a while."

He started past her, his entourage following.

"Please, my lord!" she called after him. "It is important; perhaps more important than the defense of this place."

He listened but did not stop.

"It has to do with your recent travels."

Derek whirled to face her. Something piqued his curiosity; not only her words, but the way they were delivered.

"And what travels would those be?"

"I think you know the ones I speak of, but I do not wish to mention them here."

He eyed her. *What did this woman know? Could he afford not to listen?*

"Time is short, my lord. I must speak with you before it is too late."

The sword master advanced, ready to skewer. "You dare threaten the lord?"

"Whoa! Hold," Derek commanded.

The man paused and bristled at being called off. "M'lord, she is a witch. She is not to be trusted."

"I must see to a few things. I won't be long. Wait for me at the steps to the keep. We'll talk then."

The woman nodded, then hissed at the sword master.

Derek pivoted and walked to the castle gate. There he instructed the masons, though it was difficult to stay focused on the task with the woman's words echoing in his head. *It has to do with your recent travels.* Did she truly know something about his time travel? Perhaps the better question was if she knew how to stop it.

He brought the masons to the archway and explained where and why he wanted stone removed. Derek left them to work out the details and fell into a brisk pace toward the keep. The woman was not in sight. A band drew tight across his chest. He increased his speed. His eyes swept the grounds, but she was nowhere to be seen.

He stopped and did a three-sixty scan of the yard. The woman had disappeared.

"Here, my lord."

Derek whirled, heart racing; eyes ready to burst from their sockets. His hand reached for his sword. She was behind him, but he was sure she hadn't been there a mere second before.

"I apologize, my lord. I did not mean to startle you." She pointed at his hand still wrapped around the hilt. "You have no need for that. I wish you no harm."

"You said you knew something about my, er, travels."

"I do, my lord. It was a spell cast on you by my daughter. You will remember her, of course. The woman you saved in the forest and the one who was raped by the true lord of this keep."

"Raped?" He let the word reverberate around his skull before saying, "No wonder she had such benevolence toward me. I thought it strange since I had just rescued her from a similar fate at the hands of those men."

"She was so enraged by the assault that she cast a spell, not knowing its true nature or depths. She only wanted to rid these lands of a blight and didn't understand she had affected your life as well."

Derek was dumbfounded. His entire situation had been caused by something he had no hand in.

"Do you have any idea what she's done? Do you know how far-reaching that spell was? I am from a far distant future. At this very moment, that wretched man is in my time with a good friend of mine, who he already attempted to rape. She is in danger. How can I stop the spell?"

"My lord, that is the purpose for me coming to you. To tell you of the danger you are in. The spell cannot be broken. It will go on until one of several events brings it to a conclusion."

"And they are?"

"If either of you dies, it is done."

"Okay. As much as the people here hate this Erek, that shouldn't be hard to arrange."

"But he must die here. If he dies in your world or you die here, the other will be trapped permanently."

Derek thought about the impending battle. If it happened, it would be best to avoid getting involved in the fighting. If it looked as if the keep would fall, he'd have to find a way to escape.

"But my lord, there is more. You may have noticed your time here is growing longer and the return visits to your time growing shorter. How long was your last stay?"

"More than two days."

"I was afraid of that. I should have come sooner. If you stay here more than three days in a row, you will be unable to return."

Derek stood, mouth agape. "Damn! I'm almost there now. I have to find a way to end this. How fast does the time advance each trip?"

"Unknown, my lord. I think it changes with your level of involvement in this time." She swept her hand toward the increased activity. "I'd say it is quite involved at the moment."

Derek's mind whirled in search of a solution. There had to be a way out. He needed the help of someone in this world; someone he could trust. Someone with as much to gain by ridding the world of their real lord. The answer came in an instant. Eldina. She was better off without her husband. But would she help him? Or maybe more importantly, would she believe him?

"I need you to come with me."

She balked. "Where?" She sounded wary.

"If we are to make this work out for everyone's benefit, you need to help me convince Lady Eldina."

"I'm not sure that is a good idea."

"Look, if your story is true—and I don't doubt that it is—we will need someone on our side."

"I am not well received here. No one will believe me. They will think I am the cause or that I am trying to ensnare you in some wicked magic."

"Are you?"

Her look of surprise was real. "No, my lord. I am here to right a wrong. Nothing more."

"Then I beg you. Come tell your story. I think with all that has happened in the past few days, the lady will be more receptive than you think."

The woman gave a nervous glance toward the gate, ready to bolt. Derek recognized her intent and took a different tact. "I'm not an evil man. I've done some bad things in my life, and I regret most of them. But it's important to me that somebody here knows I am not the evil lord everyone thinks I am. I especially hate the fact the Lady Eldina despises me for things I never did.

Also, my-my love in my own time may be in danger, facing the man they think I am. Please. Help me."

She stared long into his eyes, searching for verification. Then she nodded. "As my lord wishes."

"Thank you. Come."

"M'lord," the sword master said.

Derek hadn't seen the man approach. He stood a few feet away, ready to spring to his defense should the need arise.

"You have a lot to do. You have given this…woman enough of your time. Let me escort her to the gate for you."

"No. She is coming with me." He turned toward the steps and stopped. "You should come with us. I need you to ask the lady to join us in my room. I doubt she'll come if I ask. Tell her it is important and much will be explained. Things she will want to hear and things you need to know to ensure the defense of this keep."

The furrowed brow showed the man's confusion.

"Please. Just do it." To the woman, he said. "Follow me. Please."

CHAPTER THIRTY-ONE

He led them to his room where the battered woman was asleep on the chair. She stirred, then jumped to her feet, seeing Derek and the witch enter. The blanket flopped down, exposing her naked torso. Quickly, she grasped it and covered herself.

"Oh, m'lord. I'm sorry. Can I please go now?"

"Not just yet, but please get dressed."

Derek turned toward the witch to give the young woman some privacy.

"What is your name?" he asked the older woman.

"Gleena."

"And your daughter is Es—?"

"Esmarelda. Yes."

Derek remembered her. She was quite lovely and quite deadly. The look in her eyes when she cut her assailant's throat haunted him. At the time, he thought it strange that she glared at him as she killed the man. He had the feeling she wished it was his neck she was slicing through. Then she had the unexpected, overly sweet change of attitude at the cottage with her family. It all made sense now.

"Can I offer you something to drink?"

"No, my lord."

He turned to the now-dressed young woman. "What about for you?"

She lowered her gaze. "No, m'lord." She fought a sob. "I just want to go home, if you please, m'lord."

"Just a few more minutes. Please. I promise you can go soon. You need to hear this. It won't make what you went through any easier, but at least you might understand a little better."

From the hall, Eldina's angry voice came through the walls as she'd intended, Derek was sure.

"I don't care what he has to say. I have no desire to hear it. And I'll tell him to his face. The nerve of him, summoning me like one of his whores."

The door opened, held by the sword master. Eldina stormed in and stopped short upon seeing the other two women. Seeing the younger one's swollen eye and bruised face, she cried out with alarm and flashed Derek a death look. She moved toward the girl and wrapped comforting arms around her. The girl began to cry.

"Dear girl, I am so sorry for what you have endured. You have my vow it shall never happen again." Eldina turned the girl to face Derek. "This is the end. I plan to dispatch a rider to my father today. I will let him deal with you as he sees fit. I will no longer tolerate your abuse of the people of these lands. They deserve better. You do not deserve the title of Lord."

"I understand, Lady Eldina, and agree with you wholeheartedly. This type of behavior should never be allowed."

Her shocked expression told him she had not expected those words from him.

"If you will only bear with me for a few moments, I will explain."

"No! There is no explanation for this sort of action. Come, my dear. I will get you some assistance."

Seeing his opportunity slipping away, Derek spoke with force. "No. You will stay and hear me. It is very important. Not only for you, but for the future of this keep and all who reside here."

Before Eldina could object, he rapidly continued.

"This is Gleena. She has vital information to impart. Please do her the courtesy of listening as the lady of this keep. Gleena, since I don't know what happened in the beginning, please start."

Gleena glanced about with nervous energy. She stammered a few times and Eldina said, "Please, dear woman, welcome to Mountain Keep. Feel relaxed and free to speak. Forgive being placed in the middle of our problems."

"It has to do with the lord of the keep. He is not in this room."

Eldina's eyebrows knitted. "I understand you may be new here, but the lord—at least for the moment—is right there."

"No, my lady, he is not. This man is an ancestor brought here by a spell cast by my daughter."

She had their full attention. Now even the crying woman stopped and listened.

"I don't understand," Eldina said.

"I'm sure you don't, but you must listen with an open mind. You see, the real lord came upon my daughter in the woods one day and forced himself upon her."

Eldina flashed a look at Derek. "I'm so sorry for you and your daughter. The lord shall pay for his vile assault."

Gleena held up a hand to stop her. "He has been dealt with already, my lady. Just not in any conventional way. You see, my daughter has certain abilities."

"They're witches, my lady," said the sword master.

Eldina's eyes widened. "Do such creatures truly exist?"

Derek answered, "They do, my lady, and Gleena is one herself."

"Wait a minute." Eldina narrowed her eyes. "If you're trying to make us believe your behavior was because of some spell, you can end your tale there. It is too convenient an excuse since there is no way to prove it. This is low, even for a snake like you."

"Please, Lady Eldina, hear her out."

"You may not believe in witches and spells, but that does not mean they do not exist," Gleena said. "I, too, have the ability, but my daughter's power dwarfs mine.

Her anger was so great that she cast a travel spell on the true lord, wanting only to send him from these lands. And though her power is great, her experience is little. She converged two spells. The result did not only send the true lord away but caused him to switch places with an ancestor. The man standing here now is not the true lord. He is a near duplicate of the true lord."

"Lady Eldina," Derek said. "My name is Derek. I come from another world, another time. Your husband is currently in my place, as I am in his."

Eldina glanced from Gleena to Derek to the sword master, and back to Derek.

"I know this is hard to believe. If it weren't happening to me right now, I doubt I'd believe it myself. But it is, and here I am."

"No," Eldina said. "Lies. I will hear no more."

"Eldina, wait!" Derek said, his voice firm and commanding.

"You forget yourself," she snapped back. "Come, my dear. Let's get you home."

"Haven't you noticed the changes? Look at me. Am I different in subtle ways from this Erek? I am broader than he. I speak differently. I treat people differently." Derek faced the sword master. "You can't say you haven't noticed the difference. When was the last time Erek worked out on the practice field? Was my skill better than expected? Would he have led an attack against far superior forces? Did he have enough knowledge to fortify this keep? Would he have the courage to do either?"

He looked at Eldina. "And you, my lady. Certainly you felt the difference when we made love in this room."

She colored. "My lord, we do not discuss personal things in the open. And that was a mistake, never to happen again."

"But it was different, wasn't it? I saw it in your eyes. You were confused and thankful. In my time, it is a criminal action to abuse a woman. The man who did that to this young woman should be punished severely, and I would do it myself. It was not me."

"Your story lacks consistency. When did you arrive here?"

"The first time was when you stormed in here and chased that other woman out."

"Then you have been here ever since. That means it was you who assaulted us. Twice." She gestured to the girl and herself.

"No, my lady," Gleena said. "The spell fluctuates. It sends those affected back and forth until the transfer becomes permanent. That time is coming soon. If the spell is not broken, this man will be stuck here for the rest of his life."

Derek said, "Each time Erek returns, he is confused and scared and takes it out on you and those around him."

"Well, if you're the better choice, all the better. Let the spell run its course."

"My lady, I have a life in another time. I want to return there and can't do it without your help."

"Excuse me, my lord," the sword master said. "But if the spell is broken and you return to your world, who will lead the defense of the keep once Bertrand arrives?"

Derek sighed. "Yes, that is a dilemma. I carry much guilt over that. But all the more reason for haste on the preparations. Once they are in place, I know under your leadership this keep will survive."

The silence hung like a heavy burden. Eldina said, "I see no reason to send you back where you belong. You are needed here. In the lord's stead, I make the decisions, and I decide you should stay and help defend us."

"My lady, the transfer cannot be stopped. I have no control over the spell. When the spell decides, it sends me back. It could be now, or it might be in the middle of a battle."

"Can you do something to ensure he stays?" she asked Gleena. Her cold, callous tone shocked him.

"No, my lady. It is my daughter's spell, and even she cannot stop it."

"And how does this spell work?"

Derek looked at Gleena and shook his head.

"You will tell me or become a permanent guest in the dungeons," Eldina spat.

Gleena narrowed her eyes. "That would not be a wise decision, my lady."

Eldina paled at the threat. The scrape of steel filled the room as the sword appeared in the sword master's hand.

Derek did likewise and pushed Gleena behind him to defend her.

Tension held them frozen in place like its own magical spell.

"There is no cause for this," Eldina said. "Put up your swords."

The two men eyed each other.

"Darven, please," the lady said. The sword master straightened and slid the blade in place.

Darven. Well at least now he knew the man's name.

"Here's the deal, my lady. You help me, and I'll help you."

"I'm still not convinced of the validity of your claim. How can this be proven?"

Derek smiled. "The only way I know is for you to spend the night with me. You will see me depart and Erek return."

"You'd like that more than I would. I have no intention of ever being in the same bed as you."

"Think, my lady. The last time you and I shared a bed, it was quite pleasant for both of us."

She blushed again. She faced Darven. "I will only stay if you do as well."

"Actually," Derek said, "That's for the best. Erek will be in a foul mood when he reappears. He will want to take it out on you. With Darven here, he will be able to defend you."

"And how will I know when this supposed transfer takes place? You could just as well be pretending."

"The way I understand it, my body will vanish for a few seconds. That's when you need to be ready to act. Do not let him get violent with you. I don't care if he is the lord."

"And how will you help us?"

"When I'm here, I will continue to oversee the keep's defenses and fight if necessary. If Erek is here, ignore whatever he says and let Darven handle things. I have complete confidence in him."

"If he is the lord of the keep, we will not be able to ignore him."

"Then keep him locked up and out of sight. No one needs to know he's here. You were going to send word to your father about his unlordlike behavior anyway. If he's out of sight, he can't disturb our plans or assault any women."

"I don't understand," the abused woman said. "*Was* I assaulted, or is this a bad dream?"

"You were assaulted, dear, but for the moment, the identity of the man who did it is unclear."

"I don't mean to be crude, but was the lord undressed when he attacked you?"

She glanced apprehensively at Eldina. "It's all right, dear. You can answer. I would like to know where this is going."

"Yes. He was very nice at first. Then, when I refused him because he is married, he ripped my clothes off and beat me. I'm sorry, m'lady. It was wrong of me to be persuaded to come to this room, but he is the lord. What choice did I have?"

"It's all right. This is not your fault."

"Back to the question," Derek said. "Did he disrobe?"

"Yes, ah...m'lord?"

"Tell me about his skin."

M'lord?"

"How did it look?"

"I, ah..."

"Was it soft or rough?"

"I-I guess soft."

"Pale or dark?"

"Pale."

"Smooth or marked?"

"Smooth, I guess."

Derek pulled his shirt from his pants and slid it over his head to the gasps of Eldina and the abused woman.

"How dare you, my lord," Eldina said.

Derek stepped forward. "Did he have any scars like these?"

Both sets of eyes scanned his body. Eldina's mouth hung open a bit.

The other woman shook her head. "No, my lord. Nor did he have those ridges across his belly." She pointed at his almost full six-pack.

Eldina forced her gaze from his torso. "I do not remember seeing any of those either."

Derek dressed.

Eldina said, "Perhaps there is some truth to your story after all. The proof will be if you disappear, as you claim."

"Yes, but if the timeline stays consistent, it may not happen until sometime tomorrow."

"We shall see. But I warn you, whoever you are. If this magic does not occur, I *will* dispatch a rider to my father."

Derek said. "Agreed. Now, we still have much to do to prepare for battle. I need your assistance, my lady, to ask the people to do what is necessary to prepare for battle."

Though her eyes told him she was still unsure of his story, she nodded.

CHAPTER THIRTY-TWO

Derek worked tirelessly long after most others had gone in for their evening meal. If he expected the people of the keep to give maximum effort, he had to show he was willing to do that and more.

As the sun set, he was on the parapet with the master mason and carpenter. "Along the wall I need those brackets attached like I showed you, and just a bit larger than the dimension of the shields. Does that make it clearer?"

"Yes, m'lord," the mason said.

"Aye," said the carpenter. "Makes more sense now."

"Can you do it?"

"It will be tight, but we should have just enough by day's end tomorrow."

"With luck, Bertrand will be delayed and give us an extra day or two." Derek glanced at the western sky, surprised to find it was dusk. He had lost track of time. Turning to face the courtyard, he found it almost deserted. He looked at the two men. "My apologies. I did not note the time. Go. Eat. Be with your families. We'll start again early in the morning." He clapped the two men on their backs. "And thank you for your assistance."

The men were surprised by his words but bowed and left.

Derek leaned against the wall and stretched, sudden exhaustion sweeping over him. Every muscle screamed. He turned to look out across the land. Though too dark to see far, he felt strangely at peace. Ironic, considering the current crisis.

"My lord."

Derek whirled, reaching for his sword, but to his astonishment, found it was gone.

"I apologize, my lord." Darven stepped into the torchlight. "I did not mean to frighten you."

"Good God, man! You scared five years off my life."

The large man came closer. "Well, it's fortunate then that Bertrand is coming to kill us. You won't miss those years."

Derek gazed at the man, mouth agape. Darven broke into a wide smile. Derek laughed loudly.

"Yes. How decent of him to help me out."

"If you're looking for your sword, I had a man run it to your chambers."

"Oh good. Thank you. I took it off when I was climbing the tree to cut branches. Guess I forgot it."

"Considering what's coming, you may want to keep it close."

"Yes. Good advice. Is there something you need me for?"

"No, my lord. The lady wanted to know if you were attending the evening meal. I offered to come for you."

"Wasn't sure I'd be welcome. Figured I'd grab something to eat and go to my room."

"Your presence has been requested. I'm no expert, but I think it wise that you accept the invitation."

"Oh you do, eh? Last meal for the dying man?"

"Let's hope not."

They walked together to the doors of the hall. Darven opened one side and Derek entered. The hall was reserved compared to his visit during a previous meal. The mood was solemn. He wondered if it was the custom, the lady's request, the effect of an impending siege, or the result of exhaustion from the work he'd dumped on them.

Derek felt an urge to tiptoe so as not to ruin the silence, but as the door swung open and Darven entered with a full-booted footfall, he walked on.

All eyes turned to him. He kept his gaze forward, not wanting to see the fear or loathing in the eyes of the people. Instead, he focused on the lady. She locked eyes with him, her expressionless face gave away nothing. Then to his amazement, she stood as he approached.

She motioned to the large ornate chair next to hers. Relief flooded through him. Derek walked around the head table to his seat. As he closed on the lady, her face lit in the most beautiful smile he'd ever seen.

Derek took his seat, aware for the first time that the entire hall was standing. The sight was emotional. A lump caught in his throat. He bowed to the room and sat. As he did, everyone else followed suit. Like a door had opened on a school lunchroom, the hall began to fill with loud, cheerful voices.

He watched for a moment. The lady leaned forward and placed a metal plate in front of him heaped with enough food for four people.

"Eat, my lord—husband. You must keep up your strength."

"Thank you, my lady, ah…wife."

He ate what he could, but never having a great appetite, much of the food was left. His guilt at the waste was short-lived, as he remembered where he was. Nothing went to waste here. It would either go to the kitchen staff, end up in tomorrow's meal, or fed to the dogs.

Derek sat back to watch his people—Erek's people—but he felt like they were his. He lifted a goblet of strong, sour wine and sipped. He cringed at the taste. *Drinking this would take some getting used to,* he thought.

Eldina leaned close and spoke in a soft voice. "Do you wish me to come to your room this night?"

The offer both surprised and excited Derek. It must have shown on his face because the lady blushed brightly and stammered, "I-I mean to witness—you know, the disappearance."

"Huh? Oh yes, of course. I knew exactly what you meant. I mean, why else would you be there?"

He gulped the wine and coughed.

"Yes. Why else?" She drank deeply and didn't cough, eyes locked on his.

They sat in silence for the remainder of the meal. Then she excused herself.

Derek waited a few minutes before he exited. By then the hall was empty, save for a few hearty drinkers.

In his room, Derek undressed down to what passed for underwear in this time. He sat on the bed and thought through the day's activity. He made a list of things still to do. He wanted to sleep but was hesitant. If he traveled, he would need witnesses. Derek also wanted to pass on his new list of tasks in case he didn't make it back in time.

He stretched and fought back a yawn and lost. His head felt heavy and began to loll. Derek snapped his head up, hearing an audible crack in his neck, the pain waking him. Standing, he paced and rubbed the back of his neck. It didn't take long before the overwhelming urge to lie down hit him.

Looking towards the door, he went back to the bed, telling himself he'd be able to sit against the headboard without falling asleep. A knock jarred him alert. He sat up and stared around the room, confused. The door creaked open and Eldina poked her head in.

"My lord, are you awake?"

"I am now."

"Are you decent?"

He laughed. "Yes. Please, come in."

She entered, but he noticed she left the door open. She glided across the room to one of the two chairs. Both were strewn with clothes.

"I'm sorry. Just pitch them on the floor."

"The servants usually take care of that, but most are too afraid to enter for fear they'll be assaulted." She blushed. "I'm sorry, my lord. I'm not sure if that was you or not, but it is the truth."

"I understand. If you are afraid, you can leave. I do not wish for you to feel uneasy."

"No. I shall stay; at least for a while."

"Then if you don't mind, I'm going to sleep."

Derek pounded his pillow to create a soft spot for his head. He closed his eyes. The exhaustion was like a weight drawing him down into dreamland, but he only went so far. Try as he might, having Eldina in the room watching him was more of a distraction than he gave it credit. He fidgeted, changed positions, then rolled over. That was a big mistake. Facing her, his eyes forced open a slit. He watched her watch him.

"I do think it works better if your eyes are closed," she chided.

"I didn't think it would be this difficult with you here."

"Well, it was your idea and your curse," she said with a hint of sarcasm.

Rather than reply, he watched her and tried to imagine life with her on a permanent basis.

"What are your thoughts, my lord? Or perhaps it isn't smart to ask."

"I'm just very sorry for how Erek treats you. You deserve much better."

Her look hardened. "Yes, I do."

"As long as I am here, you will never have to fear abuse from me."

"Then don't go."

"I wish I had control over it."

"We shall see."

Derek rolled over and fell asleep, dreaming of Eldina.

CHAPTER THIRTY-THREE

Derek was both surprised and relieved to wake up in the same bed he'd fallen asleep in. He rolled over and found Eldina slumped over in the chair asleep. Sometime during the night, she had been wrapped a blanket. He noticed the door was now closed. Had she felt secure enough to close it, or had someone entered, covered her, and shut the door?

The bed creaked underneath him, and he stopped moving to prevent waking her. Propping his head on one arm, he studied her. Long strands of red hair hung in separated strings across her face. As she exhaled some of them lifted and fell back. She looked even younger as she slept, and at peace. He cringed at the thought.

He scooted to the edge of the bed and lowered his feet to the floor. He thought he'd been quiet, but when he looked up, she was looking back at him.

"Sorry. I was trying to be quiet."

"A mouse, you are not," she said and covered a yawn with the back of her hand.

Feeling naked. Derek grabbed his pants and stepped into them.

"Thank you for the blanket," she said.

"I'm sorry, my lady. I'd like to take credit for that, but when I woke, it was already there."

"Oh!" She looked around as if expecting to see someone else in the room. Eldina stood and folded the blanket, placing it on the chair. "I see you are still here. Perhaps you are stuck. Or maybe it is that we are stuck with you. Tell me, my lord, did you ask that woman to spin that wild tale?"

"No, my lady. I would not do that. The story is true. I did warn that the magic might not work until today."

"Yes, you did." She started for the door. "I guess it is for the best since you still have much to do. Best you get moving now." Without a glance back, she exited the room.

Derek stretched to ease his aching body. He had a busy day ahead. The kitchen was in full gear. Derek greeted the women and snatched an apple on his way to the rear courtyard.

He took a bite, chewed, and tasted something foul. Half of a worm wriggled in the white flesh. He doubled over and spit, gagging. He spit several more times, then studied the apple.

Darven stood on the practice grounds. He rocked back and forth, heel to toe, clasping his hands behind his back. Derek approached. The man turned his head. "Sleep well, my lord?"

"Slept. Not sure how well."

"I stopped in to check that you were still here. Perhaps the spell has been broken and we can count on this version of you to be a bit more, uh, lordly."

Derek frowned. "As long as I am here, you can count on me to be the best lord I can be. I'm sure you'll inform me when I'm not."

"It will be my pleasure, my lord."

That brought a smile to Derek's face. *The man was beginning to warm to him.*

"Ready to get started?"

"Aye. Thought I'd run the men through some practice first."

"Is that wise? We have so much to do."

"A soldier should never go a day without practice. It might make the difference between life or death in battle."

"All right. But maybe you can cut the session a little shorter just for today."

"We'll see how the men respond."

"Fair enough. I'm going to start making the rounds to see how much progress we've made."

"Very well, my lord."

Derek went first to the armory. The one-armed man was busy bundling arrows.

"Good morn, m'lord."

"And to you. What's the total?" He motioned toward the arrows.

"We had less than two hundred in stock. Yesterday we cut and made another hundred."

Derek nodded. "I need that to be a thousand."

"A thousand, m'lord! That will take a lot more time and much more makings."

"Get to it. Do the best you can. I'd hate to lose a battle because we ran out of arrows."

"Aye."

"Fret not, sir; you have done well. With a full day ahead of you, imagine how much more can be accomplished."

Derek left the man grumbling to himself and moved on to the blacksmith. The man was busy pounding on a long sheet of heated metal. Sweat poured from his face, droplets sizzling on the metal. His arm rose and fell in a steady rhythm. Though his body was well-muscled, his right arm was half again the size of the left.

The man looked up but did not stop his work. Derek watched for a moment before asking, "Is that the first?"

The smith shook his head. "Second. First is around back for your inspection."

Derek walked through the shop and out a back door. Leaning against the wall was a sheet of pounded metal. It was not uniform in thickness, but Derek didn't think it mattered. And as hard as the smith was working, he thought it best not to mention it. As long as the ends were close to the same size, it would work.

He stopped next to the smith and shouted to be heard over the clanging. "It looks good. I'm having the masons and carpenters build slots for the sheets to fit in. It doesn't matter if the thickness varies, but it has to be the same size along both ends or it won't fit into the slots." He pointed to the area of importance.

"Perhaps if the lord had given me more time to accomplish this task, it'd be done more to his liking."

"Do the best you can, master smith. I'd hate for the gate to collapse and the keep be taken because we were unable to fortify it."

The man looked up and glared at him without missing a beat on the metal.

"You're doing well. If you need more help, just ask."

"More help'd just get in the way. I'm better off doing it myself."

"Whatever you decide. Oh, and on the next pieces, leave two holes on one long side." He pointed. "About here and here."

The smith went back to pounding, the noise drowning out his mumbling.

Next on Derek's list was the master carpenter. He found the man on the parapet with the mason. The mason, a small lean man, was chiseling away mortar between two stones. He stopped after only a few strokes of his mallet. The taller man held up an L-shaped piece of wood and slid it into the spot the mason had created.

"That's it," the carpenter said.

"Okay. Leave that one with me to use as a template. You're going to make them all this size, right?"

"That's the plan."

Derek said, "Looks like you've got things moving."

"Yes m'lord," they replied in unison.

"Good. How goes the shields?" he asked the carpenter.

"Got a few done, but I'm going to need a lot more wood to do this entire space."

"I'll have Darven send you the men you need. What about you, master mason?"

"Now that we have the proper depth, I'll have my apprentices start creating the niches. I will be setting the stones for your track today." He sighed, as if not wanting to continue.

"Go on, man. Speak your mind."

"M'lord, I just don't know about digging out the walls."

"What's the problem?"

"Time and manpower, not to mention that it will weaken the structure."

Derek nodded. "Keeping Bertrand's army away from the gate will be important. Once they reach the gate's arch, they cannot be seen from above. I need those slits so our men can get to them."

"I understand, m'lord. I will do the best I can. I'm just speaking as you asked."

"What you are working on now is the priority. Get that done, and we'll worry about the other if we can get to it."

"Very good, m'lord."

"Thank you for all you've done. We will be successful because of your hard work."

He climbed down and stood next to the gate, staring at the wall while he took a bite of the apple. He chewed, remembering the worm, and looked at the apple. No worm. He continued chewing. A few minutes later, Darven joined him.

"Darven, I need a solution."

"And the problem is?"

"The mason is hesitant to carve out the wall, which I can't blame him for. But if the enemy gets under the arch, they can pound away at the gate without worry. Even with the steel plates in place, given time, they may still be able to break through."

The two men stood in silence for a long time before Darven said, "M'lord, why does the metal gate have to go all the way up?"

Derek got a glimmer of an idea and wondered if it was the same as what Darven was thinking. "Explain."

He stepped under the arch and looked up. "An attacking force will not be able to shoot into the courtyard unless they bring something to climb on."

Derek listened, realizing Darven was talking out his idea with himself. He turned and studied the space from different vantage points, then said, "Instead of building five plates, as you call them, what if we build only four?" He drew his sword and touched it to the stone where eight feet would reach. "That will leave space above for our men to stand on something and shoot at the invaders."

Derek stepped inside the arch and envisioned Darven's plan. He saw no flaw. "That's brilliant, Darven. Plus, it will lessen the burden on the smith and the mason. So with four sheets, an archer needs to be three to four feet off the ground, depending on his height, to be able to have an impact."

He looked side to side. "We should be able to get at least six men across. Yes. It should work. I'll tell the masters. Darven, send any available men to assist the armorer and the carpenter. Both of them need wood. Then, see to some sort of shooting platform for inside. It has to be sturdy enough for six men to stand on and easy enough to move fast. Maybe something like the benches in the hall."

Darven nodded and put a hand under his chin as he thought. Derek headed off to find the mason, excited the plan was coming together.

CHAPTER THIRTY-FOUR

By noon, the plans were well on their way toward completion. Ten men and six older children were cutting down trees. The mason had one side of the stone track set and his apprentices had chiseled grooves in the entire front wall. Derek found it hard to believe that whoever had designed the keep hadn't built the wall higher or the parapet lower.

The armorer had a dozen men and women putting together arrows. The carpenter's apprentice supervised the setting of the wooden L-brackets. The carpenter himself was instructing four men how to place the shields.

As the entire keep broke for a midday meal, a cry rang out from the wall. "Rider! A rider approaches!"

Somewhere in the courtyard, a woman screamed. No sooner had the words left the guard's mouth than the people broke into frenzied, high-speed motion.

Derek raced for the parapet. At the top, he ran to the man who sounded the alert. "Where?"

"On the road cresting the horizon, m'lord."

Derek strained to see him. The man must have great vision. He shielded his eyes with his hand. A tiny dot appeared on the road, the dust his horse created more noticeable than the rider.

Darven joined him. He leaned out over the wall for a better view. He straightened and said, "It's Martin, the man I sent to the castle. He will have news of the battle."

He climbed down to the ground and Derek followed.

Several guards stood at the gate, ready to close it, should the word be given. More men carrying weapons ran across the courtyard.

Derek estimated it took the rider ten minutes to make it to the gate. A man stepped forward and took the horse's reins as the rider jumped down.

"M'lord," the rider said between short breaths, as if he was the one doing the running. "The siege has ended at the castle. The enemy packed up and retreated. Once they were out of sight, I left to report."

"That's good news," said Derek. "Well done."

"Did you see which way the army went?" asked Darven."

"No, sir. I didn't think it important. I thought you'd want to know the fighting has ended."

"Yes. Yes, of course. See to your horse."

"Thank you, sir. M'lord."

As he led his horse away, Derek noted the worried look on Darven's face.

"What concerns you? I thought you'd be happy the siege ended."

"I am, my lord. My concern is where they will go once they leave the castle. If home, then yes, I'm happy. However, if they decide to try a smaller holding, they might come here."

That sobered Derek's good mood. He shouted after the rider. "Did you travel the entire way on the road or did you cross the river?"

"Didn't want to chance the river crossing alone, m'lord."

"Okay." He waved the man on and made some mental calculations before speaking. "So if Martin left before seeing where Bertrand went and it takes three days' journey to travel by road, figuring that he was moving faster than an army, we have at best two days. At worst, one."

"If they're coming here."

"Yes. If."

Derek paced. "They're coming, aren't they?"

"Aye."

"I guess we better step up our efforts, then."

"Let's eat first," Darven said. "Who knows when we might be able to have a meal together again."

The hall was alive with the news. Derek took his seat and listened and watched. He wondered if they realized the castle's good news might be the keep's bad news. He wasn't about to destroy the pleasantness, at least not until they'd finished eating.

As the meal wound down, Derek stood and pounded on the table. The hall went silent.

"You have heard the news. It is good, to be sure. However, I must warn you that just because the castle is no longer in danger does not mean we are safe. We need to finish our tasks, even if the threat never comes. It will be done for whatever may come our way. I know it's neither easy nor popular. You've achieved so much already. Let's not leave the job half done. Ah, thanks."

He strode from the hall, the echo from his boots the only sound.

The afternoon was much the same, but Derek noticed less intensity and drive to the effort. Darven sent two riders out to relieve the other scout. An hour before sunset, the second gate track was done. The wooden shields had been set in the wall along the front. The armorer reported two hundred more arrows finished, which was halfway to Derek's goal. The blacksmith, though happy to have one less metal sheet to pound out, was still angry about having to do the first one. He was nearing completion of the third section.

As the sun set, Derek and Darven stood on the parapet and looked out over the land. Derek pictured the crops flattened by a thousand men ready to lay siege to the keep. Did Bertrand still have two thousand men after his sneak attack and his failed effort at the castle? If he only had eight hundred, would it matter? Thinking he could stop the eventual fall of the keep was folly.

He had to find a way to lessen the odds even more and delay the attack for as long as possible. All day he'd been trying to figure out ways to do that. An idea occurred based on the minutemen of Revolutionary times.

"I have an idea to delay Bertrand's army, but it will take skilled men who may lose their lives in the process."

Darven said, "This is war. They may lose their lives anyway."

"I want to send ten archers out on horseback to the bridge."

Darven caught on immediately and stood erect. "Narrow passage. Great ambush."

"Exactly. They need to hold them as long as possible, then retreat. They can move down the road, set another quick ambush, and ride away. If they harass them enough, it will cause loss of life and time, and frustrate the advance. Perhaps it can buy us a day or so."

"I shall see to it in the morning."

It was the end of another long day, but not as exhausting as the previous one had been. Still, when it came time for sleep, he was more than ready. He patted the older man on the shoulder and went to his room.

Derek hadn't given any thought to traveling all day. It bothered him that he was getting used to his new world, like it was a given he'd spend the rest of his life there.

He sat in bed and added up the hours. If his count was right, he had now been in this world for more than two full days. Less than a day was all he had left before the change became permanent. *What about Jackie?* He prayed she was safe.

Would he travel tonight? He hoped so, because if he woke in the same bed, it meant he was that much closer to being the lord of the keep. As romantic as his creative mind found it, this was not his time or his world. He needed to go back, if only to finish his book.

His story had lost credibility with the lady, so he doubted she'd come tonight. Still, he fought to stay awake in hopes she would return.

He was in twilight when the door opened with no proceeding knock. Eldina entered, saw him awaken, and glided toward the chair without speaking.

"My lady, please. Sleep in the bed. I'll take the chair."

She stopped. He saw the idea had appeal. Then he remembered he had to be in the bed to travel, or so he thought. How did he explain that to Eldina without sounding like he was only trying to get her into bed?

"Or perhaps you will trust me enough to share the bed? I promise I will stay on my side."

"I'm not sure of the wisdom of sharing a bed. After all, I only have your word that you won't attack me, and if your story holds the tiniest thread of truth, it wouldn't be proper to share a bed with you since you're not my husband."

"Maybe not, but we've already shared so much more than that."

Her face reddened, although Derek wasn't sure if it was embarrassment or anger.

"Come, my lady. Get on the other side. You should at least be comfortable during your vigil."

She hesitated, took two steps and stopped. then, like she was thinking, *Oh, what the hell,* she walked around the bed and sat on the edge. Derek tried not to think about the last time they were in this bed together, but the image was too strong. He turned away from her to hide the reaction.

His back to her, he felt and heard her shift into a more comfortable position. To mess with her, he turned over fast and she almost leaped off the bed.

"Just wanted to say good night." He rolled away from her, fighting back the laughter.

"You were being funny, weren't you?"

"Who, my lady? Me?"

She didn't respond, but he felt her return.

"My lady, let me stress the importance of you staying awake and not being on the bed when Erek returns. You must either quickly subdue him or leave the room."

She did not respond. He lay quiet and soon drifted into a light sleep.

It came upon him so fast that Derek was seconds from landing before he realized he was traveling. He waited until the effects wore off before opening his eyes.

"You'd better tell me something, you bastard. And it better be the right something, or I'll beat the shit out of you again."

Jackie stood over him with a rolling pin.

As fast as he could get the words out, Derek said, "I love you, Jackie."

"And you damn well should."

CHAPTER THIRTY-FIVE

Derek flopped back and covered his face with his hands. "Damn!"

"Hey bud, I don't care what you had to deal with. It couldn't have been worse than what I did."

Derek sat up. "Why? What happened? He didn't..."

"No, but he sure tried."

"Tell me." He patted a spot on the bed next to him.

"Huh! You two are alike in some ways."

"Well, then pull up a chair. The sight of you standing over me with a rolling pin is a bit unnerving."

"I got news for you, bud. Wherever I sit, I'm keeping the rolling pin. I may carry it with me wherever I go from now on."

As Jackie turned her head, loose hair fell away from her face, exposing a dark spot on her cheek. Derek bolted from the bed, causing her to jump and scream.

"What happened to your face?"

"Nothing. Leave me alone."

"Hush. Hold still."

She allowed him to brush her hair back.

"Oh, Jackie. Did he do that?"

She lowered her gaze. "Yes."

"What else did he do?"

She lifted her gaze to meet him. Anger flared to life. "Nothing. I didn't give him the chance."

He drew her close and embraced her.

"I'm so sorry."

"Don't worry. He didn't come away unscathed."

"Please forgive me for putting you through this."

"I'll forgive everything if you deliver a bestseller."

"I will. It's close. One way or another, it will be over soon."

She pushed back from him.

"What's that supposed to mean?"

"This was a very informative trip." He let her go and climbed back on the bed. Propping some pillows up, he leaned back.

"Oooh! This sounds promising. Tell me everything."

"You first. I want to hear what this asshole did."

"Deal. Scoot over."

Jackie crawled up next to him.

"Well, you asshole, you left before I got here, so when I walked through the door, he was already here. I thought it was you at first, except you don't usually walk around the apartment naked, and of course, he didn't have your scars.

"We kinda froze in place, seeing each other. When I ran for the stun gun, he came at me. He caught me and pinned me against the wall. He controlled my hands and thought he'd won, but he's never dealt with a modern woman. He was so sure of his conquest that he pressed in and rubbed his little pecker against me."

"His name's Erek, by the way."

"Who gives a fuck?"

"Tell me what happened."

"I blasted his boys with a knee and he dropped like a whore's panties at the wave of a hundred-dollar bill. He rolled, clutching his pathetic excuse for a boner, and I ran for the stun gun. Halfway there, I thought, *screw this!* and went back and kicked him a few times. After that, I had to deal with his crying. Christ! That was worse than him trying to stick me with his pin-dick like I was a butterfly."

Derek covered his mouth to keep from laughing.

"Anyway, I dragged his limp dick across the room and hoisted his ass up on the bed. I thought he was out of commission and tied his feet first. By the time I went for his hands, he'd recovered enough to fight me again. That's when I got this."

She turned her head and pulled back her hair.

Derek winced, looking at it.

"I wondered why your hair was loose. Usually you have it pulled back."

"I just didn't want you to get all butch and try to be the big caring man."

"And why is that so bad?"

"Hell, I don't know. I just didn't want you to worry about me."

"I do anyway."

They locked eyes for a long, emotion-filled moment.

"Don't pin me down with those bedroom eyes. They don't work on me anymore."

"I know. That's a helluva shame."

"Yeah. Well, hey. You want to hear this or not?"

Derek slid his arm around her and pulled her close.

"Easy, big boy."

"Finish talking."

"Funny; you never liked me talking before when we were in bed together."

"You've made it pretty clear that's about the only option left." The eye lock held longer this time.

"You were saying?"

"Huh? Oh yeah. So he slugged me. I mean full out, closed fist, punched me in the face."

"Jesus! I'm gonna kill that asshole."

"He hits like a four-year-old."

"He hits hard enough to do that."

She shrugged. "I fell, and by the time I got up, he almost had his feet untied. I was pissed and tired and not in the mood to mess with him any longer, so I zapped him…uh…a few times."

"A few times? How many is that?"

"Lost track after eight."

"Thank God you didn't kill him."

"Why is it all right for you to kill him, but not for me to? That's pretty chauvinistic."

"For the moment, neither of us can kill him."

"I stopped…eventually…but it wasn't easy. His eyes rolled up and he drooled like he was teething."

Derek caressed her arm and she leaned against his chest.

"So why can't we kill him yet?"

"I learned a lot this time. Turns out, it's a spell cast by a witch who was pissed at Erek for raping her."

"Really! Did you get the recipe for this spell?"

"Cute."

"Hey, I'm dead serious."

"Oh, I know. But anyway, this witch is young and lacks experience, so she didn't know about this little side effect. All she wanted to do was banish him from her world, but what she didn't know was to do that meant someone had to replace him."

"And the magic picked you?"

"I guess, since apparently I'm related to him."

"Well, that certainly explains a lot."

"What's that supposed to mean?"

"Oh, just that both of you have a problem keeping it in your pants. Well, *your* pants. I don't think that asshole has any of his own."

Derek averted his gaze. He was comfortable having Jackie this close now, and the reminder of his indiscretions hurt. He knew he didn't have the right to be upset, but as close as they'd become over the past few days made the slap hurt.

Jackie sensed his mood shift. She touched his shoulder.

"Hey, I'm sorry. I didn't mean to hurt you. I thought we were way past that by now." She gripped his chin and gently guided his face toward hers. "Really. I'm sorry. It's in the past. I won't bring it up again. Okay?"

His vision blurred.

"Oh shit! *You're* not going to cry, are you?"

Derek turned away and wiped his eyes, then tried to change to the topic. "You want to hear the rest or not?"

"Please. Continue."

CHAPTER THIRTY-SIX

Derek told her everything. Unless she asked a clarifying question, she stayed quiet, absorbing his words with visible astonishment. As he finished, she mulled the story over before asking, "Derek, you don't wish you were living there, like forever, do you?"

He thought about the question. "Sometimes, I think I do. Of course, if I don't find a way to break the spell, I might not have a choice."

"This is crazy. It can't be happening. This is the kind of shit that comes out of author's heads all the time, but I've never read a manuscript and thought, 'Wow! This is real!' There has to be something we can do."

"Yes. I can find a way to kill him, but it can't be here, or..."

"Yeah, I know; you will be stuck in the other place."

"I don't know how much time I have left. Each time I stay there longer. Based on the length of time for this last one, I may have only one more trip before it's permanent."

Jackie clutched at Derek and pulled him tight into a hard, emotion-filled embrace. "That can't happen. I can't imagine not seeing you again."

"Don't worry. I'll finish the book before I go."

She slapped him across the chest. "Hey, that's not what I'm talking about. But that'd be nice."

He smiled.

"Seriously, Derek. I would miss you. I mean, even though we're not together anymore, I still treasure your friendship."

"And what if that's not enough for me?"

"I'm sorry, Derek. I have nothing else to offer you."

"Then I'm better off in the other world. At least I have a wife there. Even if she does hate me."

"Please don't say that. Don't even think that."

"Why? What's the difference? You want it all, but I don't get anything."

"I don't know what to say."

"No, you've said it all. I'm going to get some sleep before I start writing. You should probably go."

He rolled onto his side away from her and pulled the pillow down under his head.

"Derek."

He didn't reply.

"I do still love you. I'm sorry it isn't the way you want it to be."

Yeah, he thought. *Me too.*

He woke four hours later. To his surprise, he found Jackie curled up next to him, snoring softly. He watched her for a moment, then got out of bed. He went to the bathroom, dressed, and sat down at his laptop. For several minutes, he stared at the screen, then shifted his gaze to the sword. He touched the scabbard, memories flooding back. As the story replayed in his mind, he put his fingers to the keys and typed.

Hours went by. It was as if he were nothing more than a conduit as the words flowed through his body from some distant source. His desire to finish before being transported for good was his driving force.

He didn't glance up when Jackie placed a coffee cup on his desk. He was only vaguely aware it was there. He briefly glanced her way when she came out of the shower wearing his bathrobe. By dinner time, he risked breaking his flow by looking at her as she placed a plate with a baked chicken breast, wild rice, and broccoli on it. He ate without tasting it, not stopping.

Time ceased. It was him, the story, and the laptop. Nothing else existed. As the story reached its current stoppage, Derek pushed back from the desk and stretched, arching back over the chair. He realized darkness had fallen and glanced at the clock on his laptop. Ten-sixteen.

"I can't believe it," he said.

"Can't believe what?"

Derek jumped from the chair. It slid across the floor, toppling over as it hit the mats.

"Damn, Jackie! You scared the shit out of me. When did you get back?"

"Honey, I never left."

"You've been here the whole time?"

"I didn't want to disturb you. You were deeper into the zone than I've ever seen you. Did you finish?"

"As far as I can for the moment."

"Oh. Does that mean you'll be going back?" She sounded concerned.

Derek walked toward her, a need to hold her driving him. "I don't think I have a choice. If what the witch said is true, it's going to continue to happen unless I can find a way to stop it." He held out his arms for her, but she stepped back from his reach.

"Are you sure you want to end it?"

The question surprised him, but not because she asked it. He was surprised at his lack of an answer.

She stepped into his embrace and pressed her face against his chest. "You do want to stay there, don't you?"

He held her. "Would it really matter?"

"How can you even ask that? You may be a dumb ass dip shit, but that doesn't mean I don't still have feelings for you."

Derek placed a finger under her chin to lift her face. Jackie resisted at first, then allowed it. Her eyes were full of tears. He tried to speak but the words were stuck in his throat. Their eyes held, and slowly their lips were drawn together. They touched, then repulsed like a static charge had sparked. A fraction later, they dove toward each other, embracing in a frantic passionate kiss. A hunger engulfed them, stealing their breath.

They broke apart and reconnected more frenzied, the need unquenchable.

Jackie pulled him back toward the bed. He did not resist. Why she was allowing this to happen did not matter to him. He wanted her; needed her desperately. As her legs hit the bed and she scooted back, Derek broke the lip lock, looked at her, and to his disbelief, asked, "Jackie, are you sure about this?"

"No, so don't make me think about it."

She clawed him up on the bed, her nails biting deep into his back. She spread her legs and he crawled between them, kissing her hard again. She pulled at his shirt, yanking it over his head, and tossed it to the floor. She shoved him on his back and unbuttoned her blouse. It joined his shirt on the floor. She unfastened her bra, whipped it off and flung it, but before he could get much of a glimpse, she was on top of him again, pressing down in a fierce attempt to meld with him.

He slid his hand between them to caress one of her small, pert breasts while she worked on his pants. He kissed her neck. She tore his pants down, leaving several long scratches from her nails. Her hand found his erection and she stroked it as she attacked his mouth with hers.

Derek moaned, then his eyes flew open wide. "Oh God, no!" The traveling feeling was coming.

Jackie broke the kiss, misunderstanding his exclamation. "Don't you dare—"

"Please God, not now."

The way he said *please* made her stop and look at him.

"I'm sorry." The bottom fell out of the bed. "Get off the bed, Jackie!" he screamed, but he was traveling and had no idea if she heard or understood him.

"Jackie!" he shouted.

As the other ball of light approached, Derek put his hands on the side of his vessel and tried to push it into the path of the other one. Although the ball of light did not move, he discovered his hands extended outward as the wall gave way, taking the shape of the push. Desperate to stop his doppelganger, he reached as far as he could, hoping the briefest of contact might throw Erek's bubble off course, perhaps even sending him to a different world.

The bubble rushed past, mere inches from his reach.

"Damn! No! Jackie!"

CHAPTER THIRTY-SEVEN

Seconds later, he landed. Derek pounded the bed wildly with his hands and feet like a three-year-old having a meltdown.

The door flew open and Darven charged in. "Listen, you coward. I don't care if you are too afraid to stand and fight, but you owe it to the people who will fight and die here today to at least make an appearance and bolster their confidence."

Derek sat up. "Huh?"

Darven scooped up some clothes scattered on the floor and pitched them at Derek. "Get dressed now, or so help me, I'll drag you naked and dangle you over the wall for Bertrand's archers to take target practice on."

Derek stood and dressed. "Darven, what's happened?"

The large man paused and bent to study Derek as if he were an exhibit in a freak show. "Is that you? The other Erek? Have you returned?"

"I just arrived," Derek said, pulling on his boots. "What's going on?"

"Saints preserve us. Bertrand is in sight. He should be here within the hour. Hurry! The people must see you on the wall."

"How is that possible? He wasn't in sight when I left. It should have taken him at least two days to get here."

Darven studied him. "You have been gone near four days. Your plan to stall them worked. It bought us an extra day, but they are here now."

Derek grabbed his sword and strapped it on. He walked toward the door, but Darven stopped him. "The knife, my lord. Take the knife. If they breach the wall, the parapet does not offer ample room for swords. You will need to get close to dispatch your opponent, and you will need the knife."

What Darven called a knife was almost the size of a short sword. He slid the scabbard into the sword belt and the two men left the room.

While they jogged down the stairs, Derek said, "Have all the defenses been set in place?"

"They are finishing up the east wall now. The steel shield for the gate is done, but no one knew how you wanted them placed."

"Damn! That will take the longest. We have to hurry. Gather ten men and two heavy ropes."

They exited the outer doors, and as Darven went to gather the men, Derek ran for the ladder that led to the top of the wall. Once there, he was met with silence from the men and a line of wooden shields, erect and standing at attention.

He stepped forward and looked out over the land. A few stragglers ran toward the gate. The head of the army was in view, but the end was not. A lance of fear pierced him numb for a moment. How big was the invading force?'

He lowered his head and forced his breathing to a steady rhythm. Clearing his mind, he went through a mental checklist of things to do. The space between the shields was about eight inches. That gave the archers enough room to shoot in a wide arc.

He looked up and down the line of defenders. There were precious few of them. "Does everyone have enough arrows?"

"How do we know what's enough?" one man asked.

Despite his nervousness, Derek smiled. "Good question. I suggest you make every shot count. Use the shields for protection. Shoot and duck back while you set another arrow. Don't stand there and make yourself a target. If they set the shield on fire, let it burn. That will prevent them from scaling the wall in that spot. Once it burns through, knock it down on top of the invaders. Remember, you are defending your home and your families. We stand together."

"Begging your pardon, m'lord, but while *we* are standing together, where will you be?"

A few others grumbled their agreement.

"That's a fair question. I will be here at your side. We will fight together. This is my home too. If the bastards want it, they'll pay a high price to get it."

"My lord!" Darven called from below. "We're ready."

Derek climbed down the ladder, jumping the last few feet. He ran through the gate, stopping at the crowd of men. Eyeing the metal shields, he noted one did not have the holes he'd requested, but then remembered one had already been done before he gave the order. That had to go first.

"All right. I need five men on that side and five on this one," Darven commanded, and they stood ready. "Darven, take those two ropes and have the men above throw them over the arch so they dangle on this side."

Darven looked at the steel plate, clearly confused.

"We can handle this. I need those ropes for the next one. Hurry."

Darven ordered one man to pick up the ropes, and they climbed the ladder.

"On my call," Derek instructed. "We will lift this shield, walk under the arch, and set the bottom into those two tracks." He pointed to the newly constructed stone.

"It will be heavy. Do not go too fast. If you lose your grip, call out so it doesn't get dropped on someone. Questions?"

Some showed obvious signs of confusion, but Derek didn't have the time or patience to explain further.

"Okay. On three." He bent and slid his fingers under one end. The men did the same. "One, two, three. Lift!"

A chorus of grunts burst out. The men strained under the weight, but the shield lifted. "Now step. Step. Step." Derek gave the command twenty times before the shield was close to its placement. "Set it down."

The men panted, sucking in deep breaths.

"We're almost done." He pointed to an opening in the front of the track. It was going to be tight, but they had to make it work. "We have to lift it high enough to slide the bottom into these two spaces. Once it's in, the rest will be easy."

The men didn't look so sure.

"Come on." He counted to three again and the plate rose. With the plate touching the track, but not quite high enough, he shouted for Darven to bring more men. The extra hands made the difference. Derek guided one end while Darven did the same on the other side. The ends slid in and the men walked the top of the plate forward. The fit was snug, and for a moment Derek feared it would not go in, but with a hard push, the metal slid down and dropped with a thud.

A small cheer of victory rose from the already exhausted men. But with three more to go, Derek wondered if they'd have enough energy left to fight.

"Darven, send the masons to close in those holes. The rest of you follow me. We have to move fast."

Derek showed them how to tie the ropes through the two holes. Then he instructed Darven to grab another ten men and put five on each rope. This time, with men pulling on the ropes and lifting, the metal plate rose with ease. The men walked it into the arch, where it was hoisted to the top of the track. Derek had to climb to guide the end into the slot, but once in, the plate slid home with little trouble.

"Quick, men! Two more."

Now that they understood what was needed, the third and fourth plates were seated in a short time. The men took turns climbing up the ropes to get inside the keep. Derek waited until the end before taking his turn. By then, the head of the army was less than half a mile away.

Two wooden shields had been taken down to allow the men room to get over the wall. As he stepped on the platform, they were replaced. Darven came to his side.

"Let's do a checklist." Derek scanned the walls. "All the shields are up?"

"Aye."

"The arrows distributed?"

"Aye."

He had seen the spike rails were in place along the outer walls. "Have the workers continue to make them. Is the stand in place in the arch for our men to shoot over the metal shield?"

"Aye."

Derek looked around, hoping for a brainstorm of anything else he could do. Two thoughts vied for attention. "Are all available men on the wall?"

"Yes."

"What about any women who can shoot a bow?"

"Women, my lord?"

"Yes, women. Surely, we have some women capable to fight."

He gave Derek a confused, blank look.

"Bring them all together in front of the keep. I will address them."

"Yes, my lord." Darven climbed down and ran across the yard. Derek looked out at the opposing force. The leader rode to the left. Row after row followed but the rear of the column was still not in sight. Derek sighed. *My kingdom for an airstrike.*

CHAPTER THIRTY-EIGHT

Derek walked up the stone steps of the keep and turned to face the gathered inhabitants.

"You know what's coming and what may be in store for us. To have a chance to survive, everyone will have to contribute. Any of you who feel comfortable using a bow should go to the armorer and get outfitted. I will need some of you to stand here across the top of the steps. Others should go inside the keep and take a position in the windows.

"If any of the enemies get over the wall and inside the keep, it will be up to you to shoot them. We don't have enough men to help you.

"For the women and children not fighting, I expect all of you to cut bandages and prepare to help the wounded. A few of you grab buckets and fill them with water. If a fire breaks out, douse it. Don't let it get out of control. Stay calm no matter what. You know what's in store for you, should they win.

"I need six boys who can carry a bucket or torch."

He looked around the group of women and children. No volunteers raised their hands.

"Mothers, they will not be fighting, although they'll be close enough to it. As the battle develops, the enemy will use ladders and ropes to climb over the walls. I need this fearless band of warriors to stop them. I'll need two on each side. One will hold a bucket, the other a torch.

"Every time you see an opponent, the bucket carrier will dribble oil on the top of the ladder or rope. The second person will set the torch to it. Six brave lads?"

Eight hands went up from six boys and two girls ranging in age from six to fourteen. Derek told the two youngest boys to help their mothers, then sent the other six volunteers for the equipment they needed. He looked at the anxious faces. "May God be with us," he said.

"My lord!" Darven called from the front wall. "Riders approach under a white flag!"

It had begun. Derek ran for the ladder.

On the wall, Derek watched as a contingent of six riders came forward. A majestic figure on a large white horse led the way. Derek assumed this was Bertrand. The riders stopped, and Bertrand signaled to one of them. That man drew his bow, set an arrow to the string, and fired in a high arc. It fell ten yards short.

Derek gave Darven a quizzical look.

"They're making sure they are out of range of our archers, my lord."

Derek nodded his understanding. "Huh." He turned to the nearest archer. "May I use your bow for a moment?" The nervous young man was only too happy to give up the bow. Derek drew back the string to test it. It would do. He nocked an arrow and took aim, then angled the bow up a few more degrees before releasing it. The arrow shot into the air, reached its pinnacle, then descended, sticking into the ground ten yards beyond the riders. The group turned in circles as the horses stamped and whinnied. The startled riders looked ready to flee until Bertrand barked at them.

Some of the men cheered. Derek handed the bow back and smiled at Darven.

"If you knew you could reach him," Darven said, "Why didn't you bury the point in his black heart?"

Derek stopped smiling and looked at the group of riders. The thought hadn't occurred to him. That was stupid. To save face, he said, "They were under a white flag."

Darven frowned. "Indeed."

"Do they want me to ride out there?"

"Yes, my lord, but it is permissible to send a delegate. I will meet with them."

"No," said Derek. "I'll go. I want to take the measure of this man. I want to get inside his head if I can."

"Inside his head? Are you speaking of magic?"

"No, Darven. I want to mess with him." Derek could see that didn't help Darven understand any better. "I want him to fear us rather than the other way around."

"Ah! But, my lord, how will you get to him? You can't pass through the gate."

"Lower a rope and I'll climb."

"Do you plan on lowering your horse as well?"

Darven was making his point, but Derek was annoyed.

"Then I'll walk."

"No. That will be a mistake. You will be out there with no protection. Their horses can run you down before you ever reach the wall. Let me go."

"Do you have so little regard for your archers? I will stay within range. If Bertrand makes a move toward me, he will have to come into range. Shoot him. That may end the war. If the opportunity presents itself, I may take him out myself."

"White flag, remember?"

"Hey, you're the one who wanted me to shoot him."

"My lord, there is no honor in murdering your enemy."

"No, but we all may live longer. Don't worry. I plan to challenge him. Winner takes all."

Darven exhaled a long blast of air.

"In that case, you should let me go."

"Darven, these people need you a lot more than they need me."

"And again, I say I should go. No offense, My Lord, but I'm a better fighter than are you."

"I can't argue that. All right. I won't challenge him. But I am gonna screw with him. Get a rope."

Several minutes later, Derek was lowered to the ground. He looked up at Darven. "Don't let those men wander from that rope. If I'm running, I want to get to safety as fast as possible."

"Aye. Run fast."

Derek did a double-take, thinking the man was being funny, but he'd pulled back out of sight. He drew in a breath and tried to make himself look bigger, then strode with false confidence toward Bertrand and his entourage.

He stopped ten yards from the horsemen.

The stout man in the vibrant purple cloak leaned forward and eyed him with curiosity. "And who might you be?" Bertrand asked.

"I am the lord of this keep, sir. What brings you to my gates? I don't remember sending any feast invitations."

Bertrand chuckled. "You are in good humor. I like that. It's important for a man to be as happy as he can be before he dies."

"Die, sir? I don't plan on dying anytime soon."

"Plans do change."

"If you intend to make camp, please do so to the side of the road so that our daily business can resume."

"Of course. Far be it for me to come between your people and their daily routines. It would be a shame, though, to have to kill anyone who leaves the keep."

"That would not be polite or noble. We have done nothing to raise your ire or deserve your threats."

Bertrand's face reddened. "Nothing?" he yelled. "You don't remember attacking us from behind and sneaking up on my army in the night like the cowards you are?"

"No, I don't recall any such thing. Are you sure you're at the right keep? It would be a shame for so many of your men to die for your simple mistake."

"It will not be my men who die. Your entire populace shall be put to death. I will own these lands, and then return to the castle and take that as well."

"Such lofty goals. I wonder if you're the type who throws a tantrum when he doesn't get what he wants."

"Oh, I will get my way. How many men do you have guarding those walls? Fifty? Sixty? I will crush them like bugs beneath my boot."

"Brave talk for a man who stays at the back of his army and watches his men get mowed down. Your leadership abilities are a major question to those who serve under you."

"You are a bug that I will squash personally."

"I look forward to it. Perhaps we can save a lot of lives if the two of us fight it out."

The challenge made him blanch. Derek doubted the man had ever fought. But he couldn't have risen to power unless he could fight.

"Well, Brigand? Will you stand and fight, or will you pass off the challenge to one of your lackeys like the coward you are?"

The man to the right of Bertrand drew his sword. "Let me run the braggart through, Your Majesty."

"Your Majesty?" Derek laughed loud. "What could you ever be king of?"

"Your land, for one."

The other riders all held a weapon, begging for the honor to cut Derek down.

"That remains to be seen, *Your Majesty*," he said with a mocking tone and bow. "You seem to have forgotten you are out here alone with no one to help you. You are a long distance from safety. I could end this battle right now."

"You could if you were so low as not to honor your own white flag."

"As you say, I'm a brigand. What do I need with honor when I rule these lands?"

Bertrand motioned to one of his men, and he pulled his bow and an arrow. He drew the string taut. Derek saw his death on the tip of the arrowhead. Despite his bravado, his stomach clutched. His mouth went dry and his pulse quickened.

Bertrand was amused by Derek's sudden silence. His hand raised, ready to give the order to end Derek's life. "What's the matter? Not so bold with your words now, are you?"

Derek waited, ready to dodge. He didn't believe Bertrand would give the word, but it didn't ease his anxiety. Then, to his surprise, the hand fell. Derek dove as the arrow whizzed past. He rolled and came to his feet, drawing his sword.

He ran straight at Bertrand, noting with satisfaction the wide-eyed look of shock. The rider to the right moved to intercept him, sword raised high, ready to strike a death blow on top of his head. As the sword descended, Derek pivoted at full speed, like he was on a basketball court. Ducking under the horse's head, he came up next to the rider as he adjusted his sword above Derek's head. Before the blade swung down, Derek lunged upward, impaling the man through the gut. The blade fell from his grasp.

Derek pulled sideways with his sword to dislodge the man. He toppled from the horse and Derek freed the blade as a second man rode forward. He squatted behind the horse as another arrow whistled overhead. Crouching, he walked under the riderless horse, putting it between him and the second rider, but the move put his back toward the archer.

Derek swatted the horse's rump with the flat of his sword. As the horse bolted across the swordsman's path, Derek went around the scared beast, finding an opening and driving the blade into the rider's hip. He cried out and tried to turn the horse away from Derek.

Derek's luck held. As the horse moved, so did he, just in time to avoid taking a shaft in the back. Instead, the arrow bit into the horse's flank. It reared up, throwing the rider.

The other two swordsmen rushed to protect their leader. Bertrand backed away. Fear now creased his arrogant face. The archer was left alone, and he was the most dangerous threat. Derek pulled the knife from his belt, and as the archer nocked another arrow, he hurled it. He only intended to throw off the shot, which he did by striking the horse on the head. The blade didn't stick, but the frightened horse reared up and bolted, sending the arrow wide by twenty feet.

Derek charged, shouting a war cry.

The trio of riders protecting Bertrand closed around him and fled. The archer gained control of his mount, swung around, and reached for another arrow. However, by the time he had the string drawn back, Derek was upon him. He launched at the man, sword first. He caught the man in the side, the blade ripping out through his back. He screamed, kicked his horse into motion, and rode after the fleeing Bertrand.

"Who's the coward now?" Derek shouted. He tilted his head back and howled at the sky. Finished and feeling good about himself, he suddenly noticed two dozen riders bearing down on him.

"Oh shit!"

Derek turned and ran as hard as he could, knowing all the while it was a race he could not win.

The thundering hooves came closer. The distance to the wall seemed to get farther rather than closer, as if saying, *Don't bring your troubles to me.*

He ran, telling himself not to look back. *It will only slow you down.* Yet, even knowing that to be true, he couldn't prevent his head from turning. The riders were ten yards behind. They all held swords up, ready to end his life with a single strike.

Then, a dark cloud blocked a portion of the sun and passed overhead. Horses whinnied and men cried out. The pounding of certain death faded.

Derek risked another glance and found all but one rider now on the ground with multiple arrows protruding from their bodies. The lone rider had two arrows in him, one in the leg and one in the shoulder. He turned his mount and fled but did not make three strides before a lone arrow embedded in his back barrage, toppling rider and horse.

Breathing hard, Derek stopped and watched, amazed he was still alive. The horse whinnied, struggled up, and rode off. The man did not move.

A voice boomed out from the keep. "Run, you fool!" Darven shouted. He stood on the archway holding a bow.

Derek was surprised at the man's tone and choice of words until he saw another group of riders racing toward him. "What he said," he told his feet.

Though less than twenty yards, the run felt like it took forever. When he reached the wall, he had no energy left to climb and relied on the men to hoist him over. The men looked at him with a mix of respect and fear.

After his breathing had returned to normal, he said to Darven, "Fool?"

"Well, what else would you call someone standing in the open with men trying to kill him?"

"Good point."

CHAPTER THIRTY-NINE

The initial attack was not long in coming. It was nothing more than a probe, but adrenaline ran high throughout the keep. Bertrand sent only a third of his forces, his archers moving up to support them and keep up a steady barrage of arrows like deadly rain.

Derek and Darven paced the length of the walls, yelling at the men to stay calm and keep their heads down. Using Darven's strategy, they instructed the men to shoot sporadically to make Bertrand believe their numbers were even fewer than he thought.

"They're checking our strength," he said. The strategy proved out as the half-hearted charge stalled and the men retreated. "Of course it would work better, had we held back a hundred men." He winked.

"Men on the ground!" Darven shouted to those standing around afterward. "Gather up all usable arrows and hand them out. Men on the wall, you do the same."

Derek walked toward him. "Thoughts?"

"Bertrand will make us wait now to build tension. He is in control and will use it. A lot will depend on how confident he is in a quick victory." He paused to scan the ground in front of the keep. "He didn't lose but a handful of men. He will come soon, I think. Maybe by late afternoon."

"What were our casualties?"

"One man injured; a man and a woman killed on the ground."

"How?"

Darven gave him a sarcastic frown. "They forgot to duck."

Derek shook his head. He hated being responsible for others. "Stupid."

"Aye."

Derek glanced up and down the line of anxious men. Some sat. A few leaned against the wall and stared with blank eyes at the keep, lost in fear-motivated prayer. Derek empathized. He felt the fear clawing at his gut. He forced it aside and asked, "Is there anything else we should be doing?"

"Aye." He nodded toward one of the blank-eyed men. "Praying."

"Way ahead of you. Lower a few men over the wall and retrieve as many arrows as possible."

Darven turned to go and Derek said, "Darven."

The big man faced him.

"If I...if I disappear during the battle..."

"Don't."

He departed, leaving Derek with his jaw agape.

"Right."

A few women and children brought water and food to the men on the wall. The mood was somber. Most ate in silence, perhaps wondering if the morsels they chewed would be their last.

Derek took a break and went to the keep. The level of noise was cacophonous. He walked through the hall, talking ceasing as he passed. He tried to ignore it, but the silence was loud.

He paused outside his door, afraid to enter for fear of being pulled toward the bed and transported. Although he didn't think it was near the time yet, he didn't want to take the chance. By the time he returned, the battle might be over and the keep lost.

The door down the hall creaked open and Eldina exited. Seeing him, she stopped.

"My lord, is everything all right?"

He forced a smile. "Everything's grand. How is your day?"

She frowned. "You're having sport with me."

An image of the sport he'd like to have with her ran through his mind. He held up his thumb and forefinger. "Just a bit."

"Were you going to your room, my lord?"

"I was but thought better of it. I was afraid…you know…that I might disappear again."

Her young face creased with concern. She took two steps closer, arm outstretched as if to prevent him from going. "Oh no, my lord. No. You can't."

"Believe me, I don't want to. But I don't seem to have any control over the spell."

"Is there nothing I—I mean, we—can do, my lord?"

"No. And please call me Derek."

That made her blush. Derek didn't know if he'd crossed some sort of time period custom, but he thought it ridiculous that Eldina had to refer to him as *my lord* since they were married, not to mention it made him feel weird to be treated like a lord.

She bowed slightly and looked down. "Very well, my—I mean, Derek."

He smiled. Her face colored again.

"Did I speak it wrong, my lord?"

"No. No. You said it just fine. I'm sorry for smiling. I just liked the sound of *my Derek*."

"Oh." Her features clouded in thought, then brightened. "Oh!"

They stood in awkward silence for several moments before she said, "Can we win—Derek?"

He exhaled hard. "I don't know. We will give them a good fight, but in the end, their numbers are far superior."

"We still have the fallback to protect us."

"Fallback?"

Footsteps pounded on the stairs behind him, echoing loudly in the confined space. A soldier ran around the corner and stopped short, seeing the lord and lady in the hall.

"My Lord, they come!"

"Return to your post. I'll be right there."

He faced Eldina. The question about whatever the fallback was pushed from his mind by an overwhelming desire to hold her.

"I must go, my lady."

"Eldina."

"Eldina." He stumbled for words. "I hope to be able to see you again. I, uh—I..."

Before the right words formed, she rushed at him, threw her arms around his neck, and kissed him with an intense passion that made his throat constrict with emotion. He pulled her close, returning the kiss with his own deep need. They broke. Tears welled in her eyes, and his vision blurred in response.

Before he led her into his room, he gained control of his urge and pushed away. "I'm sorry, Eldina. I wish we had more time."

"As do I, Derek."

"I..."

He didn't know what else to say, so he pivoted and raced down the stairs, perhaps to his death.

In the hall, the cacophony had intensified, and he wasn't prepared for the noise level in the courtyard. Those not screaming were talking loudly. People ran aimlessly. Derek dodged and danced around them on his way to the wall. Once there, a storm of arrows descended over the keep. Several people fell to the ground as they received the deadly points.

Derek climbed in a hurry. Reaching the platform, he stepped to the wall in time to see another barrage of death falling toward him. He threw himself down against the wall. The man next to him wasn't as quick and took an arrow to his neck, the force pitching him backward and to the ground.

Damn! It is too early to start losing our people.

He looked for Darven and found him on the other side of the gate.

"Archers! Now!" he commanded.

As one, the small band of men stood, aimed, and loosed. Unable to stay hidden, Derek stood to take in the attack. What he saw iced his veins. Bertrand had sent his entire army. The ground before the keep was covered by a swarm of black silhouettes. He noted twenty ladders and one heavy log battering ram. A long line of archers kept a steady covering fire behind the charging forces.

As he watched, the racing blanket of men divided into three groups. The main host continued toward the front wall and the gate as the other two diverted toward the right and left sides.

Derek looked down to see the long knife in his left hand and the sword in his right. He had no recollection of drawing them. Looking to the sides, he saw his men focused and firing at will. He thought he should say something encouraging, but his throat was too dry to speak. He left them to their tasks.

The battle raged even without contact. By the time the first men reached the wall, the archers had depleted half of their supply of arrows. Bodies were strewn across the ground in a killing field, but the numbers were inconsequential compared to the still-approaching horde.

Derek stared, mesmerized by the sight. A loud clanging like a dull-toned bell broke him from his trance. The battering ram had reached the metal plates. The battle was on. It was real.

CHAPTER FORTY

"Draw swords!" Darven yelled. "Do not let them get a foothold."

The tip of a ladder appeared within three feet from Derek. He looked for the boys who made up the fire brigade and spotted them anchored to the ground. He stepped to the edge of the platform. "You boys! Get up here now!"

They broke from their fugue and scrambled for the ladders, the oil from their buckets sloshing down the rungs.

"Careful! You'll set yourselves on fire!" Derek admonished.

The sound of swords clanging together increased with slow but steady progression. Derek couldn't wait for the boys to get situated. He slid the knife back in its sheath and ran to a ladder, snatched the torch from one boy's hands, and said, "Follow me."

He ran to the first ladder just as the first attacker reached the top rung. He swung his sword and Derek parried with the torch. Before the man could take a backhand cut, Derek jammed the torch in his face, propelling him off the ladder and to the ground.

Derek jammed his sword's point into the wooden platform, then ripped the oil-coated torch from the bucket of the trailing boy. He wiped the dripping end across the top rung as the second assailant neared the top. Careful not to touch the flame torch to the oil, he placed the fire to the rung. It ignited in a burst, catching the man climbing. He screamed, released his hold, and plummeted, hitting a man beneath him and they both fell.

Derek hurried to the next ladder and repeated the process. He turned to the boys.

"You see how it's done?"

The boys nodded.

Derek handed the torches back. "Remember to stay away from each other. Do you have a knife?" he asked the fire holder.

The boy nodded and tried to speak but could only stammer.

"Take it out. If one of the attackers gets near the top, cut his hand. Don't try to fight him. Now go."

Derek ran back to retrieve his sword without looking to see if they'd obeyed. He gripped the sword and drew the knife, then scanned the wall to see where he was needed most. He found a trouble spot twenty yards away and raced to help. Before he arrived, one of his men was cut down. Derek ran his sword through the enemy fighter from behind. Placing a foot on the man's butt, he bore down and pulled the sword free. The man fell on top of the one he had slain.

Whirling, Derek caught another enemy swordsman jumping from the wall. Before his feet touched down, Derek's sword sliced through him. Stepping over the body, he peered over the wall between two shields and spied four more men climbing. He shouted for the fire brigade, but before they arrived, one of the fighters reached the top rung.

Derek drove his sword downward through the shoulder. He fought to hold on but after a moment, fell. The oil boy arrived. Derek yanked the oil torch from the bucket, ran it across the first two rungs and the top end sections, then stepped back.

"Fire it," he said, and the boy with the torch touched it to the ladder. In a whoosh it caught and blazed, safe for the moment. Derek moved on.

Fights were breaking out all along the parapet. Without archers to keep the enemy at bay, they climbed in relative safety. Derek saw several fires burning at the top of the wall. The boys were doing what they could, but it wasn't enough to stop the assault.

In one section, Derek saw six attackers and only two of his men. He charged them. Catching two enemies from behind, he swung the sword at one, the blade almost severing the man's arm, and plunged the knife into the second man's back. He shoved both men off the parapet to the ground, where he hoped someone would dispatch them if they survived the fall.

With his arms not yet in a position to attack, he kicked the next man between the legs from behind, doubling him over straight into the sword of the defender. Derek leaped the falling body and pushed past his own man to help the next one. They stood side by side battling two of the opposition.

His partner dispatched one as he ran his sword through the other. The third attacker managed to score a strike against the keep defender, dropping him before Derek killed him. As soon as the man slid from his blade, Derek was in search of his next opponent.

Battle lust had taken hold. He heard the growling long before realizing he was its source. He moved along the platform, his blades a blur of motion. He lost track of how many men he had faced and how much time had passed. He laid waste to all those who opposed him, leaving behind a trail of carnage.

After the next man fell, he advanced, about to strike down the next figure in his way before recognizing Darven. The man was equally possessed, his face a bloody death mask. He whirled on Derek, issuing a warrior cry. His blade descended in a mighty killing stroke. If not for his quick reflexes, Derek would have been cut in half. Still, his sword touched the top of Derek's head, nicking his scalp.

Darven offered no apology. He pivoted and looked for his next foe.

A glance showed a dozen fires. The boys had been busy. "Push the ladders over! For God's sake, push the damn ladders over!" he shouted.

He shoved the nearest one with his sword to demonstrate. "You and you." He pointed to two exhausted men. "Take up your bows and stop any who attempt to climb."

Darven ran on to the next ladder, this one aflame. He pushed it over with his sword and was on the move again, shouting commands to the men as he worked. Derek decided he should do the same in the opposite direction.

The first ladder he moved to knock down had a head in view. He lopped the top off, a mist of blood spraying over the wooden shield next to it. Before the body hit the ground below, the ladder fell sideways.

Breathing hard, he moved to the next ladder, noting the sound of sword fights was dwindling. The next fifteen minutes proved to turn the attack back. The remaining men on the ladders dropped to the ground and carried them away. Even though several of the invaders still on the parapet surrendered, the keeps men cut them down, unable to hold back the bloodlust that drove them.

A weak cheer rose from the dry, tired voices as the last enemy soldier fell.

In the fading sunlight, Derek leaned on the stone wall and watched the retreat. He glanced down to see the pile of bodies at the base of the wall. The sight made him queasy. He fought back nausea as he scanned the grounds and estimated they'd killed about two hundred men, perhaps ten percent of Bertrand's force. He had fifty archers. The kill rate should have been higher. He wondered what Bertrand's percentage was.

Turning, Derek slid down the outer wall until he squatted against it. He panned the yard. Smoke rose from a few buildings. Men carried wounded comrades to a section where others could tend to them. A headcount totaled twenty wounded. He'd have to wait for a count of the dead.

He turned, hearing footsteps approach, but was too tired to look up to see who it was. Darven slid down to join him.

"We did well, my lord."

"Did we? How many men did it cost us?"

"Not sure yet. My guess is twenty wounded and ten to fifteen dead."

"What did we start with? Fifty?"

"Once we added the young and the old, we had a few more than sixty."

"So maybe we're down by half? I wonder how many of the wounded can still fight. I doubt we can hold off another charge."

"Aye. We did well in pushing this one back."

They sat in silence for several minutes.

Darven said, "If I may say, my lord, you did well. If we don't survive the next attack, I wanted to say it's been an honor."

"Thank you, Darven. Coming from you, that means a lot." He groaned, trying to stretch out his sore muscles. "But we're not done yet. We have to plan our defense. There has to be something else we can do to drag this out long enough to make Bertrand reconsider his course."

"Without help, our options are limited."

"What about that?"

"What about what?"

"Help. We should've sent someone to the castle as soon as we saw the army approach."

"Aye. That, we should have done, and that we did."

"Huh?"

"You were, ah…away at the time. Lady Eldina sent a man over the wall so he wouldn't be seen. He was instructed to go through the woods, but he was on foot. If he is alive, he will still be two days from the castle. Even if he reaches the castle and an army is dispatched, they will have to come by the road, which leaves them three days' march."

"So we need to hold out four to five days?"

"Aye. If the lord agrees to send a force."

"Why wouldn't he?"

"Your counterpart is not the most popular man in the realm. The only hope we have is if Lady Eldina's sister can persuade her husband."

"Wow! I hate this other me."

"Aye. You are not alone. These lands would do much better if he never returned. I don't envy you replacing him, though. He has left a lot for you to overcome."

"That might be out of my hands. I may be stuck here."

"Well, *my lord*," he emphasized the words, "you may feel stuck, but we would feel relieved. But what does it matter?" He stood. "We will most likely be dead on the morrow." He winked, smiled, and walked away.

Derek sat staring out across the yard as the sun set. Yes, he would die; they all would die. But as an idea struck him, he said, "But maybe not upon the morrow."

CHAPTER FORTY-ONE

He woke with a start, grabbing for his sword. *Where the hell...?* He was on the floor in the hall with a smelly, threadbare blanket draped over him. He sat up and wiped the sleep from his eyes. The evening's memories returned in a slow stream like a scrolling sign on the insides of his eyelids. A long day had stretched into a longer night once Derek put his plan into action.

He ached from his muscles to his brain. Kitchen sounds echoed through the hall. The aroma of fresh-baked bread invigorated him. Entranced by the aroma, he stood and followed the scent. When he entered the kitchen, chatter ceased and all eyes swung his way.

He tried to avoid their eyes, not sure he would see any friendly faces.

"Can I help you, m'lord?" the short, heavyset cook asked.

He stretched his face in what he hoped was a warm smile. "That bread smells heavenly."

"Would you like some, m'lord?"

"Aye. That would be amazing."

She beamed a smile at him and gave a quick bow.

"You heard the lord. Bring him bread. Mary, bring the butter and the honey. Dora, bring that bowl of fruit. We can't have the lord too weak to fight, now can we?"

The kitchen burst into motion.

"Would you be taking your meal in the hall, m'lord?"

"Will I be in the way if I just stand here?"

"In the way? Heavens, no. Aby, fetch a chair."

"That's all right. I don't mind standing."

"Nonsense. You sit and rest and let us take care of things."

In seconds, food was piled up in front of him. He glanced around for a napkin and silverware before remembering where he was. Slipping his knife out, he carved two slices from a still-hot and steaming loaf of black bread, then speared a thick piece of ham. He laid it across the bread, placed the top slice on, then realized he'd never be able to open his mouth wide enough to take a bite. Removing the ham, he sliced the meat in half and remade the sandwich. Ravenous, he bit off a massive chunk.

He chewed, finding the meat tough. A goblet was placed close, the server backing away and curtsying with every step. He lifted the goblet to wash down the food. The strong, bitter wine helped to revive him.

Derek made it only halfway through the sandwich before a breathless teenage boy entered. "My lord! Sir Darven sent me to fetch you. They're coming."

Derek looked from the boy to the food and set the sandwich down. "Guess I have to get back to work," he said to the kitchen staff. "Thank you for the food and for your kindness."

Derek ran out of the keep and toward the ladder. To each side along the walls were the new defensive measures he'd put in place. He prayed he'd made the right decision, but with the number of men left to defend the keep, he had few options.

His simple idea had developed into a more elaborate plan. He had the men rip down the parapets on both sides of the keep. They would stand along the front wall to make a stronger defense.

While they worked at clearing away the wood and baring the ground, others took the wood and whittled spikes. They left some of the parapet sections intact and attached the spikes to them, then placed the finished product on the ground near the fence. The idea was that when the invaders scaled the fence, they'd find no foothold and be forced to drop. The spikes would slow many of them, making them easy targets on the ground. Women and some of the wounded who were unable to fight would stand at the ready with knives and swords to cut the enemy down before they could attack.

At least that was the plan. If Bertrand figured out what he was plotting, he might direct all his forces to the sides. The defenders would have nothing to prevent them from coming over the walls en masse.

He reached the wall and scaled the ladder. Darven was already there, looking much fresher than was possible. Inexplicably, his alert appearance annoyed Derek.

"Ah, finally decided to join us, eh?"

Derek ignored the jab.

"What have we got?"

"More of the same. Bertrand is starting early. He must plan on ending this today."

"Guess he's going to be disappointed then."

"That's a good thing—confidence. Let's hope it's contagious."

The horde approached at a walk in a dark wave. They were conserving energy, waiting until they were in archer range before charging all out.

Derek found a bow leaning against the wall and seven arrows laying loose on the platform.

"Where's the archer for these?"

"He's standing next to me."

Not understanding, Derek leaned back to look at the man. Darven barked a laugh. "The man standing next to me is you, my lord. I had them brought up for you. We need every man we can get since we have fewer men now."

Derek picked up the bow, pulled back on the string, and let it free. Satisfied with his power, he seated an arrow and waited. The approaching horde carried twice as many ladders this time. Bertrand had also busied his men last night.

"Archers," Darven said. As one, bows tilted skyward and strings drew back. Derek followed the commands. He knew the first few long-range shots were not aimed. They flew haphazardly, hoping with the many targets out there, they'd find a home in a body.

The command was given. "Loose."

A weak volley was launched. More than half struck home, though many into shields. They loosed three volleys before Darven shouted, "At will, men! Make them count!"

The invaders broke into a riotous charge. Again, they followed the same plan, breaking into thirds.

Derek stepped back and screamed over the din. "Archers on the ends! Target the groups going to the sides!" To Darven, he said, "Man, I hope that works."

"It only costs us much-needed sleep and perhaps our lives."

Derek stared at the big man. "You've got to work on your pep talk."

Darven winked. "What else did you have to do this day but fight and die?" He spied a head over the wall and fired an arrow. "Huh. See? Already one less." As he loaded another arrow, he said, "You can't kill them if you don't shoot, my lord." He aimed and released. "Two for me."

"A challenge, is it?"

Derek stepped between his two shields and an arrow whizzed past his face, less than an inch away. A feather etched a thin line across his cheek, burning his skin.

"You also can't kill them if you're dead," Darven said, shooting his third arrow. "Three."

Derek swallowed hard. The near-miss had shaken him. Inhaling and exhaling two deep breaths, he took his position, lined up a shot, and watched it fly. A man stumbled three steps before pitching on his face.

"I'm on the scoreboard."

"Scoreboard, my lord?"

"Never mind."

He fired his remaining arrows in a steady routine, then looked around for more. He found several stuck in the shield to his right and snaked an arm out to twist them free. He fired twice more before the invaders reached the wall. A few of the enemy grabbed the large spiked rails at the base of the wall and moved them against the metal plates at the gate, then set them ablaze. Others tipped long ladders upward toward the wall with practiced efficiency.

A ladder touched the wall two feet from Derek. He glanced around to see the fire brigade already moving toward him. Derek took the oil torch from the boy's hand and soaked the wood, allowing the excess to drip down the side rails. Exchanging it for the fire torch, he set the ladder on fire.

While reaching out, an archer from below loosed a shot that flew past his arm. He ducked back. With more caution, he peered again. The archer waited below, his string drawn back, arrow waiting to be delivered.

Curious, he changed positions and looked through another gap. Up and down the line, every ladder had a protector in place. A man stood to the side of each ladder with bowstring drawn, arrow nocked and ready.

"Do not lean out. Keep behind the shields." To the boys, he said, "They have an archer waiting to shoot when you light the ladders. Be careful. Do not lean out too far. Now go. Hurry."

The boys ran in opposite directions and regrouped. Derek looked to see where he was needed. No one came up his engulfed ladder, so he moved to an unprotected section where a ladder was in place and waited for the first arrival.

Seconds later, a head appeared, ducked below the wall, then looked again.

Sword arm drawn back level with the top of the wall, Derek said, "Boo!" and drove the blade through the man's eye. He had to push the body off the sword. An arm reached up and grabbed the top of the wooden shield to the left. Another hand gripped the right one.

Derek swung the sword, cleaving the fingers from the hand. He heard a scream as the fingers fell to the platform. As he struggled to pull the blade free from the wood, he noticed the second hand was still there. A head appeared over the top. It was two different men.

Panicked, he worked at the blade with more vigor, but the soldier jumped to the platform before the blade was free. Desperation crept through his heart and squeezed. Breathing came in short, quick gasps. Giving up on the sword, Derek fumbled to draw the knife. The wild-eyed bearded man approached, sword over his head to deliver the killing blow.

Derek managed to drag the knife out but knew he was too late. Then, in a sudden burst, the man was shrouded in flames. He screamed, dropped his sword, and swiped at the fire engulfing him. Derek stepped forward and drove the knife into his heart. The man fell, hanging halfway off the platform. Derek kicked him over. Behind the man were the two boys from the fire brigade.

"Good work, boys. Thank you. Be off."

Derek caught the next man as he leapt down. He ducked and lunged upward, catching the man under the chin. The blade pierced his mouth and continued into his brain. He looked for the next attacker and found the boys had set fire to that ladder as well. He resumed his efforts to free the sword. Still unable to get it unstuck, he successfully used the point of the knife to chip away at the wood.

With sword in hand, he turned to find his next opponent. He had plenty to choose from. He charged, catching the invaders by surprise.

Feinting with the sword, Derek ducked and slashed the first man's thigh with the knife. The wounded man lifted his leg and Derek shouldered him off the platform. As soon as his sword was clear, he drove it into the gut of the next man. His enemy dropped his weapon and wrapped his hands around Derek's blade.

Derek used him as a shield, pushing him back into his own comrades. The man gasped as the sword slid deeper into him. Derek reached over the man's shoulder and thrust the knife into another attacker's face. He fell. The man still attached to the sword tripped over the body and fell backward. Derek yanked his sword out.

With a barrier of bodies preventing the next attacker from engaging for the moment, Derek watched as a man dropped over the sidewall. A wooden stake pierced his foot, jutting through. He clutched at the wound and fell to his butt, where he was pierced again.

A wounded defender with a missing leg hobbled up on a crutch. Balancing on the crutch, he lifted a short sword and slashed it across the back of the fallen man's neck. His partially-severed head rolled to the side, lolling at a grotesque angle. Several bodies lay on the ground and other defenders moved to dispatch more. Derek saw only one attacker walk away unscathed. He took three arrows in the chest.

So far, his plan was working. But for how much longer?

CHAPTER FORTY-TWO

The line of attackers tossed their dead comrades off the platform and advanced. The narrow walkway was a blessing, as it was difficult for two men to stand side by side and fight, but it wasn't impossible. Their limited space to swing both helped and hindered Derek. The two swordsmen could not take full cuts without impeding their partner, but even without the longer-arced attacks, Derek had trouble finding an opening in either man's defense.

He parried, attacked, and parried the opposite strike. It went on like that for a long while. Derek knew the longer it took to dispatch them, the more likely he'd leave an opening. He had to end the fight now before others could join in from behind.

He threw the knife in his left hand at the opponent on the left side. The man flinched but the knife did no damage. Derek used the fraction of a reprieve to backhand a vicious cut at the man on the right, then lunged at the man on the left. The maneuver worked. The sword slid home, but with it stuck there, Derek was without a weapon.

He stepped to the side using the skewered man as a shield, just as the second man drove his sword forward. The blade sliced a long gash up his right arm. Derek winced but immediately controlled himself. He kicked out and struck the man's shin. He hopped back and prepared his sword for the killing thrust.

Before the attack was initiated, the man straightened and puffed out his chest. His eyes widened in surprise and pain and he fell to his knees. He dropped his sword and reached desperately behind him. Derek wasn't sure what had happened, but he did not hesitate. He pulled the sword loose and swept a two-handed strike that decapitated his opponent.

The head bounced once on the platform and dropped from sight. The body fell forward, displaying the arrow in his back. Derek looked down to find Eldina standing below with a bow. He blew her a kiss and she smiled and ran off to help someone else.

Retrieving his weapons, Derek moved to engage the next man. Adrenaline coursing, Derek went into berserker mode. His blades whipped from side to side in a blur of deadly motion like a human chainsaw.

He cut a path through the enemy forces until he noticed he no longer had anyone to fight. He stood alone, searching for prey like a ravenous wolf. A growl rumbled in his throat. A man approached. He saw something in Derek's eyes and turned the other direction.

"Coward," he said.

He stalked the man. Glancing back, the soldier spied him and increased his pace. Blocked by other combatants, he was forced to turn and engage Derek. Fear showed on his face. He gulped and looked ready to faint.

Derek advanced, but stopped a sword's length away. In a voice unrecognizable as his own, he pointed his sword to the wall and said, "Go. Tell Bertrand the devil fights here."

Confused, legs visibly quaking, the man could not move. Derek pushed the man's sword to the side, stepped closer, and clutched the man by the throat, pulling him close enough to smell his foul breath. "Go now or die." He released the man, turned, and paced in the opposite direction in search of his next victim. He glanced back once to see the man scampering over the wall and disappearing down the ladder. Derek smiled.

A man appeared high above the wooden shield. Derek swiped a powerful backhand cut, ripping through the man's gut. He clutched at his belly as intestines spewed out and plummeted backward to the ground.

Without thought, Derek stood between the wooden panels, leaned out over the wall, and roared. The ladder below was clear of potential attackers. He gripped the top and gave it a shove. It toppled to the ground, landing on two men readying to climb up the next ladder.

The battle raged on. Derek lost all concept of time. His right mind had gone as the violent and deadly stranger in his head controlled his actions. He paced up and down the parapet, staking out his territory. None of his men dared venture there for fear their lord was unable to tell the difference between friend and foe.

The enemy, too, knew to stay clear. The lull between attacks became longer and longer. He paced and growled when no enemy faced him. With increased frequency, he stepped into a gap in the shields and roared at the top of his lungs. Only enemy archers remained on the grounds outside the keep.

He balanced on the wall, lifted his arms to his sides, and howled like a wolf, unaware of the many arrows passing closer and closer to him. He was yanked from the wall by powerful hands. He whirled, growling and ready to cut his aggressor down, only to come face to face with Darven.

"Stay down, you fool." Darven clutched him tight and shook him. "They think you are invincible. Can't you see how they run from you? You are the reason their attack is stalling. They are afraid to face you. If one of those archers find their mark and kills you, it will be all the incentive they need to resume the attack. Keep your fool head down."

He pushed Derek away and stormed off to engage a foe. The words broke through, leaving Derek confused and exhausted. He'd never been so bone tired. All he wanted to do was lay down and sleep.

With fresh eyes, he scanned the courtyard below. The carnage amazed him. How many dead were there? A hundred? No. More. Many more. He spied his people, their bodies strewn around the grounds. Women, young men, and old men had given their lives or had been wounded to ensure the survival of the keep. The sight both saddened and buoyed him. He would not let their deaths be in vain.

With renewed determination and using his last remnants of adrenaline, Derek whirled and charged an unlucky invader who had dropped to the platform in the wrong spot. He cut the man down and hoisted the body, pitching it over the wall.

Time flew by. When the retreat was called, the sun was well into its downward arc. Too exhausted to sit, Derek flopped to the platform, then struggled to right himself. He stared, unable to think. The carnage was shocking. In his pretend fights with imaginary opponents and all his training and tournaments, Derek never had a clue what real combat in this era was like.

A figure stepped next to him. Derek was too tired to look up but recognized the boots.

Darven said, "My lord, see to your wounds."

Wounds?

He scanned his body. He was covered in blood. How much of it was his own? The sight sent waves of revulsion through him. His mouth went dry and swallowing became difficult. He had an overwhelming desire to cry. He turned his head away from Darven and choked back his sobs.

Darven bent and placed a hand on Derek's shoulder. In a soft voice, he said, "My lord, come. Let me help you."

Derek allowed the big man to get him to his feet. Once upright, Darven lifted Derek's arm and draped it over his shoulder. His taller frame made the task difficult. He got

Derek to the ladder and called down to some of the men to help him to the ground.

The men dragged him into the keep. A crude medical center had been set up in the hall. Scores of men and some women and children were spread out on the floor.

The men helped him down and Derek stopped them. "Lean me against a wall."

They dragged him back and left him propped there. "Thank you, men. You did well today. You should be proud."

They mumbled something he could not make out and left him alone. His head lolled as sleep tried to claim him. Suddenly, he heard a woman gasp. "My lord!" Someone knelt in front of him. He wanted to lift his head and look but did not have the strength.

"You're hurt." She called to someone and soon a wet cloth pressed gently to his arms. It felt good despite the pain. He knew it was Eldina. He wanted to speak but lacked the strength and ability to form the words.

He started to drift and she shook him awake. "No, my lord." He felt her lean closer. She whispered in his ear. "Derek, you must not fall asleep. You cannot leave us. Not now."

"You're very pretty," he said.

"Quick! You two men. Help me get the lord to his room."

Derek had the sensation of floating. Grunting and obscured words drifted through his limited consciousness. Softness greeted his back as the men placed him on his bed.

Eldina shook him again. "My lord! Derek! Do not sleep. Do you hear me? You cannot fall asleep."

"Then—you shouldn't—have put me—on—the bed."

The light came for him, embracing him like an old friend. He slept through the journey, waking for an instant as he landed. The vague shape of a woman hovered over him.

"I love you, Eldina."

And the lights went out.

CHAPTER FORTY-THREE

As the light seeped between his lids like a wedge forcing them open, Derek stretched. Pain brought instant alertness. His eyes sprung open and he tried to sit up, causing more pain.

"Easy, tiger. Sit back and rest. It looks like Edward Scissorhands went to work on your body."

He turned his head toward the voice. Jackie leaned over him. Another shape formed behind her. To his surprise, he saw it was Bill, her fiancé. The look on his face was a mix of confusion, anger, and curiosity.

"Oh. Company. Hey, Bill. What brings you here?"

"The fact that my fiancée seems to have moved in with her ex-husband."

"Oh. Yeah, I guess that would do it."

"What the hell just happened?" he said, more to Jackie than to Derek.

"I wish I could tell you. It's weird, and apparently, it's real. You see the difference? This is not the same person who was in the bed yesterday."

"Bullshit! Can't you see the asshole is playing you? He'd do anything to get you back."

"Bill, use your head, not your heart. Look at his body. He's bigger than the other guy."

"That's a skill that actors develop to make themselves appear bigger or smaller for the roles they take."

"His hair is shorter and way cleaner."

"Your imagination."

Getting exasperated, she said, "What about the cuts on his face and arms? Did he use some sort of acting skill to create those before your eyes? Did they appear by magic?"

Derek said, "Well, actually..."

"Shut up," she said. To Bill, she said, "You have to admit something very strange is going on. It's beyond explanation."

"The only strange thing here is him."

Jackie's anger hit a boiling point. Derek didn't envy Bill, and he silently cheered her on.

"If you can't believe what you see with your own eyes, then you need to go. I don't care what you think is going on. It has nothing to do with us getting back together. You should go before you say or do something that pisses me off enough to tell you goodbye." She pressed so close that she had to tilt her head back to see him. "You either trust me or you don't. Make up your mind, because I'm staying to see this through."

She glared at him, hands on hips. Derek smiled smugly and Bill swung a hostile look at him. His eyes narrowed and Derek thought he was about to pounce.

Bill was a big guy and in decent shape. He was good looking in a Neanderthal sort of way and made boatloads of money in the financial game. Jackie had traded up, but Derek had renewed confidence and relished the chance to take him on, though he was currently unable to rise from the bed.

"No. I'm staying. You are not spending another night alone with him." He turned and stomped to the sofa, throwing himself down in tantrum mode.

Jackie turned her attention to Derek and the anger melted from her beautiful face.

"What happened? You're covered with cuts, though none too severe. A few of them need stitches. I put butterfly bandages on them, but you need a doctor."

Derek nodded. He motioned with his chin toward Bill, asking a silent question.

She rolled her eyes and shook her head. "I'll tell you later," she whispered.

"Hey!" Bill shouted. "Don't you dare start telling secrets."

"Relax, big boy," Derek said. "We all know I'm no match for you."

"Got that right," he muttered.

Jackie leaned closer, pretending to examine one of the wounds. "Don't you start something. This is difficult enough as it is."

He gave his best sheepish look and said, "Sorry."

He scooted and tried to sit up, but his muscles rebelled. It took three attempts and an assist from Jackie. He gave a detailed account of the battle as he moved.

"God, Jackie. It was incredible. I never imagined how insane a fight like that could be. I mean, I've been in combat. I've killed and seen men killed, but there was no comparison. Most of the killing in modern combat is done from a distance. This was close quarters. Blood and guts everywhere. I was close enough to smell my opponent and look into his eyes."

The recitation stalled and he stared off into space. Then in a burst, he tossed the blankets back. "I've got to write this before I forget it."

Jackie glanced down, then behind her. "Ah, you might want to get dressed first."

"Oh yeah, good idea. We wouldn't want Bill to see how inadequate he is."

Jackie got up and Derek thought he heard her mumble, "Ain't that the truth," but it could have been his imagination.

She tossed him a robe. He climbed out of bed and slid it on. As he passed her on his way to the bathroom with his back to Bill, he pulled the robe open a bit, exposing himself. He lifted his eyebrows a few times and gave her a mischievous smile.

"You're so bad," she whispered and gave him a second glance.

Derek showered and dressed. Jackie prepared lunch for the three of them. They sat around the table in awkward silence. The only thing preventing an all-out conflict was each man's fear of Jackie.

"Did you find any way to break the spell?" Jackie asked.

Derek shook his head and talked around a roast beef sandwich. "No. I couldn't get out of the keep to find to the witches."

"Witches?" Bill scoffed. "Bullshit!"

Jackie and Derek ignored him.

"This Bertrand character has the place bottled up pretty good. I barely had time to catch my breath before the next battle started."

"How much longer is this bullshit going to go on?" Bill said.

"Don't worry your pretty little head, Bill. The end is coming soon. If I can't break the spell, I'll end up in the other world permanently. That should make you happy."

"Yeah, it sure would. How much longer?"

Derek felt the heat rise from his core. Jackie noticed the change and interrupted.

"If Derek stays three days in a row, the transfer becomes permanent. He'll never be able to return."

"Huh. Well, that'd be a shame. Is there a way I can facilitate this move?"

"Don't be an asshole." Derek thought the words, but Jackie said them.

"Hey; just trying to be friendly."

Jackie shot him her famous *shut up or die* look. Bill shut up.

Jackie said, "If I can't kill him here, somehow you have to get somebody there to kill him."

"I've thought about that. I'm going to talk to Darven about it."

"Wait, what's this about killing someone?"

"The only way for the spell to be broken is for either Derek or this Erek to die," Jackie said.

"So what's the downside?" Bill said.

Derek leaned across the table. "Believe me, if I'm gonna die, I'm taking you with me."

The two men glared across the mere three feet that separated them.

"The first macho fool who throws a punch loses me forever."

Both men were unwilling to be the first to break the stare, but shot furtive glances in her direction.

"Now, you," she said to Bill. "Go home and bring me some fresh clothes."

"What? He's here now. There's no reason for you to be here."

"I told you I'm staying to see this through. Do what I ask and I won't make it a command."

"How much longer, Jackie? You're asking an awful lot of me."

"I'm asking the man I plan to marry to trust me. If I can't get that, then our future is as bleak as Derek's."

"Gee thanks," Derek said.

"No problem." To Bill, "Now go. Bring me clothes for two days."

Turning her attention to Derek, she said. "And you need to get writing. I do not want this story to slip away."

"But it's okay if I do, huh?"

Her features softened. "No, Derek, it's not. I don't want that to happen any more than you do."

"I want it to happen," Bill said.

Jackie and Derek said, "Shut up, Bill."

CHAPTER FORTY-FOUR

Derek opened the file and sat organizing his thoughts while Jackie cleared and washed the dishes. He watched her work. A deep heartfelt sadness held him hostage. He was unable to start.

Jackie noticed and stopped working. "Hey, you. Get to work."

"Am I only a story to you?" he asked.

By her expression, Derek knew a sharp-witted reply was on the tip of her tongue, but when she caught his eyes, she swallowed it. She wiped her hands on the dishtowel and walked toward him. "Derek, what's the matter?" Her voice held the sincerity of real concern.

His voice quivered. "I'm scared, Jackie." He broke down, the tears falling in rivulets.

"Oh, honey." She rushed the last steps to him and enveloped him. She held him close as he cried, cooing comforting words.

As the tears subsided, she lifted his chin to see his face. Still in his desk chair, he looked up at her through blurred vision. "What if this next time is the last? I might not come back." He choked back a sob.

"Baby, there has to be something we can do."

"You don't really care. You just want the story."

"Hey!" she snapped. "That's not true. I'm torn up inside. I don't want you to go. I'd miss you, Derek. I mean, you're a pain in my ass, but I *would* miss you."

Their eyes locked and held. An energy spark ignited between them. She stroked his cheek. Her eyes grew moist. He saw her swallow. Lip quivering, she said, "Oh

God, Derek," and pulled him to his feet. She kissed him. Their passion fueled the spark into a full flame.

They pawed at each other, a desperate hunger driving them. She ripped the t-shirt over his head and raked her nails down his chest. He moaned into her mouth.

His hands slid down her shirt, stopping over her breasts. He circled them gently, remembering what excited her. He fumbled with her buttons while she clawed at his pants. She had them open before he finished his task. She dropped to a squat, hooking the pants and underwear and yanking them to the floor. He stepped out of the encumbrance and she grabbed his erection and stood. She led him to the bed before releasing him to finish what he was unable to.

Naked, she climbed on the bed and straddled him. Her face was flush with passion. She took hold of him again and lifted herself. As she guided him inside, she said, "God, you'd better not travel now."

She lowered her body slowly until he could go no deeper. Slowly, she rose, then back down. With each rise and fall, she increased the pace. Unable to hold back any longer, she went into a frenzy, riding him hard. He met her downward motion with strong thrusts. Their skin slapped.

Gasps and moans melded together. His hands found her nipples and gently rolled them, knowing how it quickened her climax. She cried out louder with each stroke. He'd forgotten how loud she could be. Part of him hoped Bill was outside the door.

In a final all-out flurry, they climaxed together in a chorus of "Oh Gods!"

They were both spent, but he maintained just enough hardness for her to start again after a few seconds of recuperation.

"Stay with me, baby," she purred and rode him in short, quick movements. She built again toward what she called mini Os. Her second one wasn't as loud, but she bent over him, exhaling over his neck.

"Oh God! Oh God!" She lay her head on his chest and said, "Oh God, what have I done?" She covered her face and started to cry.

"Hey! Stop that. Don't do that. Don't cheapen or ruin it for me. I'm not going to apologize for making love to you."

"It was wrong."

"Damn it!" He rolled her off him and stood. He paced in anger. "I thought you wanted this. I hoped you wanted me. I'm sorry that making love to me upsets you so much. Maybe it's best that I do go and never come back."

He gathered his clothes and went into the bathroom. He stared into the mirror and a rage built within him. He let out a roar and drove his fist into his reflection. The cuts brought pain, then clarity and calm. Pulling the shards from his knuckles, he ran cold water over his hand. He blotted the cuts until they only seeped, then wrapped a gauze pad and tape over them.

He dressed and walked out.

Jackie was dressed and stood frozen in place. She confused him at first until he realized he'd seen the same look on the enemy soldiers that cowered from him. Jackie was afraid.

"What? You think I'd ever hurt you?" He walked past. "I think I finally understand. You're no longer worth the effort."

He sat in the desk chair and wheeled to the laptop. As it came back to life, Jackie said, "Derek, I'm sorry. I didn't mean..."

"Don't apologize. In fact, don't speak. I have a story to finish so you can make another killing. It doesn't matter that I won't be here to partake in it, but hey, what do you care? You'll have your story."

"Derek..."

"No. Don't talk. I'm working. Your presence is no longer needed. Who cares if Erek runs rampant on the streets? I won't be here to care. Go! Now!"

He stared at the screen, wanting to pick up the laptop and hurl it against the wall. He gripped the edge of the table with both hands and forced himself to calm. As his breathing returned to a somewhat normal level, he turned and glared at her.

"Why are you still here? Leave. In fact, you're fired. What was the name of that agent you despise? LuAnn Something? I'm gonna call her and see if she wants to represent me. Now get out."

Jackie sobbed as she moved to the door. She gave him one last pleading glance and left. To his surprise, she didn't slam the door.

"I love you, Jackie," he said in a soft voice to the empty room.

Then he went to work.

CHAPTER FORTY-FIVE

Hours later, Derek reached the point in his story where he'd left the other world. He wasn't sure how to end it. If he never came back, the book would forever remain unfinished, though he didn't doubt for a moment Jackie would find someone to ghostwrite the ending.

He thought of Jackie and sighed. He knew she still cared for him. You didn't do what they'd done if you didn't still harbor some strong feelings. But he knew she'd never be happy with him again. She would always wonder if he was fooling around on her. Trust was difficult to rebuild. He knew he'd never cheat on her again but convincing her wouldn't be an easy task.

She had to be concerned about falling back into the same trap as before. Yes, he was angry about her comment. But did he blame her? She risked giving up her second chance at happiness by getting involved with him. Bill was a good guy. Probably. He'd treat her with respect. If Derek loved her as he proclaimed, he'd let her go.

He wished now he hadn't yelled at her and chased her away. He at least wanted to say goodbye.

Derek had one way to make it up to her. He closed his eyes, pictured the other world, and let his thoughts go. In a few minutes, he had a thread. He played with it, tugged at it, then finally followed where it led.

Opening his eyes, he smiled. "Yeah. That works." He spent the next four hours writing and rewriting the ending until he had it just right.

Derek pushed back, put his feet up on the desk, and reread the ending. "Jackie will love this." He closed the file and started an email to her.

Jackie,
I finished it. I hope you enjoy it and it sells well. I'm sorry for my outburst. Whatever happens, know I will cherish our last moments together for the rest of my life. I am composing a letter and sending it to my new attorney with a new will that leaves everything to you. I don't have much, but I hope it makes up for all the pain I've caused you. I wish you love and happiness with Bill.
Love always,
Derek

He attached the new book's file, read the note again, and paused the cursor over the send button. Once he pressed, there was no turning back. As his eyes misted, he clicked Send.

It was done.

He shut down the laptop and stretched. The clock displayed eleven-eighteen. His eyes burned from the strain of sitting in front of the computer screen all night.

Wine sounded good. He went to the kitchen and searched his collection. Finding the most expensive bottle, he uncorked it. *Screw letting it breathe*, he thought. He grabbed the biggest glass he had and filled it. He sat at the island and stared into the dark red liquid. The color was lighter than blood but reminded him of it just the same.

A violent shudder raced from top to bottom and back up again. He gulped the wine, feeling an urge to wash away the memory of the battle. Some went down his windpipe and he coughed several times. Anger rose. He pushed the glass aside. *Can't even do this right.*

All he wanted was a simple drink to relax and prepare him for the journey back. Why couldn't things just be easy? Across the room, the phone rang. He followed the sound to the nightstand, knowing only one person would be calling at this hour. Who was he kidding? Other than telemarketers, no one else called him at all.

Derek looked at the screen. It was Jackie. He wanted very much to hear her voice once more. He wanted to apologize and tell her he did love her but didn't want to argue with her, which was more likely to happen than anything else. He hit ignore, then shut the phone off.

Wiping the moisture from his eyes, his gaze fell on the sword. He slid it slowly from its scabbard and stared at it. It was nothing like the one he'd used in battle. This one was too pretty to abuse like that. He danced it across the room, doing familiar graceful turns and moves he used to like, knowing now they had no place in an actual fight.

Gliding to the table, he picked up the glass of wine and continued his routine. In a few minutes, the glass was empty and his sword play no longer interested him. But that was all right. It was his goodbye to the sword.

He slid the blade home one last time, then took the glass to the kitchen. The bottle was still more than half full. He thought about having another glass but didn't want to show up in the middle of a fight half drunk.

Derek wondered what had occurred since he left. Was there another attack? Did they hold it off? What had Erek done to screw it up? He probably surrendered.

Well, he might as well find out. He started for the bed, stopped, and went back to pour another glass of wine. With the bottle lifted, he paused. Pushing the glass away, he brought the bottle to his lips. He swallowed two large gulps, some of the liquid dribbling down his chin. He wiped it away with the back of his hand and went to the bed.

Propping the pillows up, he sat against the headboard and drank some more. It didn't taste like a five-thousand-dollar bottle of wine. He couldn't believe he'd spent that much on it, but that's what happens when you get drunk at a wine auction. He took another drink. He felt warm and dreamy.

He yawned, took one more drink, and set the bottle down on the nightstand. Too bad it was going to waste. Derek slid lower on the bed until he was laying down. The second yawn was longer and louder. His eyes grew heavy. He smiled, feeling the familiar traveling sensation.

A noise distracted him. The door burst open and Jackie ran in. It was too late, but at least he saw her one last time. She ran at him, a look of desperation on her face. In his buzzed mind, he thought, *Aw, that's nice.* He raised his hand and waved, and she was gone.

As the light took him, he wondered if he'd really seen her or if it was only a dream. Regardless, it was a nice image to keep.

Derek landed hard with a painful jolt. He was not in his bed. It took a moment for his eyes to adjust to the torchlit space. He was in a cave.

"What the hell is this?"

"Oh, my lord!" Eldina's voice cried out. "Is it you? Are you back?"

She scurried to him on hands and knees, coming out of the dark like a specter. "Oh! It is you!" She threw her arms around him and hugged him tightly.

Darven walked over and stopped in front of him. "Welcome back. Maybe you can get us out of the mess you got us into."

CHAPTER FORTY-SIX

As his eyes adjusted, Derek scanned the large, musky cave while Darven filled him in on what he'd missed.

"Your counterpart was not happy when he returned. His first action was to raise the white flag before anyone knew. With the gate blocked as it is, he was unable to send out a retinue, so he had two men lowered to the ground to act as his messengers. They were to negotiate terms for peace and surrender if necessary."

"And he didn't think to go himself?"

Darven gave him a look that back home meant a sarcastic, *"Please."*

"Anyway, Bertrand had no interest in surrender, peaceful or otherwise. He had the envoy killed and signaled a new attack. Without a stable presence and your leadership to bolster the men, the keep was taken."

"And where are we?"

"The fallback."

"Which is?"

"A series of caves in the mountain."

Derek furrowed his brow, trying to picture where a cave entrance was. He came up empty.

"What caves?"

"Originally a hideaway for the previous lord and lady, they were expanded over the years to hold the entire keep. The entrance was hidden behind the stable. Only a few people knew of its existence 'til now."

"How many of us are left?"

"About twenty fighting men. I moved the women, children, and wounded here once I saw the direction of the battle. At this moment, Bertrand has no idea where we are, or he'd be trying to get in."

"What protection do we have here?"

"The armorer moved as many weapons in as possible. Cook stocked the caves before the first battle. Large boulders cover the entrance, should it be discovered."

"Anything else?"

"Aye. The real lord issued orders for your arrest. I am to lock you up and not allow you to make decisions that will cause further ruin to his keep."

"Seriously?"

"Aye."

"And…?"

"And he can kiss my large, hairy arse."

Despite the seriousness of the situation, Derek laughed.

Darven shushed him. "Sound carries in the caves. We must tread and speak softly."

"How big is it?"

"There are four caves total. A long, narrow entryway. Two large caverns that run off the narrow one, then one about half the size of the other two, thirty yards farther in."

While Darven talked, Eldina stayed in Derek's arms, resting her head on his chest. He stroked her hair subconsciously.

"Show me around."

He tried to move Eldina aside, but she clung to him. "No. Please don't go."

"I'm not going far. I just want to see the caves."

He stood, but she held his legs like a child clinging to a parent.

"My lady, I'll be back. I promise." He pried her hands apart. "It'll be all right."

Derek left her there and walked with Darven. The big man snatched a torch off the wall. The area inside the mountain was larger than he imagined. Along the path, they passed the keep's remaining inhabitants. Most either avoided his gaze or glared at him. Darven led to the front passageway first and shielded the torch to prevent its flickering light from leaking out into the stables.

"I see the people have lost their trust in me."

"Aye. As well they should have. To them, you are a coward."

"Even though they saw me fighting?"

"That was then; this is now. As far as they are concerned, they are here because of you."

"Can this place be defended?"

"Aye. There are two places. One is the entryway. It is long and narrow. We dragged and rolled some large rocks across the path there." He held the torch out to reveal the barrier. "If they get in, they will be forced close together. No more than four men can fit and their attacks will be hindered. Our archers will keep them back for as long as they have arrows. Once that happens, their superior numbers will overwhelm us, but it will give the women and children a chance to escape."

"Escape? There's an exit?"

"Aye. More than a hundred years ago, the original inhabitants living in the caves had two ways in. When the keep was built, the rear entry was concealed to prevent enemy forces from coming in from behind. It will take some work, but if we are discovered, I have given directions for the way to be opened. I have assigned four men to the task of clearing the exit and leading the women and children away."

Derek nodded, understanding their predicament. "So we will sacrifice ourselves to allow them to escape?"

"Aye."

"Can the exit be seen from the keep?"

"No, not directly. It is toward the back and off to the side. They will have to hug the mountain until they are behind it for a distance of an hour's walk. If anyone comes to that side of the keep's wall, our people will be in view."

Derek pondered.

"What if we opened the way and sent them out at night?"

"Moving along the rocks at the base of the mountain would be difficult. A torch would be seen for a long way."

"But in the dark, they could move away from the mountain. They will have to rely on starlight to guide them, but by the time the sun comes up, they could be miles away."

Now Darven nodded. "It's a thought. The fear would be sound. At night, any unusual noise travels and draws attention. If they are caught in the open, they will be killed or taken and perhaps used as leverage against us."

"Aye," Derek said. "It's a gamble. But I think one worth exploring further. If anything, some of the barrier should be cleared away for a faster escape."

"I'll get men on that now."

"Should we have archers here now?"

"No. If one of them slips against the rocks and makes a sound or falls asleep and snores, we risk being heard and discovered. I have them waiting around the corner. They will know by the noise and the light that filters in if the opening is discovered."

"You've thought of everything."

"Everything but how to achieve victory."

"That and survival."

CHAPTER FORTY-SEVEN

Darven showed him the other caverns. One had a small pool of freshwater that filtered down from the mountain and disappeared underground. That was a bonus. They'd starve before they died of thirst.

Derek recognized a few of the kitchen staff as they walked through distributing bread, cheese, and fruit. The eerie silence inside the cave was appropriate.

They reached a small passage with another barrier of large rocks. Derek followed as Darven climbed over.

"This is the rear exit."

He held the torch up next to a massive wall of collapsed rock.

"How thick is it?"

"Not sure. My guess is ten to fifteen feet."

That was better than Derek had hoped. It would take a lot of time to clear the debris away.

"We need to start moving this now while we have the time and the extra manpower. We may not be able to get through it under the pressure of a defense."

Darven studied the area behind him.

"We can pile the rocks at the end of the passage where it opens to the back cave. That way, we can narrow the space to allow only one or two men to get through. If we have to protect the exodus, that will make it easier."

"And it gives us a fallback. Sounds like a plan."

Darven looked confused. "Aye, that's because it is a plan."

It took a moment for Derek to realize the man took his words literally.

"And a good one. Let's get started."

Darven went to get workers while Derek started hauling smaller rocks. He took them to the defensive barrier and dropped them to the floor on the other side. He was on his sixth trip when Darven returned.

Derek sat on a rock to catch his breath. He used the sleeve of his shirt to wipe sweat from his face. He stopped. Before now when he traveled, he was naked. He assumed that nothing from the future could go back in time. He looked down, realizing he was wearing clothing Erek would wear. Did that mean the spell was evolving as the time got closer to a conclusion?

Hearing the men climb over the barrier, Derek looked up at Darven. They did not look happy to be there.

"Problem?"

"Some of them took a bit of encouragement, but I reminded them of what was at stake. They may not be willing to work for you or fight for you, but they will fight for friends and family."

"Whatever works," Derek mumbled. He stood and stretched his already aching back muscles. "Have them form a chain. We can pass the smaller stones back faster and with less effort."

Darven arranged the men, and soon the process was in motion.

As they got to the larger rocks, two and three men worked together to haul them. The progress was slow but steady.

At what he guessed was a little more than an hour later, one of the men dropped to his knees and held fingers to a leaking crack in the cave wall.

"Air, sir."

Derek noted the comment was addressed to Darven and not to him and he chose to ignore it.

"We are close."

Derek and Darven approached the wall and felt for air in other places. They found nothing. Dropping to his knees, Derek turned the side of his face to where the man indicated. He felt it too.

"Let me have the torch." He extended an arm toward Darven.

The man hesitated before handing the burning stick to him. Derek lowered it to the hole and the flame flickered and danced. He swept it along the surface of the wall and found no other place where air seeped in.

"We're almost there. Let's pull more from the top. I don't want to risk a collapse."

They worked for another hour before stopping. Derek was confident the remaining rocks would come down in a hurry with minimal effort.

"That's good, men. Go get some rest."

The men didn't comment, but Derek knew it was more than their exhaustion.

Once they were gone, he sat with Darven on the barrier and stared at the wall. Darven's hand jabbed him on the chest. Surprised, he looked down to see a wineskin. Derek accepted and uncorked it and took a mouthful. The wine was strong, sour, and so refreshing. He passed it back.

"Thanks."

Darven took it without comment and drank.

"It's dark, so it's night. I have no idea how late, though. We need to keep track of the time and as darkness falls tomorrow, we send everyone out that we can. Have whoever leads them work your way to the east. It may take a long time, but it's the safest place for them."

Darven didn't respond.

"I want you to lead them."

"Me?"

"Yes, you. They will need someone with your leadership ability to see them to safety."

"They need their lord to do that."

"No. You've seen it. They respect you, not me. They will not follow me. Their resentment of me will lead to problems, which in turn may lead to discovery. If I were Bertrand, not knowing where we have gone, I'd have patrols riding in all directions. After a while, if he hasn't already, he will realize there is only one place we could be. Here. He will instruct his men to tear the buildings down and look for the entrance. They may be doing so now. We'll be lucky if we make it to tomorrow night to escape."

"And what will you be doing?"

"I'll be here buying you some time. I need two bows and as many arrows as can be spared. I would ask for a few volunteers to stand with me, but I know that unless you tell them, none will offer. It's all right. It's better that I stand alone and die alone."

"This is madness."

"It is my job to protect the people."

"No. That is my job. It is your duty to lead them."

"Eldina can do that better than I. She will need a good and strong adviser. That's you. If they are ever to be a keep again, the two of you are the best way to achieve it."

"I will not allow you..."

Derek whirled on him. "Whoa! You don't talk to your lord in that fashion. You work for me. I make the decisions. This is my keep. You will follow my orders or I will strip you of your position and find someone who will carry them out. Are we clear?"

Darven studied him for a long silent moment. "Aye, my lord." He swung his legs over the barrier and stood on the other side. "It's a shame you aren't the real lord here. The people would be proud to follow you." He disappeared into the darkness, leaving Derek to ponder his words.

CHAPTER FORTY-EIGHT

He sat on the barrier for a long time. Shuffling footsteps sounded behind him and he turned to see a hazy form materialize out of the darkness. As it moved into the now-dwindling cone of torchlight, he saw it was Eldina. He figured Darven had explained his plan to her and she was here to talk him out of it.

"My lady," he greeted.

She climbed up and over the rocks in an unladylike fashion and sat next to him. Her eyes were dim pale orbs, but he had enough light left to see they were full of tears. She slid her arm through his and laid her head on his shoulder. They sat together until the torch sputtered and went out.

Derek felt her warm breath on his neck as she raised up to kiss his cheek. He faced her and the next kiss brushed his lips.

"I wish things were different. I wish you were my true husband and we had the time to get to know each other. I think," she choked, "I think I would be very happy." She pressed her lips to his.

An internal struggle waged inside him. She was too young for him to be having these thoughts and reactions. He did want her, but even though sixteen was an acceptable age in this world, she was not his wife.

Funny, he thought. If she were older and they were back in his world, being married would have nothing to do with whether they slept together.

Her embrace tightened; her kiss became more impassioned. "We may not have many more chances. Please. Lay with me once more."

Derek tried to push her away, but she only increased her efforts. In truth, he hadn't tried very hard.

"Please, my—Derek. I know you want to. I can feel the heat rise off your body."

She should feel the heat from my side, he thought.

Her hands rubbed up and down his chest. Her kisses became frantic; almost desperate. She lifted his shirt and clawed at his bare skin. His resolved melted. Her hand found his erection through his pants and she squeezed it. All self-control evaporated under the white hot flame of his desire.

He scooped her up off the rocks, knelt one knee at a time, and laid her gently on the ground. He hiked her skirt above her waist as she wrapped her hands behind his neck and yanked him down. She kissed him hard, her tongue exploring his mouth.

He unfastened his pants and tried to kick them down his legs but failed. He groaned in frustration, broke the embrace, and rolled onto his butt to rid himself of the hindrance. Rolling back on top, he moved his pelvis and her legs opened wide. Settling in the right position, he entered her, conjuring a low moan from her core.

Derek took his time to slide as deep into her as possible before pulling back. Each successive thrust became faster until the frenzied pumping was more attack than lovemaking.

She squeezed around him and gasped as she felt the first sensation of her orgasm. His own was building beyond control, and he slid his hand beneath her butt and pulled her closer to him. They climaxed together and continued moving long after the ripples of pleasure ceased, unwilling to accept its end.

Breathing hard, sweat dripping, they held each other until he retreated enough to fall out of her. He rolled to the side and she lay her head on his chest, purring with delight and planting soft, moist kisses across his chest.

She whispered, "I love you, Derek."

Something caught in his throat. He wanted to say the same back to her, but he thought of Jackie. He still loved her, but he knew now any hope he held would never come to fruition. With tears streaming down his face, he said, "I love you too, Eldina."

They slept together in the last moments of peace and happiness they would know.

* * *

Morning sounds drifted through the caverns and woke them. It took a moment for Derek to get his bearings before sitting up with an abruptness that woke Eldina. She had lowered her dress to cover herself, but he lay there fully exposed. He scrambled toward the barrier, grabbing his pants as he went. Crouching low, he slid them on before standing.

He let out a cry of surprise to find Darven on the opposite side, a half-smile threatening to crack the hardness of his face.

"Morning, my lord." He shifted his gaze to Eldina as she stood to wipe the dirt from her skirt. "My lady."

"Sir Darven," she said.

"Sleep well?"

Her face beamed. "The best sleep I've ever had."

The opposite corner of his lips curled up to match the first. Derek found the smile unnerving. Obviously, the man had little practice with such an alien concept.

"Something you need?" Derek asked.

"Aye, my lord. If you will follow me."

Derek stepped up on the barrier to climb over, but Eldina snared his hand and pulled him back.

"Did you mean what you said last night?"

Derek looked deep into her soft eyes. He brushed a strand of hair out of her face. He searched his mind and his heart, and to reassure her, he said, "I love you, Eldina."

She smiled, tears streaming down her cheeks. She rose on tiptoes and kissed him. She squeezed his hand and released it.

Derek scrambled over the rocks to catch up with Darven. The big man did not speak as they wound their way through the caverns. Most were eating breakfast, though no fires were lit. The risk of being sighted was too great and the caverns would fill with smoke.

They reached the front passageway, and Darven placed a finger to his lips for quiet. Creeping to the wooden wall that covered the front entrance, they stopped and Darven cupped his ear so Derek would understand to listen.

He could hear movement on the other side of the wall. Damn! The opposition was closer to discovering the opening than he'd hoped. Time had run out.

They backed away and retreated to a point beyond the first curve in the cave wall.

"We need to create a diversion to draw them away from their search."

"Whatever we do needs to happen fast. My guess is they'll find the entry in the next quarter-hour."

There wasn't much time to formulate a plan. Derek spoke the first and only thing that came to mind.

"I need to get out the back and make myself seen. Bertrand will send every man in his army after me."

Without waiting for a reply, Derek took off at a run. Darven struggled to keep up. As they ran, Derek gave instructions.

"Get the men ready to defend and prepare everyone else in the back cavern. I'll need a bow and some arrows and a few men to help make a hole to crawl through."

Their dash through the caverns sent a rush of nervous chatter after them. Somewhere along the way, he lost Darven but assumed he was carrying out orders. Reaching the back barrier, Derek hurdled the rocks and searched the pile, deciding the rear wall the best place to crawl through.

He tested several spots before settling where he hoped would be the best chance to get through without being crushed. He dug out a few smaller rocks before others joined him.

"Pull from here and here as fast as you can. No, move that one. Yeah, that's good."

Within minutes, light poured in. He lowered to the ground and looked through. It wasn't big enough. The only way to widen the tunnel was to crawl inside. He did so and grabbed rocks, but there wasn't enough room to pass them back. Each time, he had to crawl back out and go in for the next one. The process was long and birthed ever-increasing anxiety. With each passing second Bertrand's men came closer to uncovering the opening.

He had opened the tunnel halfway when one man grabbed his arm.

"Let me, m'lord. I'm smaller. I can work on the other side."

"Go," Derek said. Why were they being nice to him?

He looked at Darven who shrugged. "I said you were under a witch's spell. Sometimes you were a hero, other times a cowardly fool. I told them to ignore the fool if he returns."

The man dove into the opening and wriggled like a child pretending to be an alligator. He stopped with only his feet sticking out. Derek feared the man's movements would bring the wall down on him and not only crush him but causing a longer delay; however, the man was still for only a few seconds before pulling himself through and disappearing.

Derek peered through the tunnel and a grinning face looked back. The man reached in and pulled out rocks. He made short work at widening the gap.

"Try it now, m'lord."

Derek wiggled in. He made it to the midway point before getting stuck; the claustrophobic feeling closing in on him and panic lancing his soul. Whimpering spilled from his mouth.

"Hold, m'lord. I see the problem." The tunnel rat crawled in from his end, grabbed a rock from each side, and retracted. The space created was just enough, and Derek couldn't crawl out fast enough. The freedom of the other side gave him such relief and he had to fight back tears.

They passed his bow and a quiver holding eight arrows through and his sword and knife. The other man said, "Good luck, m'lord."

"Push a few rocks into the gap, but not too many in case I have to come back in a hurry. If I'm not back by nightfall, fill it in."

"Yes, m'lord. I'll tell Sir Darven."

"Good man." Derek didn't wait for him to scurry back in. He ran along the mountainside, stopping at the keep wall. He strapped on his blades and pressed against the stone. Hearing no alarm, he crept toward the front. With the parapets torn down, he had little fear of being discovered until he reached the front.

Derek stopped and crouched at the corner. Above, he caught sporadic movement as men paced their posts. He scanned the grounds in front of the castle. Carts dotted the land as men collected the bodies of their fallen comrades. Derek wondered what they would do with the corpses.

Bertrand's camp was still where it had been. Was the man still there or had he moved into the keep? Derek hadn't counted on that. He hoped they were all inside. Pursuit would be delayed since the gate was sealed shut.

He had to do whatever he was going to do now. He looked at the woods. They offered the best cover and the only real chance of escape. The horses were still at the camp, which made sense since they were not able to climb walls. That meant horsemen might run him down before he ever reached the limited safety of the forest. He looked from the camp to the tree line and estimated his chances of covering the nearly hundred yards before a rider could mount and pursue. It was a slim chance.

Oh well. What difference did it make if he died here or in the caves? He had to protect his people.

His eyes stopped at the point where the keep abutted the mountain. He scanned upward, thinking he might be able to scale it. Feeling the weight of lost time, he broke into a run. His eyes were already searching for foot and handholds before he reached the spot.

He slid his arm through the bow and placed his foot on a protruding rock. In seconds, he was halfway up. If they ever recaptured the keep, he would have to remember to have the masons chisel here.

He strained to reach his fingers above the wall, seeking a grip to pull himself the rest of the way up. His foot slipped and he started to fall but pushed off with his other one. Lunging for the wall, he managed to snare just enough of the stone ledge to hold him.

Finding purchase again, he muscled his way to the top and leaned over the stone. He allowed a three-second rest before snaking his leg on top of the wall. Once he was sitting with his back pressed to the mountain, he slipped the bow free and seated an arrow. Now he needed a good target. He passed over several soldiers, stopping on a fat man wearing a cape. Perhaps he was an officer.

Derek tried to set up an accurate shot. He loosed the arrow and it sailed past the man, landing three feet behind. It skidded across the ground and the man slowed for an instant to gaze around.

Derek immediately nocked another arrow. As the officer continued, Derek adjusted his aim and fired. This one pierced the man through the back. He dropped to his knees and snaked a hand behind him to find the source of the pain.

It was a long time before his cries for help were heard. Four soldiers ran toward him. Derek took his time, waiting for them to stop moving. As one of the soldiers bent to the officer, Derek shot. The arrow bore through the man from behind. He fell over the injured man, pinning him to the ground.

A moment's confusion by the other men gave Derek the chance to nail another one. This time, the arrow drove deep into his target's chest. In an instant, the men were running and shouting the alarm. Crouching, Derek rose to the top of the wall and walked heel to toe toward the front. The nearest guard spotted him and drew a sword. Ten feet away, Derek stopped and lifted his bow. As the man turned to run, Derek loosed the arrow. He stumbled and fell off the platform to the ground.

The courtyard was a buzz of movement. Men ran for cover or rushed toward him. Several stopped to shoot arrows. He jumped to the platform as two arrows flew overhead. He set the next arrow to string and hit one of the enemy archers.

Two guards ran at him. He drew his sword, met the first man, and grabbed his arm after knocking his thrust aside. Derek turned the man in time to take two arrows in the back from his own men. He let the body fall and engaged the second man. They exchanged attacks before Derek saw an opening. He squatted and lunged, stabbing the man in the thigh. He cried out and hobbled backward.

It was time to go.

CHAPTER FORTY-NINE

Derek climbed over the wall and hung to lessen the distance of the fall so as not to sprain or break his leg. The wooden spike rails had been moved aside and were not a threat. He kicked away from the wall and let go. The landing wasn't pretty, but other than feeling some rocks bite into his back as he rolled, he wasn't hurt.

He got to his feet and ran with all his strength. A glance behind showed a group of men mounting horses.

At fifty yards from the trees, he glanced again. Four men rode toward him as another twenty mounted. He ran harder but already felt winded. Adrenaline pushed him, and fear stole his breath.

By the twenty-yard mark, he knew he'd make the trees, but the first riders would be right on his heels. He reached back and pulled one of his last two arrows. The effort to seat it caused him to slow, but he had to make his pursuit think about coming on too fast.

In one motion, he slowed, pivoted, and drew back the string. He drew a bead on the lead rider. He was close enough for Derek to see his eyes widen in shock. He hugged low to the horse and Derek adjusted. The arrow embedded in the rider's shoulder. He pulled to the other side and his horse veered into the path of the next rider.

Two for one. That helped. He grabbed the last arrow and raced for the trees.

The riders slowed, now knowing Derek was a lethal threat. He reached a tree, catching his breath, and used it as a shield. He drew the arrow back, and from his periphery noticed the second wave of riders angling for the woods a hundred yards down. They would cut him off and surround him in seconds.

Derek slacked the string and ran deeper into the trees. He needed to find the thickest section of branches and undergrowth to hide in, knowing the likelihood of evading the riders was nil. Still, as an area presented itself, the slim idea of a plan began to form.

He ran into the thick cover, branches ripping at his face and arms. He dove to the ground, wiggled beneath a leafy plant, and waited. He heard but did not see the horses. He could not wait long to make his move. Within minutes, the entire area would be swarming with men beating the foliage for him. He drew the sword and set the bow and arrow down.

The ground reverberated with hoofbeats. A few rode by and several stopped. The men talked about who should do what. Two horses stepped into his covered area, their riders cutting at the greenery with swords. As one horse passed two feet to his left, Derek moved into a crouch and prepared to launch. Waiting until the rear legs were even with him, he stood, grabbed the rider by his leg and tunic, and tore him from his mount.

He slammed the man to the ground, pulled his knife, and drove it through him. He snatched up the bow and arrow and went after the horse, snagging the reins. The beast shied away, but Derek reeled him in as the other rider turned to see what the commotion was about.

Spying Derek climbing on the horse, the rider shouted the alarm and kicked his horse forward. Blade held high and ready to deliver the killing blow, he closed swiftly.

Seated on the confused horse, Derek drew his last arrow back, aimed and fired almost point-blank into the rider, toppling him backward off the horse.

Knowing the others would be closing on him soon, Derek reared the horse into a turn and kicked its flank hard. The frightened horse ran hard and fast. It burst from the woods and raced along the front of the keep. Taken by surprise, the archers who had fired were well behind the racing animal. The riders heading for the trees reined in their mounts to change course, allowing Derek to get a good lead on them.

His new path held no place to hide for a long way. Trees and mountains were on the horizon, but the distance was deceptive. His mount would be long tired by the time they arrived at anything usable for cover. He pressed on, allowing the horse to run as it wanted. Derek made no effort to glimpse his pursuit. He knew they were there and that there were many of them. Glancing back would only slow him down and make him more anxious.

He rode on. A myriad of thoughts rushed through his brain. If this was to be his end, he wanted to remember everything. He wondered if Jackie enjoyed the ending of his book, even though what was happening now was not what he'd written. He thought about Eldina, the young and beautiful woman he made love to last night. He should feel guilty but didn't. What did that say about him? Was it wrong?

Certainly not in this world.

The mountains still looked to be an eternity away. He smiled to himself that the sun was rising behind him. Wasn't the hero supposed to ride off into the sunset?

Hero. Is that what he was? He didn't feel like one, but he had done things he'd never expected to do, certainly not in his world. His thoughts fell on the young witch who had cast the spell that caused his predicament and how she must have suffered at the hands of Erek. Did he hate her for creating his current situation? No. Erek deserved to be punished. But *was* he being punished? After all, he was in Derek's world; out of place, confused, and afraid, but still alive. Derek didn't have the luxury of looking toward a future. He hoped at some point that his twin in time would get what he deserved.

Beneath him, the horse began to falter. Its strength faded and with it, his lead. But his pursuit should be having the same problem. To his surprise, the trees and mountains appeared larger now.

Derek risked a look back. They were coming; many of them, but to his surprise, they appeared to be a long way back. If his horse survived, he stood a chance to reach the trees at least, even if escaping was beyond reality.

He allowed the horse to slow but kept it running. With hope blossoming, Derek worked on a plan to evade Bertrand's men. With grudging sluggishness, the mountains grew. The trees looked attainable. The small army of horsemen closed on him, but he still had a safe lead. A mile from the trees, Derek spurred the horse into a full run.

"Come on, baby. Give me a little more. We're almost there."

With a half-mile to go he'd maintained his lead. He was going to make it. A quarter-mile and fresh adrenaline hit his bloodstream. The horse had nothing left to give, though, and slowed to a walk.

No! Not now.

Though he kicked and yelled, Derek was unable to coax more speed from the exhausted animal. He was thankful it was still moving. The pursuit, however, had gained at a scary rate. Derek hopped down and ran, yanking on the horse's lead. He needed the horse in the woods to act as a decoy.

The horse trotted, though clearly against its wishes. They reached the tree line and Derek forced the horse onward, darting around trees. Once the riders were out of sight, he leaped on the horse's back and urged it forward. Fifty yards in, he discovered a stream. Perfect. The horse stopped to drink and Derek jumped down. He pulled the reins until the horse was in the stream. He let the horse drink for a few seconds, then turned it downstream and slapped its haunch.

The sharp crack echoed. The horse leaped forward and ran through the water. Derek turned and ran in the opposite direction, hoping the horse would go far enough to lead the riders away.

He splashed through the water, coming out on the opposite side. Almost immediately, the ground inclined. The angle rapidly sucked his energy but he pushed onward. His survival depended on getting far enough up the side of the mountain to be out of sight from below. That would allow him to turn north and eventually double back to the keep.

He had a long way to go, but there was still a lot of time left in the day. He wanted to be back before nightfall; before Darven began the exodus. He wanted to see Eldina one more time. The thought of her spurred him on and soon he was above the height of the trees and beyond sight of his pursuit.

Derek lost track of time and distance. Traversing the mountain was tedious, having to watch every foot placement to prevent falling or creating a rockslide. Twenty yards above, he noticed a level area. He climbed, straining to reach the plateau. Once there, he rolled over the edge and sprawled on his back, unable to move.

He wasn't sure how long he lay there, but when his eyes opened, the sun was on its descent. Somewhere below, the whinny of a horse reached his level. Derek crawled to the edge and peered down. He saw no pursuit, but his gut told him they were there somewhere, and closer than he'd hoped.

Rolling away from the edge, he stood in a crouch and ran. He had little fear of causing a slide on the plateau. He ran as far as he could on the flat area, then slowed as the angle increased and he went back to careful foot placements.

Derek walked another hour before angling downward. He descended cautiously, watching for movement and alert to sounds. He reached the tree line with what he guessed would be two hours of sunlight left. He still had the wide-open ground to cover, then had to go around the back of the mountain. He was not going to make it before dark. Resigned to failure, he said a silent goodbye to Eldina and an apology.

He stopped at the stream for a long drink. He would never drink from a stream back home, but here he gave it little thought. Besides, he rationalized, he'd be dead long before any parasites took him. His body wanted to refuse his commands to move, but in the end, gave in and complied. The effort promised much pain the next day, should he survive the night.

If he survived, it was pain he'd gladly accept.

CHAPTER FIFTY

He exited the woods thirty minutes later and started across the open ground. In the dimming daylight, the keep was only a dot on the horizon, and it had taken a while to locate it. He was farther north than he'd thought. He tried to coax his legs into a jog, but after a few short strides, they refused to obey. He settled into a fast-paced walk.

To take his mind off the distance, he thought about Jackie. He let the movie of their lovemaking play out in slow motion, savoring each second; not for the physical pleasure, but because they had shared the intimate moment. If that was his last time with her, at least it was memorable, though he wished it hadn't ended in the way it did. He didn't blame her for being angry and confused. She'd let her emotions and past feelings for him control her actions. He was glad she did, but he no longer felt the hurt from her rejection. He would always love her and would take that last memory with him until the end of his life, however short it promised to be.

By the time the scene faded from his mind, he was surprised to see how much ground he had covered. In the final moments of dusk, Derek estimated another hour of travel at his current pace. That was motivation enough to convince his legs to jog.

Though the distance was closing, the keep disappeared in the darkness. Sporadic torchlight dotted the area, appearing to float. Farther to the right, larger fires glowed, displaying the camp. Derek tried to discern if there was any importance in the small number of fires. Had the majority of the invaders moved into the keep? If so, was it for protection, or had they discovered the cave's entrance?

He increased his speed and length of stride with little protest from his body. Reaching the mountain, he veered left to avoid tripping over any outcroppings of rock. He didn't move far enough, however, and his foot caught something. He fell, swearing. He rubbed his scraped shin, then hobbled off at a slower, more cautious pace.

Frustration bloomed from his exhaustion. The mountain seemed endless, but finally he reached the far end, realizing for the first time the mountain stood alone and apart from the other ranges. How strange that was. There were mountains to the north and of course, to the west where he'd just been, but this one stood like a sentinel guarding the rest.

Derek felt his way along the wall in the dark. He stopped and closed his eyes, forcing an image of the tunnel into his mind to find clues to its location. If he remembered right, he'd crawled from the interior of the mountain less than halfway from the keep. So he was a little more than halfway, coming from this direction. But how far had he gone?

He walked bent over, searching for any anomaly in the rock surface. It was impossible. Forced to crawl, he no longer felt like he was making progress. Derek first had to find a placement for his knees to avoid resting on a stone. Then he dragged his hand along the base of the mountain and repeated the process.

He had no idea how long he'd been searching, but a sudden out of place sound made him freeze like a hunting dog spying prey. From somewhere not far ahead, he heard the crunch of loose stone. In slow motion, he slid the knife free as he tried to pinpoint the source. The sound became constant, like something being dragged across the ground. Were Bertrand's men doing the same sort of search?

One leg at a time, he lifted his knee and placed his foot on the ground. He slowly stood, ready to defend or attack. A few seconds later he heard an exhalation and the dragging ceased. A sword scraped across leather. He crouched lower and waited, trying to pierce the night, and searching for darker forms within the blackness.

For long, anxious moments, nothing moved. Perhaps he'd alerted whoever was there and he was doing the same as Derek. Standing still was difficult. His angst grew as he expected a sword to slash out of the darkness and cut him down at any second. Then the scraping returned.

Derek risked a short step, then froze again as he heard someone say, "Shush!" Now he knew at least two other people were out here. It had to be Bertrand's men. Maybe he'd figured out the only place Derek could've come from during his attack was along the side of the mountain. If that was the case, there was sure to be more than two men out here, but wouldn't they search with torches?

He backed away, wanting as much distance between him and the searchers as possible. He froze again, hearing a whispered voice. "Give me your hands. I'll pull you out." Derek mulled the words over in his mind several times in a few seconds. Maybe they were his own people. He had to know.

Moving forward, he didn't worry as much about being careful as he did distance. The dragging sound was close.

"You're free. Stand up."

Derek stopped, kicking a loose stone. The sound was like a gunshot in the darkness.

"What was that?" a frightened voice whispered.

"Shush!"

Silence surrounded them again. If this continued, the outcome would be death, and alerting the enemy with the noise of a sword fight. He decided to take a chance and announce his presence.

"It's Lord..." He suddenly realized he had no idea how to announce who he was, so he lied. "Ah, Erek. Who's there?"

"Lord who?"

"I am the lord of the keep. I crawled out of the tunnel earlier today. I was helped by a man who crawled out first to make the tunnel wider." He paused. No reply. "Sir Darven and Lady Eldina are inside, along with about twenty men and many women and children."

"M'lord, if it is you, step forward and show yourself."

"I would have to be right on top of you to do that. Ask me a question about what's inside that only I would know."

"A question?"

"Yes. Ask me something so you can verify who I am."

Derek grew frustrated, then angry at the prolonged silence. Then a female voice said, "If that is you, m'lord, how many caves are inside?"

"Three. Two side by side and one behind them. There's a passageway leading from the keep which splits and leads to each."

"M'lord, it is you!" she said.

Movement to the front startled him. A shadow advanced as if materializing from spirit form. Derek jumped, pushing the knife out. The man leaped back.

"M'lord, it's me. Jerald. I led you through the tunnel."

Derek was unable to make out his facial details, but the voice was unmistakable. "Of course. Jerald. What are you about here?"

"Leading the women and children away."

"Good. I'll help."

They spent the next hour pulling people from the tunnel. He hid when one of the men whispered, "Here, my lady." He wanted to see her, to hold her once more, but feared the goodbye might make noise or prevent her from fleeing. He wanted her safe more than he wanted one last kiss.

With everyone outside, Jerald and three other soldiers led the caravan away. Derek watched until the last man was out of sight, which took only seconds. *Be safe,*

Eldina. He crawled through the opening. Before he made it all the way, his hands connected with a large stone. To his surprise and fear, he realized they were filling in the tunnel. He didn't want to get trapped inside the tunnel and retreating backward was difficult.

Feeling an air-constricting panic tighten around his chest, Derek pushed as hard as he could on the stone and shouted, "Hey! I'm in here! Help!"

Through the rocks he heard muffled voices. He pushed on the rock in front of him and it moved. Not much, but enough to give him hope. He scooted forward and yelled again. "Help!" This time when he pushed, the rock moved a short distance before making contact with the one behind it. He pushed harder, but the rock did not budge.

Derek dug his toes into the side of the tunnel for leverage and pushed with everything he had. The rock moved, but not nearly enough. However, some of the rock walls behind and above him gave way, kicking up dust. He gasped for air. The tunnel offered little room to expand his chest. He felt a full-blown panic attack about to erupt. With no idea if he could back out, he lost it and screamed as loud as he could. Pulling the rock toward him, Derek rammed it, clacking it against the next one several times before he felt the rock give.

Seconds later, the way was clear and he saw a torch in front of the opening.

"Oh, thank God!" he said. A face appeared next to the opening. The flame lit only half of the man's face, but it was enough for him to recognize it.

"Darven, get me out of here."

CHAPTER FIFTY-ONE

A goblet of water was pressed into his hand. He had trouble getting his breath back; the thought of being trapped in the tunnel until he died proved to be a tough image to erase.

Darven said, "They were back working in the stable toward the end of the day. Their voices came through enough to hear they were chasing you. We feared you'd been captured—or worse."

"Aye," said Derek falling into the vernacular. "I shot a few of them, then stole a horse and fled. They gave pursuit, but I lost them in the woods and mountains to the west. I freed my horse and made my way back on foot in the dark. It took longer than anticipated." He took a long drink, finally feeling his body relax.

"Where are we now with things?"

"As far as I can tell, no one is in the stable. We probably have until morning before we're discovered."

"So we have enough time to get the rest of the men out?"

"Aye. But if they come in and find us gone, they will chase us. If we put up a defense here, we can stall, giving the others a chance to get far away. They will believe the survivors are all here."

Derek nodded. It was a good plan, but he wanted half the men gone. No sense all of them dying.

"How many men do we have?"

"Counting you and me, eighteen."

"How many of them are married with children?"

He frowned. "Perhaps half."

"Send them out now while they can still catch the others."

"My Lord..."

"It's an order, Darven. We can hold out here with half the men, given the narrow passages. Why should they all sacrifice their lives? I've already told you I want you gone. Take some of the men and go."

"If you want to order some of the men to go, that's fine, but don't try it with me. I will not go. There are not enough men here to make me."

They eyed each other, though neither gaze held any anger.

"Very well. Pick the men to leave. Explain to the others we will follow once we've delayed any pursuit long enough to ensure their safety."

Darven knitted his brows.

Derek explained, "If they think they are being sacrificed, they will fight an uninspired battle, knowing the end is inevitable. But if they believe there is hope for escape, they will fight hard for survival. I'd rather they have hope."

Darven left without a word. A few minutes later, he returned with ten men. Derek told them they might have to clear some debris away but should be able to get through. He wished them luck. Without much discussion, they lined up and one by one crawled into the tiny tunnel. The first one took a lot of time, but once the path was reestablished, they disappeared at a steady pace.

Once the last man had gone through, he rolled a large stone in front of the opening from the outside. Darven lifted a heavy rock and placed it in the opening at his end.

"Darven, don't. Leave it open. I doubt anyone will find the entrance before the attack. We can leave one man here to guard our backs. It should be easy to dispatch any intruders."

He set the rock aside.

"Well, I'm going to finish my wine and get some sleep," he said.

After he left, Derek stretched out on the barrier and drifted off.

The morning came too fast. Before he'd settled into a decent nightmare, Darven was shaking him awake.

"They are coming."

That was all he needed to hear. Derek swung off the stone barrier and followed the big man. They reached the front barrier as an ax bit into the wooden wall that covered the cave. They didn't spend any time finding the entrance, but instead were making their own.

Six men stood behind the barrier with bows and the remaining arrows. Two more guarded the rear entrance.

"You two kneel. You two stand." He motioned. "You two are in reserve."

"If I may, Sir Darven, have them rotate shots. First the kneelers, then the standers. With the passageway so narrow and having so few arrows, we don't want duplicate kills. The men on the left target the left, and the men on the right target right."

The ax struck again. The blade protruded through the wood on their side.

"The two men in reserve, draw your swords. If anyone gets close, you step up and protect the archers. If we run out of arrows, we will hold them here for as long as we can. If we need to retreat, run to the back barrier. We will hold there and try to escape."

A thought struck him then. "We will need time. You." He tapped one man on the chest. "Take two bows and six arrows and place them behind the rear barrier."

He nodded and ran off.

A third strike and wood splintered off.

"Douse the torches," Darven said. "Let their eyes strain to find us." The flames sputtered out. "Everyone! Duck."

A face filled the open space. "I feel air," he said. "I think there's a cave."

"Let me see," a voice said.

Derek leaped up and over the barrier. Knife in hand, he kept to the side of the passageway as another face peered in. "You're right. It's too dark to see anything."

Someone commanded, "Well, don't stand there. Take it down."

The ax blasted into the wood again. This time, Derek reached up and grabbed the ax head. The man wielding it yanked hard but the blade did not budge.

"It's stuck in something."

"Pull on it, you weakling."

The man grunted with his effort and Derek released his hold. The ax flew back and the sound of metal hitting floor reached his ears. Swearing and laughter followed.

"Here, let me do it."

The next man swung and the ax head ripped through a section all the way inside and met little resistance. Derek missed as he tried to snare it, but on the next swing, the ax hit more wood and he held it in place. Again, the men on the other side jeered. On the second tug, Derek released it, though not with the same satisfying effect.

"It's catching on something."

The blade hit again a few inches to the left of the last one. Derek caught it, but with the hole wider now, a man put his face to the gap and looked in all directions, stopping on Derek.

Feeling cocky, he said, "Hi," and jammed the knife into the man's eye.

A scream erupted, followed by a cacophony of voices. A chorus of curses assaulted him, but the ax did not fall again. He managed to stall them, but how long could he keep it up? It might have been better to let them break free and deal with them. It might have been a much smaller force than they'd surely have to deal with now.

Oh well; too late now. Derek walked back to the barrier and climbed over.

"Did you enjoy that?" Darven asked.

"Yes. Actually, I did."

"Hopefully you'll enjoy what comes next just as much."

"Only time will tell. Oh, and I think I just bought us some time."

"Aye. They will be more cautious, but now they know we're here."

"They were gonna find out sooner or later. Let's keep everyone out of sight until they come in."

They only had to wait thirty minutes until they heard voices on the other side of the wall.

Someone with authority had taken command and the axes fell, one after another. The wall splintered, creating larger and larger holes.

The defenders grew antsy. Five more swings and a hole opened big enough for a man to run through, but no one came. On what must have been a silent command, six men moved into the opening and drew bows.

"Derek said, "Stay low. Let them fire as much as they want. You two men in reserve: go around and collect as many arrows as you can.

"Fire!" The command given, the six arrows flew through the narrow path and overhead.

"Stay down," Darven said. "I'll tell you when to get up."

Another flight of arrows entered and passed harmlessly. The two chasers ran to gather as many as they could find. After the third volley, the commander ordered the advance. Derek wondered if it was Bertrand who gave the commands. If they could take him out, the army might retreat, or so he hoped.

Darven said, "Archers."

The four men got into position as a mass of humanity filled the passage.

"Bottom two," Darven said. "Loose."

The two arrows whisked away.

"Top two, loose."

"Bottom."

"Top."

Darven called out each round. The archers fired; the bodies fell. The accumulation became their own barrier on the floor, making it more difficult for the invaders to advance.

"Need arrows," one of the bottom men said.

One of the men in reserve handed over the arrows he'd collected.

The attack slowed. They no longer sounded anxious to get inside. The attackers knew that whoever was in front was dead, sapping all motivation to advance. Voices echoed in the caves, becoming louder until someone in charge issued a do-or-die order, which translated to die-or-die. Regardless, a loud rumble of warrior cries erupted; the sort used by men working up their courage to do something they knew may result in death. In a rush they came, row after row of moving walls of flesh.

They hoped to overwhelm the defenders fast, but to their credit and Darven's steadying presence, they mowed the rows down until they had to climb over the bodies. The advance slowed. Then the men entered with shields in front, which made a great difference in the limited space. Shortly after that, the limited supply of arrows ran out.

The enemy didn't notice at first, but when one man and then a second tried to move forward and wasn't shot down, the rest grew more confident and the charge was renewed. With swords drawn, Derek and company met the attack. At first, no headway was made. The limited space hindered swordplay. The man in the middle to Derek's right held a shield, further making strikes more difficult.

Derek's strategy evolved to knocking weak sword thrusts aside and stabbing with his knife. The men pressing behind could not see what he was doing, so with each opponent that stepped forward, he used the same gambit. Bodies fell and piled. Wounded men were pulled to the back. The replacements looked endless.

Someone grabbed the shield off the defender to Derek's right and yanked it down, pulling the man forward. Before he could release his grip and step back, a sword flashed downward, cleaving the top of his head off. His body was dragged across the barrier and men stepped on top, but Darven filled the gap, and in a few quick, deadly cuts, backed down the breachers.

Derek's arm grew tired. Twice, blades nicked him. They didn't have much time. Retreat was inevitable, as was death. He said, "Send whoever's behind us to the fallback. Have them grab the torches and douse them. Have one of them take a torch into the left cavern. Maybe we can buy some time to regroup."

Darven's absence was felt immediately, as now two enemy soldiers turned their attention toward him. Derek was pressed to keep the swords away from him. He no longer worried about attacking, being far too busy trying to keep the blades from penetrating him.

To his relief, Darven returned fast. His sword flashed and the middle attacker's forearm fell on the barrier. The soldier held up his stump and screamed, which kept another soldier from filling his space.

"Clear your foe, and then we run," Darven gasped out through ragged breaths.

Derek increased his effort, feinting with the knife and driving the sword home. He yanked it back, turned, and ran with Darven a step behind. The third defender at the wall didn't make it one step before an enemy cut him down.

Derek ran into the darkness, praying he didn't hit a wall. Thundering footsteps followed, but they were unfamiliar with the caves, and in the dark were forced to slow their pursuit.

He was amazed they had made it this far. Survival did not seem to be reality. That did little to buoy his spirits, though. Death was still chasing him.

CHAPTER FIFTY-TWO

Darven twice grabbed his arm and guided Derek in the right direction. They made a turn and in the distance saw the flicker torch light.

They reached the barrier, scrambled over, and collapsed to the ground. Surprised to still be alive, Derek took a headcount. They were down to six, though one was wounded through the left bicep. The two men left to guard the rear still had arrows.

"Can you crawl?" Derek asked the wounded man.

"Yes, m'lord."

"Good. Get through the tunnel. Do it now. You'll be the slowest of us and you'll need a head start."

The man looked at Darven, who nodded his agreement. He went to the tunnel.

The echo of voices bounced around the cave walls, leaving Derek confused as to where the men were. He looked at the man holding the torch. "Put that out. No sense leading them here any sooner."

The flame was extinguished and darkness swallowed them.

Derek said to one of the men, "Give the first man another minute and follow him."

"Yes, m'lord."

"Then you," Derek said. "And you," to the last man. "Hand me that bow."

The man brought both sets and placed them between him and Darven.

Derek heard the second man begin his trip through the tunnel.

Though he was nothing more than a dark silhouette, Derek faced Darven. "If they don't find us by the time the last man is gone, we should try to escape as well."

"You go."

"What? No. You go first."

"I am not trying to be valiant, my lord. The truth is, I'm too large to fit through the tunnel. If I go first and get stuck, you will not be able to get out. I have to go last."

Derek had no argument.

Movement in the caves sounded closer and echoes bounced into each other, giving false impressions. Light danced off a wall in the distance. They finally had sense enough to light the torches. It wouldn't be long now.

The third man began his escape crawl. The noise he made sounded like an alarm. Derek took the bow and his few arrows and turned to peer across the barrier.

Darven said, "Keep down below the rocks. Perhaps they will think this place deserted. Even if they don't, we'll have surprise for our initial attack."

Derek thought it through. It was as good an idea as any. He slumped down and lay on his back. He set the bow down and grabbed his sword. If they did come to look, he'd be too close to use the bow. He closed his eyes and felt exhaustion pull him down. In a panic, he commanded his eyes to open and sat up.

Oh no, you don't. You're not taking me. Not this time.

The notion gave him pause. How long had he been here this time? This was the second night. One to go. If he traveled now, he wasn't close to staying forever yet. If he traveled at all, it would be sometime tomorrow night. If it didn't happen, then the spell was done. This would be his new home for the rest of his life.

Darven nudged him. "They're coming," he whispered.

Derek flexed his hand on the hilt. He thought of how he would attack from that position and adjusted his grip to facilitate the strike. The light played across the cavern's ceiling.

"See anything?" a voice said.

"Nothing but that pile of stones."

"Check behind it. You go with him."

Derek could tell there were at least three. He decided survival was possible.

He waited, his heart pounding like he'd run a race. The light stayed in one place, but shadows played on the wall behind him. He readied; muscles tensed.

"I don't see anything here," one said.

"Same here," the second man said, but his head appeared above Derek. For a moment he froze, perhaps not sure what he was seeing, but Derek knew that wouldn't last. Before the man could utter a word, Derek exploded off the floor and drove his sword through his jaw and into his brain. Before the body hit the floor, Darven ended the second man.

While the torchbearer stared open-mouthed, Derek bent to grab the bow.

"Hey! Hey!" the man shouted as he backed away. He turned to run. "They're..."

An arrow struck him in the back, pitching him forward. The torch flipped through the air like a juggling club and landed on the floor. He was right; only three. Derek held his breath, hoping no one heard. After a minute with no response, Derek stepped over the barrier to retrieve the light and put it out, but before he could reach it, several men carrying torches came into the cave. They stopped, seeing Derek and the bodies, and then charged.

Before Derek could turn and run for the safety of the barrier, an arrow whizzed past him and dropped the first man. The others were quick to retreat. He leaped the stone wall, and in one motion bent and scooped up the bow and arrows. He now had three and needed to make each one count.

He knelt next to the wall, an arrow aimed and ready. The barrage came less than a minute later. Now, however, someone with some sense controlled their efforts and had orchestrated the attack. Archers knelt and fired, not so much to hit as to keep their heads down. The men in front held shields. It worked. Derek had little chance to aim, but when he peeked, he saw two lines of men making their way along the wall.

He ducked an arrow, crawled behind the barrier toward the sidewall, and popped up again. Arrow drawn back, he released at the closest man, who was within fifteen feet. The arrow struck where aimed under the shield and sunk into the man's leg. Derek dropped for cover and readied the next arrow. He moved a few feet to the right and came up firing. This time, the arrow struck the next man as he bent for the shield dropped by the wounded soldier.

He took a chance, knowing he might not have the time to seek cover and get off his last shot. An arrow buzzed past his face. The hesitation it caused allowed the men to charge. He fired near point-blank into the first man's chest, then threw the bow at the second man.

Derek ran to recover his sword, pivoting just in time to block an overhead strike that could have split him in two from the head down. The blow was fierce enough to buckle his knees, but he pushed up hard off the ground and punched the man in the side of the face. He spun away, leaving an opening for the next man and a second of delay for Derek to retract his knife.

The sound of metal on metal filled the passageway as more men moved into the space. They would have no chance to escape. This was where Derek would die. He shouted a defiant cry at the thought of death and threw himself into an all-out berserker assault. One after another, his opponents stepped up and fell away. He lost track of time and the number of kills. Still they came, and the weight of the sword and his waning adrenaline began to take their toll.

Growing tired, he took minor cuts and barely avoided killing blows.

A grunt from his right, warranted by an attack from all sides, brought concern. Darven had fallen. As the press of the enemy increased, Derek considered lowering his weapons and accepting defeat, but his determination to live wouldn't let him. He would go down fighting.

If only that cursed spell would cause him to travel now. It would be more fitting for Erek to end this way. That was not to happen, though. His blade flashed back and forth in wild swings; each time, the weight dragging his arm lower.

As first one blade and then another pierced him, he knew his time had come. No longer with enough strength to wield it, the sword fell from his hand.

To his surprise, he felt the hardness of the rock wall at his back. He had nowhere to go and no way to stop the final stroke that would cut him down. With several arms drawn back and ready to finish the job, battle lust in each man's eyes, Derek dropped the knife and closed his eyes.

"Hold!" a voice shouted over the din.

Three points pricked his skin before halting their thrusts.

"If you kill that man, I will have your heads."

The men stopped short. Derek felt their hot, foul breath in his face. One man growled at having to stop his kill. His face twitched and Derek wondered how long he could hold back his blade before giving into the desire to kill. A hand clasped the man's shoulder and yanked him backward, ending the immediate threat.

Derek glanced down as the blade points were withdrawn from his chest and abdomen. The men parted and Derek looked up to see a large man approach. Black hair covered most of his face. He wore a tattered black cape, a silver breastplate, and gauntlets. His eyes scanned Derek from head to toe. Bertrand.

"You are—excuse me—*were* the lord here?"

Derek's throat thickened and he was unable to speak. There was no sense denying it. He swallowed hard and nodded.

"I dare say you don't look like much, and I'm impressed. When you first came to me, I didn't believe you were capable of such fierce fighting. I was told you were a weak-kneed coward, but you have proven that to be untrue."

He was obviously talking about Erek. Derek swallowed again to make sure his voice did not crack and said, "You have won. The keep is yours, but not its inhabitants."

"No, I see that. Still, it wasn't them I have come for. My sole purpose for taking this keep was to punish you for interfering with my attack on the castle."

"Yeah. I see that went well for you."

Bertrand gave a half-smile, then backhanded Derek across the face with his metal-gloved hand. The blow staggered him, and although he struggled to keep his feet, he bounced off the wall and fell to his knees.

"No matter. Your efforts have only delayed the inevitable. After I took the castle, I would've come here anyway. Nothing has changed except the order of attack. I will have these lands and be their king."

Derek tried to get to his feet, but Bertrand put a foot on his chest and shoved him back down.

"On your knees is a good look for you, especially now that I am your new king. If you don't die from your wounds too fast, I will parade you in front of the castle wall so they can see no more help will be coming."

So that would be it, then. They would kill him at the castle for all to see. At least he'd saved Eldina. That counted for something. He glanced over at Darven's body.

Sadness drained his remaining energy. He slumped, ready to die. His shirt was covered in blood; sprayed dots of crimson from those he'd killed and long streaks and large blooms of his own. With any luck, he'd bleed out before they reached the castle.

"Bertrand said, "See to his wounds. I don't want him to die before we arrive. You hear that? I'm sparing you for now. You have a three-day reprieve before your execution."

Derek was lifted and carried from the caves. Before he made it outside, he slipped into unconsciousness.

CHAPTER FIFTY-THREE

Derek woke later to find his wounds bandaged and his hands and legs bound. He was laying on the dirt of the practice field behind the keep. Men and horses moved around the grounds, but no one paid him any attention. Trying not to move and alert them he was awake, he scanned the grounds through eyelid slits, searching for an escape route.

He thought about the spot where the keep met the mountain, then remembered he'd ordered the platform taken down. There was no way to get to the top of the wall. He was coming up blank as a nervous buzz circulated through the keep. Men ran toward the front as if following orders. Voices grew louder and carried concern. Activity ceased in the center of the yard and increased around the walls. Tension fell over the keep, and he realized they were getting ready to defend.

An electric excitement coursed through him, matching that of his enemy, but for different reasons. He rolled now to see if he could determine what set off the sudden action. He saw nothing, and knew it was the perfect diversion.

Derek rolled to a sitting position and used his fingers to work at the ropes on his feet. With little knowledge or experience, whoever bound him had tied his hands in front, but they knew how to tie a knot. The process was too slow. He looked around, his gaze stopping on the ruins of the stable and the cave opening beyond. If he could reach the cave, he'd be able to work at the knots unobserved.

He got to his knees, pushed off the ground with his bound hands, and managed to get to his feet. He began hopping toward the cave and felt stupid, like an overgrown rabbit trying to evade its hunters. The stable grew closer, spurring him on. Trying to move too fast, he miscalculated a jump forward and pitched off-balance. He caught himself before falling to the ground, but it stalled his momentum.

As he pushed back to his feet, he heard voices behind. Two men came toward him. A voice yelled, "And where do you think you're getting off to?"

With fear sparking new energy, Derek hopped as fast as he could. He reached the ruins and tried to hop over debris left from the destroyed building. Misjudging the height, his foot caught. Unable to prevent his fall, he hit hard, cutting his knee on a jagged piece of what had once been the rear wall of the stable. Before he could right himself, the two men were on him.

One kicked him. "I'll teach you to make us have to chase you." He kicked him again.

"Hey! Easy now. The king wants him alive."

They lifted him roughly and Derek pulled his legs up to his chest.

The man who kicked him punched him in the chest, expelling the air from his lungs. "Put those legs down and hop, or king or no, I'll beat you near death."

He brought his arm back to deliver another punch, but before he could throw it, a blade burst through his chest, arching him backwards. Derek and the other guard watched him drop. The other man's surprised look matched Derek's. Before the guard could react, a dark form lunged and impaled him as well.

Having no support, Derek fell. He looked up, fearing he was next. The blade descended and Derek lifted his hands in a useless defense. The sword stopped, slid between his wrists, and sliced through the rope. Shifting his focus from the sword to the man, he let out a gasp.

"Darven! I thought you were dead."

"As was the intent." He cut the bonds on Derek's legs. "Now, you going to lay there all day, or you want to escape?"

Darven extended a hand and Derek took it. He was hauled to his feet. His body complained from the multitude of cuts and bruises. Darven held one hand pressed to his side. Blood seeped through. He'd been wounded; perhaps severely, but it hadn't prevented him from rescuing Derek.

Darven jumped over the broken wood and disappeared into the caves. Derek hesitated only long enough to remove a sword and a knife from the dead guards before following.

They raced through the caverns, slowing as the light faded behind them. Darven grabbed a torch from a sconce.

"Darven, do you know what's happening?"

"As far as I can tell, another force has appeared."

"Do you know whose?"

"My guess is it's the lady's family."

The sentence was elating. The chance of rescue and seeing Eldina again was too much to believe.

They reached the back barrier where Derek had made his not-so-final stand and climbed over. He stopped and stared down at the tunnel. He turned to Darven.

"There will be no arguing. You must go. Now."

"But it's too small for you. No matter what you say, I'm not leaving you alone."

Darven's eyes narrowed. He looked like he was about to attack. He drew in a deep breath to either launch a verbal tirade or grab Derek and force him into the tunnel, but before he could do either, they heard commotion coming from the tunnel.

They moved to the sides of the opening and held their swords aloft, ready to drive them down through whoever entered. A few minutes later, a head popped out. Derek was already in a downward thrust when he recognized Jerald, the tunnel rat who had clambered out of the tunnel to lead the people away.

"Hi, m'lord. I'm returned!" He spoke majestically, like he was Christ rising from the dead. Derek expelled a blast of air, relieved he hadn't skewered the man. As Jerald dragged his body from the hole, he said, "You wasn't about to kill me, was you, m'lord?"

"What are you doing here, Jerald?" Darven asked.

He stood and said, "Rescuing you, sir," as if it were something as simple as fetching a horse.

"By yourself?" Darven asked.

"Well, of course not, sir. Even I couldn't do that."

Then they heard someone else coming through.

"I brought friends, I did. Lots and lots of friends." Jerald gave them a wide toothless smile and bent to help the next man out.

Thirty minutes later, a combined force of two dozen men from the keep and the castle stood in the small passageway. Their leader said, "That's all, m'lord."

The man said, "Lord Benton has given us an hour to get inside before he will assault the keep. Then he will give the signal to attack from inside and make our way to the gate.

The gate. Derek moaned. "Twenty-four of us will not be enough to lift those metal plates. Not and try to fight."

"Metal plates, m'lord?"

"Did you come up from the front with the main host?"

"Yes, m'lord. But the gate was wooden, not metal, just as it has always been."

Was that possible? Had Bertrand done them all a favor by taking them down? He thought about when he was bound on the ground. It hit him then. Horses! They had horses inside. They wouldn't have lifted the horses over the wall. "They took the barrier down."

Jerald smiled. "Yes, m'lord. All down it is."

"Split your force. Half with you and half led by Sir Darven.

"Me, m'lord?" Jerald said. "Does that mean I'm a Sir too?"

"Win the fight and don't get killed and we'll see. Now, one to the right; the other to the left." Derek scanned the men. "How many have bows?"

"Only four, m'lord."

"They'll come with me. Let's go."

As they walked to the front of the caves, the parties were divided. Sounds of battle reached them. Derek let the assault groups go first before leading his men straight for the keep at a run. He leaped up the back stairs and into the kitchen. Food was out everywhere, but the room was vacant.

"Swords out. This way," Derek said. He ran into the hallway, slowing as he reached the hall. It, too, was empty. He raced for the stairs.

The door to his room stood open. Inside, he found two men ransacking his belongings. He assumed they were searching for valuables. Lot of good valuables would do them dead. He attacked the first man and cut him down before he could free his sword. He felt no guilt killing an unarmed man.

While the others finished off the second man, he ran for the tower steps. The overhead hatch had already been opened. He stopped and peered out. Four archers stood loosing arrows from long range.

Derek turned to the others, placing a finger to his lips. Then, with as much stealth as possible, he climbed to the top and crept toward his prey. His sword was already halfway through its slash before any of them noticed him. The man fell and Derek kicked him off the roof. Turning, he plunged his blade into the next man's side, even though one of Derek's men had engaged him.

In less than a minute, all four men had been killed. His archers set up and fired at the men protecting the wall. Derek picked up one of the dead men's bows and prepared to do the same.

He stared out over the inner and outer yards at the mass of humanity bent on destroying each other. It was at the same time so different, yet much the same as the modern conflicts he'd been in. Killing was faster with guns but bows and swords were more brutal.

He set an arrow to the string, targeted, and loosed. He watched the flight and felt satisfaction upon seeing it strike. He seated the next arrow, and while searching for his next target, spied Darven and his men locked in a fierce battle on the grounds to the left of the gate.

As he watched, Darven felled a man, then took an arrow that spun him to the ground. A shard of fear lanced Derek's heart. He scanned the parapet for the culprit, finding him already targeting his next shot. Derek quickly sighted on him. His shot was rushed, but he hoped to distract the man if he didn't hit him. Before the arrow landed, he had another ready to go.

The first arrow passed inches in front of the man's face. He jumped back and looked for the source. By the time he spotted the men on the tower, Derek had already released the arrow. The man nocked his arrow and drew back on the string, then pitched backward over the wall as Derek's arrow burrowed into his chest.

Derek leaned on the short wall and stared at Darven, willing him to move. To his relief, the big man was on his knees and pushed up to his feet using his sword for balance. Jerald ran over to help him and the two men set off to find their next opponent.

Derek grabbed another arrow, sighted along the platform, and stopped on a man wearing a black cape. His eyes narrowed and a red mist veiled his vision. He released his breath in a steady flow and let the arrow fly.

It sailed true at the so-called king's back. Before it struck, one of Bertrand's men ran behind him and took the arrow through his neck. He fell into Bertrand, who whirled and slashed at the already dead man.

He noted the protruding arrow, determining its origin. His eyes scaled the keep, stopping on the tower. His eyes locked with Derek's and hatred traveled the distance, sending a chill through Derek's veins.

Bertrand raised his sword and pointed it at Derek. Understanding, Derek nodded and tossed down the bow. Roiling anger gripped his gut. He pivoted and ran for the stairs to put an end to both the usurper and the assault on his keep.

CHAPTER FIFTY-FOUR

Derek sprinted down the stairs and out the front doors. With fighting all around him, he stood on the steps and searched for Bertrand. He spotted the man just in time to see him point and issue a command to two of his archers.

Derek dove to the side as the two arrows ricocheted off the stone steps. He hit, bracing against the impact and losing the sword in the process. Before he could scoop it up and run for cover, an enemy soldier charged him. Derek dodged and punched the man in the side of the head. The blow knocked him off balance, away from Derek and directly into the path of the next flight of arrows.

Before the body hit the ground, Derek retrieved his sword and raced for the safety of the parapet on the far side of the gate. An arrow hit the ground between his feet. Another whizzed past his face. He leaped bodies, pivoted around fights like a running back going through the secondary line. He reached the wall, out of breath and bravery. He pressed the outer stone wall like he was trying to become part of it. Out of view from the archers above, he calculated the odds of reaching Bertrand. He should've known the brigand was too much of a coward to face him.

Fighting was fierce on the platform above him. Bodies littered the courtyard. He did not see Darven or many of the defenders. If they didn't get the gate open soon, they'd be dead and the counterattack would be thwarted.

As if in response to his thoughts, the boom of a battering ram sent a vibration along the wall. Derek sucked in air, hoping courage was riding on the current. With grudging acceptance that he had no other choice, he peeled his body from the wall and forced his legs to carry him to the gate.

Eight men stood behind the massive wooden gates bracing long poles against them. The crossbar bowed inward under another assault, but not enough to threaten the gates' integrity. Derek assessed the situation. The poles had to come down to hasten the gates' demise, but to topple the poles, he needed to eliminate the eight guardians. He pressed against the wall again.

His eyes roamed the keep's facade, stopping at the roof. The archers were still there. An idea bloomed. He waved his arms overhead to get their attention but they were focused on the fighting above him. Extending the sword overhead to gain more height, he tried again and the sword hit the bottom of the platform. Frustrated, he stepped from underneath his protection and waved frantically, but the only attention he drew was from an enemy swordsman.

He jumped backward to avoid the slash, then met the second attack with his sword. With a quick flick of his wrist, a basic move learned from his fencing instructor, he rode his weapon over the top of the other man's and lunged. The sword scythed a line up his opponent's arm to his elbow. The sword fell as his enemy clutched his arm, and Derek swung the sword like a bat, catching the man across the face and carving deep into the skull.

He backed away and tried to wave again to no avail. Scanning the ground, he spied a bow and one arrow next to an archer felled from above. He ran to snatch them up and raced back to the wall. Setting the sword against the wall, he sheathed the knife and set the arrow to the bowstring. Derek targeted the closest archer, moved his aim to the left a bit, and fired. The arrow soared upward. The archer shifted position and for a moment, Derek feared he'd hit him. The arrow shot past his ear by only inches and got his attention.

The archer drew back the string and searched for the culprit. Spying Derek waving his arms, he targeted but pulled up an instant before release as recognition passed over his face. Derek pointed toward the gate. The man didn't seem to understand what he was trying to convey. Derek picked up his sword and tried again, using the blade to extend where he pointed, but his contact was slow on the uptake.

Derek was forced to walk to the edge of the gate and point at the men under the arch. Before he got his message across, one of the men supporting the poles saw him and attacked. His strike was clumsy, missing and hitting the ground. With a backhand cut, Derek removed the man's head from his body. It bounced and rolled under the arch in front of two of the other men. They growled at Derek and rushed him, but before they came within striking distance, they were cut down by a flurry of arrows.

Derek looked up, nodded, and gave a thumbs-up, but then wondered if they understood what he meant. The archers shot two more men before stopping. Derek looked at them and gave a *'What's going on?'* shrug. The archer pointed to his eyes and shook his head. Derek got the message instantly. From their height, they had no angle to see that far into the arch. Derek was going to have to go in and get them himself.

He sighed. It was never easy. *Three against one. What could go wrong?*

He slid the knife free and stepped into the arch. Two men were facing the gates, but the third had a sword in hand and saw him coming. He tapped one of the other men, who nodded and watched his partner advance on Derek. Unlike his two previous opponents, this man knew what he was doing. Derek tried several moves to end the fight in a hurry, but each was countered with ease.

A lance of fear clutched at his gut and puckered his anus. The man attacked with a ferocious flurry of cuts, slashes, and lunges. Derek gave ground under the steady assault, barely blocking or deflecting each one. Forced back after a vicious slash, he tripped over the body of his last kill and fell on his back.

His foe stepped forward with sword raised and a smile on his lips. The sword descended in a blur. Derek closed his eyes and tried to roll out of the way. He felt no pain and thought he'd rolled clear, but when he opened his eyes, he saw the man standing over him, his smile and sword replaced by three arrows and a sneer. He staggered two steps and dropped to his knees in a death stance.

Freaked by the entire encounter, Derek got to his feet and scrambled away, then turned and saluted the archers. Anger and fear sent an animal-like growl from him. Without thought, he charged the remaining two men.

The man facing him stepped over a pole and waited for his attack. Instead of stopping to engage, all common sense was gone. He swatted the extended blade aside enough to continue running. Lowering his shoulder, Derek plowed into him, driving the surprised man back into the gate. They hit with the force of the battering ram from the other side.

Derek kneed the man in the groin and he dropped. He kicked at the underside of one pole and found it was firmly planted. He kicked at it several more times before it gave ground. Two more kicks and it fell, bringing the attention of the last man. Before he got in range, Derek leaped another pole. In midair, he stabbed the blade through the man's throat.

He tossed his sword and knife down and put his shoulder into lifting and pushing another pole. It was slow going. His strength depleted rapidly. He felt weakened from spent energy and blood loss. Grunting and feeling little give, he almost fell as the pole gave way suddenly.

He turned to see Darven standing there, a smug look on his face. A broken arrow protruded from his chest. "Needed real muscle."

"Kiss my ass."

Together they made short work of the remaining poles, then fought to lift the heavy crossbar. They were forced to lift one end at a time, but even with that accomplished, they could not move to the other side without the beam sliding back in place.

The gate thundered again, this time creating more give in the wood. Breathing heavily from the exertion, Derek said, "I've got an idea." He went to get his weapons. He jammed the sword point-first into the ground near the gate and held the knife.

The two men got underneath the beam and pushed up. They grunted and strained. The end free, Derek lifted the knife, and as soon as the crossbar had cleared its support, he jammed the knife into the gate underneath the beam to prevent it from dropping, and he knew it wouldn't hold long under the extreme weight of the beam. They had to work fast, but they had no strength left to finish the job.

Taking a minute to catch their breath, they moved to the other side as the ram struck again. The wood would give, but it would still take time. They bent to raise the other side just as Bertrand and three of his men entered the arch.

CHAPTER FIFTY-FIVE

"We have a dilemma," Darven said.

"You think?" Derek asked. He picked up his sword and reached for his knife before remembering he no longer had it.

"Aye. I do. And I think one of us has to fight and the other lift the beam. Unfortunately, I'm the better fighter and the stronger man."

"No one likes a braggart."

"Aye. They do. I can't let them kill you, so I'll fight. That way, if I die, I'll no longer care if they kill you."

The three men started forward, cautious about their approach. It looked like Bertrand was staying back to watch. That lowered the odds a bit for the moment.

Readying to meet them, Derek said, "We could just fight them together."

"Aye, but if we both go down, no one will be here to lift that bar."

Derek realized the sounds of battle within the walls had diminished. How long before Bertrand could send others against them? Darven was right. This was their only chance. "Pick."

Darven growled. Derek understood that was his answer and ran for the gate. As he was shorter than Darven, his leverage was hampered. His effort was at maximum, but the beam lifted grudgingly. Through narrow slits, Derek watched as Darven engaged the three men. Two went for him and the third attempted to go around and make for Derek.

With the fluid, graceful moves of a dancer, Darven parried attacks from both foes, then pivoted and stuck out a foot to trip the third man. He toppled face first, but the move opened Darven up for a thrust. He arched back and whirled, slapping the sword from the second man away.

Fear for his friend and failing the keep sent a surge of power through Derek and the bar rose. The wounded Darven met his foes with renewed energy, driving both men back.

The fallen man got to his feet and retrieved his sword. Derek had to choose whether to drop the beam and face the man or continue and risk being run through. He shifted position and lifted his sword in weak defense. The move lowered the beam inches. The pounding of the ram pushed the gate into him, almost knocking him to the ground. He struggled to maintain the progress he'd achieved.

The man stalked toward him, sword ready to pierce him. Derek glanced to see Darven's progress. One of the enemies fell to the ground as Darven stabbed him, but before he retracted his sword, the other man slashed him in the side. Darven fell to one knee.

"No!" Derek screamed, and the boost of adrenaline drove the beam upward. The swordsman brought his arm back and shot it forward. Derek made a feeble attempt to block the thrust, managing to turn it aside at the last second. The blade impaled the gate, and for the moment, Derek was safe. He used it to his advantage.

With the last push, the beam cleared its latch and Derek pitched it to the ground. The swordsman pulled his blade free and Derek swung his sword in a wild and desperate attack, severing the man's arm. A gout of blood rained on the gate as sword and arm fell. The man dropped to his knees, clutching the wound.

Too exhausted to lift his sword, he looked up to find Bertrand advancing on him with a cruel and evil visage. A glance told Derek that Darven had fallen and took the last man with him.

It was between himself and Bertrand now.

He forced his hand upward, knowing he no longer possessed the strength to defend, let alone defeat the man. Still he stood his ground as the man approached. His hatred matched what he saw on Bertrand's face.

Derek readied himself, deciding to put everything he had into one attack. Maybe he'd get lucky.

Bertrand shouted and charged. As the two men thrust their weapons forward, the battering ram struck one last time. With no crossbeam, the gates blasted open, the left side hitting Derek from behind and throwing him forward. The pain was more intense than he'd ever felt.

He was face to face with his enemy. A wild-eyed look appeared on Bertrand's face. As men streamed in around them, Derek's eyes fluttered and his gaze fell. Both men were pierced through, their opposite's sword holding the other man upright.

Derek did not know how long they stood like that, but he was aware of voices all around him. As his vision narrowed and darkness closed in, he was vaguely aware of hands touching him.

Dreamy images danced before his eyes. First of Jackie, then Eldina. He was smiling just before he succumbed.

* * *

He was falling. In his subconscious, he understood what it meant. He forced his eyes open, expecting to see Jackie. To his surprise, he discovered he was still at the keep. He was in bed with a heavy quilt covering him, giving the impression of being weighted down.

He attempted to uncover himself but was stopped by pain.

There was movement to his left. He turned to see Eldina rising from a chair near the bed.

"Oh, my lord. Derek." Tears flooded her eyes and further words failed. She placed her hands on his arm and laid her head on the pillow next to him and cried.

Derek tried to shush her; to comfort and soothe her, but his mouth was too dry to emit words. Eldina lifted her head to gaze at him. Her tear-streaked face could not hide her beauty. He slid his arm slowly from under the covers and wiped the tears from her cheek.

"What...What..."

She understood his nonquestion. "The battle is over. My sister's husband's men finished what you started. He said he was wrong about you. You are very brave and worthy of me. You are severely wounded. They say," she choked, "they say you may not survive." She lowered her head and sobbed.

Derek tried to absorb her words. So after all he'd been through, it was going to end here anyway. He wondered if the doctors could save him in his own world. He looked at the sobbing woman. Did she care that much to be this upset? Did he? The answer was yes. He lifted a hand and stroked the back of her head.

"Eldina."

She lifted her head.

"I need to travel." His voice was weak. Derek had the feeling there wasn't much time.

"No." She clutched him, causing a spear of pain. He winced audibly.

"Eldina. I have to."

"No. I won't let you."

"Listen to me. If I don't go, I'll die."

"But what if you die in your world? I'll never see you again." She pulled a knife—his knife, he realized—from a table and held it over him. "I'd rather kill you now than lose you."

"I have a better chance of surviving there than here. Besides, the spell will bring me back anyway."

"Oh, Derek. I want you here. I don't ever want to see your twin," she shuddered, "again."

"You might not have to. I may not go back. This might be the end. If I'm here through the night, I'll be here forever or until I die, which won't be long. But you have to promise me not to interfere if I start fading."

He looked at the window. It was dark. Nighttime. He might not have much time regardless. He guessed just a few more hours and the transfer would be permanent. That meant he didn't have long to live.

"No!"

"Eldina. It's my only chance. Our only chance. If I can get proper medical attention, I might survive and come back. Don't you want the chance to be together for a long time? We can have that if I go back."

Her hand trembled, the eighteen inch blade dangling above him.

"But how will I face that monster? I refuse to let him touch me again."

"So when he lands, kill him."

She stopped crying abruptly, a look of stunned shock on her face. "I can't. Even if I want to, there are strict laws against such acts against nobles. I will be executed."

"Not if you can prove he was abusing you."

"It matters not. I am his property to do with as he pleases. To injure him in any way will bring shame to my family. They will be forced to disavow me. They will," her hand went to her neck, "cut off my head."

"Okay, then let me do it." He reached up and took the knife from her. "I'll take it with me and when we pass each other, I will drive this knife into him." He didn't remind her that to do so would break the spell, and he'd no longer have a way back to her. The thought saddened him, but even though he wanted to return to her, deep inside he understood this wasn't where he belonged.

"If he's not dead when he arrives, let him bleed out before calling for help."

"But people will still think I killed him."

"No. They already think I'm going to die from my injuries. Just say I tried to get up and fell on my knife. No one will doubt that."

"But..."

Before she could finish her complaint, Derek felt the energy shift around him. To his relief, he knew he was traveling. He might yet live. He clutched the knife tighter. Whatever happened, though...whatever the cost, he would end Erek's life, if only to prevent him from hurting Eldina.

"Eldina, it's happening. I'm going."

She wrapped her arms around him, but he did not feel them, nor did it feel like she had a solid grip on him.

"No!" she wailed.

"I'll be back. I'll take care of Erek. I love you."

And the light surrounded him.

CHAPTER FIFTY-SIX

The first thing he noticed when he adjusted to the falling was that he no longer held the knife. He supposed that made sense. It was the same reason he always arrived naked. Things from the other world did not exist in his world. Still, he needed to end Erek's miserable life.

Pressing his forehead to the bubble, he saw the second ball of light coming. He pushed with both hands on the bubble to get it to move. The effort caused severe pain throughout his body but he had to work through it. He pulled back and hit the bubble again. He couldn't be sure, but it felt like it moved. He tried again, knowing time was short.

Then again, what if the bubble popped? Would he die and float for eternity in the void?

He had no idea, but since there was a good chance he was going to die anyway, he shoved again. He noticed fresh blood dripping down his torso. The measures the so-called doctors of the other world had used to stop the bleeding were not effective.

Derek looked for the second ball. It was close.

Very close.

His bubble had moved. He began shoving it hard and fast. He saw Erek's terrified face in the other bubble as he realized what Derek was doing. His mouth opened in a soundless scream. One more good push and Derek would have it.

The two orbs rushed forward on a collision course. Despite feeling elated at accomplishing the feat, a wave of fear enveloped him as he anticipated the contact. He sat back in the bubble away from the point of impact and slipped on the now blood-slick interior.

He lifted his hands in front of his face as if it would be enough to deflect the impending damage. Three seconds. Two seconds. The bubbles adjusted course and passed inches from each other, close enough for the twins to make out clear features of their doppelganger.

"No!" Derek shouted at the fast-disappearing ball of light. "Eldina!"

He dropped to his butt, placed his head in his hands, and wept.

* * *

Eldina screamed as Derek vanished. "No!" But there was nothing she could do. He was gone, but somehow she knew he'd come back to her. "Yes. He'll be back," she said to reassure herself.

Something on the bed drew her attention. It was the knife. She breathed a sigh of relief and reached for it. She was glad Derek had dropped it. She didn't want him to kill Erek. She was not stupid. If he succeeded in killing Erek, the spell would be broken and Derek would never return. She could endure Erek one last time. She would not let him hurt her, but she had to keep him alive.

Someone knocked on the door as she picked up the knife.

"Come," she said and turned to see Darven enter. His torso was wrapped in bandages. Suddenly she heard a whoosh and felt a heavy, painful impact on her arm. She gasped out in pain as she tried to free her hand from the sudden weight.

Yanking her hand away, she looked to see Erek had arrived. But something was wrong. His expression was pained; tormented. He clutched at his chest. The knife blade protruded between his ribs. She looked down in shock at her now-empty hand, then back at her husband, the lord of the keep. He turned toward her and his mouth worked, but only pained gasps came out. He extended a bloody hand toward her, but she leaped from the bed with a cry of fright.

She watched as Erek breathed his last breath, his hand flopping over the side of the bed.

Eldina lifted her gaze to meet Darven's.

"I-I-I..."

He rushed to her side and wrapped his arms around her to offer comfort.

"Shush now, child. We'll figure something out. Remember that everyone thinks he's going to die anyway. We can handle this."

But she was no longer listening. His words were the same ones Derek said. *Everyone thought he was going to die anyway.* "Oh my God. He's gone."

Darven said, "Aye, my lady, but don't you worry none. I'll tell everyone he died from his wounds. You will face no punishment as long as I am here."

But he didn't understand. Her concern wasn't for Erek, but because with his death, the spell was broken. She would never again see Derek, the man she loved. She put her head on Darven's chest and cried for a long time.

* * *

Derek landed on the bed clutching at his bleeding stomach.

"Oh shit! Derek! Bill, help me. He's hurt. Call 911."

Jackie stood by his side and ripped off the pillowcase.

She pushed his hands away and pressed it to the wound. "Derek, can you hear me? Hurry, Bill. I think he's dying."

Then all went dark.

* * *

Derek had no idea where he was in his dreamy haze. His first conscious thought was that he had made it to Heaven.

An unfamiliar black face leaned over him. "Hey Derek. How are you feeling, honey?"

The look of confusion must have shown on his face.

"Don't you worry none. You're in good hands. You're in St. Charles Hospital. I'm Arenthia, your nurse. I know you have lots of questions—believe me, we've got a few ourselves—but you are going to be fine. We're taking great care of you. You'll be up and around in no time." Arenthia rambled on while she checked his vitals. Soon her voice faded and sleep reclaimed him.

He woke again with clearer vision. This time, the first face that came into view was Jackie's.

"There you are. Thank God. Arenthia said you'd woken up, but I had to see for myself. I'm so glad you're all right. You scared the shit out of me. And poor Bill may never be the same. He's still trying to rationalize what he saw."

Derek tried to speak, but the words came out as a jumbled croak.

"You don't have to talk. I can talk enough for both of us. You just rest and get better, because once you do, I'm gonna put your sorry ass right back in here for scaring me so bad. "

He closed his eyes. He was going to live. Traveling had come at the perfect time. Had it somehow known of his peril and moved to heal him? Did that even make sense?

Well, as much sense as anything else.

He rested for a few minutes, listening to Jackie prattle on. How much longer did he have before his last travel? He thought about Eldina and the battle, but mostly about Eldina. Then his thoughts drifted to Darven. He'd seen the big man go down. Had he died? He realized for the first time that Darven was perhaps the best friend he'd ever had, even though he'd known him for only a short time.

He realized he was crying when Jackie comforted him. "Oh, baby. It's okay. You let it all out. I'm here for you." Her hand caressed the side of his face. She patted something soft on his cheeks to wipe away the tears.

She hugged him close and rocked him until he quieted and drifted to sleep again.

The next time he woke, the room was empty. He looked around. A monitor and drip bag stood to the left. A few vases of flowers lined the countertop in front of the bed. The chair near the bed on the right was empty, save for a blanket.

Sunlight seeped around the drawn blinds. How long had he been there? How long would it be until he traveled? If he had to wait until he got back to his own room in his own bed, perhaps it was time to move to a new apartment and buy a different bed.

Derek allowed himself to think of Eldina. He wanted to see her but knew his next trip would be his last for this world. His world. Yet even though the change was drastic, he found he longed to be there with her and with his friend. Why did he have to travel to another time and place to find love and friendship?

The door opened and Jackie and a man in a white lab coat entered. Derek assumed he was a doctor.

"Good. You're awake," Jackie said. She leaned over the bed and kissed his forehead. "This is Doctor Nuxhall. Doctor, this is world-famous," she turned to face Derek with a hand near her mouth, as if to prevent the doctor from hearing the next part, "in two different worlds," she dropped her hand, "author Derek Lawson."

Nuxhall extended his hand and Derek gave him a weak shake.

Over the next twenty minutes, he addressed Derek's condition, wound and injury care, and how much longer he had to stay.

"You've got a lot of stitches holding you together inside and out. The wound was quite severe. We're fighting an infection, but I think we've got that under control. If all looks good tomorrow, we'll send you home. I'll give you a list of restrictions and a note if you need an excuse to miss work. As an author, do you have a boss?"

"Yes," Jackie said. "That would be me. And believe me, I'm a slave driver."

Derek nodded. "I can attest to that."

They talked a few more minutes before the doctor left.

"I'm so glad you're okay, Derek."

"You must not've liked the ending and want me to do a rewrite."

"No." She pressed her lips into a fine line. "I love the story. It's fine. In fact, it's wonderful. I already submitted it to the publisher and told them they were getting a bargain. There's going to be an auction for the movie rights. It's going to be bigger than your last one. And you were worried about not being able to write a better story."

"Yeah. I only had to transport to a medieval world and almost die…several times, I might add…in order to do it. The question now is, how will I top it? Teleport to the future?"

"Why don't we enjoy this one for a while before worrying about the next?"

"Okay, but you realize I won't be here for it, right?"

CHAPTER FIFTY-SEVEN

Her face fell. "Don't say that, Derek."

"Why? It's the truth. I didn't break the spell. I was there almost three days last time. This time, it will be more than three days, which makes the change permanent. It's going to happen. We both need to come to grips with the reality."

"There has to be something we can do."

"Not that I've found."

"I can't believe this is happening."

"But it is."

"But you'll miss the release of your new book. You'll miss the premiere of the movie."

"Guess you'll have to enjoy both without me."

"It's not fair."

"Don't worry, Jackie. Maybe I can continue to write and have the manuscripts held for you by some delivery carrier to be delivered sometime in the future. That way, my legacy will continue and you'll still make bundles of money."

"You're an asshole, you know that?"

"I should; you've told me enough."

"Well, I'm saying it again. Asshole." Her voice rose in anger. "I don't give a damn about the books or the money, you dumbass. I'm worried about you. If this magic does continue, I'll never see you again. You'll be out of my life forever."

"If I'm such an asshole, what does it matter?"

She shook her head and calmed. "God, you're so stupid." She whirled and stomped out.

Derek didn't see her again until he was discharged. He was rolled out the door in a wheelchair. Jackie pulled up and the transporter helped him into her car.

"Thought you were mad at me."

"I am, but who else would pick you up?"

He thought about how sad that was. The truth was, he had few friends now. He'd lost most of them after Jackie left. The rest drifted away because of the reclusive lifestyle he'd settled into after the divorce. He only had himself to blame; not that it mattered anymore. Now that he was leaving forever, the lack of close relationships was a blessing.

They drove the rest of the way in silence. Derek felt like Jackie had already shut down on him. But he didn't blame her. After all, he was leaving her again.

His thoughts drifted to that last night they'd spent together making love. For a moment while the passion still burned within him, he'd allowed himself to hope things could get back to the way they were. That she'd forgiven his sins and was his again. That life was about to be good again. He'd felt whole for the first time since he'd messed everything up. But it had only taken a few seconds to dash that happy thought. It served a purpose, though. He realized for the first time that he would never be with her again.

Ever.

Until that moment, he'd always held out hope that someday she'd come back and give him the one more chance he so desperately needed.

That was for the best too.

She pulled up to the curb in front of his building and the doorman opened his door and helped him out.

"So good to see you again, Mr. Lawson. We were all worried about you."

"Thank you, Marvin. I appreciate that."

"You want me to help you up to your apartment?"

"Thank you, Marvin," Jackie said. "We'll manage."

"You don't have to see me upstairs. I can do it."

"Now you're being an ass again."

Derek started to reply and thought better of it. Jackie and Marvin each took an arm and guided him to the elevator.

Once inside, Jackie said, "Okay Marvin, I've got it from here."

"Yes, ma'am."

The doors shut. The ride reminded Derek of the traveling bubble, but in reverse.

The doors slid open. Mr. Jenkins was just entering his apartment. "Back to try it again, eh?"

Derek's anger sparked, and he started to reply, but Jackie cut him off. "He's fine. It was just an accident. Thanks for your concern." Her reply, though more polite than Derek's would've been, still had an edge of sarcasm that made him smile.

Jackie unlocked the door and Derek entered. He stood in the center of the room, staring at the bed. She closed the door and stood next to him. "What?"

"Guess I should just get this over with. I mean, why wait? I've got nothing left here, and the book's finished—unless you want me to write the real ending?"

"I love the ending the way it is and shut up. You do have everything here. You just want me to feel sorry for you."

He smiled humorlessly. "No. That might have been true once, but..." He shrugged. No need to rehash it. "You should go. I want to make this last trip alone."

He walked toward the bed, but before laying down, he scanned the room for the last time. He sat on the bed and swung his legs up. Settling into a comfortable position, he noticed she had come to the bed.

"I was serious. You don't have to be here."

"Yes, I do."

"Well, climb aboard." He patted the bed next to him.

She shook her head. "No, not this time. We need to talk."

"Seriously? We've already broken up."

"Don't be an ass. This isn't easy for me." She sat on the end of the bed so she could look at him. "Derek."

"I know. I know. It was a mistake."

"Listen to me. I have to say this. For both of us. Yes, it was a mistake. I do love you, Derek. Part of me always will. But I've moved on. I love Bill, and I *am* going to marry him. I'm not placing blame. That's all in the past. It just…ah, hell." Tears flowed, and she wiped them away like they were an annoyance. "It just is what it is. I will always feel close to you and want you in my life, but just as a friend. It can't be anything more ever again. I will not say I regret what we did. It was important for both of us, I think, but for different reasons. Please tell me you understand and are all right with it."

He reached across the bed and squeezed her hand. "I do love you, Jackie. I always will, but I understand and wish you happiness. Don't worry about me. I'll be fine. Take care of everything for me."

"Oh, Derek."

"Do me a favor?"

"Sure."

"Please go."

She looked at him for a long moment, a pained expression on her face. She stood, wiped the tears with her palms, and walked away. She stopped, turning back to place a soft, loving kiss on his forehead, then disappeared through the door.

No longer able to control his emotions, he cried up until he started to fall.

CHAPTER FIFTY-EIGHT

Three days later, he sat at his desk staring at his computer screen, the blank page glaring back. He'd been there before, but this time, he felt no pressure. The story was already percolating.

He fell asleep that first night, surprised to find he was still in his apartment when he woke. He waited in bed almost the entire next day, thinking the transport might occur at any second, but it never came.

By the morning of the next day, he began to believe the spell had been broken. But according to the witch, there was only one way that could have happened—if either he or Erek died. And he was still alive. Various theories played out in his mind.

Maybe Erek had been injured in much the same way he had been. Going back to his world deprived him of the medical attention needed to heal him.

Or if Darven was still alive, he killed Erek to protect Lady Eldina. Derek could see that happening. He thought Darven would enjoy the kill.

But it was the last scenario that scared him most. Had Eldina finally had enough of the physical and verbal abuse and killed the man herself? If so, what end had befallen her? Was she on trial for murdering the lord of the keep? Was she executed; her beautiful head severed from her body? It was too much to absorb. Derek had strong feelings for her. He found himself praying for the transfer, if only to discover what had happened to her.

By the end of the second day, he knew it was over. He was to remain in his own world. The notion brought about much introspection. It was time to rejoin the world and begin socializing again. He thought about contacting his old friends to try to reconnect.

Early on the third day, Derek exited the shower, drying his hair with a towel, to discover Jackie and Bill standing in his apartment. He shrieked with surprise and covered himself with the towel.

"What? What the hell are you doing here?"

Jackie raced toward him and threw herself into his arms, the towel pressed precariously between them.

"Oh God, Derek! It's you! It's really you! Did you go back at all? Are you here for good?" She smacked kisses all over his face.

"It didn't happen. I've been here the whole time. I think the spell is over."

"Ahem!"

The two of them looked to see Bill holding the towel, which had slipped down. At first, Derek thought Bill was mad and they would have words or worse, but he merely said, "It would be nice if you would stop pressing your naked body against my fiancée."

He smiled, breaking the tense moment as Derek took the towel and covered himself and Jackie backed off. But Derek swore he saw her glimpse down and smile.

"Welcome home," Bill said.

"Ah, thanks. Let me get dressed."

"Good idea."

They sat around the kitchen table and talked for hours. They had lunch, and Derek realized he liked Bill, giving him a chance for the first time. As they were leaving, Jackie gave him a big hug and kissed his cheek. "I'm so glad you're still here."

"Thanks. Me too." Yet he felt a touch of sadness, like part of him was missing.

Jackie noticed. "Hey, it'll get better."

"Yeah." He smiled but felt no warmth.

Bill offered his hand and Derek shook it warmly. "I'm not sure what I saw, but I'm not going to question it or even think about it. I'm just glad it happened to you and not me."

He laughed and Derek did too, like they were old friends.

Jackie sent Bill to get the car. When they were alone, she smiled, her lips straining to reach their full range.

"Derek, I have a meeting later today with those bidding for the movie rights to your book. I expect it to go high."

"Great!" He watched her fidget. "Why don't you say what you're trying to tell me?"

"Oh, Derek!" She reached across the table and took his hand.

"Bill and I set a date."

"It's about time."

The comment stymied her for a moment; perhaps unsure if he was being sarcastic.

"I'm happy for you. Truly."

"Bill can never know about what we did, and it can never happen again."

"I understand. You don't have to worry about me saying anything. I wouldn't. Not ever. Of course, I'll always remember it. It was really good like it used to be. In truth, it helped me realize that it's time to move on."

"You mean like closure?"

"Well, if I remember right, it was more open than closed."

She slapped his arm. "Asshole." Her smile beamed brightly. "So we're good, then?"

"We're good. I'm good. You and Bill are good, and my book is going to be great."

"That's what I like to see. That old confidence coming through loud and clear."

"With that in mind, once it's released, I think I'd like to do a book tour."

Her jaw fell open. "Seriously? You've always hated doing appearances."

"Well, it's time for a change. I need to rejoin the real world. It might be fun."

"Oh, I doubt that, but as soon as we have a release date, I'll set it up."

They stood. They walked to the door in silence. He opened the door. Their eyes met. Hers filled and she moved closer and pressed her lips softly against his. It wasn't just a peck, and there was no tongue, but it was extremely passionate. She broke, placed a hand on his chest, and walked out.

As Derek moved to shut the door, Jackie shouted down the hall. "Now sit that fine ass down and write me the next one."

He stepped into the hall. She was waiting at the elevator.

"I knew you liked my ass."

"Yep. Always did."

She stepped into the waiting car and the doors closed on her.

Derek stood there for a few minutes, sorting out his feelings. He decided he was all right.

Hours later, sitting at the desk, he replayed Jackie's phone call after the auction. It had been a staggering amount. He'd opened a beer to celebrate but hadn't touched it after the first sip.

The screen was still blank, but an electric energy buzzed through him.

Huh. Space.

The future.

He smiled as he typed, *Twins in Time Book 2: Space Travels.*

It was a terrible title, but the words flowed like water. Once he started composing he realized it was a sequel. He would get to see Eldina again, if only in the images he created on paper. The story would write itself. He smiled as he worked.

Wait 'til Jackie reads this one.

Epilogue

Six months later.

Jackie had been right. The book tour was tedious. It hadn't been bad at first, but the constant travel and repetition wore on him. Still, it had been successful and was coming to a close. Initially, he'd balked at the European portion, but once there, he'd been able to enjoy the sights and meet many new fans.

He sat in a small, quaint bookstore on the outskirts of London. The proprietor was a middle-aged woman who gushed over his latest bestseller. She was sweet but a little over the top, as far as her praise and attention were concerned.

According to Jackie, the movie production had just kicked off. She had worked an invitation for him to visit the set, but he declined. The silence that followed spoke volumes to them both.

He had one more day in England before flying home. He contemplated taking a drive into the countryside, hoping to find someplace familiar to help him reminisce. Over the past few months, he'd done extensive research, looking for the land or the people of his travels, but had come up with only vague possibilities. Derek had concluded it didn't exist; at least not in this dimension.

He signed another copy, smiled, and shook the young man's hand.

"An honor, sir."

"Thank you. And thank you for your support."

He sneaked a glance at the line and saw it was near the end. The next person slid her copy of the book onto the table. Derek took it, opened the cover, and said, "Who shall I make this out to?"

"If you don't mind, I'd like it made out to my grandmother. She's such a big fan. When she heard you were coming, she made me promise to come. She's a bit old and doesn't travel well."

Derek looked up and smiled. The woman's reddish hair hung loosely over her face, covering much of it. "Well, you tell her I said thank you."

"Of course. She'll be so thrilled."

"And her name?"

"Eldina."

The pen froze on the paper, leaving a smudge line.

Derek looked up. The woman brushed her hair back, revealing eyes that he knew. Vibrant green eyes that had once bore straight into his soul. Eyes he'd never forget. She smiled. His heart fluttered, and he stood up so abruptly that the chair tipped over.

"Eldina?"

"Yes. Is everything all right?" she asked, a look of concern on her face.

The proprietor beelined for the table. "Is there a problem here, Derek?"

"Ah, no. No. No problem."

The young woman grew nervous. "Did I do something wrong?"

"No, dear girl. No." He took the chair the proprietor righted and sat down. "I'm sorry. The name brought back memories." Derek studied her face. *My God! It's her. How can that be?*

"Were they bad memories?"

"No. Well, not all."

"For a moment, you looked like you'd seen a ghost."

He nodded. "I thought I had. You look exactly like someone I once knew. Her name was Eldina."

"Like the lady from the book? Is that who you named her after?"

Derek could not take his eyes from her. "Yes."

"I think my grandmother was so taken by the story since it is her name."

"Is it a family name?"

"Yes. It dates back a few centuries, or so I'm told. We're descendants from a lord in a small remote land."

That made Derek pause again. *It couldn't be.* "Do you know where this land is?" He became aware of sweat breaking out on his forehead.

"I have an idea from the stories that have been passed down, but I've never been."

This was too much to take in. He had a strong desire…no, a desperate need to talk to the woman in private. "I would very much like to hear more. Will you be around for a while?"

She blushed. Another memory flooded his brain. He wanted to take this woman in his arms.

"Ah, I hadn't planned on it. This is quite a distance from my home. It will take nearly two hours to get back."

"What if I take you to dinner." He added quickly, "Just to talk. I-I don't know how to explain it, but I have a feeling this is extremely important."

She hesitated, looking uncomfortable.

"Please."

"Okay." But her tone indicated she wasn't sure of her decision.

"I'll be done in a few minutes."

He signed the book, *To Eldina, my medieval muse. With all love and affection, Derek.* As an afterthought, he wrote *Lord* in front of his name.

He tried not to cheat the final few people of their time, but he hurried as best he could, keeping one eye on the woman, praying she wouldn't duck out on him.

Thoughts and memories swarmed through his mind, making it difficult to keep his attention focused on the remaining fans.

Once done, he thanked the proprietor. He left walking with the young woman, leaving the storeowner speechless. It wasn't until he was out the door that he realized he had agreed to go to dinner with her. Feeling guilty, he ran back into the store and found the woman still standing there, looking as if she'd been slapped.

He rushed to her and wrapped her in a big embrace. With a peck on the cheek, he said, "I'm sorry. I need to speak to this woman about some research. Can I meet you for breakfast tomorrow morning?'

She was still blushing from the kiss and stammered that he could.

Derek and the young woman sat in a pub and ordered food. He had no idea what to say or how to broach the subject. He was so overwhelmed with emotion and possibilities that he stumbled over his words. He took a long draw on his pint, set the glass down, and took a deep breath.

"Mr. Lawson, what is going on?"

He asked her name, and she told him it was Deirdre. He smiled and looked into her eyes. The depths drove another memory through his brain. He saw something else in her features. She looked like Eldina, but she wasn't a dead ringer. There were subtle differences. He was confused at first. He'd seen that face somewhere else. "I would love to hear more about your ancestors. How far back do you know?"

The question made her nervous and he wondered if she was hiding something. He cocked his head to the side in a quizzical manner.

"I have to confess. Although my grandmother did insist on my coming, I would have anyway. Ever since I was young, I've been told stories of our family history that made little sense to me. I always thought of them as fairy tales, but recently, my grandmother has been very insistent that I know the whole story. The history is handwritten in an ancient family tome. I have to admit, it bears a striking similarity to your book." She shook her head and looked away. "I can't make sense of much of it. It can't be real, but how is it that your story is like my family's?"

He thought of his Eldina. Her image floated next to Deirdre's face. No, not quite. They weren't a perfect mirror image. Then it hit him. *A mirror.* He knew exactly where he'd seen that face before.

"I would very much like to visit your grandmother and see that book."

"You would?" Genuine surprise registered across her lovely face. "Why?"

"What if I told you that the events of the story are real and there's a good chance we're related?"

ABOUT THE AUTHOR

Ray Wenck taught elementary school for 35 years and was also the chef/owner of DeSimone's Italian Restaurant for more than 25 years. After retiring, he became a lead cook for Hollywood Casinos and then the kitchen manager for the Toledo Mud Hens AAA baseball team. Now he spends most of his time writing, doing book tours, and meeting old and new fans and friends around the country.

Ray is the author of thirty-eight novels, including the Amazon Top 20 post-apocalyptic, *Random Survival* series, the paranormal thriller, *Ghost of a Chance*, the mystery/suspense *Danny Roth* series and the ever popular choose your own adventure, *Pick-A-Path: Apocalypse*. A list of his other novels can be viewed at raywenck.com.

His hobbies include reading, hiking, cooking, baseball and playing the harmonica with any band brave enough to allow him to sit in.

You can find his books on your favorite online sites.

You can reach Ray or sign up for his newsletter at raywenck.com or authorraywenck on Facebook.

Ray Wenck

Other Titles

Random Survival Series

Random Survival

The Long Search for Home

The Endless Struggle

A Journey to Normal

Then There'll Be None

In Defense of Home

Danny Roth Series

Teammates

Teamwork

Home Team

Stealing Home

Group Therapy

Double Play

Playing Through Errors

The Dead Series

Tower of the Dead

Island of the Dead

Escaping the Dead

Pick-A-Path Series

Pick-A-Path: Apocalypse 1

Pick-A-Path: Apocalypse 2

Pick-A-Path: Apocalypse 3

Stand Alone Titles

Warriors of the Court

Live to Die Again

The Eliminator

Reclamation

Ghost of a Chance

Mischief Magic

Twins in Time

Angel's Angels and Fairies

Short Stories

The Con   *Short Stop: A Danny Roth short*   *Super Me*

Super Me, Too

Co-authored with Jason J. Nugent

Escape: The Seam Travelers Book 1

Capture: The Seam Travelers Book 2

Conquest: The Seam Travelers Book 3

The Historian Series

The Historian: Life Before and After

The Historian: The Wilds

The Historian: Invasion

Bridgett Conroy Series

A Second Chance at Death

Ray Wenck

CPSIA information can be obtained
at www.ICGtesting.com
Printed in the USA
LVHW052034100621
689923LV00008B/858